MINES OF MARS:
ARSIA MONS

BOOK 3

ROBERT A. SPHAR

MINES OF MARS: ARSIA MONS

BOOK 3

ROBERT A. SPHAR

DEDICATION:

I would like to dedicate this book to the loving memory of my parents, Allen and Mary (Max) Sphar. They helped me to become the person I am today and everything that I am, I owe to them. They were supportive of me and my brothers during the years when we were trying to find a direction in life. This is not the direction that anyone ever expected that I would go in, but I hope they would be proud.

Thank you both.

We all love you.

CHAPTER ONE

"It looks a lot like Pavonis," Lorna said as they entered the Arsia Mons complex. "The tunnels are smaller, but not that much different."

"What are you going to find for us to do here?" Al asked.

"Hell, I don't know. Mike, do you have any requests on what we should look for?"

"Christ, if you can find half of what you found in Pavonis I'll be happy."

The tunnel they had entered was about half the size of the ones in Pavonis Mons. Five hundred feet high and two hundred feet wide. The light was still dim this far out on the perimeter, but the shapes were familiar. Rooms dotted the sides as they proceeded.

"Should we wait for the others?" Lorna asked. "We're going to need to bring more people back here. We don't have enough resources with us to do much good."

"Mike, how long can you stay? Shall we have a look around?" Al asked.

"I can spare a little while. My shuttle is scheduled to pick me up tomorrow afternoon. I'll need to be back by then. I guess we could look around for a while."

"We can get you back out in the morning," Lorna said. "I'm surprised that there's so little dust here."

"Yeah, I noticed that too," Al said. "What's the air like now?"

"Still bad, but it's getting a little better. The pressure is the same as in the other complex," Lorna said. "Sean, what do you think of this place?"

"You never cease to amaze me. I wasn't sure you had a chance in hell of finding anything here, if you ever even made it in. I didn't think there would be anything but a mountain here."

"You doubted me. Shame on you."

"You'll learn that she's not often wrong," Al said. "I'd have thought you'd have figured that out already."

"I've seen her come up with some pretty fantastic stuff," Sean said. "This just seemed like such a long shot."

"We had information indicating that there were several more locations on Mars," Lorna said. "It seemed logical that this might be one of them. I'm betting that we can get into Ascraeus Mons, and maybe Olympus Mons too before we're through. Why don't we go to the center of this place and have a look around?"

"That seems to be the place to start," Al said. "Arnold, can you read me?"

"Go ahead."

"We're in the complex and headed for the center. Girls, did you copy that?"

"We hear you Al," Brittany said.

"Us too," Patty said. "I don't have enough supplies to last too long in here though. I did manage to do a computer dump but didn't take time to restock."

"Can you last until tomorrow?"

"Yeah, that's no problem. I could even stretch it for another day after that."

"Mike needs to get back out tomorrow afternoon," Al said. "We'll decide on what to do this evening. I'd like you all to split up at the first intersection you come to and take a different way to the center. It'll give us a head start on mapping."

"We'll go left," Brittany said. "Patty, we'll see you this evening."

"Race you to the center," Patty said. "We'll go right."

"Arnold, since you and your people are new to this; maybe you'd better go straight and follow our tracks," Al said. "The dust is minimal so you can close up a little if you want. When the light gets better, we may stop and look around for a minute. If you catch up with us, stop."

"Understood," Arnold said.

Arsia Mons is one of a string of three volcanoes on the western plains of Mars. The string runs from Arsia Mons to Pavonis Mons in the center, and then on to Ascraeus Mons to the northeast. Far to the northwest of Arsia Mons is the giant Olympus Mons, towering almost seventy thousand feet above the barren red landscape.

An archeological find was made in one of the mines of Mars just over a year earlier. It led to the discovery of the complex hidden inside Pavonis Mons that opened the door to this discovery. Al was in charge of that mine and Lorna was brought in to explore what they had found. Along with her daughter Eve, Lorna worked her way through a dangerous maze that uncovered information that had been guiding them ever since.

"Eve's going to be pissed when she hears where we are," Lorna said.

"Yeah, but maybe she'll have time to cool down before we get back," Al said. "This is going to be fun, coordinating two operations at the same time."

"We can turn a lot of it over to Arnold and his people. It's down to their area of expertise now anyhow. We've done about all we can."

"This evening, we need to go over what kind of additional personnel we're going to need to get headed this way," Mike said. "God, I wish we didn't have to wait six months to get people transported from Earth. That's one of the biggest hassles of the operations on Mars."

"You can't plan for everything up here," Al said. "Especially when Lorna keeps finding new stuff for us to look at."

"That's true," Mike said. "It was a lot simpler when all we were doing was mining. We had our supply chain pretty well established for that. Now you keep throwing a monkey wrench into my system."

"Yeah, but we're making money," Lorna said. "Not to mention a little history. You can't tell me you're upset at the challenges we give you. Are you?"

"Of course not. The work you've done has revolutionized how we're going to do business on Mars. The Martian miner is going to up the production by at least double. Also, being able to grow some of our own food will save millions of dollars. No, I'm not upset. You keep at it. I can tell you now that I'm authorizing a bonus of two billion for each of you."

"Only two?" Lorna asked. "Well, I guess I can get by on that, but I may have to work part time to make ends meet."

"If you need any references, let me know," Mike said.

As they continued into the interior of Arsia Mons, Lorna worked the mapping system on the Mars cruiser. The cruiser was inspired by what Al thought they might need when they reached Pavonis Mons. The old crew cars were battery powered and had limited range. He laid out the specifications and let Sean actually do the design work.

During the time they were waiting for the facility at Pavonis to be built, Al and Lorna had tried to anticipate every eventuality. They had done a good job of it, but were still held up on several occasions, waiting for technology to catch up with them.

The cruisers were designed to carry six passengers, but after they were deep into the inner complex of Pavonis Mons, they had to rethink things and with the ingenuity of Patty and Brittany Thompson, they settled on a four-seat version. The rest of the space was taken up by a large computer system for the mapping system that Patty and Brittany designed and installed in one of the early models. With the enclosed environment, the cruisers could be driven on the surface of the planet as well as inside the complex where the air was too bad to sustain life for very long. The small reactor gave the cruiser an unlimited range.

"Do you think we'll find another garden in here?" Mike asked after a long silence.

"Probably," Lorna said. "It wouldn't make sense for them to have to transport all their food from Pavonis. I was just looking at the overlay of the surface map onto the map we made on the way over here. While the two volcanoes are similar in size, Arsia may have a slightly smaller complex. We started up into it farther from the outer perimeter of the mountain."

"I see what you mean," Al said. "We may find what we're looking for in a couple more hours. When the air is good enough, I need to stop and stretch though. Being cooped up in here is going to be a problem soon."

"Give it another half hour," Lorna said. "It's getting better, but not as fast as I'd hopped."

"I'll try, but if it's not better by then we may have to break out the air packs. The light is getting better. How long until dark?"

"Three hours," Sean said. "That's not going to give us much time to look around."

"No, but we can start as soon as it gets light in the morning," Al said. "Did you ever figure out how the light works?"

"As far as we could determine, there must be a collector of some kind on top of the mountain," Sean said. "By transmitting the light through a crystal of some kind, they were able to simulate day and night. Actually, day and night is exactly what they had. We still haven't figured out how they distributed it inside the mountain though. So many questions."

"And so few answers," Lorna said.

* * *

"Martin, this is Jen. Where are Al and Lorna?"

"I'm not sure, but from what I've been hearing on the radio, they must be a long ways away."

"What do you mean a long ways away?"

"It sounds like they've gone exploring again. I just caught a few words of it. I think they found a way to get into Arsia Mons."

"Christ, you're kidding. How did they do that?"

"I don't know," Martin said. "We'll have to wait for an update. What did you need them for?"

"We've been cruising around in here for a day now and it looks like it'll be the better part of a week before we can get an idea of how big the upper garden is. We've run up against a few roadblocks, but nothing major to report."

"Don't get lost in there. I'm going to need you back out here as soon as you can get done in there."

"Hey, I have a map now," Jen said. "We'll check in again this evening."

"Ok. Take care of things. I'll talk to you later."

"Later bye."

* * *

"Martin, this is Eve. What did you say about where mom is?"

"It sounded like they found a way into Arsia Mons. That's what I thought I heard. I only caught bits here and there."

"Mother, where are you" Eve said.

"We're exploring again," Lorna said. "Patty found a way into Arsia Mons."

"And just when were you going to let us in on this?"

"We're just looking around. We'll be back in a couple of days. Try to tie up the lose ends there so we can get started over here."

"This sucks, mother."

"Yeah, but I can't help that right now. We'll come back out tomorrow or the next day and show you what we found. Get things started there and then we'll change the focus to over here. We're going to have to do this one a little different. We may not have all the people we need, so get ready for some more long days."

"Ok but let us know when you're coming back."

"We'll stay in contact. We laid out repeaters on the way over and we'll place them everywhere we go. If you need anything just call."

"Alright, but I'm not happy with you."

"You'll get over it—or not. Lorna out."

"Do you believe that?" Eve said.

"Relax, baby," Brian said. "She must have had a good reason for going without you. You'll get your chance over there."

"Relax, he says. Yeah, right."

* * *

By the time the Arsia complex started to dim, they had traveled for nine hours. The tunnel system still resembled the one in Pavonis. They had counted twelve side tunnels so far and there was no end in sight. As

6

far as they could see was the same as what they had driven through since entering the light.

"We can keep going," Al said. "I don't know if it will do much good though."

"I'd like to see if we can find anything," Mike said. "Can we go on for an hour or so?"

"Yeah, but let's take a break," Lorna said. "My butt went to sleep an hour ago. Arnold, we're going to stop for a few minutes. How far do you think you are behind us?"

"We were the second ones in, so probably not far."

"Come on up to where we are. We'll wait on you."

"Ok, we'll be along in a few minutes."

"Al, pull over to the right," Lorna said. "We might as well look this place over while we're getting the circulation back."

"I'll stop at that intersection," Al said. "We can take a look in some of the rooms."

"It'll be dark in a few minutes. We won't be able to do much more tonight."

"Yeah, but we can get in far enough to get a fresh start in the morning. Mike, you're going to have a long day tomorrow."

"I don't mind. Especially if you find me something to look at. I may have to call and have the shuttle delayed though. I guess you know I'm going to have a shitload of work to catch up on when I get back."

"Isn't that the way it always is," Al said.

"Sometimes it seems like its better not to go anywhere, so you don't have to do all the stuff that you should have been doing when you get back," Mike said. "You guys seem to mess up my schedule fairly regular these days."

"We apologize," Lorna said. "Would you rather that we didn't?"

"No, that's alright. You just keep coming up with reasons for me to come out here and visit. Every time I do, you make us big money."

Al pulled to a stop at the edge of the intersection. They all groaned as they got out.

"I'll tell you one thing," Lorna said. "The trips back to the complex are going to be a lot farther in between."

"That means setting up a mainframe in here somewhere," Al said. "Let's see if we can find a good place to set up a command-post."

"How many portable habitats do you have left, Mike," Lorna said. "We're going to need several more in here before we're done."

"Not many. You've already used up most of the ones we have. We're working on getting more of them put together, but you've stressed out manufacturing almost to the limits. Trying to give you everything you need and still keep the planet running is one of my daily challenges."

"Well, I think we're paying our way though," Lorna said as they went into a room close to the corner of the intersection.

The interior of this room was again similar to the ones at Pavonis. However, they had a look that suggested that they might have been inhabited more recently than the others they had seen.

"Look," Lorna said. "There are cushions on the stone furniture. They're not very good, but you can tell what they are. We didn't see any of this over there."

They walked through the rest of that set of rooms and two others before Arnold pulled up and stopped. They emerged from the third set of rooms when they heard the cruiser.

"That's a hell of a drive," Arnold said as they got out.

"Yeah, but we've done worse ones than that," Lorna said. "Our people have been doing that every day for several weeks. Most of it around in circles, but that doesn't make it any easier."

"Just the number of hours involved is impressive," Al said. "They've done a hell of a job."

"When did you plan on stopping for the night?"

"We're thinking we need to go in another hour or so," Al said. "We want to get in as far as we can. According to the map that we've been making as we came, we should be getting close to the center."

"Patty, Brittany, can you hear me?" Lorna called on the radio.

"We're here," Patty said.

"Us too," Brittany said.

"We stopped at the thirteenth cross tunnel. When you get to that one, we're going to go in another hour. We'll camp in an intersection and let you know which one it is."

"Just let us know," Patty said. "When we turned at the first one, it took a half hour to get to the next one headed back to the center."

"Us too," Brittany said. "Do we have a plan for tomorrow yet?"

"Not yet," Lorna said. "We'll discuss it when we get together later."

"See you then. Brittany out."

After a break of fifteen minutes more, they climbed back into the two cruisers and continued on. They ran abreast and were separated by fifty feet or so. The minimal amount of dust that they were encountering wasn't a problem.

After they had been back on the road for an hour, Al pulled a little ahead of Arnold and then stopped at the next intersection.

"Girls, we're stopping at the sixteenth cross tunnel," he said as he stopped.

"We're coming up on number fifteen," Brittany said. "We'll be along soon."

"We just past fourteen," Patty said.

"Arnold, ease your cruiser over here and we'll set up camp," Al said.

"What kind of camp is there to set up?"

"You haven't seen our toys in action, have you?"

"No, I couldn't even get the map to work on the way in."

"We'll fix that," Lorna said. "The young ladies in the other two cruisers are the ones that designed the system. I'm sure they can get it to work."

"We probably just never figured out how to turn it on."

"We can fix that too. They can give you a full rundown on how it works."

Al guided Arnold to a point where they were about fifty feet apart and had the backs of the cruisers facing each other.

"Come over here," Al said. "Mike, have you seen how these work?"

"No. I've heard about them, but never actually seen them in action."

When they were all assembled. Al started the sequence to deploy the portable habitat that each cruiser carried on the back. First the back hatch opened, and the habitat started to unfold. When it was fully extended, Al pushed the button to start the inflation process. In a matter of two minutes the habitat was fully extended and inflated, ready to use.

"That's cool," Arnold said. "I thought we'd have to sleep on the ground."

"It has all the comforts of home," Lorna said. "They're considerably smaller, but most of them are there."

It was almost another hour before Brittany showed up; followed fifteen minutes later by Patty. They parked so that all four habitats were pointed toward the center of the circle. The crew of eleven gathered in the center for a brainstorming session.

"First thing we need to do is rig a composite of the three maps," Al said.

"Three?" Brittany asked. "What happened to the other one?"

"We didn't check them out on the system," Lorna said. "Can you take care of that?"

"Oops. Yeah, I can take care of that."

"Patty, can you make a composite disc so we can all have all of the map that we have so far?" Al asked. "According to the map we made, we should be close to the center of the mountain. I figured we'd run into another garden, but so far, we haven't."

"Yeah, I can combine them, so we all have everything," Patty said. "Which one doesn't have a map to download?"

"That one," Al said pointing to the one Arnold had driven.

"I'll get right on it. Sis, you'd better show them how it works, or we're going to have to go looking for them."

"Come on guys. Mapping 101 is getting ready to start," Brittany said leading Arnold and his two people to their cruiser.

"I'll get us something to eat," Lorna said. "Sean, want to give me a hand?"

"Sure."

"Al, I'm still amazed at the qualities you pull out of your people," Mike said. "Those two girls are amazing."

"I can't take much credit for that," Al said. "They had the ideas before they got here. I just gave them the support and stood back and watched. Without them, we still wouldn't know where we were over in Pavonis. We would have had to pull every survey crew on the planet in there and still it would be a year or more to get all the information we have now. I'm proud of them."

"You bring out the best in your people. That's one reason I knew you'd be the one to handle the mine you were at. With it hanging on the side of the chasm like it is, it's a tough assignment."

"Bill has taken good care of it though. I knew he would. We worked that thing for almost two years together. He knew as much about it as I did."

"By the way, I gave that magnetic rock a name the other day. Don't tell Lorna, but we're calling it lornacite. When she leaves this planet, her name is going to be on a lot of things."

"I talked to Bill before we left over there the other day," Al said. "He's starting to ship it in mass. They'll soon have enough of it stockpiled to do whatever they want with it. When we opened up the two big deposits in the back of the mine, he moved several crews in there and went right at it."

"We're still trying to figure out if we can ship it back to Earth. The way it screws with the navigational equipment has us worried. We may have to work with it here and install it into whatever they decide they want to use it in. I did hear that they were trying to develop a new engine for space travel. They've opened up some old designs that weren't practical without this kind of material to power them. They say it could cut the transit time to Earth by half, or more. The advances you've sparked have been fantastic."

"All in a day's work. None of it would have been possible without Lorna and Eve. We might have figured out the stuff in the mine eventually, but I doubt if we'd ever have gone to Pavonis, much less here."

"Alright you bums. It's soup," Lorna said coming out the back of the habitat.

Sean had come out a couple minutes earlier and set up a small table that was attached to the side of the habitat. They all gathered and ate. Brittany continued to answer questions about the mapping system as the meal progressed. Arnold was fascinated at how it worked.

"How are you coming, Patty," Al asked as they finished eating.

"I'll have you a working copy in a half hour. I still have one computer to download. Then we'll have to upload the composite in all four, but that will only take a few minutes."

"Let us know when you have it. We'll need that to make plans for tomorrow."

"I'm about finished eating," Patty said. "I'll get right back to it. It's nice to have someone fix dinner for a change."

"We'll take care of the clean-up if you can get that disc," Lorna said.

"Deal."

"Arnold, are you ready to finish your lesson?" Brittany asked.

"There's more?"

"We've incorporated several variations that I haven't gone over yet. You can run the basic system with the information you have now, but it will really hum if you do a few more things."

"Lead on. Mike, that's the most fantastic thing I've seen in years," Arnold said as he followed Brittany back to the cruiser.

"Learn all you can," Mike said. "You and your people are going to have a lot of catching up to do. At some point though, you're going to have to lead the way instead of following."

"We have to crawl first. Your people have done more than anyone could have expected."

"Yeah, now it's your turn."

Thirty minutes later the disc was complete and installed in all four systems.

"It's ready, Al," Patty said. "I have it set up on the outside monitor on your cruiser."

"Thanks, Patty. Everyone, gather around so we can see where we are," Al said.

He studied the map as they all started to gather. It mostly confirmed what he'd thought it would.

"Ok, it's pretty simple for now," Al said. "Tomorrow, we'll continue on like we were today. We have to find the center so we can establish what we have. I suspect it's like Pavonis, but these spokes aren't coming together as fast as I had expected. By the time they get in this far they should be closer than they are. That may indicate that the hub of this wheel is farther south."

"It was closer to the south than the north, in Pavonis," Lorna said. "Over an hour closer."

"If we extend these lines out and allow for a reasonable distance at the hub," Al said. "We're still an hour from it. Girls, you go back to your tracks in the morning. Meet us farther in. Mike, what time do you need to get back out?"

"I'll call and delay the shuttle until the following morning," Mike said. "I'll give it until 1200. After that I'll have to get started back."

"You may want to ride with Patty then. There's no telling where we'll be by then. Everyone, we'll set up the same coordinate system we have in Pavonis. Compass points for everything between the center and the outer rim, numbers for the rings. For right now, we'll use the rings from the outside, to the inside. After we get the interior better defined, we may reverse that set of numbers. We came in on 030. That's the way back out."

"I'd like to stick with you and Lorna for a while in the morning," Mike said. "I know that's going to make us rendezvous somewhere later, but if you think we can work it, I'd like it that way."

"We can make it work," Lorna said. "We're all going in the same direction."

"Ok, that's the plan. Arnold, can you move to the west and come in more from due north?"

"I don't see why not," Arnold said. "If I have any problems with the mapping system, I'll call Brittany and have her explain it again. Maybe she could make sure I have it started right before we leave."

"We'll get you off on the right foot," Brittany said.

"I guess we'd better get some sleep," Al said. "Sweet dreams."

* * *

The complex started to brighten at 0600. Lorna was already up when the first rays started to illuminate the massive tunnel. To her surprise, Mike was outside looking toward the interior of the mountain.

"Penny for your thoughts," she said as she walked up behind him.

"I just wanted to catch the first light in the new place. It was really dark when we got here last night. These places amaze me. The biggest difference between here and out on the surface is there are no stars in here."

"Yeah, and you don't freeze, and you can breathe, among other things."

"Well, yeah, that too."

"They are wondrous places. The more we find the more questions we have."

"Where is it all going to end?" Mike asked.

"I don't know. We'll keep looking for that point, but I think we may be a couple years away yet. Can we support it for that long?"

"That shouldn't be a problem now. Even if you don't find anything else, I can justify it to the board. We'll use what you've already found to kick the production to a point that they may have to double the transport ships to haul it away. That would be a shame, wouldn't it?"

"Yeah, that would be a shame. All that capital outlay would dent the profits for a while. I imagine they may squawk all the way to the bank."

"You're a very wealthy woman, did you know that?"

"I had an idea that would come," Lorna said. "That's not why I'm here though. When Eve and I started up here, we scoured everything we could get our hands on. We tried to figure out why no one had ever found traces of life. I'm more convinced than ever that it's out there. We never dreamed of finding anything like this though."

"Well, it's about time to roust the others. We have a long day ahead of us. Besides, I need my coffee."

"Yeah, and I need my tea."

* * *

They all spread out again at 0700. The objective for the day was to find the center of the complex. Within an hour they had succeeded. Al and Lorna, along with Mike and Sean, rolled up to the opening at 0800. It looked like an industrial complex.

"This should be interesting," Al said. "Everyone, we found it an hour in. You should be coming to it soon. Check in when you get there."

"Will do, Al," Brittany said.

"We copy," Patty said.

"Us too," Arnold said. "What did you find?"

"An industrial complex. Let us know what you find when you get there."

"Let's take a look," Lorna said. "This may be harder to figure out than some of the other stuff we've found. Sean, I think you've found a new home."

"Yeah, no kidding. After we look around for a few minutes, let's make a run around the perimeter and see if we can find the best place to set up operations. I may have to steal a couple of your habitats."

"We'll figure out something," Al said as they got out.

They walked into the edge of the area and found giant machinery as far as they could see. After about a half hour of working their way in and out of buildings and through storage yards, they came to an open area. It was several hundred yards across and three hundred feet wide. The ground here was polished stone, as smooth as glass. There was virtually no dust to be found in this open area. As they walked across it, Lorna looked back and the footprints they had made seemed to disappear.

"Shit, look at that."

"What?" Al asked.

"Where we walked and tracked the dust in; it's disappearing. It's like its being vacuumed up."

"I don't see it."

"Watch. I'll go get my feet dirty again and track it back out here. Watch what happens."

When her feet were dusty again, she walked back toward them. They approached her, looking behind her. The dust seemed to be repelled. Some of it went up into the air and the rest slid toward the edge of the opening.

"Now, that's weird," Mike said. "Sean, what could cause that?"

"I'm not sure. It looks like they have different polarity or something. Like magnets trying to push each other away."

"What would it do if you put a habitat on it, I wonder?" Lorna asked.

"I don't know," Sean said. "I guess we could get something here and bring it out a ways and see what happens. Al, give me a hand. There's a beam over there that I think we can handle."

"Ok. Which one?"

"This small one. It may give us what we need to know."

They grabbed a small piece of steel-looking material that was about ten feet long. When they placed it in the center of the clear area, it slowly started to move to the side. By the time it reached the edge, some hundred feet away, it was moving very fast and accelerating. It crashed into the debris that was around the edge.

"Does that answer your question?" Sean asked.

"Yeah, I guess it does. We're not feeling any effects from it though. It's not trying to throw us out."

"It must be a magnetic effect of some kind," Sean said. "That wouldn't affect us. We're not metal. The dust must have a lot of metal in it."

"Yeah, but it can't be all metal," Lorna said.

"I don't know. We'll have to look at it."

"Let's move on," Al said. "There's plenty more to see."

As they left the clearing, Al's radio started to crackle. Then it became clear.

"Al, this is Brittany. Where the hell are you?"

"We're here. What's up?"

"I've been trying to call you for ten minutes."

"We were investigating something strange. It may have messed with the radios. Where are you?"

"We're at the opening west of you. Patty should be about to the one to the east. We're going to go in and look around a little."

"Be careful. Things in here may not be what they appear."

"What do you mean by that?"

"Just watch your step. Keep to the open areas as much as you can until we have a chance to get some engineers over here."

"Ok, whatever you say. Brittany out."

"Al, this is Patty. We're entering what looks like a giant parking lot. There are some strange looking rides over here."

"Patty, this is Sean. Keep your eyes opened for anything that has a flat top on it. We may find something over here to do some of the things we need to finish in Pavonis."

"Ok, we'll look around. Patty out."

"What are you looking for?" Lorna asked.

"Hell, I don't know. There might be some kind of equipment that could give us access to the library shelves over there. Something that could extend up high enough to reach most of the information on those high shelves. My guys are working on a couple ideas, but we're not sure they'll work."

"This place could be a gold mine," Mike said. "Imagine what we could do if we could harness the alien technology in here."

"There are a couple years of clean-up though," Al said. "We're going to need a lot of engineers and mechanics to figure out what we have. God, this thing keeps getting bigger all the time."

"I delayed my shuttle until tomorrow morning, but maybe it's time I went out now," Mike said. "It may take us twelve hours to get back to the outer complex. I don't know what you're going to find here, but it's going to require a lot more help than you have available. I can't help you much here. I can help back in my office."

"Ok," Al said. "Patty, we're going to come to you. I think it's time you took Mike back out. He needs to get back and you're low on supplies. We'll be there in an hour or so."

"Ok, Boss. We'll look around and meet you back at the cruiser in an hour."

"See you then."

"What was that?" Lorna asked. She stared and pointed up high and far to the south.

CHAPTER TWO

"What's what?" Al asked.

"There. Up high. I thought I saw a big bird or something," Lorna said.

"You're kidding!"

"No. I'm not kidding. It went behind that tall structure to the south."

"Maybe you'd better take her with you, Mike."

"Damn it. I'm not hallucinating. There was something there."

"Yeah," Mike said. "I believe you. We'll call it a Lornavulture, or something."

"Damn you two. Sean, I could use a little help here."

"I believe you," Sean said.

"Look, you asses. If I say I saw something, I saw it. At least a think I saw it. It was only a glimpse."

"Ok. Don't get so riled up about it," Al said. "We'll keep our eyes open. What did it look like?"

"Just a big bird in the distance. It was so far away that I couldn't really tell, and I only saw it for a second."

"Let's work our way back out," Al said. "We need to get over and meet Patty."

* * *

"Patty, where are you?" Al asked an hour later. "We're at your cruiser."

"We'll be there in a few minutes. We got sidetracked looking at some of these things. There's some cool stuff in here."

"Ok. We need to get Mike headed back to the complex. Hurry every chance you get."

"Ten minutes."

"Ok. See you then."

"Let's get out and have a look while we wait," Lorna said. "Sean, maybe you'd like to take a look at some of this stuff and see if it'll help you."

"I knew there had to be more than we found at Pavonis. There just wasn't the right kind of transportation to support a whole society. There wasn't any kind of construction equipment or anything like that. Damn, look at that line of cranes."

"You should be able to get something in there to work for us," Al said.

"Yeah, I think so. Then we have to figure out how to get it over to Pavonis. Mike, we may have to fix up a low-bed trailer that we can pull with a rover or something."

"Great. Another project to work on. I'll see what I can work up when I get back. You might want to call your guys and see if they have any ideas."

"We'll do that," Sean said. "Al, I think I need to spend the rest of the day here. Can we work that out?"

"Yeah, I think we can do that. I may need to go have a look at the other areas and then come back."

"Just leave me a snack. I'll be fine. There's Patty. Maybe she has a better idea of what's in here."

"What kept you?" Al asked.

"Back in there a couple miles, there's some really cool construction equipment," Patty said. "I just love that kind of stuff."

"Did you see anything that looked like a forklift?" Sean asked.

"Yeah, there are several different kinds. Some little ones for handling small stuff and some of those that telescope out a long ways, so you could reach up high. There may be more too. We had to turn around about there so we could meet you."

"Can you drive in there?" Al asked.

"I think you can if you pick your way in," Patty said. "It's pretty cluttered in places."

"I need to be headed back," Mike said. "We have a long way to go."

"We're ready," Patty said. "Al, do we come back here when we come back in?"

"Yeah, I think we'll all be over here for quite a while. Until I tell you otherwise, this is home. When you come back in, branch out at the first intersection and start working your way back to here. In the next couple days, we'll try to find a place to put a command-post. It'll take us a week or so to get a supply chain set up in here. We're going to have to stretch things for a while."

"Can we hook up to one of those small trailers and bring in extra supplies?"

"That's not a bad idea. Get with the support crew and have them set you up when you get out there. They may have to bring one out from the interior. Mike, we're going to need a habitat soon."

"I'll get one headed this way. It'll be there by the time you figure out a place to put it."

"Patty, take a day before you come back," Lorna said. "That'll give us a chance to look around. Besides, you need a break."

"Yeah, we do. Let's hit the road."

Alex climbed in the back and Mike rode up front while Patty drove. Al, Lorna, and Sean watched as they drove away.

"Sean, do you want me to stay here with you?" Lorna asked.

"You can if you want."

"Do you mind, Al?"

"No. I'll cruise around and see what else there is to look at. Meet me back here before dark. You'll need to pack a lunch to carry with you."

"I'll take care of that," Lorna said. "Be back in a minute."

"What do you think you can find in there, Sean?" Al asked.

"I don't know. I'm hoping there might be something to get us up high in the library over there. Other than that, just see what's there, I guess. There may be more of those boring machines too. I'll keep an eye out for them."

"You might see if there's anything with a sealed cab. It would be helpful for getting them to the other side."

"I'm thinking we're going to have better luck finding a trailer to haul them on. I don't know what we're going to pull it with though. What about bringing in a rover? They have a lot more power and weight."

"We'd have a hell of a time getting it inside."

"We could open it up with one of the miners. It wouldn't take that much to tunnel over that far. Slim and Joe could do it in a day or so."

"Ok, I'm ready," Lorna said.

"What all do you have in there?" Sean asked.

"Just the essentials," Lorna said as she shouldered the backpack she was carrying.

"Let me take that."

"No, you can take it when I get tired. There's enough to tide us over until dark."

"You two get started," Al said. "I have miles to travel."

"See you here this evening," Lorna said.

Al climbed into the cruiser and was gone in moments. Sean and Lorna looked into the distance and started toward the opening.

* * *

By lunchtime Lorna and Sean were four miles into the interior. To that point they hadn't found anything that they thought they could use. There had been several variations of cranes and forklifts that had possibilities, but nothing else really grabbed their attention.

"Let's grab a bite to eat," Lorna said.

"Ok. We can sit on that bumper over there."

"Shit, look there."

"I see it this time. It does look like a big bird. It seems to be circling that tower in the distance. It must be huge for us to be able to see it from here."

"How far away do you think that is?"

"Several miles. I don't think we can get there and back today."

21

"At least you saw it this time. I think Al thought I was nuts. What do you make of this place so far?"

"It's a fantastic find. There's enough construction equipment in here to do anything we want, if we can get any of it to run. Those hi-reach forklifts might get us a start in the library at Pavonis. It looks like they may reach as much as a hundred feet. That won't get us all the way up, but it'll give us a hell of a start. All we have to do now is figure out a way to get them over there. I doubt if they move all that fast and it's a long ways. We'll have to haul them somehow. I'm still working on it."

"We've seen so many different types."

"Yeah, and I'm sure there's many more to be seen. Now, what did you put in there to eat?"

"Just a few sandwiches and some water. Take your pick. God, it's so quiet in here."

"Most tombs are quiet."

* * *

Mike checked his watch as Patty drove out of the complex, headed back towards the Pavonis compound. It was 1400.

"Smitty, this is Mike."

"Yes sir. What can I do for you?"

"Contact my office and have them delay the shuttle until tomorrow morning. We're headed back, but it's going to be late before I get there. Also, have you talked to Slim lately?"

"Slim's here in the complex. He came out about an hour ago. Do you need to talk to him?"

"Yeah, can you round him up for me?"

"I'll get back to you in a few minutes. The shuttle may have taken off already. Do you want them to go back?"

"Leave that to them. They can find a room there somewhere if they prefer. Mike out."

"What do you think of our cruisers," Patty asked, as they waited for the call.

"Amazing. You girls did a fine job on them. I had a chance to spend a little time with Brittany and Johnny when they were at the hub working with the engineers. Now I'm pleased to have a little time with you and Alex. I enjoy exchanging ideas with bright people."

"She's the one with all the brains here," Alex said from the back seat.

"You were smart enough to team up with me," Patty said. "That should count for something. Mike, what do you make of all this stuff we're finding?"

"I've been trying to figure that out. Lorna has certainly turned this planet upside-down. Until she leads us to the end of the trail, we can only speculate. From what we've seen since yesterday, they appear to have segregated different areas to do different things in. The complex at Pavonis is mainly agricultural, while this one seems to be industrial. I guess they figured they didn't mix for some reason."

"You think they traded back and forth?"

"I think that's a logical assumption," Mike said. "We need more information."

"Mike, this is Slim."

"There you are. I need you to see about getting ten of the miners moved out to the outer complex. Al and I talked about it last night, and I think it's time to kick-start production around here. How long do you think it will take you?"

"If I hijack some help—maybe two days. Is there a rush on it?"

"We might as well get started. I'll arrange for transportation to move them to the other mines. I'd like you to put together a crew that can go with them and train other crews. It will probably mean you'll be gone from here for a week or two."

"Joe and Jim are already up to speed on it. I may have to dip into Bill's crew for other miners to teach."

"I'll call him in the morning and see if I can soften the blow a little. From what I've heard, he's still bitching about us not returning Larry and Burns."

"Yeah, he did mention that when I was over there the other day. Maybe you can convince him it'll only be temporary."

"Well, he's had the benefit of the machine for several days now and I think his production has been padded enough that he can spare them. You concentrate on getting the machines out to the complex and let me know how many people you need."

"We may have to do this in pieces," Slim said. "The transport can only haul three at a time. It'll take them several days to make the trip to some of the other locations. We're a long ways out."

"I'll get them moved. You'll have to teach the transport drivers how to drive them so they can unload them. When we get them on the ground, I'll send a shuttle to pick you up. I think three crews of two will work for a start. I'll borrow three from Bill."

"Get Dan and Jeff if he'll let go of them."

"Anyone else?"

"Bill's little brother, Josh. He worked with us too. He picked up on it right away."

"He's not going to like this," Mike said.

"I think it would be a good idea to take some safety and security measures too. The machines will be there before we get there. Someone might get evaporated if they try to use them without learning how first."

"Good idea. I'll have a talk with each of the managers before they're delivered. Will you still be at the complex this evening?"

"Yeah, I'll put together a crew and go back in tomorrow morning. It's too late to get much done today. Do the mines have a mapping cruiser we can use?"

"They all have at least one," Mike said. "I'll see you this evening, probably late though."

"I won't be hard to find. Talk to you later."

* * *

"Brittany, this is Al."

"Go ahead Boss."

"Where are you?"

"On the south end of the inner circle. We've been stopping and looking around a little and haven't made very good progress today."

"I'm on the south-west side and I left Sean and Lorna back on the north side. I guess I'm closer than you are. I'll head back. Keep coming around the circle. You may not get back to where we are tonight, but that's alright. We'll compare notes later."

"Ok. When are we going to branch out and start our systematic search of the place?"

"Once we get the center mapped. I want to see how it lies compared to Pavonis. Call me in the morning if you don't get to where we are tonight."

"Ok, will do."

"Arnold, status report," Al said.

"We've gone into several openings into the center section. In a few years I think we can figure it all out."

"Can you survive on your own tonight?"

"Yeah. Where will you be?"

"I dropped Lorna and Sean off at 015 on the inner circle. I have to go back and get them."

"We're south-east of there. Maybe two hours away."

"You can come meet me if you want. You're closer to them than I am. I'm almost four hours away."

"Maybe we'd better go hook up with them. It may be after dark before you get there."

"Good. I'll meet you there and we can compare notes. Tomorrow we may need to spread out a little more. We'll go over that tonight."

"See you then."

* * *

"How far to the opening?" Lorna asked as the light began to fade.

"Maybe two miles," Sean said.

"Al, we're running late."

"Good, so am I. Arnold should be there any time though. I'm still an hour away."

"I'm glad I thought to put in a couple lights. Did you find anything today?"

"I found several more parking areas full of various types of equipment. The rest of it looks like manufacturing facilities of some sort. That's about it."

"We didn't fair much better. We have several machines that may help us in Pavonis, but still haven't figured out how to get them there."

"I'll see you soon."

"Ok, see you soon."

"Lorna, this is Arnold. Can we come in and get you?"

"I think so. It would certainly be nice not to have to walk the last couple of miles. Where are you?"

"I think we're where you went into the complex. There's a lot of footprints here and two sets of cruiser tracks."

"I'll shine my light up and see if you can pick it out."

"Yeah, I see it. We'll work our way toward you. See you soon."

"Great, my feet hurt."

* * *

"Mike, are you about ready to go?" Slim asked at breakfast the next morning.

"Yeah, the shuttle came in last night and they're getting it ready to go now."

"Joe and Jim are getting things ready inside. I talked to them last night and they're drafting some of Sean's engineers and some support people to drive the Martian Miners out here. They're giving them all lessons now. I think we can have them out here by tomorrow night."

"I'll get the transport headed this way this morning. It'll take them until tomorrow sometime to get here. They'll have to rest up a little before they head back."

"I'll wait out here and make sure the transport drivers get trained too. If they have any trouble getting out here, I'll be here to handle it."

"It sounds like you have this handled. I'd better get out of here. I have a lot of things to catch up on."

"Come back when you can stay longer."

"With everything that's about to happen around here; that may be soon."

"What all did they find over there?"

"Industrial and manufacturing stuff mainly. It'll take a lot of time to sort it out. I imagine they'll be back in a day or two."

"I'll walk you out to the shuttle," Slim said as Mike started to leave.

"I believe this is going to take on more of a life of its own than it already has. Lorna's still convinced that there's a way to get to the other volcanoes. She thinks there's a tunnel in a little nitch somewhere that we've been driving by. The one to Arsia Mons was almost missed. Patty said they almost drove right past it."

"We'll have to go over the map real close when we get it complete. Well, it looks like they're waiting for you. Have a good trip."

"Thanks. I have to get back to the hub so I can get some rest. I'll see you later. Call if you need anything."

"We always do," Slim said. "We always do."

"Yeah, I noticed that."

* * *

"Al, this is Brittany."

"Go ahead. Where are you?"

"We made better progress after we talked to you yesterday. We'll be to where you left Lorna and Sean yesterday, in about thirty minutes."

"We'll wait for you here. I'd like to see what you have for a map."

"We mapped the entire inner circle and think we need to go south and see if we can figure out where the southern boundaries are. After we go back out and download maybe we could do like Lorna and Eve did and map the outer ring. That would answer a lot of questions."

"I'll think about that while you head this way. See you in a few minutes."

"Ok, Brittany out."

"That *would* answer a lot of questions," Lorna said. "Maybe Eve and I could run half of it while she runs the other half with Johnny."

"We've put a lot of responsibility on those girls," Al said.

"Yeah, but they've handled everything we've thrown at them and asked for more. I'm a little apprehensive about having them running around in the dark for weeks at a time too. That doesn't alter the fact that it has to be done."

"Of course, you're right. We'll have them make a run to the south and map out what they can before they have to go out and download the information. We should be going out about the same time. We'll talk about it."

"It has to be done."

"Sean, do you have any idea where you want to set up in here?" Al asked.

"Either here or back where we came in first. That would keep the supply chain as short as possible. This is going to take some time. Also, we saw Lorna's bird again yesterday. I saw it this time."

"If there's a bird flying around in there, there has to be a food supply somewhere," Lorna said. "That means another garden or something."

"Brittany may have seen something in her travels," Al said. "We'll ask her when she gets here. Could you tell anything about it?"

"Just that it was very big. It was a long ways away and we could still pick it out."

"It seemed to be circling that tall structure in the distance," Sean said. "Maybe it has a nest there or something."

"Can we drive in that far?" Al asked.

"We got in several miles, and I think you can go at least that far," Lorna said. "We might be able to pick our way in farther."

"Arnold, maybe you could go to the south end and work your way back inside," Al said. "We'll work our way in from here. Map everywhere you go."

"When will we start looking out away from the center?" Arnold asked.

"Let's see if we can get a handle on the size of this place first. We'll go back out tomorrow and gather up reinforcements. Patty will be coming back in then. I need to call and get someone set up to come in with her. I don't want anyone over here alone. It's too far away to get to them if someone gets hurt."

"I've been thinking," Lorna said. "Maybe the way to handle this is to get everyone lined out and send them this way. We can run a couple of cruisers around the outside and fan out with the rest. We still have a couple areas to explore in Pavonis, but I think they can wait for a while. We need that command-post also."

"We're provisioned for several more days," Arnold said. "We can stay a while if you want to send Patty back in."

"There's Brittany now," Al said. "Let's see what she has for a perimeter map of this inner area. Britt, how'd you make out?"

"Ok, I guess. We have it mapped back to here, but we didn't see anything special."

"Can you pull it up on the outside monitor so we can all see it?"

"Sure, just a second."

They all gathered around the monitor and gazed at the image she had displayed. The circle wasn't as round as they had anticipated. It was more egg shaped. They calculated that it was over a hundred miles across and the long axis was half again that much.

"We didn't look into many of these openings after we talked to you yesterday," Brittany said. "When we needed to stop and stretch, we'd look around a little, but we didn't go into any of them."

"Going south is a good idea," Al said. "We're going to drive into the center and look around. You have supplies for several days yet, see what you can find down south."

"How about if we go out at about 195 to210 degrees and work our way back to where we came in? That way we'd be back at the point where we could go back and download."

"Yeah, that would cover about half of the outer circle," Lorna said. "We could get Patty to pick up the other half when she comes back in tomorrow."

"Ok, but be careful," Al said.

"We always are," Johnny said.

"This place gives me the creeps," Al said. "Be very careful."

"What do you mean; gives you the creeps?" Lorna asked.

"I can't explain it yet. I have a feeling that wasn't there in the other complex. Everyone be on your toes. It's probably my imagination but be careful. Arnold, you guys come in from the south and we'll go in from here. Brittany, you work your way out to the south-west and then come back to the east. When you get back to where we came in, head out and download. We'll get Patty to take the other half."

"When you get to the south end, keep an eye out for a tunnel leading to the ring of stones we saw on the satellite photos," Lorna said. "I'm betting there's one on the southern extreme of the loop."

"We're probably looking at three days to get back to the exit," Brittany said. "It's kind of hard to tell until we get down there but judging from the length of what we have here, where we came in, that's my guess."

"Ok, let's get started," Al said. "Keep in contact."

* * *

"Slim, this is Joe."

"Go ahead."

"We're about ready to head out. I have ten of the Martian Miners lined up and we had to draft four of the cruisers for support. They'll meet us about dark."

"Any idea when you might get out here?"

"Well, judging from when we took the other one out a few weeks ago, late tomorrow afternoon. We'll have to do the last few hours on air packs. We're also going to clean a path on the way out. I have three miners set up to sweep the dust as we go. I think we can get rid of most of it that way."

"Good. Keep me informed of your progress. If you need anything, just call. Smitty can find me here."

"Slim, how are things going?" Patty asked as she entered the control room.

"Not too bad. What the hell did you guys find anyway?"

"Well, I found the way into a tunnel that headed south. We came back out and got the others to go with us. About four hundred miles south-west of here we found the way into Arsia Mons. When we got to the center of the complex, we found an industrial sight of some kind."

"That should be interesting. What kind of stuff was in there?"

"Just a bunch of machinery and stuff. There's also a lot of mobile equipment and construction equipment. Sean was really excited about it."

"How are they going to handle it?"

"I don't know yet. I came over here to give Al a call so I can figure out where he wants me to start."

"I'll raise him for you," Smitty said. "Al this is control."

"Go ahead, Smitty."

"Al, this is Patty. What's the plan of attack for tomorrow?"

"We'd like you to run the outer ring so we can define this place. Brittany is working from the south-west back toward where we all came in. We'd like you to hang a right at the first intersection and go around the edge until you intersect with her tract. We're going to be inside the inner circle most of the day. If you happen to find any tunnels leading out away from the center, do a little checking on them too. I don't know if the outer ring is where we came in."

"That sounds reasonable. Are you going to be around for a couple days?"

"That depends on what we find in here," Al said. "We should head back out and get things lined up for a full-scale assault on this area. We should know more tonight."

"I'll give you a call when we leave here in the morning, in case there are any changes," Patty said.

"Talk to you then. Al out."

"Looks like you'll be spending a few days in the dark," Slim said.

"Yeah, it looks that way," Patty said. "I don't mind the first couple days, but after that it gets to me a little. Alex seems to handle it better than I do."

"It's one of those things that you either can or can't handle very well. Eventually you can get used to it though."

"We've spent most of our time, Brittany, and I, out in the open. We weren't exposed to this underground environment until the last year or so."

"You seem to have adapted pretty well. God, that system for mapping has saved us all. Without it we'd still be running around not knowing where we were or where we were going."

"We started working on that on the trip here, from Earth. Hollie sure helped work the kinks out of the program for it. I don't have the programming skills she has."

"She's done a lot of that. It's what got her on this crew in the first place."

"Well, I'd better go see if Alex has the cruiser ready to go for in the morning."

"Good luck"

* * *

"How far have we gone?" Lorna asked.

"Almost eight miles," Al said. "It's slow going, but it's better than walking."

"Look. Above that tall structure. There it is again."

"Well, I'll be damned. I see it too. God, it has to have a wingspan of twenty feet at least."

"It may be more than that. It's hard to tell because we're still so far away. See, its landing on top of that tall building."

"Where does it get its food? It has to eat."

"I'll bet we find another garden connected to this place," Lorna said. "That's the only explanation that makes any sense. And it has to be easily accessible from here. There hasn't been any sign that it ventures outside into the tunnels. Surely if it did, there would be places where it had landed, and we'd be able to tell."

"I won't argue with you. It's just one of the questions we'll have to answer. Hang on a minute. Brian, this is Al."

"Yeah, Boss."

"We need a habitat trailer brought out to the outer complex. Mike is sending us a habitat to bring to Arsia Mons. When can you get it brought out?"

"I can have it out there tomorrow. We're getting several cruisers ready to support the miners that they're transporting out now. They'll have to catch the miners before dark, so they have a place to bunk for the night."

"Send it on out. When can you and Eve join us over here?"

"As soon as we can figure out how to get there, I guess. Hollie may have to stay over here for a week or so, but I think we're about finished until we can figure out a way to get up high in the library."

"Ok, meet us at the outer complex tomorrow night. We'll have a long day today and tomorrow, but we need to start breaking teams off and getting them out to the Pavonis complex. Start calling in all of the mapping cruisers and have them downloaded by tomorrow night if possible. We'll get them lined out when we get there."

"That may not be enough time for some of the ones on the north end," Brian said. "We have three up there. I can get the rest in by then though."

"Get all you can. I'll call Hollie and have her take care of the ones we decide to leave there."

"Will do. Is there anything else we need over there?"

"Yeah, a big butterfly net."

"A what?"

"Never mind. I'll explain when we get out tomorrow night."

"Ok, whatever you say."

"See you then. Al out."

"You aren't thinking of trying to catch that thing, are you?" Lorna asked.

"No, not really. We do need to keep an eye on it though. Who knows what kind of complications it might cause."

"Al, look to the north-west," Sean said. "What do you make of that?"

"Where?"

"There. It looks like a big hole in the roof of this place."

CHAPTER THREE

"You might be right," Al said. "It could be the center of the old volcano. That's something we didn't see at Pavonis."

"Could there be another level above this one?" Sean asked.

"Why not," Lorna said. "There was inside Pavonis. How are we going to get up there?"

"Patience," Al said. "We're just getting started over here. If there's another level, there has to be a way to get up there. We'll just have to go find it."

"Again, the more we learn, the more questions we have. I just get impatient."

"Al, there's a beam across the road ahead," Sean said. "We may have to find another way to get any farther."

"Let's stop and take a look," Al said as he pulled to a stop short of the beam.

As they climbed out, they stopped to look around. To the south loomed the tall tower they were trying to get to. In the distance to the west were several other tall towers spaced unevenly, dotting the horizon. The soil here was dry and dusty, but not as bad as what they had encountered inside Pavonis Mons. The condition of the structures and equipment around them was good, considering the length of time they had been sitting idle.

"Think we can move that thing?" Al asked.

"It looks pretty heavy to me," Lorna said.

"Let me see if I can get that forklift-looking thing started," Sean said. "If I can get it started, we shouldn't have any problem moving it."

"While you guys mess with this, I'm going to have a look around," Lorna said.

"Don't go too far," Al said. "This won't take long."

"I'll be close. Just give me a call when you're about ready."

As Sean went toward the machine he'd been looking at, Lorna wandered into a factory building that was close by. Once inside, she found herself in the edge of a very large warehouse. There were a few crates around the edge, but for the most part it was empty. The roof was well over a hundred feet high, and it appeared to be almost a thousand feet long.

"Al, this might be a good place to set up a habitat," she called on her radio.

"I thought we were going to set it up in the tunnel," Al said.

"This building is more than big enough. I'm thinking there may be a power source connected to it too, if we can find it and get it to work."

"God, woman, you're awful optimistic aren't you."

"Yeah, but what the hell. If you dream, dream big."

"Sean has this thing started, so head back this way. We'll be ready to go in a minute."

"Ok, I'll be there in a minute."

"Arnold, how are you guys doing?" Al asked while he waited for Sean.

"We're just entering the south end of the complex. We're going to try and pick our way into the center."

"Yeah, that's what we're trying to do too, but the going is slow. See what you can do."

"Ok, we'll keep in touch."

"Al, this is Patty."

"Go ahead."

"We may be able to get into the outer ring by mid afternoon tomorrow. We'll try to get an early start. Where's Brittany hiding?"

"She headed southwest this morning, but I'm sure she's nowhere near the outer ring yet. We got off to a late start."

"Patty, we're kicking it out on a course of 210 degrees," Brittany said. "That should put us about straight across from where you come in. That should split it in half."

"Ok, we'll take the north and west sections," Patty said. "See you around."

"Roger that. Brittany out."

"You kids be careful," Al said when the chatter had subsided.

"Will do, Boss," Patty said.

"Us too."

"Sounds like they have a handle on things," Lorna said as she walked up behind Al.

"Yeah, I just hope they take it easy. Here comes Sean."

Sean rolled past the cruiser and lifted the beam out of the road. When the road was clear he parked the machine to one side and got out.

"It's going to take us several hours to get back out," Al said. "Maybe we should just head back out and go back to the Pavonis compound. This can wait until another day."

"Yeah, I guess it can," Lorna said.

"Let's head back," Al said. "We have a lot to do to get everyone lined out and get them in here."

With the tight confines of the inner area of the cavern, Al had trouble turning the cruiser around.

"Why don't you try the four-wheel steering?" Lorna asked.

"We haven't used it much," Al said. "I forgot it was there. Do you want to drive?"

"No, you're doing fine. I'll shut up."

"That'll be the day. That—will—be—the—day."

* * *

"Joe, this is Slim. How are you doing?"

"Not too bad. We stopped at the edge of the good air and spent the night. We've been on the road again this morning for a couple hours. I estimate we'll be there late afternoon."

"That sounds good. Al and Lorna will be here this evening. And the transport should be in late tonight."

"We'll be ready. It's going smoothly. It just takes a long time."

"How are your escorts doing?"

"We're bored to tears," Sharon said.

"Oh, baby, relax," Joe said. "We need you to stay close in case there's a problem."

"Yeah, I know, but this is the pits, poking along behind you."

"How's the dust back there?"

"There isn't any. You're making a clean sweep of it."

"That's good, isn't it?"

"That's very good. Now see if you can get a little more speed out of those things. Sharon out."

"Yes, dear," Joe said and laughed.

* * *

At 2100 that evening Al pulled into the small dome of the Pavonis compound. The three domed structure was a welcome sight. As they maneuvered into the center dome to park in the maintenance area, a small contingent gathered to greet them.

"Mother, what have you gotten us into this time?" Eve asked as they got out of the cruiser.

"Did you get a look at what Patty downloaded?" Lorna asked.

"Yeah, and it looks a lot like what we have here. Do you have any idea how big it is yet?"

"No, but in a few days we'll know more. Patty and Brittany are working their way around the outer ring now. Brittany will be the first one back here with the new information. That won't be for a couple days though."

"Have you gathered up all the cruiser crews?" Al asked.

"There are still two that can't be here until the day after tomorrow," Eve said. "They were clear up on the north end. I told them to work their way back here for a download, but not to worry about it too much. I figured it wouldn't hurt to leave two crews here."

"That will give us twenty-two crews to map Arsia," Lorna said. "That should be enough."

"Slim, what's the status on the Martian Miners?" Al asked.

"We have ten of them lined up waiting for transport. Joe led them out this afternoon. We've been going over a deployment plan for them and need to have you look it over. It's going to take several days to get them delivered. I talked to Bill back at the mine this afternoon and he's not happy with us, but he'll get over it."

"What did you do to him?"

"We hijacked Dan and Jeff from him and I'm still working on getting Josh too. You may have to help me with that one."

"Lorna, let's go have something to eat and get Smitty to call the crews together," Al said. "I'd like to get some of them headed in first thing in the morning."

"Eve, can you download our cruiser for us?" Lorna asked. "Put the information on a disc and bring it to the dining hall so we can put it up on the big display."

"Sure. Anything else?"

"No, it's been a long day and I need food. That's all I can think of for now."

The small band started their migration toward the dining hall as Eve and Brian connected the cruiser to the port for the download. The large number of cruisers and Martian Miners made navigating through the center dome awkward. They had never had this many in one place at any one time.

Most of the cruiser teams were lounging in the dining hall when they walked in. Lorna got on the phone and placed a call to Smitty in the control room to gather everyone else.

"We're going to get something to eat, and then go over what we have with you," Al announced to the gathering. "Get ready. Here we go again."

As they finished eating, Eve came in with the disc Lorna had asked for.

"You guys get around," Eve said as she handed the disc to Lorna.

"Put it in the computer and bring it up on the big display," Lorna said as she finished her second glass of tea. "I may live after all."

"Let me pour you another glass," Al said. "You're on."

"Gee, thanks. Ok, listen up everyone," Lorna said as the map of the two Mons flashed to life on the giant monitor at the end of the dining hall. "We're all going on a little trip. As you can see, there's work to be done to the south. We'll assign areas to each team in the morning before you head out. We'd like you to concentrate on the spokes first, and then work the rings. The first run inside will be only for three days or so. By the time you come back out, we'll have things better defined.

"We don't have much more of an idea what's there than we did when we started exploring the Pavonis complex. We've defined the center and some of the spokes close to the entry point. The outer rings are being mapped now and should give us a better idea of the size of the area we'll have to cover. Any questions?"

"How long does it take to get over there?"

"About six hours. That's going to mean that you'll have less time to work for now. We're working on getting a computer set up at this location, close to the center of things," Lorna said indicating the spot where they had decided to put the first of the habitats. "Once that is accomplished, we'll restock and download there. We have in an order for several more cruisers that we'll use mainly to run supplies between here and there. We'll rotate crews back out here for a couple days off when we can.

"We need this defined as quickly as possible. We have four crews here that are made up of engineer types. They'll be assigned to the central hub of the complex for now. Al, do you have anything to add?"

"Just this. There are strange things over there. We've seen what appear to be giant birds of some kind. Watch yourselves in there. I have a strange feeling about this one. Now, go get some rest. We'll start assigning areas at 0700. You'll be going in on fifteen-minute intervals starting at 0800."

"What do you have in mind for us?" Brian asked.

"We'd like you to take Eve and work your way into the center hub," Al said. "There's a lot you can look at in there. Eve can work with you for now. Most of the work is just mapping the area. The others can do that. We'll be back over there after we get things lined out here."

"Al, the transport just arrived," Slim said. "It looks like they brought several more cruisers. Joe and I will see that they get unloaded."

"Thanks Slim. I guess you'll have to set this one out for now."

"Yeah, it sounds like Mike has plans for us for a couple weeks. Can you make that call to Bill for me?"

"I think we're done here. Let's go to my office and see what we can offer him to persuade him."

"We'll see you in the morning," Lorna said as Al and Slim left.

"Get some rest. You look like hell," Al said over his shoulder.

"Gee, thanks."

* * *

"Bill, I'm not disturbing you, am I?" Al asked when Bill answered the phone.

"Hell, yes, you're disturbing me. What's the idea of stealing all my people?"

"Easy, Bill. We're not stealing them this time," Al said. "Just borrowing them a few days at a time. How many crews do you have trained on the miners so far?"

"Everyone has had a turn at it. Production has tripled and they had to put on another transport just to haul it away. That thing puts out some high-grade shit. The boys at the mill won't have much to do if you get everybody one of them."

"Would you like to have another one?"

"Damn right. Who do I have to kill to get it?"

"Just loan us some of your guys for a couple weeks. I'll see to it that you get another one when we get them to the other mines. Fair enough?"

"You strike a hard bargain, but I guess it'll be worth it in the long run. How many of these things do you have?"

"About forty," Al said. "When we can get them distributed, everyone will have at least three of them. You'll have four if I have anything to say about it. You'll also be the first to get the next wave of them."

"When will you need them?"

"Not until we can get them delivered. Slim will be handling the logistics of this. He'll let you know."

"So, you want Dan and Jeff to start with, right?"

"And Josh," Al said. "We're going to be running three training crews at a time. We won't have them for long."

"Alright. Have Slim give me a heads up when they need to be ready. I'll have to juggle things around while they're gone."

"Thanks Bill. Talk to you later."

"I could only hear one side of that," Slim said.

"You're all set. Just let him know as soon as you get the shuttle scheduled. You can go by and pick them up."

"Why was he so hard to deal with on this?"

"I don't know. When you see him, ask him."

"You'd better get some rest. You've had a long day. I'll see to the cruisers and get the miners loaded."

"By the way, where's my wife? I kind of lost track of her."

"She's in your room. I had her brought in today. She's due for a day off too."

"Good. Thanks."

* * *

When morning dawned, Al was standing in the control room gazing at the eastern horizon. Smitty was just coming in.

"Looks like another clear day," Smitty said.

"Aren't they all?"

"Well, yeah, except when the sand kicks up. We haven't had one of those in a long time though."

"We're due. How are things going here?"

"Hell, it's like a ghost town. You guys have almost everyone inside. We get a few that come out for downloads and the supply people that get things ready to go in. Other than that, there is not much to do. I monitor the radio traffic to keep tabs on everyone. I can get a fairly good picture of things from that. I still want to make a run in there."

"You could go in for two or three days now if you want. Slim and his crew will be here waiting to deploy and train people on the miners. They can back up Albert. He seems to be doing alright. You could make a supply run into the area where the library is. That would give you the lay of things."

"Is there someone who could go to show me around?"

"I'm sure we can find someone. Alice has been in there several times. How about her?"

"Yeah, I'd like that."

"I think she kind of likes you," Al said.

"Is she out here now?"

"Yeah, she's been running supplies. I saw her last night. I'll set it up. You can leave when we get things lined out."

"Great. I'll get with Slim. Albert just went off shift so one of them will need to hang around here today."

"After you talk to Slim, pack a bag for three days or so. I'll set it up with Alice. Meet me in the maintenance area in an hour," Al said as he left.

Lorna was getting the crews lined out in the dining hall when Al walked in. Three teams were already at their cruisers preparing to leave.

"Al, I had them go in and branch out after they get in past the outer ring," Lorna said as Al joined her. "I assigned each of them to a spoke and that should give us the best coverage."

"That should work out fine," he said. "Where are the four engineering teams going in?"

"I've spread them out a little. They can find a place to go in on their own. I just suggested that they hit it from all sides. Eve and Brian are going to go back to where we were yesterday. Brian has to get the habitat dropped off and set up first. Two of the other teams are going to meet them straight in from the entrance. They can help get it set up. With the ten extra cruisers that came in on the transport, we have more machines than we do drivers for a change. I thought you and Mona could take one and Sean and I could take another."

"How are we stacking up inside Pavonis?"

"Martin and Jen are still working on the upper garden. They have several people each. Hollie has the other nine that came with Arnold and twelve more. She's got control of the two cruisers that are still inside Pavonis too. I've split the supply chain 70/30. Most of them will now be going to Arsia."

"Mona is getting a computer ready to go in when the habitat is set up. We'll take it in with us when we go. Where's Alice?"

"She's getting ready to take another load to Hollie. Why?"

"Smitty wants to go for a ride. I'm going to pair them up. He deserves to have a look around. Slim and his crew will be on standby until the transport delivers the machines. They can watch over things here."

"You'd better catch her. I think she was about ready to leave."

"Ok, see you in a bit," Al said as he left.

The center dome was littered with cruisers. Al had to look around for a few minutes to find Alice. She was getting ready to leave when he caught up with her.

"Alice, hold up for a minute," Al said, stepping in front of her cruiser.

"What's up Boss?"

"You've been running solo for quite a while. Can I get you to take a passenger this time?"

"Yeah, I guess so. Who?"

"Smitty. He's been baby-sitting out here all this time and hasn't had a chance to look around in there. Do you mind?"

"Not at all. He's fun to be around. His sense of humor is a little strange, but once you figure him out, he's a lot of fun to be around. Yeah, I'd like that. Where is he?"

"He'll be along soon. He had to get someone to cover for him. Just hang out until he gets here. I need him back in three days. In the meantime, show him the sights. After you drop off your supplies at the library, maybe you could come back by way of the upper garden. You won't have any problem being stuck out there with him alone?"

"If there's going to be a problem, it'll be him that has it," Alice said. The look in her eyes gave Al the impression that she was going to enjoy this trip.

"Stay out of trouble," Al said.

"Yes sir!"

* * *

Late that afternoon Al was seeing the last of the cruisers depart for Arsia Mons. They had managed to get twenty-eight teams into the maze that had to be unraveled. They had scattered them all around the outer area and designed search patterns for them to follow. Over the course of the next few weeks, they would determine the extent of the Arsia complex.

"Al, can you meet me in the office?" Lorna called over the intercom.

"What's up?" Al asked when he got there a few minutes later.

"There was a message from Mike when I got here. I thought you should see it."

"What does he have on his mind?"

"Here, take a look."

Al took the fax sheet and read through it.

"There's sandstorm brewing. We haven't had one of those since we got here. We'd better get with him and see how bad it might be."

"I'll get him on the line. Give me a minute."

"Mike, how bad is this storm going to be?" Al asked when they made the connection.

"It could be the worst one we've had in five years. They still don't have it defined. It's coming out of the Hellas crater. They say it may blanket the entire planet in less than a week."

"We should be alright here. We can supplement our supplies with the stuff from the garden. The transport left here this morning with the Martian Miners. What's this going to mean for the crews we were going to send with them?"

"I have three shuttles dispatched to you, full of supplies. They may be the last ones you get for a while. We can run it in rovers if we need to, but if it gets too bad that won't even last long. The other mines will have their regular transport runs to bring in their supplies. If it gets too bad, we may have to send a transport to you too."

"That's a last resort. I think we can hold out for quite a while. Do you really think it'll get that bad?"

"Well, we'll keep that option open. Sally just brought in an update. Shit, the winds are forecasted to reach three-forty. That's almost double what we usually see. You guys better tie things down out there. You don't have any kind of protection from that kind of wind. The complex should handle it, but I'd take preparations to go underground if I were you."

"This is going to get a little hairy, isn't it?" Lorna said.

"You might say that," Mike said. "There's an outside chance the complex could disappear."

"That sounds serious enough. We'd better see what we have to nail this place down with."

"Lorna, get on the radio and get Brian back here," Al said. "We may need to put in a couple more sets of blast doors in the lower tunnel. If we lose the complex, that would be all we'd have to shield us from the storm. Have Slim get everyone rounded up and start hauling everything inside. Recall the last ten cruisers to give them a hand. The new exploration can wait until we have this handled."

"Sounds like we'd better bring most of them back," Lorna said.

"Go take a head count and see who we need."

"Ok, I'll be back in a few minutes."

"Al, is there anything else I can do from here?" Mike asked.

"No, not really. Thanks for the warning though."

"I'll get you all the supplies I can get there before it hits. That's about all I can do for now."

"Don't take any chances with the shuttle crews. We won't be able to go out looking for them if they go down. Also, we may lose contact during the worst of the storm. The link to the satellites may go down and we don't have a hard wire connection to you from out here."

"We'll talk again before this hits," Mike said. "Keep me informed."

"Will do," Al said and hung up the phone. He redialed the main weather station at the hub just as Lorna came back in.

"This is Al, at Pavonis. I need an update and most important, I need to know when it's going to get here."

After listening for several minutes, he kind of cringed as he looked at Lorna.

"Ok, thanks. Keep us updated out here. We're real vulnerable," he said as he hung up the phone. "Do you remember that little storm you went to the hub in last year?"

"Yeah, I remember. Is this going to be that bad?"

"That was like a breeze on a pond compared to a hurricane in the ocean. No one has seen one like this, not ever. It's still building, and it keeps shifting directions. He said the way it's coming out of the Hellas crater, there's no way of telling where it's going to go until it breaks out.

"We need to get everything that has wheels on it headed this way to haul all our supplies inside. Some of them will have to use the air packs to get in far enough to get to the better air."

"Slim has everyone this side of Brian and Eve turning around," Lorna said. "That will leave seven of the ones that left this morning continuing to Arsia. There are only twenty people that were going to be staying out here. The rest have been inside. Joe and Jim are rounding them up to handle the shuttles that are coming and to get things lined up to go inside. Where do we take everything?"

"The upper garden in Pavonis," Al said. "There's food and water there. If we have to hold out for a long time, that's the logical place to start. Give Martin a call and have him start coordinating things from that end. We can take care of it out here and make a few runs too."

"Al, this is Slim. We have a shuttle on final."

"Already? I didn't expect them this soon."

"It's the normal run, I think. How many were you expecting?"

"Three."

"Where are we going to put all this stuff? Three shuttle loads is a lot of supplies."

"Start sending it inside as soon as you can. We have several of those small trailers we can pull with the cruisers. Take it to the upper garden for now."

"Ok, we'll start sending the food in first."

"Martin's going to take care of it on the other end. He doesn't know it yet though."

"Al, instead of dropping this on Martin, I think I should take one of the first loads in," Lorna said. "We're going to need to coordinate things better than we have a plan for right now. We may have to shuttle some of the food to other habitats. I hope we have the capability to keep the refrigerated stuff from spoiling."

"Ok, go get things lined out in there. I'll contact control at the hub and see just when the other shuttles are due to arrive. Have Slim get you lined out."

"I'll contact you when I get there so we can get the supplies to the right spots. Eve and Brian won't be back until late this evening. They were over halfway to Arsia when we called them back."

"We'll just have to do the best we can. By the time you get to the upper garden, I should have a better handle on what we're going to have to do to weather this thing."

Lorna left and Al watched the horizon to the south-east. For the moment there were no indications of how bad the storm might be, or even if there was one.

* * *

Deep in the depths of the Hellas crater, the lowest point on Mars, the swirling winds churned at incredible speeds. Even the immense proportions of the crater couldn't confine them for long. On occasions like this the magnetic forces of the planet became unsettled, leaving the surface of the planet vulnerable to the whims of the forces of nature.

Hellas crater, which spanned almost one-tenth of the planet's surface, in the southern hemisphere, was a half a world away from the complex at Pavonis Mons. It is still uncertain what caused this giant crater. Some speculate that it was the contact point of a giant meteor strike. The corresponding area on the opposite side of the planet is known as the bulge.

Perhaps there was a strike large enough to indent the surface in this area and the force was so great that it caused the far side to bulge. If there was an event of this magnitude, it would most certainly have killed any life on the planet. The area, still largely unexplored, asked many questions, but revealed few answers.

* * *

It was late afternoon when Lorna arrived at the habitat in the upper garden. Martin and Jen were there to meet her.

"What's all the commotion?" Martin asked.

"There's a big sandstorm brewing," Lorna said as she got out of the cruiser. "We're relocating everything into the mountain. Mike said there was a chance the complex outside might not take this one."

"We could be cut off from the rest of the planet?" Jen asked.

"There is that chance. Most of the mines are located where they're protected from the full force of this kind of wind. We're not."

"How much will we have to work with?" Martin asked.

"They're sending us three or four shuttle loads of food and essentials. That may be all we get for a while. We need to stockpile most of it here. Al thinks this is the best place to set up."

"I agree. We have the capacity to sustain ourselves indefinitely. Jen has a lot of the garden mapped out and found three areas where we can rig cold storage. There are CO2 outcroppings. Jen said you found something similar in the lower tunnels too. Is that right?"

"Yeah, we found one source. It could be used that way, I guess. Where are the ones up here?"

"Come look at the map I made," Jen said as she led the way. After pulling the map up on the monitor she continued. "You see this area. It took us a long time to get there, but as you can see, we had already covered most of the area inside the garden by the time we got there. You'll have to excuse the erratic look of the map, it's still only a preliminary sketch of what all is in there. If we go east, they're only twenty miles away."

"Martin, do we have any engineer types here? We've moved everyone around so much that I can't keep up with where they all are."

"A couple of Sean's guys came up from the library area this afternoon. I'm sure they're still around. What do you need them for?"

"I'd like Jen to take them to those CO2 outcroppings and have them look things over. Jen, can we find another way in there without going through twenty miles of garden?"

"Yeah, now that we know where we're going. There are several other ways in there. We just have to pick the closest one. I can try to take them in here, it's the closest," Jen said, indicating an entrance just beyond the area they were looking at.

"God girl. Take any help you think you might need. There should be an extra cruiser here, take that too if you need it."

"I'll go round them up," Jen said as she left.

"Al and I will be shuttling supplies along with the rest. Can you handle things here?"

"I'll shuffle things around a little," Martin said. "How long do we have?"

"We don't know yet. The best guess we have right now is three days. Al should be getting a better idea on that. He may know more by now. I guess I'd better check in with him."

"You can use the radio in the habitat. It looks like you could use a glass of tea."

"That does sound good."

* * *

"Al this is Lorna."

"I was wondering when you were going to call," Al said.

"Can you load Sean up and send him in. We're going to need his help getting some kind of refrigeration set up in here. Have you found out any more about the storm?"

"It's still building. They think it may come at us from the southwest this time. I'll get another update in a couple hours. Sean's right here. What do you need him for?"

"Jen found three outcroppings of CO2 in the upper garden. We need to see if we can use them for refrigeration. We also have that one we

49

found in the lower tunnels. We could make a cold storage out of it pretty easy."

"I'll get a load and head that way," Sean said. "Do you have anyone looking at things yet?"

"Martin said a couple of your guys were here somewhere. I don't know which ones. Jen's rounding them up now to take them over there to have a look. We might have an idea of what's here by the time you get here."

"How many of those alien truck looking things do you have there?" Al asked.

"Al, we have fifteen of them working in this area," Martin said. "They should all be coming back to the habitat soon. What do you need them for?"

"In order to get everything we need moved, we may have to stockpile it inside and have them pick it up and take it on in. We can get it far enough with the cruisers to reach the good air. Send them out first thing in the morning, with every available person you can lay your hands on. By the time they get there, there should be enough stuff for them to get started."

"Ok. Anything else I can do here?"

"Just figure out how to feed us all. If this thing lasts for more than a couple weeks, we could have a problem."

"Al, are the transport ships going to be able to reach the hub?" Lorna asked. "You may want to ask Mike about that."

"They'll probably have to stack up in orbit. If it gets as bad as it sounds like it will, they might have a problem. I'll check with Mike. I'll talk to you later."

* * *

After the conversation with Lorna, Al's focus changed from the immediate situation that they faced, to the long range. Lorna was right. With almost a half a million people to take care of, the supply stockpiles at the hub could be depleted in just over a month. He placed a call to Mike.

CHAPTER FOUR

"Mike, this is Al."

"I hope your day is going better than mine," Mike said when he answered the phone.

"We'll be ready here. Lorna posed a question to me a few minutes ago. Will you be able to receive supplies from the transport ships from Earth?"

"We've been looking at that. The conditions may get so bad that that may be impossible. The next question may be how long will it last? We have stores for four to six weeks. Some of the perishables may not last that long, but we hope the storm will die down before that happens. The transport ships may have to stack up in orbit and wait for a break in the winds. What were you thinking?"

"I haven't had much time to think about it yet," Al said. "We're not worried about the long haul here. I'm more worried about the rest of you at this point. It may come to a point where we may have to start supplying you with the food you need. You have a lot of mouths to feed."

"Let's hope it doesn't come to that. We don't have any way to get it from there to here."

"No, but we have the ability to create one. We could tunnel from here. Bear with me for a minute; I'm just thinking out loud. We need to set up a contingency plan. The biggest problem I see that we face is communications. We won't know how bad things are there until it's too late. Do we have time to establish a hard wire connection?"

"No, I don't think so. The storm is about ready to break loose and head this way. I just got an update a few minutes ago. They say you'll get it first this time and they say it'll be midday, the day after tomorrow. That leaves us less than forty-eight hours. It takes almost twenty hours just to drive it in the transports."

"Can you divert the transport that's hauling the Martian Miners? Divert it to the hub."

"Yeah, but I don't see what good that will do."

"Look, if this thing gets as bad as you say it's going to, we're all in a lot of trouble. The only hope of outlasting it may be what we have here. If we lose communication, we'll be fine, but you may not be. I'm just trying to think ahead."

"I see your point. What do you have in mind?"

"I'm not sure yet, but I think it would be a lot better if you divert the miners to the hub. If we decide to tunnel, we can work it from both ends. If they're spread out, we'll have to do it all from here."

"You're talking hundreds of miles of tunnels. Most of it through areas we know very little about. You can't just follow the roads."

"Do you have a better idea?"

"No."

"Run it past some of your people. We'll look at it here and see what we can come up with. I'll get back with you in the morning. Sean's here with me and we'll look it over."

"Talk to you then," Mike said and hung up.

"He has a lot on his mind," Sean said.

"We'd better see if we can take some of the load off," Al said. "Let's go take a look at the map and see if we can see any problems with this hair-brained idea I just had. I may have gotten us in over our heads."

"No, I don't think so. The only problem I see is the terrain. There are several areas that we don't know much about. How big would this tunnel have to be?"

"Big enough to handle a transport, or maybe two. We may have to supplement their food supplies for a while. Also, it would give us an uninterruptible supply line for later. If we can develop the gardens to feed most of the planet it would be a good idea to have a way to get the supplies there in all kinds of weather."

"We'll need to stay three or four hundred feet below the surface. That's going to give us an interesting line. I wonder what all we'll find on the way?"

"This could be fun. Can we ventilate it well enough so we don't have to work in suits?"

"I think the complex here can support that. The problem will be getting circulation that far away. What happened with those fans that Brian had sent over from the hub?"

"We had time to install two of them to start circulating the air to the outer rings. They managed to get the air cleaned up in a couple areas. The problem with them is there are so many different directions for the air to go, it's hard to channel it."

"That won't be a problem in a tunnel. We may have to set up a series of airlocks to keep control of it though."

"Ok, here's the surface map," Al said as he displayed it on a large monitor in the computer lab. "What do you think?"

"The shortest distance is always a straight line," Sean said. "Or in this case the great circle route. Another thing to consider is an actual straight line. If we angle down to the depth that we'll need, we can draw a line directly to the hub. That would give us the actual shortest distance."

"Look here. We're going to have a problem here. This finger of the chasm is too close to the line we're looking at. If we break into a fissure or something, our people are screwed. We'll need to stay north of that. Shit, this isn't going to be as easy as I'd hopped."

"It looks like we'll have to leave here on a heading of 065, and run to a point northwest of the hub. Then we can turn southeast. That's the most feasible line I can see."

"It'll be a long haul to go that way, but I agree. Can we do this?"

"Yeah, I don't see any reason that we can't. You have the people available, don't you?"

"We can make do with the ones we have, but I'd like to have more. This will be a 24/7 operation. To carve out a tunnel that size and that long, well, nothing of this magnitude has ever been tried. I'd better see if I can call in a little help. Without this tunnel, the rest of the people on the planet could be in peril. This place sustained millions of people for a very long time. I think we can adapt and manage alright, but they'll be screwed in less than two months. They rely almost completely on the regular transports from Earth."

"Ok, where do we start the tunnel?" Sean asked. "Once we determine that, we can get started."

"I'd like to start around the upper garden, but I'm worried about opening up that much in that area," Al said. "I guess we'd better drop down to the lower garden somewhere and start there. We'll have to go in and look it over before we decide for sure. I'll have to think about this a little more. It's all kind of snowballed in the last hour or so."

"Snowballed yes, but it's a good plan. We can make this happen."

"Lorna's expecting you to be there tonight. I'll come in early in the morning and we can look around. By the time I get there you should have a handle on what she's looking at. I'll be able to get with Mike again and see if we even need to pursue this. Right now, the most pressing thing is to get ready here. If we get caught with our pants down, we can't help anyone."

"I'll get loaded and go on in. I'll give this more thought on the way. You might want to run it by Slim and his crew, and Brian too. It won't hurt to get everyone thinking about the same thing while we do all this other stuff."

"We'll go over it at dinner. You might want to grab a bite before you leave. It's going to be 2100 or so by the time you get there."

"I'd better go. If you come up with anything, let me know."

"I will."

After Sean left, Al studied the map for a while and put in a call for Slim to bring his crew to the computer lab. When they arrived, he laid out the situation and what he'd been thinking about.

"I don't see a problem doing that," Slim said. "It would be a big job, but with the alien technology it should be a snap."

"I'm thinking about getting Bill to bring over Dan and Jeff. He's going to have a fit, but I think I can get him to see the problem. We're going to have to run this balls out to have a shot at doing any good. I haven't had time to run all the numbers yet, so I don't know how long it will take."

"We could use the help," Joe said. "You could always go over his head."

"And I will if I have to. I think he'll see the big picture. Hell, we've made them all rich over there."

"Yeah, and they'll want to survive to spend it," Slim said. "I think even I could get him to go along this time. He sure got independent after we left over there."

"It's his operation now," Al said. "You can't blame him for doing what he thinks is best."

"Is this the route you're thinking about?" Slim asked.

"Yeah, unless someone has a better idea. We'll have to stay well north of several of the branches of the chasm that reach well to the north, and then we'll have to navigate up into the hub. That's where it might get a little hairy. Look it over and see what you come up with."

"It would be a good idea to have a direct navigational link with the other end," Jim said. "What I mean is, we have all the elevations and GPS coordinates, but we don't have it linked through the cruisers that we'll be using to do the actual navigation. What if we went over there and drove one of the cruisers back to establish that link?"

"That's a hell of an idea," Al said. "I may just have to keep you guys around. Jim, you, and Joe catch one of the shuttles and go check out things on the other end. Get one of the cruisers and come back tomorrow. It won't give us everything on the surface that we'd like to have, but it will establish that link. We'll use that cruiser to do the navigation if we do this thing."

"There's a shuttle due in two hours," Slim said. "There should be two more tomorrow."

"We'll go get ready," Joe said.

"I'll get you lined out with what you'll need on the other end," Al said. "I'm sure Mike can grease the wheels for you. He's pretty busy with all the other preparations, but I'm sure he'll have time to help you."

"That shuttle should be ready to leave here about 1900," Slim said. "You should even have time to get a little rest."

After they left, Al studied the map for a few minutes more and then placed a call to Mike.

"Are you staying busy?" Al asked when he finally answered.

"You have no idea how busy I am. What do you need?"

"I'm sending Joe and Jim in on the next shuttle. I want a cruiser for them to drive back tomorrow. Can you set them up?"

"Don't you have enough cruisers? We just dropped off ten more yesterday morning."

"I know, but this one could mean the difference between life and death to the operations on this planet."

"We don't have any of those here. I've had to pull all the people off the projects with a low priority and move them around. I don't think we have any completed units ready to go."

"Then we'll bring one from here. What we need is a navigational link between the two complexes. We're working out all the details on the tunnel idea between the two complexes."

"I haven't had time to look at that. I did manage to divert the transport with the miners aboard. They'll be in here late tonight."

"Mike, we may only have communications for another forty-eight hours. What do you want us to do when that happens?"

"Call me in the morning. And tell Joe to come see me. I'll have to give that some thought."

"Do you have an open area inside one of the domes that we can target with the miners? We don't want to come up under your office."

"In the production area. We've just completed a new dome. We haven't had time to put a lot in there yet."

"Ok, I'll have Joe go over it with you in the morning. Can you have Sally get them a couple rooms?"

"Done, now I have to go. Call me at 0700. Get your licks in before everyone has a shot at me."

"Good luck," Al said and hung up. His next call was to Bill at the mine where they had made the discovery that had gotten all this started. The mine he'd been in charge of until he and Lorna had moved their operations to Pavonis Mons. "Bill, I need help."

"This is going to cost me," Bill said.

"Yeah, but not as much as we've made you. I need you to bring Dan and Jeff over here tomorrow. Before you blow up, let me explain."

With that, Al launched into his explanation. For the next half hour, he did the best he could to impress the seriousness of the situation on Bill.

"Shit, they said it was going to be a bad one, but I never figured on any of this," Bill said finally.

"Can you spare them for a little while?"

"We'll be there by lunch, unless you need us sooner?"

"No, that should be fine. I'll wait and go inside after you get here. Can you spend the night? The storm shouldn't be here until late the following day."

"We'll have to check the weather when we get there. I'd like to go inside and look around."

"Good. Come as early as you can. I'll be here somewhere. I'll give you the fifty-cent tour."

"I'll roust them out early and get on over there. See you then."

With that done, Al worked his way over the proposed route again. Zooming in as close as he could and still maintain clarity on the monitor. He'd adjusted the route a little to stay well away from the obvious hazards. Then overlaid it on the map of the inner complex at Pavonis. By adjusting the track to a likely spot on the lower complex he was able to get an idea where would be the best place to start the tunnel. The track lined up with the spoke that laid on the same heading as he had decided on.

* * *

"I thought you'd be here an hour ago," Lorna said when Sean parked next to the habitat.

"I would have, but you sparked an unusual conversation. One that still isn't settled yet. What did you figure out here?"

57

"Jen isn't back yet. Let's go give her a call."

"Ok Jen. We'll come over in the morning," Martin was saying on the radio when they walked in.

"What was that all about?" Lorna asked.

"They're spending the night at the entrance to where they went in. They want us to come over in the morning."

"Do you feel like a little drive?" Sean asked. "That way we'd be there first thing in the morning. Al's going to want answers as soon as he gets here."

"Yeah, let's go on over that way," Lorna said.

"I'd better stay here," Martin said. "If you need me, just call."

"I'll drop that trailer here," Sean said. "Can you get it unloaded? I'll need to take it back out when I go."

"Sure thing."

"It's good to see you again," Lorna said as they drove away a few minutes later.

"You saw me this morning."

"But now we're alone again."

"Yes, we are, aren't we?"

* * *

Sean and Lorna pulled up just after first light to where Jen and her group were parked. They were just beginning to stir. They had carved a path through the thick foliage that had overgrown this entrance to the garden.

"Are you going to sleep all day?" Lorna asked as they got out.

"We got settled late," Jen said. "We didn't expect you for a while."

"We came part way last night."

"Oh, I see."

"Yeah, you probably do. What did you find in there?"

"In a couple miles, there are three outcroppings of CO_2. We looked them over and think we could construct something to keep the cold in. It might be easier to use the one on the lower level though. It would be a lot easier to wall it off as the main storage place."

"We'll look at both of them," Sean said. "Can we get in there now?"

"Yeah. Just follow our tracks. You can't get lost. We'll grab a bite of breakfast and join you in a few minutes."

"Jen, are you still having fun?" Lorna asked.

"Yeah. I have all these guys to do whatever I want. What more could a girl ask for. It's kick-ass."

"You just keep kicking their ass and we'll see you in a little while."

"Ok," Jen said as they started to drive into the garden.

Lorna looked back and saw her roust the others out of bed.

"Where in the hell did you find her?" Sean asked.

"Actually, she found us. We took a liking to her right away and included her. She didn't have the background for a lot of this, but she made up for it in enthusiasm."

It was slow going through the path that they had carved out. There were areas where it seemed well groomed and others where it was all grown together. The trees here had large leaves and even larger fruit. When they reached the spot they were looking for, Sean parked.

"They found the right stuff alright," Sean said. "We could erect a tent of some kind over each of these to get started. I do see the problems they were talking about. It would take a lot of construction to get this serviceable as a refrigeration set-up."

"Can we make it work, short-term?"

"Yeah, short-term. We'd better go take a look at the other spot; the one on the lower level. We can't do much here until we round up the stuff."

"Ok, let's go. Al will be here soon. We may not have time to get there before he comes."

"Give him a call," Sean said as they turned to leave.

* * *

"Al, this is Lorna."

"Go ahead."

"We can't do a lot with the area inside the upper garden. Sean says we can make it work in the short term. We're headed for the one on the lower level. When are you coming in?"

"Not for a while. Bill is bringing Dan and Jeff over this morning. I'm not sure when they'll get here. I'll bring them in with me."

"What are they coming over for?"

"Hasn't Sean told you what you stirred up yesterday?"

"Not yet, but I have a feeling he's about to."

"Let him fill you in. I have to call Mike."

"Ok. Keep us posted."

Al placed his 0700 call to Mike.

"You're punctual," Mike said when he answered.

"Just following orders. Have you seen Joe and Jim yet?"

"They just left. When you guys throw together a plan you don't mess around."

"Did they explain it to you?"

"Yeah, and I can't find any fault with it. If this thing lasts long enough, it could make the difference between survival and extinction."

"I've been going over the numbers and it's going to take a hell of a long time to get there. If we're going to do you any good, we need to get started. Can you do any of it from there?"

"We don't have anyone who knows anything about the miners."

"Can you catch Joe and have him call me?"

"Yeah, he was headed over to make sure the miners got unloaded alright."

"Do we have a go for the tunnel?"

"Hell yes. It won't cost shit and it could save all of us."

"That's all I needed to know. We'll take care of the rest from here. I do need to talk to Joe though."

"I'll see to it. Talk to you soon."

"Al, Bill's on the radio," Slim called over the intercom. "He'll be here in an hour or so."

"Slim, when's the next shuttle due?" Al said when he called Slim.

"It should be here any time. The other one is scheduled for about 1200. That should be the last of it."

"How's it going getting the stuff inside?"

"We're holding our own. We're just stockpiling it about two hours in. Martin is going to pick it up from there. We dropped off several loads last night and have ten more ready to roll."

"I'll be over in a minute. Can you handle things here for a day?"

"No sweat, Boss."

"When Bill gets here, I'll take them inside and go over our plan. I just got a go from Mike."

"Have you ever tried to do anything like this before?"

"No, nobody has. It would be too much to even consider without the Martian Miners."

* * *

"Slim, where's Al?" Joe asked when he called. "He wanted me to call."

"He's just walking in."

"Hello," Al said when Slim handed him the phone.

"You wanted me to call?"

"Joe, we have a go on the tunnel. I've been thinking that it's too risky to tunnel up blind from here into the hub. I need you to start a tunnel from there. Run it small for now and we'll try to connect with it. Can you do that and still get back here?"

"Yeah, I think so. It'll be a hell of a long day, but we don't have many options left."

"Call Mike and he'll tell you where to start. When you're done, have them put in a double set of doors and keep them closed. Then get your asses back here."

"Got it boss. I'll call you later."

"Looks like they're in for a long day," Slim said after Al hung up.

"Yeah. There's going to be a lot of that for a while. Where's that shuttle?"

"On final. We'll have him in the barn in fifteen minutes. Bill should be here before it leaves."

"How are you for manpower?"

"Not too bad. I broke up some of the cruiser teams and reassigned them. We'll keep hauling stuff in as long as the domes hold. I think they all understand how critical this could get."

"Sorry I've dumped this on you. I should be doing most of this."

"I've been watching you. You're way busier than I am. I can handle this for now. All the lives on this planet could hinge on what you do now. That's a little more responsibility than I care to take on, but you seem to thrive on it."

"It comes with the territory."

* * *

Joe and Jim drove into the last production dome at 0800. It was one of the larger domes in the complex.

"They seemed to be getting larger every time they build a new one," Joe said.

"Where can we start?" Jim asked.

"We need room to enlarge it later. Let's set up two hundred feet from the edge. We'll go due north for now. Let's go get the miner."

When they returned a few minutes later, a crowd gathered around the machine. Joe didn't stop to talk to the admirers; he just fired up the laser systems and went to work. Jim parked the cruiser and joined him inside the miner.

The initial cut was small by the standards of what they had cut at the mine for Bill. It was just enough to get the miner lined out and headed down. As the hole opened up in front of them, Jim worked the cutters while Joe drove the machine. When they had established the angle that they wanted to go in, they stopped and drove into the beginning of the tunnel.

"This is drawing a crowd," Jim said.

"Yeah, but we don't have time for that. Fire it up again. I have us set on the angle we need. Just run it level with the tracks for now."

As the rock ahead of them evaporated, Joe eased the miner forward. After an hour they were down almost four hundred feet, and the tunnel was almost a mile long.

"Let's level it out here," Joe said. "When we get it level, we'll open it up a bit. That'll give us a bigger target to shoot for."

After another half hour they had opened up a monstrous cave under the Martian surface. It was three hundred feet wide and a thousand feet long.

"I think we can find that," Jim said.

"I hope so. Let's go get the cruiser and map this and get the hell out of here."

Soon they rumbled out of the opening into the dome. As they climbed out, they were deluged with questions.

"Sorry, we don't have time for this now," Joe said. "Jim, can you go map that while I secure this machine?"

"Be back in a few minutes."

* * *

"Bill, glad you got an early start," Al said when they climbed out of his rover.

"We checked the weather early and the storm is on the move already. It broke out during the night. They estimate it should get here about 1400 tomorrow. What's the latest that you hear?"

"About the same. You should be alright if you get headed back in the morning. Let's get started."

"Al, can you give us a better idea what we're trying to do," Dan said as they climbed into Al's cruiser. "Bill told us some of it, but you have more information than he does."

"The situation is getting a little tense. If this storm gets as bad as they are predicting, the whole planet could be isolated. The transports should be able to run alright, but the ships coming from Earth may not be able to unload their supplies. That means we'll have to survive on the supplies we have on hand.

"Mike figures we can last about four to six weeks before things get tight. What we're planning to do is tunnel to the hub from here."

"Shit, that's a long tunnel," Jeff said.

"The way I have it figured," Al said, "it'll be over eight hundred miles. We have to angle north quite a ways to be sure we don't get into any of the fingers that come off of the chasm. While we're at it we might as well make it as big as we can. We may have to run two transports at a time through there."

For the next hour Al explained what he wanted as they drove into the mountain. They hadn't made it in far enough yet for the full scope of the complex to be evident. When they got to the point where they could see the light ahead, the whole scope of the complex became more graphic.

"Christ," Bill said. "What did you guys get into here?"

"Welcome to the city of Pavonis Mons," Al said.

"How big is this place?" Dan asked.

"Four-hundred-mile radius from the center. It has another level too. It's about two thousand feet above us. They knew how to get it to stand up too. We've only found one place where there was a cave in."

"Al, this is Lorna,"

"Where are you?"

"Lower level. 180 and number six. Do you remember where the CO2 deposit was? That's where we are."

"I remember it. We'll be there in a few hours."

"Did you find Bill?"

"Lorna, what did you get these old miners into?" Bill asked.

"Hey Bill. You finally decided to come see us."

"Al didn't give me much choice. He had to call for help."

"We all need a little help from time to time. I'll see you when you get here."

"Looking forward to it."

* * *

When they arrived, Lorna and Sean were going over the map displayed on the outside monitor on the cruiser.

"What did you figure out?" Al asked.

"We can make a hell of a deep-freeze out of this place," Sean said.

"Did you see Eve and Brian?" Lorna asked.

"They came in last night," Al said. "They're helping Slim get everything inside. Brian also has to move his entire shop inside the blast doors. We can't afford to lose that."

"God, do they have enough help?"

"If we cram too many people in there nothing will get done. They'll be tripping over each other. It's all working for now. Sean, what do you need to make this happen?"

"Just a blast door setup to bridge this area. We were able to get to the other side while we waited for you. It's a dead end. All we need is to close this off and insulate it if we can."

"Get the dimensions to Brian so he can work on it. I'm going to go have a look at the area where we want to start the tunnel."

"Did you find a spot?" Sean asked.

"Yeah. One of the spokes on this level lines up with the heading we want to take. We'll go out as far as we can and start there. I'll take Dan and Jeff to have a look at it and then bring them back to pick up a miner so they can get started. Joe and Jim will be back this evening and join them."

"Where'd they get off to?"

"I sent them to the hub to close the link on the navigation. They were going to start the tunnel on that end and then head back. We couldn't afford to just tunnel up into the hub. There's no telling where we might come up."

"Good thinking," Sean said. "We'll stay on this for now. Is there anything else we can do?"

"You might arrange to have a cruiser delivered to Dan and Jeff. They'll be somewhere on the 083 spoke down here. I'm not sure exactly where yet. The most important thing is to keep the beginning of the tunnel in the good air."

"I don't think I'd go much past ring fifteen," Lorna said. "If you're going to pull a lot of air into the tunnel, you'd risk getting the bad stuff if you go much farther than that."

"That's about where I thought we'd look. I'll have to take Bill back out tonight. He'll have to leave early in the morning to beat the storm. I'll talk to you again in a while."

"Ok, we'll head back up and help Martin," Lorna said as they got ready to leave.

* * *

Al pulled to a stop three and a half hours later. They were stopped at the intersection of ring fourteen and spoke 083. It was an immense intersection; one of the largest in the whole complex.

"Ok, guys," Al said. "This is home for the foreseeable future. We got a break here. The intersection is plenty large enough to let us do our thing. I think we need to start on the eastern edge of the intersection and make a shallow grade until we get down five hundred feet. Start right out in the middle so we still have access to the stuff on both sides. I'll have to get someone in here to block things off, so we don't have anyone drive into the large hole you're about to make.

"The transports are basically a thirty-five-foot square, looking at them from the front. Let's make the tunnel a hundred and ten feet wide and sixty feet high. You'll need to keep a good arch on the top to help support it. Drop it down on about four percent until you get down a hundred feet or so, and then make it two percent until we get to the four hundred feet. We have a long ways to go and there's no reason to dive down right away. Any questions?"

"No, I don't think so," Dan said. "You've laid it out pretty well. How far do we go before we get out from under the mountain?"

"About a hundred miles, more or less," Al said.

"The scenery on this road is going to suck," Jeff said.

"Yeah, but it'll make the trip quite a bit shorter than the surface route. We won't have to worry about sandstorms either. Let's go get you a couple miners so you can get started. When you drive them over here, use the lower cutters to wipe the dust out. Get as much as you can. Dust is a real problem in here."

* * *

Three hours later they all met back at the starting point of the new tunnel. Dan set up the first cut while Jeff parked the back-up machine. Once they had started, Al and Bill watched until they were well on their way. The tunnel started to take shape rapidly. Dan and Jeff had had a lot of practice on the miners recently and it was evident.

"They seem to be getting the hang of that thing," Al said.

"Yeah, they've been working with it every day since you guys turned it over to us," Bill said. "You should see what they've done with it. The mine is almost double the size it was when you were there last."

"You must be getting rich."

"We're doing pretty well."

"Let's get you back to the complex. It'll be late by the time we get there."

As they left Al called Lorna to check in.

"Lorna, we're headed out. How's everything going?"

"So far, so good. I'll be headed out soon for another load too. I'll probably see you out there."

"Did you find someone to deliver the cruiser to Dan and Jeff?"

"Yeah. Hollie and Sharon are headed that way now. Have you heard from Joe and Jim?"

"No, not yet. I'll call them when I get back to the complex. They may even be there by then."

"Al, this is Slim. They checked in a few minutes ago. They estimate they'll be here about 2100."

"Copy that, Slim. How'd they do at the hub?"

"They made a hole down four hundred feet and a chamber three hundred by a thousand feet to shoot at."

"We should be able to hit that. I'll be back in a few hours. Keep things going."

"We may not be able to get it all done until tomorrow night. Brian's doing pretty good relocating his stuff and the last of the supplies are about ready for transport."

"We can still work even after it hits. We'll have to watch how the storm develops."

"Ok, Boss. See you soon."

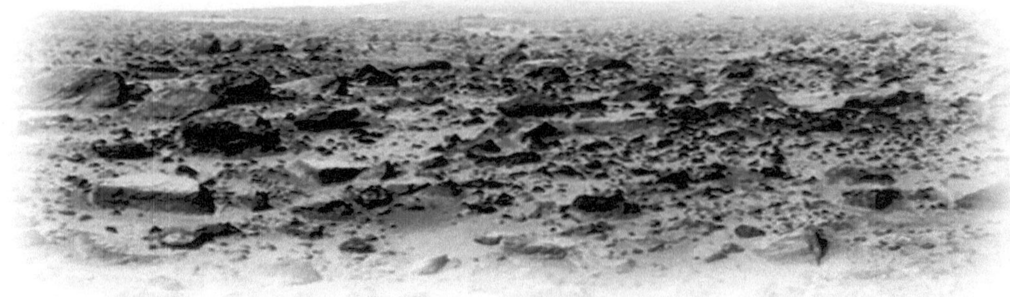

CHAPTER FIVE

As the sun set that night, Joe and Jim sped back toward Pavonis Mons. The red hue of the western sky was darker than usual. They still estimated that they would be back into the Pavonis complex by 2100. Joe had the navigational system on, and the autopilot locked on the navigational beacons. They were cruising west, toward home.

"Slim, have you checked out the sunset tonight?" Joe asked on the radio.

"Sorry, I haven't had a chance. Is it a good one?"

"Yeah, and from the sound of things it might be the last one we see for a while."

"That's the rumor. Where are you?"

"About two hours out. This has been a long day."

"Dan and Jeff got things started this afternoon. I don't know how far they'll get though. Your two ladies took them a cruiser to bunk in. You probably won't get to see them until you get back inside."

"We'll live. We won't enjoy it, but we'll live. Is Al around?"

"No, he's still inside with Bill. They should be out soon though. What do you need?"

"Nothing. I just wanted to give him an update on what we did at the hub. It can wait until we get there."

"I relayed what you told me earlier. He seemed to think that was good."

"Ok, see you in a couple hours. Joe out."

* * *

As Al and Bill approached the outer complex the traffic got a little heavy. Cruisers were going both ways as fast as they could go. Al had trouble merging into the flow of traffic headed into the upper level of the complex.

"Damn, must be rush hour," Al said.

"They're sure headed somewhere in a hurry," Bill said. "Slim must have built a fire under them."

"It would seem that way. Let's go see what's left."

As they drove through the last couple miles of the tunnel, they saw equipment stacked everywhere. There were two lanes for the traffic, but everything else was covered with Brian's equipment. They worked their way into the small dome and parked.

"Christ, Brian, what are you doing?" Al asked.

"You said to get it inside. I don't have time to haul all of it two hours in. Once we have to close up here, then we'll have plenty of time."

"I can't argue with that. Keep after it. How long can you work tonight?"

"Until we get done. Just keep the coffee hot. We don't know how much time we have."

"Do what you can. I'll give you what help I can."

"It looks like I'll just be in the way here," Bill said. "Maybe I should get started back tonight."

"Let's go to the office and call on the weather. That might give you a better idea if you want to crash for a few hours or not. No sense getting too carried away."

When they reached the office, Al placed a call to the hub.

"What do you have for us on the weather?"

"Most of the southern hemisphere to the south-west of you is blanketed," the controller said. "It looks like you'll be covered by sun-up. That should be just the leading edge of it though."

"What kind of winds can we expect?"

"Big! We're clocking some of it coming out of the crater at over four hundred miles an hour. I hope you're ready for this. Hell, I hope we all are."

"We're not ready yet, but we will be. Call my control room if you have any updates. We're trying to monitor things from there."

"We'll try. It's getting pretty hectic around here."

"We're relying on you to keep us posted for as long as you can. Talk to you later."

"How bad is it?" Bill asked.

"You might want to fire up your rover. If you wait until morning, you might have an extended stay with us. He said it should be here by daylight."

"As much as I'd like to weather it here, my place is at the mine. I'd better go."

"Grab something to eat as you leave. I'll go with you."

An hour later Al and Bill walked to where his rover was parked. Joe and Jim were just coming in through the airlock.

"Bill, what the hell are you doing out of your hole?" Joe asked as they got out.

"Just bringing you some help. How's the weather."

"Surprisingly calm. I don't think that's going to last though."

"Al, thanks for the tour. I'd better head home. Keep these bums out of trouble."

"That's a tall order," Al said. "Good luck. Give us a call when you get there. We'll have someone in control to take the call."

"I'll do that—Later."

"Later, Bill," Joe said as he climbed into his rover. "Al, we had a chance to see some of the forecast stuff while we were there. This is the worst one on record. Bill's in for a hell of a ride too. It'll be coming right across the chasm at them. It'll be hard to hide anywhere."

"Yeah, but we can't worry about that right now. We need to concentrate on what we have to do. What kind of shape are you two in?"

"Good, why?"

"Mind a little overtime?"

"I thought we did that already today."

"This thing is due about sun-up. We still have a lot to do."

"We'll grab a bite and lend a hand," Jim said. "What can we do?"

"Help Brian. We'll also need to get a couple of big computers ready to go. We can wait to take them inside, but I want them ready."

"We'll be back in ten," Joe said.

* * *

They worked through the night. Everyone pitching in to move as much of the complex as they could. Lorna and Martin showed up with twenty more people, about 2400, and that helped. Sean came along an hour later with ten of the alien trucks. They had to make part of the trip wearing air packs, but that didn't seem to matter.

Al and Lorna stood in the control room as the sun started to rise. To the south-west an ominous wall of dust and sand was about to descend on them. Al got on the phone.

"This is Al at Pavonis. This may be the last chance we have to communicate with you."

"Al, this is Mike. I've been here monitoring things most of the night. Are you ready for this?"

"We hope so. We'll continue to take things inside as long as we can. As it's getting lighter here, we can see it coming. I'm beginning to understand how they must have felt thousands of years ago."

"We've been watching it on satellite pictures. I doubt we'll have that option for long. Be safe and good luck."

"Do you have any last-minute instructions for us? Lorna's here with me."

"Be safe and stay alive. Do you have any idea how long it will take to tunnel to here yet?"

"Just a guess. It looks like about five weeks, give or take. We'll have to do better than twenty miles a day to match that. We'll be there sooner if we can."

"Hopefully we'll still be here."

71

"If your engineers are right about how the domes are rated, you should be alright."

"If they're not; I'll fire the whole lot of them. Mike out."

"He's not happy," Al said after he hung up.

"Can you blame him?" Lorna said. "The whole planet may be coming down around his ears."

"No, I can't blame him. I hope this is an exercise that's not going to be all that needed. When we break through on the other end, I'd like to see a bunch of smiling faces. I doubt that's going to be the case though."

"We can only do so much. Even with the speed of the Martian Miners, it's still going to take a long time to go that far. We'll just have to stay after it and see what happens. In the meantime, we have a job to do here too. Did Bill make it back last night?"

"Yeah, he called about 0130. The wind had picked up some, but it still wasn't that bad. He's had them tying everything down there too."

"Not that it'll do that much good. They don't have the self-sustaining environment like we do. They can move into the mine, but without the oxygen generators they can only last so long."

"They're better off than the other locations though. They have the water supply in the dig that will help them. The others don't have that."

"How long do you think we can stay out here?"

"Until the rafters shake. I really don't know. We'll just have to play it by ear."

"Everyone has been at it for a full twenty-four hours. They won't be able to keep this up much longer."

"They'll hang on a little longer. There's still a lot to do. We'd better go see if we can help. This thing will be on us in less than an hour."

* * *

By 1400 that afternoon the day had almost turned to night. The sand and dust were so thick that the sun could hardly penetrate it. The wind speed was still building and had reached two-ninety. The preparations had started to slow down a couple hours earlier.

"Brian, what else do you need?" Al asked as they surveyed the center dome.

"We've taken almost everything that isn't a structural part of the domes. We have several computer setups inside also. There just isn't much else we can take."

"You've done a hell of a job here," Lorna said. "Why don't we get everyone inside and let them get some rest. We can monitor the conditions here by the pressure readouts on the blast doors. Al, I think it's time to evacuate the complex."

"I'm going to make one more call to the hub. I doubt it'll get through, but I should try. You two get everyone headed inside. We'll see where we stand after we get everyone rested up. I'll meet you here in a few minutes."

When Al reached the control room, he looked at the readouts and reached for the phone.

"Hub control, this is Al at Pavonis."

All he could hear was the static of the storm. It was official; they were alone. Alone to face the worst storm that man had ever encountered on this barren world. They were also in a race against time to reach out to the other inhabitants, which would probably need their help by the time they could reach them.

"Ok, get them all inside," Al said when he returned to the small dome. "Brian, drop the pressure in the domes to half. It'll still be good enough if we need to come back out here and it might keep them from blowing away."

"I'll set it and be right behind you," Brian said.

"We'll wait in the tunnel," Lorna said. "Use the management priority lockout to secure the blast doors."

* * *

By 2000 everyone had made it safely to the habitat at the upper garden. The entire crew looked like they'd been whipped.

"Gather round people," Al called. "For now, just find a place and get some sleep. We'll deploy all the habs on the cruisers and there's room for thirty in the main habitat. There should be enough room for everyone to have a good bed. You've all done an outstanding job getting us as ready for this storm as we can get. Our thanks to all of you. Get some rest."

73

"You need to take your own advice," Lorna said. "Find your wife and go to bed."

"Yes dear."

* * *

"Al, Lorna, is any one there?"

"Yeah, what do you want?" Lorna managed to get out and answer to the radio call.

"This is Brittany. We're at the complex to download our cruiser and can't get in through the blast doors."

"Oh, hi Britt. We locked it up. Come to the habitat at the upper garden. We'll try to get you downloaded here."

"What the hell's going on?"

"We'll explain everything when you get here. What time is it?"

"0900, are you still in bed?"

"I was. I guess I'll get up now though. Head this way. We'll see you this afternoon. What did you find over there?"

"It's about like you thought it would be. I talked to Patty on the other frequency this morning. She's about to where we started. Arsia isn't as round as Pavonis, but it seems to be similar every other way."

"Good girl. Bring it here and we'll have a look at it. Lorna out."

"They don't seem to have any idea what's going on," Sean said still trying to wake up.

"No, they must have been on the other radio frequency this whole time. I thought about recalling them, but they couldn't have gotten here in time to be much help."

"Let's go see if anyone else is awake. I think I'll need a nap later."

"I think that's going to be the order for the day. Moving the rest of the stuff can wait a day."

When they entered the main habitat there were signs of life. Some of the ones who hadn't been on the all-night work crew were up. Franco was working in the small kitchen and muttering to himself.

"What's the problem?" Lorna asked him.

"This is most unprofessional behavior. These lazy people should have been up and working two hours ago," Franco said. "How long must I work in these primitive conditions?"

"Look, you primadonna son-of-a-bitch, this is as good as it gets. These people worked for over thirty-six hours without a break while you sat here on your chunky ass. They deserve to sleep in a little."

"I don't have to take this. I'm leaving on the next shuttle?"

"Look, asshole, there are no more shuttles. We're cut off from the rest of the planet. Haven't you been paying any attention to what's going on around here?"

"All Franco is interested in is his kitchen. When can Franco go back to it?"

"Franco, hello, is there anyone at home in there. There may not be a complex left on the outside. It may already be gone. What we have here is all we're going to have for a very long time. Now shut up and fix us something to eat."

"Ooh, I think you ruffled his dainty feathers," Sean said after he stormed off.

"I didn't feel like putting up with his shit this morning."

"Who's shit?" Al asked as he and Mona sat down with Lorna and Sean.

"Franco. He's in one of his moods. I must have left my tact and diplomacy in my other pants."

"Nothing but water soup for you for a week," Mona said.

"Hell, I need to lose a little weight anyway."

"How long have you been up?" Al asked.

"Just long enough to piss Franco off. Brittany called and woke me up. They were trying to get into the complex to download their map. I told them to come here."

"Good. I think this will be a light duty day. We'll concentrate on getting everyone settled here. We may have to relocate some of them down to the habitats at the library."

"When do you want to take Joe and Jim down to get with Dan and Jeff? We're going to have to get that going."

"I'll send them down in a little while. I may not be able to go check on things until tomorrow. We still have to get all that stuff moved in here. Sean, can you get with Brian and see about getting the refrigeration system up and running?"

"We'll have a temporary setup later today. Most of it will take a day or two. The distances we have to cover make it a little difficult."

"Do what you can. Lorna, can you see about the crews in Arsia. We've been out of contact with them for over a day. That makes me a little nervous. You may have to go over there and set up shop for a while."

"Yeah, I've been thinking about that. I'll wait until I get the information from Brittany early this afternoon. We may have to break off a crew and get that habitat set up over there. Brian left it halfway between the two complexes."

"We'll work all that out," Al said. "Sean, you may need to get Brian to work with you. Slim can handle the crew moving everything on in here. Where are we going to put everything?"

"I might have an idea on that," Martin said. "There's a large area inside the garden. It has water and a large open area. We might want to move this habitat in there and stockpile everything in the open area."

"Have you seen this place?" Al asked.

"No, but Jen said it's easy to get to. We can get her to take us in and show us where it is. If you want to know anything about the inner areas of the garden, she's the one to talk to."

"Where is she?"

"She's inside now, but I can get her back in a few minutes. She just left a little bit ago."

"Call her back. We'll go take a look."

"Al, the priority is to make sure all our people are taken care of," Lorna said. "We have three habitats in the library area; can't we move one of them back up here. We have over a hundred and fifty people to get settled."

"I've been thinking about that. We have to start developing alternative foods. Martin will be in charge of that. In a day or two we can move another habitat up here. I'm also thinking we may need two over in the Arsia complex. We have this one here, one down by the lower garden, three in the library area and one headed for Arsia. That's six total. If we pack them to capacity, we have room for everyone. We have more than thirty cruisers. Each of them can support four people.

"There's something else we need to think about. In just over a month, we may have almost half a million people to take care of. Consider that while you go about your daily routine."

"Well, it's not like we don't have the housing for them," Sean said. "It might not be the most comfortable, but it's dry and safe."

"Al, Jen will be back in fifteen minutes," Martin said. "Finish your coffee and we can go take a look."

Twenty minutes later they piled into three cruisers. Lorna and Sean went with Jen. The others followed. She led them into the interior of the garden, winding through the heavily laden fruit trees. After about fifteen miles, she stopped in a large open area.

"This is the largest area I've found so far," Jen said after they had all gathered. "There may be better places, but I haven't had time to look everywhere. There's a pool of water about in the center. Martin has tested it and its good water."

"Good work. We may just have to keep you around," Al said.

"You're going to have a hell of a time getting rid of me now," Jen said. "This is my garden. I know more about it than anyone here. If you need something, I'll find it for you."

"We're not looking for your replacement," Lorna said. "Can you figure out how to feed half a million people?"

"If we take the seeds that are in the fruit and veggies that we're eating, maybe. They grow at an incredible rate here. We may all have to revert to being vegetarians, but yeah, we can do it."

"We've been drying all the seeds we can get our hands on," Martin said. "I've been working with a test area. The results are phenomenal. We can grow tomatoes the size of your fist, from a seed, in five or six days. They're really good too."

"Do you think you can figure out a way to feed that many people?" Al asked.

"The diet may not have everything in it, but yeah, with all the varieties of fruit and veggies in here, I think we can. It might get a little old after a while because of the lack of variety. They won't starve though."

"Keep after it. Brian, we need to set up a habitat in here," Al said. "We can pull the one from the lower garden. After you get that set up, we'll see about moving another one from the library area to Arsia. I want two of them over there. When you go down to get the habitat by the lower garden, get with Sean and see what it's going to take to set up a wall to seal off the area we want to use for refrigeration. A couple of Sean's men are working on a temporary set up here somewhere."

"I'll need a trailer and two cruisers," Brian said. "We can have it set up in here by late today."

"Good. Martin, when he has that done, move your operation in here. Then we can move the habitat you're using now, in here too. This will be our new Pavonis base of operations. I really need to go check on my miners."

"We all have plenty to do," Lorna said. "Take Jim and Joe and get out of here. We'll set up one of the big computers in here when it's ready. We'll use this as the main download station."

* * *

By mid afternoon, Al had reached the beginning of the tunnel where he had left Dan and Jeff. Joe and Jim had followed him in the cruiser they had brought from the hub. He led the way down into the new tunnel. They had done well yesterday, for no longer than they had had to work at it. He clocked it at twenty miles to where they were now. Not bad for a day and a half.

"How are you doing?" Al called to them on the radio as he got out.

"Humming along," Dan said.

"Take a break. We need to have a look at a couple things."

"We'll be right there."

Al went to the cruiser that Joe and Jim had brought and had them bring the map up on the outside monitor. When the others had joined him, they all studied it.

"As you can see," Al began. "We have a hell of a long ways to go. Dan, you guys made about twenty miles. How long did you work at it?"

"We're making about a mile an hour. We've tried to push it harder, but it doesn't work very well. With the tunnel this big, that's about all we can do."

"Can you stretch it out if you cut down the size of the drift? Maybe cut it down to half."

"Yeah, maybe half again what we're doing now. It'll be too small to run two transports through though."

"Cut down the size. At the end of each shift, make a large section for say a half hour. We may have to come back and widen it out later. The main thing is getting there as fast as we can. Joe and Jim will relieve you this evening. We'll work twelve-hour shifts. The relief crew can bring up the other miner and both cruisers."

"Al, is four hundred feet enough of a cushion?" Joe asked. "Once we get out from under the mountain, we don't know much about the surface contours."

"Maybe you're right. Take it down to about a thousand feet. Make the grade fairly gradual but get it on down there. We don't want the transports to have to pull hard for too long. Call if you need anything. We'll have Hollie and Sharon come bring you supplies tomorrow morning. Do you need anything else?"

"Where are our girls?" Jeff asked.

"That you'll have to arrange for them for yourselves. I can't do everything for you."

"Dan, we'll bring up the spare miner and your cruiser," Joe said. "We'll be right close if you have a problem. We'll set the radios to frequency four. That way we won't have to listen to everything going on."

"Ok, we'll switch when we start again," Dan said. "Al, you look like shit. Didn't you get any sleep?"

"None of us have gotten much since I dropped you off. I'll explain this evening. I have to go now."

With that, the meeting broke up. Dan and Jeff went back to work, and the others went back out. Joe and Jim to get the other equipment, Al to go on to other jobs.

* * *

As the day progressed, everyone noticed that the light was very subdued. There were several comments made about this to Lorna.

"It's the storm," she explained. "It's blocking some of the sunlight. Get used to it. It may even get worse."

"This has been a long day," Sean said. "Brian and I have been trying to figure out a way to block off the area that has the CO2 upwelling in it. It's going to be tough to do without something to reach up high."

"Can you use something from Arsia Mons?" Lorna asked.

"Yeah, if I can figure out a way to get it over here. Any ideas?"

"Drive it or haul it."

"Gee, thanks. You're a lot of help."

"There has to be a way to do it. We just have to find it. Can we get by with the temporary setup in the upper garden, at least for a week or so?"

"It'll serve the purpose."

"Take Brian and Eve over there and figure it out. When Al gets back, I'll come too."

"There comes Al now. Let's talk to him."

"How's it going here" Al asked when he climbed out of his cruiser.

"Pretty good," Lorna said. "I think I need to take a crew to Arsia and look for a way to get up high enough to work on that bulkhead in the lower tunnel. They have things figured out except for how to get up high enough to seal the top."

"Sean, we're going to need to build several large blast doors in the new tunnel too," Al said. "Keep that in mind. The guys have cut down the size of the tunnel. We'll still be able to get through it with the transports but won't be able to have two-way traffic. They can do a little over a mile an hour. That means it's going to take us almost five weeks to get to the hub. I hope there's something left when we get there."

80

"We might be able to find some raw materials in the center of Arsia," Sean said. "I'm afraid we're going to run out of stuff to build things out of if we can't. Pretty soon that's going to become a priority too."

"I'd like to have a double set every fifty miles or so. That's going to tax our capabilities pretty bad though. You guys go ahead and take Brian and Eve to Arsia. Slim can watch over the transporting of things in here. Sean, you know what we need. Keep in touch."

"I'll go round up the kids," Lorna said.

"Kids?" Al said.

"You know what I mean."

* * *

"Wake up call," Dan called into the radio. "Are you going to be ready to take over in an hour or so?"

"Yeah. Where the hell are you?" Joe asked.

"About ten or twelve miles ahead of you. By narrowing down the tunnel, we were able to make good time. Think you two can keep up?"

"We'll be there soon, and we'll find out. Keep hammering at it while we get a bite to eat. We'll bring your cruiser with us. You may have to get the other miner moved up."

"We can do that. See you soon."

With that out of the way, Dan pushed the miner ahead again. There was almost no mineralization in the rock that they were boring through. It was almost a constant reddish black. Jeff worked the controls for the laser-cutters. They emitted a faint green glow and that made for a strange scene ahead of them.

As they moved forward, the tunnel just seemed to magically appear ahead of them. Before Joe and Jim arrived, there was a slight change in the appearance of the rock. It looked like it had been more of a sedimentary stratus.

Jeff started widening the focus so they could make a turn-out in the tunnel. In only a few minutes they were back up to the size they had been before, a hundred feet high and about three hundred wide. After about a half mile of this they began to narrow it back down.

"Are our seats warm?" Jim asked as they pulled up behind the miner.

"Yeah, and you're welcome to them," Jeff said. "How's our line look?"

"You're dropping at about two percent. It's held fairly steady since we talked earlier. The line is good too. You're down to nine-fifty. Think that's enough?"

"I think it should be. If there's a fissure this deep, we're screwed anyhow."

"If you'll stop, we'll take over."

"Gladly."

"How's it running?" Joe asked when they met behind the machine.

"Just humming along. It's really going pretty good," Dan said. "We made the wide spot and narrowed it back down. It's already set for the next run. You might give us a call an hour or so before it's time to swap again. Jeff's a heavy sleeper, and he snores."

"There are two cruisers. Hell, you can each sleep in one. Are you going to move the other miner up now?"

"Yeah, we should keep it as close as we can."

"We'll go ahead and level it out. Can you check it to make sure we're not climbing too much when you get back?"

"Sure. Do you think you'll have enough tunnel made by then?"

"We'll try. See you in the morning. That sounds funny standing here in the dark. Hell, it'll be dark all day tomorrow too."

"Kick ass. We'll be close if you need us."

Joe climbed onto the miner first and dropped through the top hatch into the driver's seat. Jim worked his tall frame into the other seat and fired up the cutters, adjusting the cut just enough to start them leveling off. After five minutes Joe moved them into the new cut and Jim readjusted things for the level cut again and they were off.

"You're still going down about a quarter percent," Dan said when they returned some forty minutes later. "That's probably good enough for now though."

"Ok, get some rest. We'll be out ahead of you somewhere," Joe said.

* * *

"Mom, are you up?" Eve asked early the next morning.

"No, but I'm awake," Lorna said. "What do you need?"

"How bad is this storm going to get?"

"I can't answer that. Nobody can. We're safe enough in here. Why are we talking on the radio when we're parked next to each other?"

"I don't know. Is Sean done sleeping yet?"

"He is now. We might as well get around and have a bite. We need to be over there as soon as we can. It's going to take us a few days to sort that place out."

"Ok, we're up."

They had only made it a third of the way the night before. After getting a late start, that was about all they could handle after the couple days they had put in. The habitat on the trailer was still somewhere ahead of them. Brian and Eve would hook up to it when they reached it. His crew would be leaving the upper garden about the time they got up and would join them inside Arsia Mons.

"Sean, what does the metal look like over here?" Brian asked as they finished breakfast. "I haven't had a chance to see any of this stuff yet."

"It just looks like metal, why?"

"Can we weld it?"

"I imagine we can. I never thought of that. Can you get your crew to swing by and bring a welding set-up with them?"

"That's what I was thinking. We have all the raw materials we could ever need if we can work with it."

"We'd better get started," Lorna said. "We can have a look around while we wait for them."

* * *

"Al, this is Brian."

"Go ahead, Brian. How far did you get?"

"About a third of the way, I guess. I need you to catch J. D. for me and send him to where we stockpiled everything out of the maintenance shop. I need a cutting and welding set-up. We may be able to use the metal in Arsia Mons to make what we need."

"They're just getting ready to leave. I'll let them know. Let me know what's going on over there."

"We will. Talk to you later."

After Al had sent the support crew on their way he went and located Martin. He was in his make-shift lab in the habitat.

"How much food can this place produce, in a pinch?" Al asked.

"More than enough, I think. We might have to adjust our diet a little, but the regeneration rate is phenomenal. We've gone in and picked several areas clean. Within a week they're ready to harvest again. I've never seen anything like it."

"Why isn't there rotted fruit, waist deep in there then?"

"Why, after thousands of years, do their machines still work? Why any of this? I can't explain it. It's so self sustaining that, short of letting the planets atmosphere in here I don't think you can kill it. It's almost like it grows on demand. The more you need, the more it produces."

"They'll be here later this morning with the other habitat for your little village in the garden. When they get that one set up, have them move this one in there too. Use them for anything you need. I have to go check on the tunnel. I may spend a day or two down there. Call me if you have any trouble."

"I won't have any trouble; I'll turn Jen lose on them. She'll whip them into shape."

"She's a dynamo alright. Where is she?"

"Over talking to Brittany, I think."

"See you later. I want to have another look at that map before Brittany goes back to the other side."

Parked in the center of a mass of cruisers was Brittany and Johnny's cruiser. It took Al a few minutes to locate them. Johnny was off somewhere, but the girls were there looking at the map displayed on the outside monitor.

"Young ladies, what are you up to?" Al asked as he approached.

"I was just asking Brittany about the other side," Jen said. "It looks awesome, from the map here. When do I get to go over there?"

"Soon enough. I'm relying on you to keep things running smooth here," Al said, leaning on the side of the cruiser. "Jen, I really am relying on you. I don't want to scare you, but in a few weeks, we may have to bring the entire population of the planet in here. Your garden may have to feed them all, at least until we can reestablish the supply lines from Earth. You said it yourself; you know more about that garden than anyone else. You're doing a fantastic job. More than anyone could have expected or asked for. Thank you."

"Hell, I'm just having fun exploring," Jen said.

"This is the best job anyone could have ever asked for," Brittany added.

"And you, young lady. I'm so proud of what you girls have done; well, thank you too. Can you show me that map again?"

"Sure, Boss. And thanks for the praise. We circled the eastern edge. Patty should be done with the western side by now too. Maybe you could have Lorna head her off. There isn't much reason to keep coming all the way back here. In a day or two we'll have a computer set up over there too."

"I talked to her about that last night before she left. She'll handle it."

"See how this whole section of the tunnel, over there, is so much straighter than Pavonis," Brittany went on. "The whole complex is laid out that way. It's kind of egg shaped. We'll have to see some of these others mapped before we can get the whole picture though. What do you think?"

"Well, it kind of depends on what Patty found. I'd like to get a look at that half of the map. Can you have a copy sent back this way as soon as one is available?"

"I'm sure some of Brian's crew will be coming back soon. We can send it with them. When do you think you'll be headed that way?"

"I don't know. I'll have to see how things go here."

"I've been studying this map all the way back from the other side," Brittany said. "Where's the best guess to tie into the upper level, assuming there is one?"

"I'm almost positive there is one," Al said. "We saw a hole in the center of things. I'm sure there's something else up there. You want to go looking for it?"

"I was thinking about that. Do you think we can find it like we did here?"

"Give it a try. When you get back over there, get Patty, and go see what you can find. There are several others that can concentrate on the lower level. Keep in contact with Lorna though."

"Al, I'll be in the garden if you need me," Jen said. "I have work to do if we're expecting all this company."

"Ok, Jen. Good luck."

CHAPTER SIX

It was mid afternoon when Sean and Lorna arrived at the spot where they were going to set up the main habitat for Arsia Mons. Brian and Eve had stopped to pick up the trailer and would be along in an hour or so.

"I think this is about as good a spot as any," Lorna said.

"Yeah, I don't see any reason to search for a better spot. It would just make it harder for everyone to find. Have you heard anything from Arnold in the last few days?"

"No, we've been so busy with the other preparations that I haven't checked on them. I guess we'd better do that. Arnold, this is Lorna."

"There you are. We thought you'd forgotten us. We're running low on supplies and may have to head back out soon."

"Where are you?"

"We started on the south end several days ago and have just about made it all the way across to the north. There's some amazing stuff in here."

"There's no reason to go back to the main complex. We had to evacuate it day before yesterday."

"What for?"

"There's a monster storm blowing out there. The worst any human has ever seen. We've moved everything inside the mountain. When do you figure you'll be out of the center?"

"By late today. We can see the edge now. All we have to do is figure out how to get there. Where are you set up now?"

"We're where the entrance tunnel connects to the center. We're going to set up a habitat there and get it supplied. When you get out, come on over to here. We'd like to hear what you've found."

"It'll be after dark, but I think we can make it tonight. See you then."

"Lorna, this is Patty."

"Go ahead."

"We're headed back that way too. How long are you going to be there?"

"Until sometime tomorrow. We'll be somewhere around here for longer than that, but we may be inside the inner complex. Did you find anything interesting?"

"Just a lot of dark tunnel. It's good to get back out into the light again. It doesn't seem as bright as it was though."

"It's not. The storm has blocked a lot of the sunlight. There's no way for it to get to the sensors that transmit it into the mountain. It's a bad one. We're cut off from the rest of the planet."

"That can't be good. How long will it last?"

"There's no way of telling. We'll tell you all about it when we see you. Have you run across any of the other teams?"

"We haven't seen a sole. Where's Brittany?"

"She's in the upper garden in Pavonis. She'll be headed back this way soon."

"Patty, this is Brittany. Wait for me where Lorna is. Al wants us to take on a new job. I'll explain it when we get there."

"Ok, Britt. Where are you now?"

"We'll be there mid morning tomorrow. Just wait there for us."

"Ok, see you then. Lorna, we'll be there late this evening. Patty out."

After running a check on the other teams, Lorna and Sean sat back and waited for Brian and Eve to get there. About an hour before dark, they showed up. The trailer had slowed them down more than they had anticipated. Sean and Brian managed to get the habitat unloaded from the trailer and started to put it together.

"Brian, I've had enough," Sean said as it started to get dark.

"Good. I didn't want to be the first one to quit. I'm beat."

"We have dinner ready," Eve said.

As they finished eating, Arnold and his two buddies showed up. Patty was not far behind.

"Guys, this is home for a while," Lorna said as they all sat around discussing the situation.

"It could be a lot worse," Arnold said. "We could be out on the surface."

"With everything else that's going on, we still have work to do here," Lorna said. "Al has a handle on things on the other side. We're going to have to support them with a lot of stuff from here. Arnold, what have you been able to come up with?"

"There's a wealth of building materials in there. I'm not sure how easy it'll be to work with. The look and feel of most of them is different than what we're used to. Whether we can cut and weld them like we do steel, well, I just don't know."

"We have equipment coming for that," Brian said. "We'll know soon enough."

"Transportation is going to be tricky too. We found a couple big trailers, but I don't think the cruisers can pull them if we load them. We haven't found anything here that we can adapt to have an enclosed environment. The only way to use them would be in suits. That would be a long haul in a suit."

"Hopefully it won't come to that," Sean said. "I'll call Al and have him bring the rover inside. That might be a little tricky, but it looks like we're going to need it."

"I don't think he can get it through the blast doors," Brian said. "We didn't design them to handle anything that big."

"They can't just make another tunnel either," Lorna said. "Hell, the domes may not even be there anymore."

"We designed them to withstand winds of over five hundred miles an hour," Sean said. "They'd better be there. If they're not, then we're all alone on this planet. They're built just like the ones at the hub."

"The hub is sheltered from the direct blast of the storm, by the ridge that almost surrounds it," Brian said. "The spaceport is at risk, but I think the hub will withstand it."

"Let's hope so," Lorna said. "I've been to most of the mines on the planet. Johnson at number nine is at risk too. They have a little protection, but not as much as most of the others."

"Al will take care of that end of things," Sean said. "We'll go inside and see what we can find to help get him there. Arnold, we need a way to get heavy equipment and materials back to the other side. Any ideas?"

"There are several large trailers inside there. The problem is how to pull them. There are vehicles that can do the job, providing you can get them to run."

"We've had some luck there. This stuff seems to be remarkably resilient. Can we get across to Pavonis with any of this stuff?"

"With air packs or suits, yeah. With the bad air in the connecting tunnel, that's the best we can do. That would be a miserable ride. We'd have to escort them all the way with cruisers."

"Well, if that's the best we can do, that's the best we can do," Lorna said. "In the meantime, keep looking for other options. We can make the difference if the problems get as bad as Al thinks they could. Whatever we do here, we have to get anything Al needs and get it to him. Guys, we have to win this race. Brian, when we go inside tomorrow, you need to work up ways to handle the materials they'll need."

"We're working on several ideas. We'll have to wait until we can get in and look around. I haven't even had a chance to glance inside the inner area yet."

"I know you haven't. I didn't mean it to sound that way. I guess I'm a little edgy."

"God, mom," Eve said. "Give it a rest. We'll get on it in the morning."

"I think I will," Lorna said. "I'm going to bed. It's been a long week."

"Yeah, and they're not going to get any easier for a while," Sean said. "Good night, everyone."

* * *

Al was on the road early the next morning. He'd spent the night at the habitat at the upper garden and needed to be at the new tunnel. He knew they would call if they had any problems, but also knew he needed to give them all the support he could.

It was midmorning when he arrived at the tunnel sight. As he descended into the new tunnel, like he usually did, he looked at the rock in the sides. There were trace elements of minerals, but nothing to write home about. He wondered if they would encounter any large deposits that they could come back to and mine.

They had tunneled for three-plus shifts now and had made good progress. At the end of each shift, they made another turnout. Dan and Jeff were well into their shift when he arrived.

"How are you guys doing?" Al asked as he pulled up behind the miner.

"Not bad," Jeff said.

"From the looks of the map-readout, you're about a thousand feet down. What are you planning to do from here?"

"Just go that way. We do take requests though."

"No, that's fine for now. You have about six hundred miles on this heading. Don't let it climb up too much. In a few days we'll be close to the first of the long arms of the chasm. I want to be at least this deep when we get there."

"We've got it leveled out fairly well now. We're not sure how the curve of the planets surface will affect things, but it's something to think about."

"I'll run some numbers on it and get back to you. I don't think it's that big of a problem, at least not yet. When we get ready to make the turn in a couple weeks, I'll have you an answer."

"Joe and Jim should back behind us somewhere."

"Yeah, I passed them on the way in. They looked like they were sleeping soundly."

91

"We're experimenting with ways to get a little more out of this thing. So far, we haven't been able to get much more out of it."

"If you can manage to keep up the pace you're on, you'll do fine. I'll be back about the time you guys swap again."

"Ok, Boss. We'll be up here somewhere."

As Al made the turn and headed out, he saw a hint of color in the wall. He stopped and got out to inspect it. When he got back in, he called Dan and Jeff again.

"How much mineralization are you finding?" Al asked.

"Just spotty," Dan said. "You must have seen that vane we just passed."

"Yeah. Too bad there isn't more of it."

"Do you want us to mine the stuff if it gets to be substantial?"

"No, not now. We can come back and take it out later if we need to. You'll probably run into more of it after you get all the way out from under the mountain. Looking at the overlay map, that should be this evening sometime. How's the air holding up in here?"

"It's showing signs that it might deteriorate, but it's holding for now. We monitor it constantly. What do we do when it gets bad?"

"I hope we can stay ahead of that," Al said as he drove away. "They're looking into that now. It shouldn't be a problem for a while. Keep air packs in the miner though, just in case."

"We have six in the back compartment. That should be enough to get the cruisers up here."

"Ok, I'll be back this afternoon," Al said. "See you then."

* * *

"What do you think?" Brian asked after he and Sean had looked over several trailers.

"I think they'll work fine. The problem is still the same though. What do we pull them with?"

"We can adapt something to fit under the front of the trailers and pull them with a cruiser, as long as we don't load them too heavy. There are a couple dollies over here that might do the job."

"That's going to put a lot of strain on the cruisers, especially when we go to climb up out of the connecting tunnel."

"We may have to tie two of them together when we get that far. It's worth a try. Our other options are a lot less attractive."

"I can't argue with that," Sean said. "Where did the girls get off to?"

"Exploring, I guess. I saw them leave a couple hours ago."

"I hope they get back before dark."

"Me too, but I wouldn't bet on it. Eve's been anxious to get over here ever since she found out about the place."

"Yeah, this one's different alright," Sean said. "I have a feeling it's going to be a gold mine when we get a chance to go through all of it. I looked at some of these buildings and they may be the answer to our problem of building all the blast doors that Al wants. We also have to figure out a way to duct the air to the front of the tunnel. That's going to be a challenge, as fast as they move with that thing.

"I've seen some stuff that might work for vent bag. It's over that way, somewhere. We'll need to put it together and just lay it on the ground. We can use some of those fans you have in Pavonis to generate the air flow. We may need to do it in small areas, with airlocks in-between. That's the only way I can see to take control of the air flow."

"We'd better get on it then. They're probably twenty miles ahead of us already."

"The air from the complex should sustain them for quite a ways. I mentioned that to Al, and he said he'd have them keep an eye on it, but you're right, we need to get this figured out. We don't want to be the reason they have to stop."

"They finally got here with the welding set-up," Brian said. "I had them get several samples from around the area close to the habitat to play with. As soon as they get some results from that, we'll know which metals we can work with. That should give us the start we need."

"Are the others getting the habitat set up?"

"Yeah, they should be done by the time we get back. I'm going to send them back to get the other one from the library area as soon as they let me know they're done. One of the other crews is working on getting Martin set up in the garden. In a few days we'll be back to a normal routine again. If any of this can be considered routine."

"I guess its routine for here," Sean said.

"Brian, we're done setting up the habitat. What do you have for us next?"

"Head back and Al will tell you where to get the next one. We want to bring it back and set it up next to that one. It'll take you a couple days, but we need you back as soon as you can. I'll have your next job lined out by then. Bring an extra cruiser back with you too."

"Got it Boss. See you then."

"They took care of that in short order," Sean said. "I didn't think they'd be done until dinner time."

"They're getting the hang of those things," Brian said. "If we have to try pulling one of those trailers with a cruiser, I want an extra on stand-by."

"If we try that, you might want to go along. The first trip may be interesting. Think we can get them a load by then?"

"I think so. Let's head back and see how the welding experiments went."

* * *

"Lorna, where are you two hiding?" Brian called on the radio.

"Shit, look at how late it is," Lorna said to Eve.

"Hi, baby," Eve said. "It looks like we might be a little late. We kinda lost track of the time."

"Now, why doesn't that surprise me? Where the hell are you?"

"Uh, thirty miles or so in."

"I guess there's no need to wait dinner for you, is there?"

"Uhhh, probably not. We can manage dinner ourselves."

"I guess you know this means I have to bunk with Sean. Does that make you happy?"

"Uhhh, no."

"Me either. You two are going to be the death of us. Are you even going to try to come back tonight?"

"Well, maybe not. It would be late, and we'd have to do all this again tomorrow. There's no sense going over the same terrain every day."

"Alright but get your butts back here tomorrow night. We have work to do."

"Ok, baby. Talk to you tomorrow."

"He didn't sound so happy," Lorna said.

"He'll get over it. He always does. Where to next?"

"I still want to see what's in that tall structure to the south. I've been trying to pick my way over to it for the last hour. It's still several miles away though. How long before it gets dark?"

"An hour, maybe two," Eve said. "Isn't that where you said that big bird-thing was?"

"That's the place. Are you game?"

"What the hell. We'll catch hell when we get back anyhow."

Lorna continued to pick her way through the roads that were littered with fallen debris. Fallen by the ages of neglect by a culture that no longer existed.

It was full dark before they reached the structure.

"We'd better bed down here," Lorna said. "I want to be able to see what we're doing when we get there."

"Sounds good to me. You're cooking, right."

"God girl, when are you ever going to learn to cook? It's a good thing Brian is a good cook. Otherwise, he'd starve."

"Yeah, isn't it great?"

"I give up. Lay out the habitat. I'll find us something."

* * *

Al pulled up to the back of the miner as Dan and Jeff were getting out. Joe and Jim were there with the two rovers. Dan and Jeff would move the spare miner up to this point before going to bed.

"You guys don't mess around," Al said as he walked up to the small group.

"You said kick it in the ass," Dan said.

"And it looks like you did just that. Having any problems?"

"No, except those alien seats get awful hard after a while," Jeff said. "The miner is working great. I've been watching the air quality and it's beginning to show signs of dropping. It's still good though."

"I talked to Brian and Sean a little while ago and they're working on that. The problem is that you guys are going so fast, they don't think they can keep up with you."

"That could be a real problem," Joe said. "We can't slow down though."

"No, we can't do that. I'm going to look in the domes tomorrow. I want to see how they're holding up. That might give us an indication of how urgent this really is. I had the monitor station checked today and the winds are over four hundred miles an hour. The domes are rated at over five, something over five. I'm having a little trouble getting the engineers to give me a hard number. I don't think they really know."

"I was here when they put down the anchor bolts for the center dome," Joe said. "They took them down as far as the equipment would let them. Hell, they're down almost fifty feet. That should withstand a hell of a blow."

"Look, the only way these domes and the rest of them too, will stand up to this kind of wind, is by sheer luck and the fact that the atmosphere is so much less dense than it is on Earth. Be prepared to continue this process when we get to the hub. We may have to tunnel to each of the mines too. I'm thinking about bringing another miner up here when we get to the point where we can branch off to Bill's mine. I just don't know how bad it's going to get."

"Slim can train a few more of the brighter ones to do this," Dan said. "Hell, you guys trained us."

"We're not to the point where we have room to do that yet. We may bring some of them up here and have them work with you. That would take some of the burden off of you too."

"Hell, Boss, we can handle it," Jim said.

"I know, but they might as well get in on some of it too. I'll go over who we have and see what I can come up with. In the meantime, just continue the way you are."

"How long do you think it'll take us," Jeff asked.

"You're making about twenty-five miles a day. That would make it just over thirty-three days. That's well under what I told Mike it would take. I just hope they're still there when we get there."

"Is that really a concern?" Dan asked.

"I'm afraid so. I'll keep you posted if I learn anything. Any more questions?"

"No, I don't think so," Joe said. "Jim, we'd better get started."

"See you tomorrow. Do you want me to have the girls come fix breakfast?"

"That would be nice," Jim said. "Can you spare them for a day or so?"

"I'll see what I can do. Go to work."

Joe and Jim mounted the miner and in moments were cranked up and inching their way away from Al and the others. Al watched as the tunnel magically appeared in front of the miner. It still amazed him the way the aliens had managed to engineer this marvelous machine. He still didn't understand it, but as long as it worked, that didn't matter.

"You guys get some rest," Al said finally. "You've earned it."

"We will," Dan said. "We have to move the other miner up to here. That gives them enough time to get far enough away that we can actually sleep. This will get old after a while, but we'll stick with you for as long as it takes."

"That's all I can ask for. See you tomorrow. I think I'll spend the night at the library. It's not so much of a commute back to here."

"How's Slim doing, getting the supplies moved in?"

"He should be done in a couple more days. Then he'll be bringing some of it down here so they can start building the blast doors. I don't think we're going to be able to have nearly as many of them as I'd like to, but I guess we'll have to make do."

"We'll get there, even if we have to do it with air packs," Jeff said.

"I hope it won't come to that, but it might. See you tomorrow."

"Ok, Boss. Get some rest. You look like shit."

"Thanks, I needed that."

"Just trying to help."

Al climbed into his cruiser and turned and left. The drive to the library was about two hours and he wanted to be there before everyone went to bed. On the way, he went over the events of the last few days. He couldn't find anything he'd missed, but he was sure there had to be something. When he arrived, the two domes of the habitats were still blazing.

"What's this, a social club?" he asked when he walked in.

"Hey, what are you doing down here," Hollie asked. "We were beginning to think you had forgotten all about us."

"No, I'd never do that. It's been pretty hectic for the last few days. Are you having any luck here?"

"Some. The translations aren't yielding much, but we're getting a lot of it scanned. What's going on in the outside world?"

Al sat down and gave them all a run-down on the situation they were facing. All they knew about it was what they'd been able to pick up on the radio. Since they were primarily listening to an alternate frequency, that wasn't much.

"God, what's going to happen?" Sharon asked.

"We're all going to do our jobs and not worry about things we can't control," Al said. "Worst case, we may have to bring close to half a million people in here to live until we can rebuild the hub. The aliens managed; so can we. By the way, Joe and Jim wanted me to ask if you'd like to come have breakfast with them."

"That would be nice," Hollie said. "Things here are under control. A lot of the time we don't have that much to do."

"They're working the night shift, so they'll be getting off about 0700. It's about a two-hour drive. You can spend the day, or even two."

"It would be nice to see them," Sharon said.

"Then get up early and go see them. Things here will be fine. I'll show you how to get there."

* * *

It was a grey morning, well after the sun should have brought light to the inner complex. The array of fiber optic-like tubes must be getting obscured by the dust and sand. Al had been up since Hollie and Sharon had left two hours earlier. He had a pad of paper in front of him, listing the things he thought he still needed to do. The list was getting longer, as he worked his way through his fifth cup of coffee.

"Good morning, Al," Melissa said, coming up from behind him.

"God, you scared me."

"Sorry, I didn't mean to."

"I was just lost in thought. How have you been?"

"Not too bad. Have you been keeping Slim busy?"

"Yeah, but he should be finished with his current project in a day or two. I'll send him down to hang out here for a few days before I send him off again."

"I didn't hear you come in last night, or did you come in this morning?"

"No, I got here last night. Melissa, we're in a hell of a fix here. I explained most of it to the others last night, but you need to know what's going on too." With that, Al launched into his explanation of the situation. When he had finished, he just watched for an indication of what she was thinking.

"Has the board been advised of the situation?"

"I'm sure that Mike took care of that. There's an outside chance that he may still have some communication with them, but we're cut off. We will be for several weeks."

"What can I do?"

"Just keep going the way you are. The others will start to ask questions soon. We need to keep them informed, but not scare them. We're in better shape here than any of the other installations. We have no way of knowing how long this storm will last, or what kind of damage it might do. The miners are working as fast as the alien machines can go, to get to the hub. We'll also branch off and try to get to Bill's mine as soon as we get to a place where we can do it. We have to get out almost four hundred miles before we can risk it."

"When will that be?" Melissa asked.

"Sometime next week. At that time, I'll need Slim almost full time in the tunnels. Hollie and Sharon went over to visit with Jim and Joe. When Slim gets out there, you can do the same. You might need to kind of watch over things here for a day or two, until they get back."

"That pair has everyone so organized around here that I don't have much to do. Can I be of more help somewhere else?"

"Possibly, in a day or two. I'd like someone to look over the accommodations around the upper garden. We may have to put up a lot of people. We may need to have a place for them to live."

"I can set up there somewhere and do that. Where's Lorna?"

"She's watching over Arsia Mons."

"Where the hell is that?"

"I figured you'd heard about that by now. We found the way into Arsia Mons. We've had a team over there for over a week. I guess I'll have to keep you more up to date."

"I guess so. What did you find?"

"It's mostly an industrial complex. There may be another level too, but we haven't had time to do much exploring. Come out to my cruiser. I have a map of what we have so far."

When Al displayed the map of the two volcanoes overlaid onto the map of the tunnels, it was amazing.

"So, this is a whole other find?"

"Yes ma'am. Patty stumbled onto it and called us to go check it out. It's going to make all the difference in the world, with the resources it has. Machinery and materials. Brian and Sean are over there evaluating the situation now. Hopefully they'll have more information later today. That's where we're going to get most of what we need to work in this new tunnel."

"Lucky timing. What would you have done if that wasn't there?"

"The best we could." Al said.

"I guess that's all any of us can do. I feel so bad about how we got started when I first arrived. I'd like to apologize again."

"You misunderstood your directive, that's all. Look, we got all that sorted out a long time ago. Let it rest. You've made yourself one of the team. That's what's important. What we're doing here, now, could save the lives of all the people on this planet. You've helped make that possible."

"Still, I was wrong."

"God, woman, yes you were wrong. That's behind us. Can you watch things here? I have to go see if our domes are still there."

"Don't worry about us. We'll be right here." Melissa said.

"I may have to send some of the others down here later. We don't have enough room to house them all up there."

"Send them down. We can handle another thirty or so. That would about max us out, but we'll make room."

"Good. I'll see you in a day or two."

"Tell Slim I miss him."

"I'll do that," Al said as he climbed into the cruiser.

* * *

"How'd the welding go yesterday?" Sean asked as they all started to surface for the day.

"We found several different types of metal that we can work with," Brian said. "Now, all we have to do is find them inside. They're going to start looking close to the entrance after they get something to eat. Can we get one of those trailers out here?"

"I think so. We'll go give it a try in a few minutes. I talked to Al last night. He's going to try to get the rover inside today. If that doesn't work, well, we'll have to make do with the cruisers. They should handle it as long as we don't load them too heavy."

"We'll take Jones with us when we go in for the trailer. He can run the crane if we need it. The others can scour the area for something to load on it. We'll have to use our cruiser until we get one back from the other side."

"We need to have them bring that big computer over here too," Sean said. "We can do the downloads here and just send a disc to Al with the crews that make the runs."

"I'll set it up. I wonder where those damn women are."

"That's a good question. I guess we'd better call them and find out."

"I'll do it," Brian said picking up the radio. "Eve, it's time to get up."

"Uhhh, ok, I'm up."

"No, you're not. I can tell by the way you sound."

"Well, I'm getting up. What happened to the sun?"

"It's on vacation, like you. Where are you?"

"Just south of Lake Michigan, hell, I don't know. Where do you think we are?"

"A little testy this morning?"

"Hush. I'm entitled once in a while. Mom, where are we."

"Brian, we're about a mile from the vulture's nest," Lorna said. "Do you understand where that is?"

"No, but Sean says he does. He wants to know what you're doing clear down there."

"Just looking around."

"Lorna, damn it, you shouldn't be down there," Sean said. "We don't know what that thing we saw was."

"Yeah, and if I don't come have a look, we never will. You guys relax. We can handle ourselves."

"If that thing is as big as I think it is, you can't."

"Then we'll just jump out and scream at it. It'll be a lot more scared of us than we are of it. We're going to have a look before we come back. You're too far away to stop us, so give it up."

"Christ, woman."

"Shut up and help Brian. Lorna out."

"Don't you turn that radio off—damn you, answer me."

"Give it up Sean," Brian said. "We may not like what they're about to do, but she's right, we're too far away to stop them."

"Shit, I'm going to kill her."

"I'll hold her for you when they get back. Otherwise, she's liable to kick your ass. I've seen her in action."

* * *

"Now that we've had our wake-up call, let's get something to eat and go find that damn bird," Lorna said. "Do you believe them, trying to tell us what we can and can't do?"

"Yeah, I believe it," Eve said. "It didn't work any better for them than it did for anybody else though. You could have been a little more tactful you know."

"No, I couldn't have. They woke me up and that's as good as it gets when they wake me up."

"What's for breakfast?"

"It's your turn to cook." Lorna said.

"Oh, cold cereal. Ok, that works for me."

Thirty minutes later they pressed the buttons on the side of the cruiser and watched as the habitat folded up and stowed itself in the back of the cruiser. Lorna climbed to the top of a pile of debris and searched for a path to get to the tall structure that they had almost made it to the night before. She could make out a way to get part way, but the last half mile or so would have to be on foot.

"We'll have to stop here," she said when they ran out of road.

"We need the exercise. Let's go."

They snaked their way through the rubble for over a half hour before reaching the base of the structure. It stretched toward what would normally be the sky, some thirty stories or so. It appeared to be almost the size of a city block at the base. It was almost like exploring a large city after a major war.

They picked their way into the building and worked their way up several floors. There were no windows, but the light managed to filter in from above, somewhere. By the time they had managed to get up to within a few floors of the top they were exhausted and had to rest.

"Was this your idea?" Lorna asked.

"Hell no, it was yours. I thought we decided not to go climbing stairs anymore. We did enough of that at the mine a year ago."

"I remember. That was worth it; this will be too."

"It had better be. What was that?"

CHAPTER SEVEN

"What was what," Lorna asked.

"Mother, listen. There's a noise coming from up there somewhere."

"I can't hear anything."

"Just listen for a minute," Eve said.

After several minutes they heard what Eve had been talking about. It was a deep throaty sound, coming from above them. They looked at each other and eased their way up another flight of stairs. They could see more daylight now and the sound was a little louder. They had to cross to the other side of a large room to get to the next set of stairs. In the center of the large room was a hole that seemed to go most of the way to the ground.

As they climbed the next set of stairs, the sound grew louder. Almost sneaking up the stairs, they hugged the wall. When they got to the top, where they could barely see into the room, Lorna stopped and motioned for Eve to do the same. The roof of the building was gone, except for a few remaining strands that dangled from the corners. In the far corner was the giant bird-looking thing they had seen. It was sitting on a nest.

"Mom, what's that?" Eve whispered.

"Damned if I know. Hand me that camera."

Lorna snapped several pictures and they started to leave. Just then, Eve knocked a brick off the step she was on. The bird scrambled off the nest and lunged toward them. They both screamed and bolted down the stairs. The bird stopped dead in its tracks. When they reached the bottom of that flight of stairs they looked back. It wasn't following.

"Where is it?" Eve asked.

"We must have scared it. I know it scared me. I did manage to get a couple shots of it after it got off the nest though. I wonder what it eats."

"There sure isn't anything in here for it to eat. It has to get it somewhere else."

"Patty and Brittany went to look for the upper level yesterday. I wonder if they found anything yet."

"Call them and ask," Eve said.

"Patty, Brittany, report in," Lorna said over the radio.

"What's up?" Patty asked.

"Have you found anything yet?"

"No, we just got to the outer area an hour ago. What do you need?"

"When you find the upper area, and you will, watch out for big birds."

"You're shitting us, right?"

"No, I wouldn't do that about something like this. We just encountered one and it's bigger than anything I've ever seen. I'm talking an elephant with wings."

"Now I know you're shitting us," Brittany said.

"Britt, this is Eve."

"Go ahead."

"It's the biggest thing I've ever seen. She's not exaggerating one bit."

"Girls, listen, we've seen them flying around in here before," Lorna said. "We can see them from fifty miles away. I'm not kidding. Watch your step when you find the center of the upper level. They have to feed somewhere and it's not down here."

"Ok, we'll play along," Patty said. "We'll watch out."

"Lorna, this is Sean. Where are you?"

"At the top of the tall structure to the southwest of you. Well, we're down several levels. We got pictures of it this time. Up close and personal pictures."

"Get your asses out of there."

"It's more afraid of us than we are of it."

"If I have to come get you it's going to hurt."

"We'll see you tonight, Lorna out."

* * *

It was early afternoon when Al rolled up to the blast doors that blocked the way into the domed complex that had been their home. Slim was close by and came to see what was going on.

"What's up Boss?"

"Slim, let's take a look and see if we still have a home," Al said.

"We should be able to tell by the pressure differential on the second set of doors," Slim said.

"That's what I was thinking. Let's have a look. Did Brian close all the airlocks between the domes?"

"Yeah, I'm sure he did."

They inspected the first set of doors and found there was no pressure differential. They opened them and went in and closed them again. The second set was a different story. While they indicated there was still some pressure in the small dome, it wasn't as much as they had had in there when they left.

"I think we'd better throw on a suit," Al said. "It looks like there's some kind of a problem in there. We need to tie off to the blast doors too when we go in there. I don't want you to blow away. There's nobody to catch you for several hundred miles."

"I don't have a problem with that."

They returned a few minutes later, encased in the latest suits that were available. They were much more flexible than the ones they had used even a year before. Al tied them both to a loop that they always put on the doors. When he opened the blast doors, they could see the full intensity of the storm raging above them.

"Christ, would you look at that," Slim said.

"Let's see if we can get a little closer," Al said.

When they reached the top of the incline, they could see the reason the pressure was low. There was a small tear in the airlock into the next dome, and the center dome was half gone.

"Well, I guess that answers our questions," Al said. "Fortunately, the other facilities have some protection from the wind. We get the full force."

"We'd better lean on that tunnel," Slim said. "They may be alright now, but if this continues to increase, they won't be for long."

"They're moving as fast as they can. The miners are fantastic machines, but they do have their limits."

"Could you put two in there side by side?"

"I never thought to try it. We might be able to. Let's try to seal off that leak and get back behind the blast doors. The rover that I came to get is in the third dome and I don't think we can reach it."

"Yeah, this doesn't look good."

"How long do you have until you're done moving stuff inside?"

"I can turn that over to someone else. There isn't that much left. Hell, Smitty can manage that detail. What do you need me to do?"

"We have to figure out a way to move that tunnel along faster, or we're going to be the only ones left on the planet. If we can move two miners in there together, maybe we could move three or four. Whatever it takes."

"We'll need more people."

"Get some of the engineers or Brian's crew. I don't care where you get them, just get them."

"I know several we can hi-jack. Shall I take them somewhere out of the way and train them?"

"We can set up something in the tunnel. There's plenty of room behind the miners. How many do you think you can come up with?"

"Enough to run three miners, on three shifts. That's in addition to the ones you have working now."

"That's a dozen people. Where are you going to get them?"

"Five from engineering and seven from Brian's crew," Slim said. "We're going to need that many trained. We may not need to use them all, all of the time, but eventually we'll need them all."

"And more, probably. See if you can get two more. We can put them with Joe and Jim. We need to cut back their hours a little. Ok, get Smitty to take over here. Swing by the library and see Melissa too. I talked to her this morning, and I think she could use a little reassurance."

"I haven't been able to get back in there for almost a week now," Slim said. "Do you have the coordinates for the tunnel? I'll need several cruisers too. They'll need a place to sleep and eat."

"We can arrange that. Break off what you need from this detail here. It might slow them down a little, but they'll have to live with that."

"By the time I get everything lined out it might be tomorrow before we can get started."

"That's fine. You might do a little practicing with the multiple miners in the same tunnel too. Also see if one person can run one. If they can it might make it easier later on. I'm going back to the tunnel to see the other crews and talk to them about trying that too. Maybe they can come up with some ideas. Line them up where the tunnel levels out and go north a ways. That's as good a place as any for them to practice."

"Ok, we'll be set up and running by lunch tomorrow," Slim said as they finished the patch job on the airlock. "There that should hold as long as the dome holds."

"See you tomorrow. I'm going back inside."

"We'll be there."

* * *

"We have two trailer loads," Brian said. "I guess I'd better head back in the morning."

"Leave Jones with me and I'll get more ready to send that way," Sean said. "We have the habitat set up and we'll have the computer ready in a day or two. It looks like we're about set up here."

"I may hi-jack the other habitat that's headed this way and set it up in the tunnel for a while. I think that's where we need to focus our attention. We'll need a large crew to fabricate these doors. We're going to need those fans soon too."

"I'll have them to you as soon as I figure out how to make it work. We'd better have Al send that habitat into the tunnel where he wants the first set of doors installed. You're right; you'll need a work camp. I'll get a crew lined up here to get the stuff located and loaded so we can get them headed back that way as fast as we can."

"Where are those damn women?"

"I don't have a clue. They should have been back here by now."

"Well, look there. They did get out of there alive after all," Brian said as Lorna and Eve drove up.

"Hi, guys. What's up?" Lorna said as they got out.

"If you two can't stay out of trouble, we won't let you play together anymore," Sean said.

"What? All we did was look around."

"And damn near give me a heart attack. What's the big idea of going in there looking for your damn bird without us along?"

"Well, pardon me all to hell. We have a job to do too. We can't help much with the tunnel and all that, but by God we can still do our job. That's our job!"

"Damn it, you know what I mean."

"I know exactly what you mean. Because we're women, we can't handle ourselves. That's exactly what you mean."

"No, damn it, I mean we don't want anything to happen to you because we'd miss you too much."

"That's a little better," Eve said, trying to defuse the situation. "Come on, let's get something to drink and see if we can download these pictures."

Lorna scowled at Sean but went into the habitat to get something to drink. They bantered back and forth for almost an hour before things started to settle down. They were able to download the pictures to a laptop computer in the habitat and show them to all that were there. The bird looked to be replile-ish but was clearly a bird.

"What are you going to call this one?" Sean asked.

"I don't name them; I just find them," Lorna said, still fuming.

"We need to have everyone watch out for these," Brian said. "At least until we figure out a little more about them."

"Unless there are a lot of other animals in here, they have to be vegetarians," Lorna said. "Otherwise, they would have died out a long time ago. Why would the alien civilization bring something like that in here to begin with? That makes two large animals in the complexes. Why are they here?"

"Maybe they bred them for meat," Eve said. "One of those things could feed a lot of people for a long time. I wonder what they taste like."

"Hell, maybe they're just big chickens," Lorna said.

* * *

When Al reached the end of the tunnel, it was almost time for another shift change. Joe and Jim were waiting for Dan and Jeff to stop.

"About ready to go at it again?" Al asked.

"Yeah, just waiting for them to give up. How are things in the outside world?"

"Not good. Slim and I went into the small dome today. Half of the center dome is gone. The others seem to be holding up alright. We need to move this thing along a little faster."

"Any ideas on how to do that," Joe asked. "We're pushing it as hard as we can. Twelve or thirteen miles in twelve hours is about all we can do."

"What if you work two of them together? Can one man run one of these?"

"Yeah, I think so, but it wouldn't look very good."

"I don't care what it looks like. When we get the other machine moved up here, you two give it a try. If the other complexes are as bad off as ours, we may be too late if we keep at it this way."

"Joe, we can change the focal points and work half of the tunnel each," Jim said. "That should give us at least half again more tunnel than we've been getting."

"Yeah, I guess it might. We'll give it a try. What's Slim up to?"

"He's gathering up another crew and he's going to train them back behind you. We'll need to start branching out to the other installations soon. Bill's first, but before long we'll need to head for each of them."

"Shit, I hope Brian and Sean come up with a way to build some blast doors soon," Joe said. "We're opening up a hell of a hole here."

"I think the complex can support us for a while," Al said. "The air quality hasn't dropped off too bad. They'll figure something out. I think the key is going to be to just keep the air moving."

"Al, how far have we come so far?"

"About seventy miles, why?"

"If we had a parallel tunnel, we could duct the air in through one and out through the other," Jim said. "We can't use air ducts like we would in the mine because they can't keep up with us. If we establish the other tunnel and connect them with small cross tunnels, they could be ducts. Look, we can't just put in doors and fans. All we'll be doing is running the same air around in circles. This way we can control it."

"That's a hell of an idea. You might have just earned a bonus, providing there are any bonuses to be had. I'll get Slim started on it. You guys keep going here. We don't need to make any turns for a while. Just keep hammering on it."

"They finally gave up," Joe said as Dan and Jeff climbed out of the miner. "As soon as they bring up the other one, we'll try working them together. We may have to draft them to help us get started."

"I don't think they'll mind," Al said. "I'll explain things to them."

Joe and Jim went to work, and Al explained the situation to Dan and Jeff. He gave them a rundown of what had been proposed and sent them to get the other miner. When they returned with it, instead of parking it out of the way, they fell in beside Joe and Jim.

"Joe, how do you want to do this?" Dan asked.

"Set the focal points in the center of the tunnel to just overlap. Then adjust the other beams to hold half of the tunnel. As long as we can keep them together in the center, we should be able to keep the same cross section, more or less."

"Ok, are you two going to be able to handle both machines?"

"We'll have to until we can get more people trained. Slim will take care of that. Let's set it up and give it a try. Once we get the cut established, we'll take over."

"Here we go," Jeff said.

They both started narrowing the focus of the beams and the pattern started to take shape. Once they had them adjusted, they started moving ahead. Al watched intently as they pulled away from him. He got in his cruiser and followed them for the first half hour. The tunnel was indeed growing at a faster rate, almost twice as fast.

"It's looking good, guys," Al called on the radio. "Now, can you do it with only two of you?"

"Let's give it a try," Joe said. "Ok, guys, stop now."

"We'll watch things for a few minutes," Dan said as they all got out. "Al, can you give us a ride back to the cruisers?"

"Sure thing. I want to watch things for a few more minutes."

Joe and Jim split up, each taking a miner and started up again. They hadn't disengaged the cutting beams, so all they had to do was drive the machines forward. It was soon evident that they would be able to make this work. They followed the two machines for a few minutes and then turned to go back to where the two cruisers were parked.

"Joe, Jim, good luck," Al called to them as they left.

"Thanks, Boss. Will you be around tomorrow?"

"Probably, but I'll have to get Slim set up too. I think we'll try the two-tunnel idea. If you can do this with two, maybe they can do it with three and catch up before long."

"It's worth a try."

"Keep the tunnel to the smaller size from now on. If we're going to have two, we can make them one-way."

"Roger, Boss. See you tomorrow."

Al dropped Dan and Jeff off to get some much-deserved rest and headed for the habitat at the library. It was 2130 when he arrived there. He could see that Slim and several others were there already.

"Slim, did you have any luck?" Al asked.

"I have the crews we talked about. When I explained the situation, I had no problem getting volunteers. How are they doing?"

"Flying. They tried out the two-miner idea and it worked well. Melissa, can you print out a map from the system in my cruiser?"

"Sure, be right back."

"Slim, we came up with a way to ventilate the tunnel that might just work. I want you to take your training crew into the tunnel and set up a parallel tunnel to theirs. Make it large enough to handle a transport, but not any bigger than you have to. Stretch it out and try to catch them. They'll be about a hundred miles ahead of you to start with, but if you use four miners, to their two, maybe you can catch them in a few days. When you do catch them, we'll put in a cross tunnel to connect them. By then we should be able to get some doors and fans set up to move the air where we want it."

"That's a hell of an idea," Slim said. "Where did that come from?"

"Jim suggested it. This is a hell of a crew we have here."

"Here's your map," Melissa said.

"Here's where we go," Al said, laying out the map. "Work your way in where the tunnel flattens out. It's large enough from there out into the complex. You'll want to go have a look at it in the morning. Pick a spot in here somewhere."

"This looks like they're making turnouts," Slim said pointing to the map. "We could start just behind the place where they made the first one. That would give us a bit of a jump on catching them."

"That's as good a spot as any," Al said. "Make the junction as big as the ground will allow, then narrow it down and get after them. I'll run some new numbers as soon as I see how fast they'll be able to go. We may be able to get there in half the time I'd expected. I just hope we won't be too late."

"We'll make it. The large dome, here, seemed to be standing up pretty well, and the domes at the hub and most of the other mines are sheltered some. We should be alright."

"We can't afford to slow them down much, so you'll have to catch them. If we have to, we'll work in suits."

"I'll have a better idea of what we can do in a day or two," Slim said. "I'll cut the junction and then we'll get after them."

"Al, this is Sean," a voice came over the radio.

"Sean, go ahead. How is it going over there?"

"Brian and some of his guys will be headed that way in the morning with two loads of materials to build the blast doors you want. They'll have to pull them with the cruisers so the trip will be a slow one. Did you get the rover inside?"

"No, the center dome is half gone. We couldn't get to it."

"Well, we'll have to do it the hard way, I guess. Can you head off the other habitat that you were going to send this way?"

"Yeah, don't you need it over there?"

"Eventually, but Brian wants to have one as a base to work out of in the tunnel. When that's finished, we can bring it over here."

"Slim says they have it loaded and were planning to leave here in the morning. I can send them the other way. Is Lorna staying out of trouble?"

"No. I'll send you some pictures she and Eve took this morning. That's kind of a sore subject right now."

"Did she find her bird?"

"You might say that. From the pictures she took, it looks like they were on the menu."

"That's not good. Tell her to stay out of trouble."

"You actually think she'll listen to me?"

"No, but it won't hurt to tell her."

"I'm pulling Arnold and his two guys in to help gather materials on this end. We'll see if we can figure out how to duct the air in the tunnel for you."

"We have that taken care of. All we need is some blast doors and some fans. I'll tell Brian what we need when he gets here. Just find us something to build all this stuff out of."

"We have a handle on that. It'll be a trick getting it over there, but we'll do it somehow. How many cruisers can we use to shuttle the stuff with? We need to run them in pairs. To pull the incline on that end, we may have to hook them together. We could use one of those truck-things if the air was better."

"Do the best you can. I'll send you six cruisers tomorrow. Will that be enough for now? I may come over in a few days. We're still working the kinks out of what we're doing here."

"That should do it for now. Brian will probably stay over there to take care of things in the tunnel. We'll support you from here."

"Ok, talk to you tomorrow."

"Sounds like things are starting to come together," Slim said. "That find over there couldn't have come at a better time."

"I don't know what we would have done without it," Al said. "Man, I think I'm going to bed. Move ten or twelve miners to the tunnel tomorrow."

"I have that many located. We'll get them headed that way in the morning."

"Good night, all," Al said. "I give up."

* * *

When the crew started to stir the next morning, the light hadn't yet made its appearance. Al was up before almost anyone else and went around checking the progress with the various crews that were working from that area. Some progress was being made, but nothing of much note. He put that all out of his mind and focused on the problem at hand. He was able to head off the habitat and send them to the new tunnel and told them to wait there for Slim.

"We're headed for the lower garden area to get the miners," Slim said. "Anything else we can do for you?"

"No. I'll meet you over there after a while. I'm headed back in to check on how Joe and Jim made out last night."

"Ok, we'll get started. I'm sending five cruisers to different locations to pick up the miners. I have seven guys that have at least moved them. I split them up and showed them where to go. Hopefully they won't get lost. I'll go to the one closest to the new tunnel and get it moved over so I can cut the intersection. By the time some of the others get there, I may have that done."

"Find a place to put that habitat. Brian's going to need it for his crew when he gets here tomorrow sometime."

"I'll take care of that too. See you on your way back."

* * *

When Al finally made it to where the two cruisers were parked it had taken him almost three hours instead of two. The two miners were well away from the cruisers and making good time. Joe and Jim were just finishing eating when Al stopped.

"How'd it work last night?" Al asked.

"Like a charm. We made almost twice as much tunnel as the night before," Joe said. "They were late getting up here because we went farther than they thought we would."

"That's good. It's going to be an all-day trip to come check on you pretty soon. Hell, I may just have to come in here and stay."

"The more the merrier," Jim said. "Do you think Slim can catch us?"

"I don't know, but he's going to try. They're moving into place now and will be running parallel to you soon. When we get some doors and fans installed, we'll cut a couple cross tunnels and see how your idea will work."

"Working the machine alone is a challenge," Joe said. "When you get some help trained, it might be a good idea to double up again. As you may have noticed, the tunnel sides are a little erratic."

"I did notice that, but the heading is still true enough, so don't worry about it. Slim will have them up to speed in no time. He's bringing a bunch of spare machines in with him too. When we get to a point where we think we can branch off, we'll use some of them and go visit Bill. I'm worried about them."

"Bill's a smart cookie. If it gets too bad, he'll take them underground. They have that tunnel we made them. They might not be too comfortable, but they'll survive."

"I hope you're right. With the direction this one's coming from, they're exposed pretty bad. You guys better get some rest. I'll try not to wake you up when I come back through. I'm going up front for a while. I want to see how this operation is going."

"I think you'll be pleasantly surprised. We were a little skeptical at first, but it seemed to work fine."

"See you later," Al said as he left.

When he reached the machines, they were almost three miles ahead of where Joe and Jim were parked. He watched as the green glow made the tunnel magically appear in front of the machines.

"Do we have company?" Dan called over the radio.

"Yeah, it's just me," Al said. "Are you getting the hang of it?"

"It's different, I'll grant you that," Jeff said. "Once you get the feel of it, it's not too bad though."

"Can you keep it up for a few days?"

"No problem. When we get done though, we're going to need a long shower. Can you arrange to have our cruisers restocked? Our supplies are running a little low."

"That I can arrange. I might even be able to have someone rig you a portable shower. Would that help?"

"Hell yes. We're getting a little ripe here, Boss," Dan said.

"I'll see what I can do. Anything else I can do for you?"

"No, we're fine. Just keep us lined up with where we need to be."

"At this rate, we'll need to make a turn in about three days. About the time we make the turn, we'll branch off and head for your mine. I want to connect to as many facilities as we can."

"Think they're in the same shape we're in, with the domes I mean."

"I hope not, but we won't know that until we get there. I have to round up the schematic of the tunnels over there too, so we can try to hit them."

"You brought back a copy of the map you made over there when you were tunneling to the areas in the back, didn't you."

"I have a copy. I just don't know if it made it inside here when we evacuated. Can you guys handle things for a couple days? I want to stick with Slim and make sure he gets off to a good start. He has a lot of catching up to do."

"Sure, Boss. That's no problem. We'll call if we have any problems."

"Joe has the navigational information you'll need later. It's in their cruiser."

"We've been watching it as we advance. So far, so good."

"I'll see you later."

When Al returned to the beginning of the tunnel, Slim had just arrived, and the miner was due soon.

"Let's set up the habitat just behind you," Al said. "That should be close enough for Brian to work with."

"I was just looking at that," Slim said. "I'll need a little room to get started. I figured to go in here, where it starts to narrow. Shorty's bringing the first miner. I'll get him to work with me until we get the tunnel started."

They went to where the crew that had brought the habitat was parked and told them where to put it. They worked with them until the miner arrived. Slim climbed into the operator's compartment and Al took a perch on top where he could watch what was going on. They positioned the machine and Slim started the cut.

Fifteen minutes later they had the intersection established. It angled to the left, north, and went in for several hundred feet. It also started to shrink in size. When they finally made the turn, so they were parallel with the other tunnel, they were a thousand feet north. By this time another miner had arrived and came up to where they were.

"How did they do this?" Slim asked

"They just cut half of the tunnel each," Al said. "Set them side-by-side and overlap the center cut a little and go. When you get a good spot carved out, that's where we'll put the first set of doors. Brian will be here late today or early tomorrow to start on that."

"Shorty, can you handle the cutters?" Slim asked.

"I think so. It may be a little erratic to start with, but I'll get the hang of it. I watched what you were doing when we cut this section."

"Ok, I'll take the other one and get someone up here with you. Michael can drive for you. Let's see what we can do. I'll instruct you on the radio if you need it."

"We're ready," Shorty said.

Al stood back and watched as they adjusted their focus for the cut. When they were ready, they started to advance. The edges were ragged for the first twenty feet and then started to smooth out. The pace they were moving at was slower than the one Joe and the others were doing, but they were off to a good start. Al turned and walked back out to where his cruiser was parked. Two more miners showed up then and he directed them to follow Slim and followed them into the tunnel.

"Slim, want to try another one in the mix?" Al asked when they pulled up behind them.

"We can. Let us work this way for a few more minutes. We're just getting the hang of it."

"I'll leave you to it. Just remember, they have a hundred-mile head start on you."

"Yeah, I know. We'll see if we can catch up. That's going to be hard to do with the rookies though."

"Give it a try and if it doesn't work, I'll trade some of them out and move Joe and Jim back here to help."

"Let us see what we can do. Can you come back in a couple hours?"

"I'll give them a hand with the habitat. Call if you need me."

* * *

"Mr. Al. Mr. Al, this is Franco. Are you hiding on one of these radio frequency things. I need to speak with you at once. Mr. Al?"

"What is it Franco," Al asked when he stopped laughing.

"Mr. Al, these conditions and most unsatisfactory. I insist that I be allowed to go back to my kitchen."

"That's not going to be that easy. Your kitchen isn't where it used to be."

"What do you mean it is not where it used to be? Franco simply cannot work in these primitive conditions. I am a Master Chef, and this simply will not do."

"Franco, shut up and listen to me for a minute."

"Mr. Al, I simply will not stand for this kind of treatment."

"Franco—shut up! Your kitchen is spread all over the planet's surface. There's a storm on the surface and we're cut off from the rest of the planet. What you have, what we all have, is all there is. If you want to leave, go ahead. You won't get fifty feet. Now shut up and get back to work. You have a job to do just like the rest of us."

"Mr. Al, I must protest. I simply will not be treated this way."

"Put Martin on the radio," Al said finally.

"Yeah, Al," Martin said a moment later.

"Draw him a picture, would you. I can't seem to get through that thick head of his."

"I'll try again, Al. He's pretty upset."

"I'll be upset if he doesn't calm down. Tell him there isn't even anything God can do about this situation. He'll just have to ride it out like the rest of us."

"Ok, Al. I'll take care of it. Martin out."

CHAPTER EIGHT

"Al, are you having a problem," Slim called on the radio.

"Mr. Franco seems to be having a little case of cabin fever. Nothing to worry about. How's it going in there?"

"We're getting the hang of it. I'm bringing another machine up. We'll try three of them for a while."

"With the tunnel the size it is, you can get four or five of them abreast. We need as much speed as we can get."

"We'll work up to that in a little while," Slim said. "We have to crawl before we run. From what I've seen with two, we may just be able to catch them."

"If you can, we'll move another machine or two in there with them and go for broke. Brian, what's your location."

"We're just coming into Pavonis," Brian answered.

"Having any problems?"

"No, not really. We had to drop one trailer and use both cruisers to pull them up the incline, but we're hooked up again and we'll be there late tonight. Very late."

"We have you a habitat set up close to the spot where you'll be working. I'll be here when you get here."

"Good. We'll need a place to sack out. We'll try to get there tonight though."

"It'll wait if you get too tired. We have a lot to show you when you get here."

"We'll be along," Brian said.

Al went back in to see how Slim was doing. They'd moved a third machine into the tunnel and had all three fired up. The pace they were moving at was noticeably faster than the one Dan and Jeff had been moving.

"Slim, do you think you can handle another one?"

"Yeah, but it's going to get a little tight. Unless we widen the tunnel, we can't use five. This is actually working pretty well."

"They have two in the main tunnel; you'll need as many of them as you can get to catch them."

"Give us five days and we'll pull along side them."

"You're on."

* * *

"You've done a good job," Al said three days later. "How will the fans work?"

"We'll have to leave the habitat here somewhere," Brian said. "We'll need the reactor to power them. The fans will pull the air into Slim's tunnel and when we cut the cross tunnels it will come back through Joe's."

"I'll go set up the cross tunnels. The air's getting pretty bad in Joe's tunnel. They're out almost two hundred miles. We need to get some circulation up there."

"Go have Slim cut through. I'll fire up the fans."

"He's still forty miles behind Joe. I guess it'll help though. Slim still thinks he's going to catch up by day after tomorrow."

"We'll rig a set of doors for the cross tunnel. We'll have to close it off when we move to the next cross tunnel."

"Ok, see you later," Al said.

It now took Al three hours from the time he entered the tunnel to get to the end. They had progressed at a fantastic rate and Joe and his crew were about to be overtaken. When he reached the green glow at the end, he parked and watched them pull away. Slim had two spare miners being driven right behind the ones that were actually doing the cutting.

"Slim, I'm going to hi-jack one of your spares and give you a little ventilation," Al called.

"Good, it's getting a little stuffy in here. I was afraid we'd have to go to air packs."

"This should help you quite a bit. Brian has the fans fired up. You can use this cross tunnel to get out until we get far enough ahead to cut another one. Do your guys driving the spares know how to cut with them?"

"You bet. Morrison, hang a right and cut us a hole big enough to drive a miner through. Al will line you out."

"Roger, Slim," Morrison said and stopped his miner. When he got out, Al met him and explained what he wanted him to do.

"We need a small tunnel right here," Al said pointing to a spot on the wall. "Twenty feet or so wide and fifteen feet high. Arch the roof."

"No problem," Morrison said. "Is this going to connect with Joe's tunnel?"

"I hope so. That's the plan at least. There may be a little difference in elevation, so we may have to adjust it after we get it opened up. Hang on a minute. I'll call Dan and make sure there's no one in this area. Dan, are we clear to cut a cross tunnel?"

"All clear unless you're breathing down our neck. Joe and Jim are about five miles behind us."

"We should have about a forty-mile cushion. Here we come. Ok, son, let's see what we can do. I'll ride with you if that's alright."

"Sure, climb aboard."

When they were back inside the machine, Morrison turned and faced the wall and adjusted the focus on the cutters and moved forward. Al watched intently as the wall started to open up to allow them to enter. Morrison moved steadily forward until the wall in front of them disappeared.

"Looks like we're about three feet high," Al said. "Can you fix that?"

"Sure thing Boss. Slim said we'd probably be off a little."

He moved the machine into the other tunnel and turned around. After readjusting the cutters, he made a smooth transition between the two tunnels. When they were finished, they got out to have a close look at the cut.

"That's pretty good work. Have you been working up front with Slim?"

"We've all been taking a turn. He keeps bringing in new people, so we have enough to do the job."

"I thought I saw a lot of new faces coming and going," Al said. "How many of you has he trained?"

"Close to thirty now, I guess. He said we'd have a lot of work to do to get to all the mines. Running five miners around the clock takes a lot of people."

"I'm surprised at how fast you've been able to catch on to them."

"We played with them a little, learning how to drive them and such," Morrison said. "Slim filled in the finer points, and we've had a lot of time to practice in the last few days."

"Thanks for your hard work."

"We're all in this together."

"Slim, I'm going to go check on Dan and Jeff. I'll get back to you in a few minutes."

"Roger, Boss."

Thirty minutes later Al pulled up behind the other set of miners. He'd clocked it at thirty-eight miles. They were a little closer than he'd figured.

* * *

Lorna and Eve were back in the interior of Arsia Mons. They had been taking short day trips looking the area over for the last several days. With Sean tied up gathering supplies for Brian, they had time to kill and thought it would be better to do something constructive.

"God, I wish I knew more about this equipment in here," Lorna said as they drove.

"Lorna, this is Brittany. I think we may have found the way to another level."

"Where are you?" Lorna asked.

"We're on the extreme east side. Spoke 90 and ring twenty. There's an increase in elevation as we've been driving for the last half hour. We're driving south in ring twenty. We'll have a better idea in a little while."

"Ok, let us know what you find. We'll head that way, but it'll be late this afternoon before we can get there. Sean, did you hear that?"

"Yeah, I heard. Are you going to go check it out?"

"We might as well. We're not doing much good in here."

"Be safe and let me know what's going on."

"We will. Lorna out."

* * *

With the cross tunnel opened, Al was able to make the trip between the ends of the two parallel tunnels in less than an hour. The air had already started to freshen in Slim's tunnel, but farther in, it was still pretty stale in the tunnel where Dan and Jeff were working. The distances were just too great to be effective with the ventilation.

"Dan, how are you holding up?" Al asked as he pulled up behind them.

"We've had to start taking hits off of the air packs," Dan said. "We don't have to wear them all the time, but we do need a little help."

"Slim should catch up with you tomorrow and that will make it where we can get the good air a little closer to you. We'll keep cutting new cross tunnels to keep the circulation as close to you as we can."

"What are we going to do when we have to branch off to Bill's mine," Jeff asked.

"I'm still working on that. We'll figure out something."

"I think you'll have to duct it across and run two more parallel tunnels," Dan said. "That's the only way I can see to get the fresh air in there."

"That's about what I came up with too. We'll be to the junction point in another day; or two at the most."

"How long will we have before we get to the hub?"

"Nine or ten days if we get a couple more miners fired up and send them in with you. I want to let Slim catch up first. We have to be able to get the air to you."

"I'm surprised we've been able to do as well as we have."

"So am I. The tunnel has a vacuum effect on the air. While you're cutting, you can actually feel the breeze coming in behind you."

"I wish it would come in a little faster," Jeff said. "Has the pressure dropped in the complex?"

"Not enough to be noticeable. The complex has so much volume that that shouldn't be a problem. The air is moving around in there though, trying to stabilize the pressure. It's good for it to do that. It's been stagnant for too long."

"Well, we're not going to be accused of that," Dan said. "I've never seen anything like this before. This is going to go down in history."

"Only if we get there in time to do any good. Do you need anything?"

"No, we're doing fine."

* * *

"We should be about there," Eve said. "This is a lot different than the tunnels in Pavonis. They're a lot smaller."

"Yeah, but the layout is similar," Lorna said. "Brittany, we're where you called us from. We can see your tracks."

"Took you long enough. Follow the tracks south. According to the mapping gear, we're on the upper level. It looks like maybe three thousand feet above the other one, more or less. You shouldn't have any trouble finding us."

"No, we can see your tracks. The only problem is it's getting late any you have a six-hour head start on us."

"Then you better lean on it. We're still looking for the center. I wouldn't think it could be that much farther. The overlay of the map on the lower-level shows that we're almost in to where we'd encounter the perimeter for the center area."

"Keep looking. We'll be along as fast as we can."

* * *

"Al, we'll catch them sometime tonight," Slim said when they stopped to change shifts. "The night crew will probably pull out ahead of them if they run all night."

"I'll be here to monitor things," Al said. "We need to get them some of this better air as soon as we can. Let's have a look at this map. I figure we need to go to the far side of the last canyon coming off of the chasms before we can turn south to intersect with Bill's mine. He has a lot of people trained in using these machines and we can use them to help us get to the hub."

"It looks like it might take two days to get down there," Slim said. "Navigating into the area is going to be a bitch. We're three thousand feet above them here."

"We'll aim for the back of the mine, well away from the chasm. Finding the tunnel in the mine is going to be the trick. I went out and retrieved the information we generated when we went over there and cut those tunnels for them. We'll have to transpose that over what we're making now. I hope the calibration of the machines are close."

"They should get us close enough to break into one of the tunnels. How are we going to break this up when we make the turn?"

"You take the tunnel toward the hub, and I'll go to the mine," Al said. "I want to see the look on Bill's face when we barge in. When we make connections there, we'll draft as much help as we can. I have a feeling they'll all be in the hole by the time we get there. Can you have the rest of the miners brought up when we make the junction?"

"That's no problem. I'll let these guys handle things here and go back and locate them. When do you plan to start branching off to the other mines?"

"I don't know if we have enough information to get to them until we get to the hub. We'll need the records from the survey office to be reasonably sure we can connect with them. We know their location, but I've never been in most of them, so I don't know the layout."

"At least most of them are well away from the chasm. We won't have that to contend with."

"I brought in all the information we had on their locations. I'll make that decision when the time comes. Want to ride over and see how the other half lives?"

"Yeah, I'd like that," Slim said.

Just under an hour later Al and Slim pulled up behind the miners that were working the main tunnel. Joe and Jim were just getting ready to take their turn in the miners and came to see what was going on.

"You're running a little late," Al said. "Problems?"

"No, we're just letting the rookie crew catch up a little," Joe said. "Where are they now?"

"We'll be five or six miles ahead of you by the time your shift is over," Slim said. "They're not really rookies anymore. Their tunnel looks almost as good as yours."

"That's good. We can use all the help we can get. When can we get some of that better air?"

"As soon as they get within a mile of you, we'll cut through and send some of it this way," Al said. "I'm figuring around 0100 or so. I'll keep a watch on things and make the call. You'll want to take the cruisers back out a ways tonight just in case I miscalculate. I'd hate to fry one of them."

"That would be embarrassing," Jim said. "When do we make the junction to Bill's mine?"

"Maybe late tomorrow. When we cut through here later tonight, I'll bring two more miners and put them with you so you can keep up with Slim. We'll bring up four more to start the tunnel to Bill's mine. You'll continue going to the hub. Brian is bringing up a blast door to install in the cross tunnel we have now. He'll be ready by the time we get ready to cut the next one."

"Jim, we don't want the rookies to make us look bad," Joe said. "Let's see how far we can get tonight."

"Dan, how are your supplies holding up?" Al asked as Joe and Jim left to go to work.

"We'll need to restock soon. Maybe you could have Hollie and Sharon bring them out. Those two are a lot happier after they get a visit from the ladies."

"I'll see what I can do. I'll try to get them out here tomorrow. Slim, let's go and let these two get some well-deserved rest."

* * *

It was 2330 when Lorna and Eve drove up and parked close to Brittany and Johnny's cruiser. As they pulled to a stop the radio crackled to life.

"Turn out the lights, I'm trying to get a little," Brittany said.

"Oh, sorry," Lorna said. "I figured you'd be through by now."

"Very funny. This is one of the fringe benefits."

"We'll be quiet. All we want to do is get to bed. It's almost time for me to turn into a pumpkin."

"What time is it?"

"2330. Go back to whatever you were doing. We'll fold out the habitat and go to bed."

"We found your upper area for you. There's another garden for you to play in."

"Good, but it can wait until morning."

"Good night."

* * *

At 0130 Al turned one of the spare machines and started cutting the cross tunnel to ventilate the main one. It took only ten minutes to cut the thousand feet and connect the two. Brian had finished the installation of the blast doors in the first cross tunnel a couple hours earlier and when the cut was complete, a rush of fresh air spilled in three hundred yards behind where Joe and Jim were working.

"Oh, that's better," Joe said a few minutes later. "Al, did you connect us?"

"Sure did. I'll send you a couple more miners now. You're about even."

"We'll move to the outside and they can fall in between us. Keep that good air coming."

"I will. Here come the others. Make room for them."

The other two miners emerged from the cross tunnel and fell in between Joe and Jim. It took only a minute for them to adjust the laser cutters and they went back to work.

* * *

To her surprise, Lorna found Brittany and Johnny fixing breakfast when she emerged from the habitat on the back of the cruiser. It didn't look like they'd been up too long, but it would be nice to eat someone else's cooking for a change.

"Johnny has things about ready," Brittany said when she saw Lorna.

"You have your own cook too."

"Yeah, he's a better cook than I am. How'd you sleep?"

"Like I died and was reborn this morning. When did you get here?"

"About an hour after dark. We wanted to see if we could find it before we went to bed. You had a long day."

"Yeah, but we wanted to be here this morning too. Any idea what we have here yet?"

"No, not yet. We haven't had a chance to look around. Where's Eve hiding?"

"She thinks every day should start at the crack of noon," Lorna said. "I rousted her out of bed, but I don't think she's functional yet."

"When you said something about a bird the other day; you were kidding, right?" Johnny asked.

"No, I wasn't. We have some pictures of it on the laptop in the cruiser. You finish getting us something to eat and I'll get it. We don't have any idea how many of them there are, but we're pretty sure they have to feed up here somewhere."

A few minutes later they all sat down to have breakfast and Lorna showed them the pictures. There was one that showed the teeth of the bird up very close.

"Damn, that looks like it got pretty close," Brittany said.

"Too close to suit me," Eve said.

"Where do you think we'll find them?"

"There appears to be an opening out in the center somewhere," Lorna said. "It comes up into here. It stands to reason that they'll feed close to that, unless there's no food there, then they'll have to branch out farther into the garden. When we saw this one the other day, it appeared to be afraid of us, but I wouldn't bet on it. Its reaction to us was probably because it hasn't seen anything like us, not in its life."

"What do we do if we encounter one of them?"

"Stay out of its way, I guess. We'll have to look at what to do. For right now, I just don't know."

After breakfast they walked into the edge of the garden and looked around. It seemed to be a combination of the two gardens inside Pavonis Mons. There were a lot of broad-leafed plants that didn't seem to bear any fruit of any kind, but there was an abundance of fruit bearing plants and trees too.

"Ok, let's make a run around the outside," Lorna said. "We need to start finding out where we are up here too. We'll go north and you go south. We'll meet on the other side later today."

"Come on Johnny, let's see what we've found," Brittany said as they walked back to the cruisers. "See you this afternoon."

"You kids be good."

"Don't spoil all of our fun."

* * *

"Al, this is Brian. We've completed the second set of doors for the cross tunnel. We'll have it installed in two hours."

"Good, they're almost twenty-five miles ahead of it now. As close as I can calculate, they're running real close to the same speed. When you get done, start on another set. We'll need another fan setup to rig into the tunnel we're going to start toward the mine. When you get this set installed, come find me. I'll tell you what we need."

"If we're going to install another fan, we'll have to rig it to a cruiser for power. We don't have another habitat we can use."

"We'll pull whatever recourses we have to, to get the job done. How many people do Hollie and Sharon have at the library? If we have to, we'll cut them down to one habitat."

"I heard that," Hollie said. "That would make it awful crowded."

"Hello, ladies. Where are you?"

"We're in the tunnel somewhere. We're bringing the supplies you asked for. Where are our guys?"

"Off out ahead of you somewhere," Al said. "How far in are you?"

"About a hundred miles or so," Hollie said. "Melissa is going to bring over another load this evening. She'll take it to Slim's tunnel."

131

"Good. You'll find Joe and Jim about three hours ahead of where you are now. They'll be glad to see you."

"This supply run is going to get to be a hell of a trip. How far did you say it would be?"

"Over eight hundred miles before we're done. We should be done in a little over a week though. See you when you get here."

"Ok Al, we're headed that way. Melissa, can you hear me?"

"Go ahead, Hollie."

"You might want to get an earlier start than you had planned. They're one hell of a long ways out here. Maybe five hours from where you are."

"Christ, that's a long ways. Slim, you'd better make this trip worth my trouble."

"You just come on out, honey, I'll take good care of you," Slim said. "See you tonight."

* * *

By mid afternoon, Lorna and Eve had almost completed half of the loop around the garden. They stopped to stretch their legs and look around when they saw Brittany and Johnny coming from the other direction.

"What did you find, Britt?" Lorna asked.

"Probably about the same thing you did. A circle around the edge of the garden. Have you found anyplace where you could drive into the interior?"

"This spot where we are doesn't look too bad. I think we might go in and have a look around. How long before you need to go back and download?"

"We can probably go until tomorrow night. Then we'll have to do something the next day. Our supplies are getting low too."

"Come on up here and we'll take a break before we go inside."

An hour later they went into the garden and split up. They were on the extreme western edge and Lorna angled northeast while Brittany went southeast. There were areas where the foliage was dense enough for them to have to backtrack and find another way around. Other areas were relatively open. As the light started to fade, they found the hole in the center that led to the lower level.

"I'd feel better if we moved back from here," Eve said. "I don't like the idea of having that thing coming and picking us up in the middle of the night."

"Yeah, there was a good clearing back a couple miles. We passed it a half hour ago," Lorna said. "We'll spend the night there. Brittany, we're going to bed soon. How are you doing?"

"Not too bad. We've found a large clearing that we're going to stop in. The trees here are completely barren of any kind of fruit or anything."

"Look around for tracks. You may want to go back out a ways before you call it a day. That's what we're going to do."

"That sounds like sound advice," Brittany said. "We'll get with you in the morning."

* * *

The storm had reached tremendous proportions as the sun set on the hub, east of Pavonis and Arsia Mons. Two of the domes at the hub had started to come apart. Over two thousand people had been caught inside them when the tops blew off. They were all lost.

"Damn it," Mike Peterson said, standing in the main control room. "Get the people into the tunnel that Al's people built. We'll only come out for supplies, and we'll do that in suits."

"I'll put the call out," the controller said.

"We just lost over two thousand people when those domes went. I'm going to fire every engineer that lives through this. Get me the engineers and send them into that tunnel; we have to make it large enough to hold almost half a million people and do it now."

"I've already called for them. They don't have any idea how those miners work."

"One of Al's mechanics, Larry something, he's been working with them. He knows how they work. Get him down there. I'll meet them there."

When Mike blasted into the new dome where Joe and Jim had started the new tunnel, Larry was already moving one of the miners into the tunnel. Mike followed him down into the cavern that had been set up as a target for them to shoot at. Larry stopped at the far end of the cavern and Mike climbed up on the machine.

"Son, how does this damn thing work?" Mike asked.

"I've never actually used it to cut anything," Larry said. "If the miners can figure it out, it can't be that hard. Climb in and let's see what we can do."

"You guys get up here and learn how to do this," Mike bellowed as he climbed into the miner.

"This is the main power button," Larry instructed as he moved into position to try to make a cut. "To drive it you just work it like this."

He showed the assorted heads that were sticking through the hatch how he'd driven it into the tunnel. Once he was in position, he started randomly moving the other levers and watching what happened. Soon he'd figured out how the focus on the cutters worked and instructed the others and told them to go get the other two machines.

"Son, let's open this thing up and see what it can do," Mike said as Larry started his cut. "I don't want to lose any more people, understand?"

"Yes, Sir."

Larry widened the focus and inched forward. Ten minutes later the other two machines fell in beside him and they all adjusted their cuts. Larry coached them on the radio as they pushed forward. As they went, the cavern started to fill with people and supplies that were being brought down.

* * *

"Slim, this is the place where I want to take off and go to Bill's mine," Al said at shift change.

"The other machines arrived an hour ago. I've trained almost forty people to run them, but some of them are still rookies."

"They won't be for long. I'll stay with them tonight and make sure things go well. You may have to baby-sit some tomorrow. I'm going to make a speed run to the mine. We'll do it with air packs if we have to. Brian is working on getting the ventilation set up, but we can't wait for that. I want to try to be there by tomorrow night sometime."

"That's a long shot, but we might be able to make it happen."

"We'll cut down the size of the tunnel, so we can go faster. I still think we need to run two of them parallel. We'll have to ventilate it sooner or later. Call back and have a supply of air packs filled and brought up. We

134

can't slow down for anything now. I have a really bad feeling about what's going on up on the surface."

"I don't know how we can do any more than we are already," Slim said.

"I don't either, but we have to try. Send me those four machines. It's time to get started."

"You got it, Boss. They'll be here in five minutes."

* * *

"Brittany, we'll work our way around to the east side," Lorna said the next morning. "You do the same. When we get to the far side, we'll meet up and compare notes. Be careful."

"We saw one of your birds a while ago," Brittany said. "Don't worry, we'll be careful. He landed behind us somewhere. I don't think he knows we're here yet."

"We found the hole in the middle last night. It's about five miles or so across. It continues up for a long ways above us. Keep your eyes open for anything going up in that direction. Hell, there may be another level above this one."

"Ok, we'll watch for anything up there. See you on the other side."

"Eve, are you ready to go?"

"Yeah, I guess so."

* * *

By 2300 that night, Al's crew was closing in on Bill's mine. He stayed close, monitoring their progress. They had decided not to cut any cross tunnels in this direction. Brian still hadn't been able to get the ventilation set up.

"Morrison, stop your tunnel," Al called on the radio. "Wait twenty minutes and cut a cross tunnel. We'll push forward here and try to link up with the mine. I don't want to open up too much at one time."

"Ok, Al. We'll hold here. Good luck."

"Ok, guys, ease it forward. I figure we're less than a mile from the main tunnel in the mine. We don't know if they've opened up any new holes."

The two miners in front of Al slowed their pace, but still kept it respectable. In just over a half hour, they broke into the main tunnel in the mine. They were six feet lower than the mine tunnel and backed off.

"Back up and angle up to the right," Al said. "Do you see anyone in there?"

"No, Boss. The tunnel is empty."

"Make me a road so I can go have a look."

Ten minutes later, Al pulled into the mine and headed for the portal at the edge of the chasm. As he drove, he noticed signs that people had been living here. When he reached the front of the mine he stopped and got on the phone. There was no answer in the control room.

As he climbed back into his cruiser, he saw lights coming toward him. It was Bill.

"What the hell are you doing barging in like this?" Bill asked, with a smile on his face.

"Just dropped by for dinner. Are you guys alright."

"Yeah, but we have some big problems. I moved everyone down here a couple days ago. We brought the auxiliary oxygen generator down and as long as the reactor doesn't crap out on us, we'll make it. How'd you get here?"

"Tunneled," Al said. "We're going to try to reach the hub and the other instillations if we can. Can you spare a few bodies to lend a hand?"

"Might as well. We can't mine shit right now. All the bins are full, and we can't ship anything until this thing lays down a little. Where did you come in at?"

"Back past number seven, I think. We're setting up ventilation to clear the air in the two tunnels. We'll run good air into here and back out through the second tunnel. There isn't enough materials available to run air ducts, so we ran two tunnels."

"How many machines do you have running?"

"We've had twelve. Eight in the tunnel to the hub and four coming this way. We have six cruisers behind the miners for support. Is your rover still in one piece?"

"Yeah, last time I checked. I brought it down here and left it in tunnel one. Do you need it?"

"We sure could use it. I couldn't get mine in here. We lost our center dome. Where are all of your people?"

"Mostly sacked out right now. We moved into the old dig. I figured there was water there and we brought all the food stores we had down here too. Al, how bad do you think this is going to be?"

"Bill, I don't know. We lost one dome, and all of the other locations are a lot older than ours. I'm afraid we're going to lose a lot of people before this is all done. Let's go see if we can get that second tunnel connected. What are you doing up this late?"

"I couldn't sleep. I was on the way up to check on things in the complex when I saw your lights. I had to come see who was wandering around."

"Morrison, this is Al."

"Go, Boss."

"Come in with your tunnel. You'll need to raise your elevation about six feet when you get closer. I'll be there when you get there."

"On our way. See you in a few minutes."

CHAPTER NINE

"I'll be damned," Bill said when he and Al drove up to where they had broken into his mine. "How long did this take you? You didn't have any of this done when I was there the other day."

"We started right after you left. I think we can get to the hub in less than a week, with your help."

Just then the telltale green glow of the Martian Miner shined across the tunnel ahead of them. Al and Bill had stopped short to make sure no one would be caught in the beam of the miner.

"Is that what you wanted, Al?" Morrison asked as he pulled into the main tunnel of the mine.

"Right on target. Can you get the cruisers up here?"

"I think so. They knew we were getting close. What do you want us to do now?"

"Call them up and we'll go take a tour before we head back. Most of you have never seen this place before."

Twenty minutes later they followed Al as he gave them a tour of Bill's mine, the mine he'd been in charge of before moving to Pavonis Mons. When they turned and went down into the pyramid room, Al stopped.

"Ever see anything like this?" he asked.

"Not me," Morrison said.

"There's more. Follow me."

Al led the way across the large room that housed the large pyramid and four smaller ones. When they reached the other side, he went into a small tunnel and turned left. Three of the other cruisers followed him. It was only a few minutes before they entered the large cavern with the waterfall on the right side.

"We used some of the structures in here to store our food," Bill said, taking over as the tour guide. "We brought some of the comforts of the complex down here to make it easier to manage. As you can tell, we're just kind of camped out until we get to where we can go back to work."

They all stopped in the middle of the cavern and Al explained that this is what led them to the discovery at Pavonis Mons and subsequently the one at Arsia Mons.

"Hey, what's all the racket? Can't you see we're trying to sleep here?"

"Charlie, is that you?" Al asked. "This is the first time I wasn't able to get you in the control room. What are you doing hiding in a hole?"

"Al, how the hell did you get here?"

"We just dropped by."

"Is the storm over?"

"No, Charlie, the storm isn't over. We tunneled over here. Want to have a look at a big hole in the ground?"

"Hell yes, but not tonight. I'm still trying to get some sleep here."

"We'll hold it down. Go back to sleep. Ok, guys, let's go back to the miners. Bill, I'll drop you at your runabout."

"When do you want us to join you?"

"Tomorrow is soon enough. Bring your cruiser and your rover. And as many people as you can. I'll get things set up on the other end. We can move your people over there if you want. They're not going to be able to outlast the storm here."

"We can shuttle them over as we can," Bill said as they left the cavern. "We're in pretty good shape here for a while."

"Bring your guys that can run the miners first," Al said. "I'd like to put on a third shift. We've been going at it twelve hours a day since we started. We may want to try a fifth miner in each tunnel too. We'll try that tonight after we get back. It's going to take them quite a while just to road the machines back to the other end."

"How far is it?"

"In the rover, about two hours. The cruiser will take a little longer. We ran it in just under thirty hours."

"Shit, that has to be a record of some kind. No one has ever even attempted anything like that."

"We wouldn't have either, without the alien technology. It would have taken us years. Here's your runabout. I'll go back to the other end and let them know you're alright and that you'll be joining us tomorrow."

"See you then," Bill said as he got out. "It's good to see you. We didn't know if we'd ever see anyone again."

"That's why we're here."

As Al turned to leave, he looked into where he knew the chasm was. Even with the powerful outside lights that normally bathed the chasm with a man-made glow, all he saw was a twisting, twirling mass of red sand.

"Joe, how are you doing?" Al asked as he made the turn into the new tunnel.

"Doing good," Joe responded. "Did you find Bill?"

"Yeah, they're alright. He moved them into the mine. They're camped in the big cavern. He'll be coming over tomorrow to give us a hand."

"Good, we can use it. These long days are getting a little old."

"We'll take care of that. We might even be able to give you a day off, as long as the tunnel continues to go. I'll be back over there in a couple hours or so. Keep after it."

"Will do, Boss."

* * *

Six days later they were approaching the cavern Joe and Jim had carved under the hub. It was decided, as they approached the hub, to aim high. Al was afraid they might encounter people in the cavern and toast a few in the process of breaking into the cavern. At 0430 on the seventh day, they broke through. They were fifty feet above the floor, which was covered with people and equipment.

"Hey, anyone home?" Al called into the darkness.

"Al, is that you," Mike called from somewhere below.

"Yeah, we just opened it up. Are you alright?"

"Well, we're a damned sight better now. Why are you clear up there?"

"So we don't toast your ass," Al said. "Clear a spot at ground level and we'll back up and come in down there. I'll hold off the other tunnel until I can see what's going on down there."

"Other tunnel, what other tunnel? Christ, how many tunnels did you dig?"

"Just two. We had too much trouble getting good air this far in, so we used the tunnels as ducts. I'll explain everything when I get down there."

"Give us fifteen minutes," Mike said. "We have a bunch of stuff to move down here."

A half hour later Al pulled into the cavern where Mike and the rest of the people from the hub were hiding from the storm. The cavern was immense, and it was also very full.

"Christ, Mike, how many people do you have down here," Al asked when they finally found each other.

"All of them. We lost over two thousand people when we lost number five and six domes. The rest of the domes seem to be holding, but we couldn't take a chance on losing another one. We had this place already started and with a little help from Larry, we enlarged it to handle everyone. God, it's good to see you. How are we going to get to all of the mines? They'll be running out of supplies soon."

"We'll just do it the same way we did this. We'll need survey information though. We don't have anything to shoot for. I went and got Bill and his people already. They've been helping us for a week now."

Mike went around to each of the miners and thanked the crew personally. When all of that was taken care of, they went to a makeshift office area.

"This isn't much," Mike said. "I think it's more than I'd have if I stayed on top though. The survey information was in dome five. I don't know how much of it we're going to be able to salvage."

"Are the computers still operational?"

"Yeah, I think so. We're still getting power from up there. They might be alright. We can go up and take a look."

"Where's the nearest terminal?"

"There isn't one in the new dome. The next one over is my guess. I'll find out where it is, and we'll go have a look."

"Do any of your computer people have the guts to stick their heads out of this hole?"

"I doubt it."

"Joe, call Hollie and Mona and have them come up here," Al said. "We'll go get the information when we find out where it is. Where's that worm that runs the computer lab. I think he should be in on this too."

"I'll find him," Mike said. "It'll start to get light in an hour or so. It would be best to wait until them."

Two hours later they suited up. Al took five from his crew plus Mike and two others from the computer lab. The eight of them went into the makeshift airlock between the two sets of blast doors. Once the pressure had been equalized, they slowly emerged into the new dome. There were signs of wear, but this dome seemed to be holding.

"Bernard, where do we go?" Mike asked as they walked across the floor of the dome.

"Across the next dome. There's a terminal there that's tied into the mainframe. We should be able to access it from there. Mike, I don't like being up here."

"Tough shit. We need access to your computers and you're going to get it for us. We have a lot of people at risk in the mines. We have to have that information."

"But—."

"But nothing. You don't get us the information we need; you don't go back in that nice safe hole. Got it."

"You'll hear from my lawyer when this is over."

"Call him and I'll send him out here to keep your dumb ass company. Now stop stalling and take us to that terminal."

As they made their way across the two domes, they all surveyed the damage. The tops of domes five and six were completely gone, much the same as the center dome at Pavonis was. There were other signs of failures too. Small sections were blown out of several of the domes they could see from where they were.

"Looks like a major rebuild job," Al said.

"It's not that bad yet," Mike said. "Once we got everyone down below, we've been making recons to check on things. So far, the one part that's held up the best is the space port. That's good. We'll be able to receive supplies from the ships that are in orbit now. By the time this thing blows over we'll need all we can get."

"We lost part of a dome at Pavonis too. The center one."

"How's everything inside?" Mike asked.

"Life goes on. It's self sustaining, to a point. We'll need to think about getting everyone over there if this thing keeps up. That might be the only place that can sustain us all."

"Shit, we have several hundred thousand people. The logistics of just getting them over there is mind boggling."

"I know, but so is the thought of supplying them with food from over there. If this storm doesn't break soon, we won't have a choice."

"There, the terminal is over there," Bernard said.

"Well, get it fired up man," Mike said. "Get me the locations of all the mines and maps of them too. I want GPS coordinates and elevations of everything."

"That's going to take time."

"Then you'd better get after it, boy. Joe, can you and the ladies keep him company? Al and I are going to have a look around."

"We'll watch over him," Joe said. "I'll make sure we get what we need. Don't get lost."

"Al, let's take a casual stroll around what's left of our lifeline," Mike said as he led the way. "I haven't been up here for a couple days."

"I'm with you, Boss."

As they made their way into the central area of the hub, they took stock of what the condition of the area was like. The tower that contained the main structure of the space port looked to be intact. This was surprising because it was the tallest structure in the complex, but it was also constructed to handle the extra weight of the transports that brought the supplies down from the supply ships.

"Think we can rebuild it?" Mike asked.

"Yeah, it doesn't look all that bad. With a few patches it's going to be just as good as new. You can have it operational in a couple weeks once the storm quits."

"Yeah, it does look pretty good at that. It's taken a hell of a beating though. And it's not over yet."

"My concern is the rest of the mines," Al said. "Can we see if we can get into the survey office? There might be something in there we can use. We can't just barge into those areas and hope we hit a tunnel. I don't have much faith in that weenie from the computer lab."

"During all this I've found out who can be counted on and who can't. There will be a few personal changes when this is all said and done."

"We're only as good as the people around us."

They walked in silence for a while. When they reached the remains of what used to be the survey office it was obvious they wouldn't get any information there.

"Al, this is Joe."

"Yeah, Joe."

"We have what we need. Hollie and Mona had to get it, but we have it."

"Go back in. We'll be along in a while. Get with Slim and Bill when you get there and lay out a course to the other mines. Mike and I will go over it with you when we get back."

"Ok, Boss. How does the place look?"

"Not as bad as it could. It'll take a couple weeks to get it operational again. We'll be along soon."

"By the way," Mike said. "Did you manage to lose Lorna? I haven't seen her here."

"She's over in Arsia Mons looking around. I left her over there. Sean and some of the others are over there too, gathering materials to support our efforts here. I've been focused on getting here as fast as I could. Those two tunnels are big enough to drive transports through. We could rig a few of them to haul people and supplies back to Pavonis. How many transports are here?"

"Only three. The others are all at the mines."

"Well, have you had enough exercise for now?" Al asked.

"Yeah, I just needed to have a look around. The board is going to be pissed when they hear about this."

"They'd rebuild it even if we all died up here. It makes them too much money to let it go. With this alien technology, it's even more valuable."

"You might be right. Shit, let's go."

* * *

"Bill, Al wants us to go north," Joe said when he got back to the others.

"Where do we take off?" Bill asked.

"With all these people in here, we'd better back off a mile or so and go from there. Here are the positions of the other mines. Some of them are down two thousand feet and some are less than five hundred. We'll not only have to go for direction, but also elevation."

"That's going to make it fun on some of these. They're close together."

"I'll clear these people out of the way so we can connect the other tunnel into here. We'll get started when we can get in there."

"We'll backtrack and get over to the other tunnel," Slim said. "Contact us when it's clear to come on. We'll stand by for your call."

Joe and Jim started moving people away from the area where the second tunnel would break through. Bill and Slim went to get the other miner ready. An hour later they opened the second tunnel into the cavern. A rush of fresh air flowed in to replace the staleness that had been there before.

* * *

Lorna and Eve had been circling the garden in the upper level of Arsia Mons for almost a week and still hadn't seen one of their birds. They had encountered several places where the birds had been but hadn't actually seen them.

"Mom, we're getting low on supplies," Eve said as they got ready to start another day. "We'd better think about heading back. Now that Patty and Brittany are both up here, we need to go restock."

"I know. I just feel like we're missing something. We'll work our way to the east side again and go on out. What do you think about a run back to Pavonis for a few days? We could use a break."

"I'd like to go see how Brian's doing. I've missed him this week."

"Ok, let's go back and see what Sean's doing and maybe tomorrow we'll take a run over there."

"Lorna, this is Patty. Where do you want us to concentrate our mapping this time?"

"I'm thinking we need to work the northeast area; around where the tunnel comes in from Pavonis. I'd like to see if there's another way to get to the upper level, close to where we come in. Other than that, just keep running your patterns. At some point we'll need to establish the outer perimeter of the upper level too. We're heading out today and may not be back for a few days. Can you guys handle things here for us?"

"Yeah, no problem. If we have any problems, we'll call. I'll try to find you that alternate way up."

"We're going to gather a few fresh samples as we exit the garden today and take them to Martin, so we'll be gone for a while. Keep after it."

* * *

Al watched as the miners started the trek to the north. He and Mike had a map laid out on the front of the cruiser and were trying to decide on the best route to take to get to the mines.

"We can go north, toward number seven," Al said. "When we get halfway, we'll need to branch off and start tunnels to number six and nine, to the west and five and eight to the east. When we get out to them, we can go on to the ones that are farther out."

"What about the ones that are south-east, toward the chasm?" Mike asked. "They're going to be a little tricky, aren't they?"

"Yeah, they are. The only one that scares me is number one. It's out close to the edge of the chasm and it's on this long peninsula-like finger that sticks way out. The area around it has fissures and isn't all that stable."

"God, I'd hate to lose that one. It was the first mine we developed. It's the smallest one, with only sixty people working it, but it's also one of the richest we have."

"Right now, we can't worry about losing production. We have to worry about the people. I'll take two machines and have Joe and Jim work one shift and Dan and Jeff work the other. They're the best we have. We'll go see if we can get to them. Bill and Slim can start going the other way for now. It's only a hundred and fifty miles. We might be able to get to them in a couple days."

"Ok, go get them." Mike said. "I'll monitor things here and start sending some people inside with every means going that way. We can't afford to wait until we run out of supplies here before we do that."

"See if you can get a transport down here. Those blast doors may be too small to get it in. If they are, make them bigger. We'll have to have access with the big stuff to pull this off."

"I'll have them get right on that. Al, thanks, you may have saved us all."

"We're not out of the woods yet," Al said.

* * *

Late the next evening Lorna and Eve pulled up to the habitat inside the upper garden in Pavonis Mons. The area was busier than they had seen it for quite some time.

"Where have you two been hiding," Martin asked as they got out.

"We've been exploring your next garden project," Lorna said. "We brought you a few samples to look at. It's not much, but we thought these particular ones looked interesting."

"Martin, where's Brian?" Eve asked.

"At the hub, I guess. That's where all the action is right now. They brought in a couple dozen people today. We're trying to find places for them to sleep."

"We can always move them out into the rooms across from the entrance," Lorna said. "They'll take a little cleaning up, but it's better than nothing."

"We'll have to find them some mattresses and such."

"The important thing is that they're safe. How do we get to the new tunnel we've been hearing about?"

"I have the directions written down. I've had to send several people that way. They're inside. You're not going to go over there tonight, are you?"

"No, but we'll be headed that way as soon as we can drag our tired asses out of bed in the morning. Before we're all done here, we're going to have tunnels under this whole damn planet. God, I'm getting tired of the driving."

* * *

"Al, we're getting close," Joe called at 2100.

"I'll be right there. Sorry about the suits, but if we hit a fissure, we're all screwed. I'm a ways back and I'll map it as I come that way. We may need to adjust the line a little."

"They're in some good ore here. I wish we had time to slow down and get it for them."

As Al drove to the end of the tunnel he reflected on how this first mine had been started. In the beginning, everything was done in suits, and it took months to do what they were able to do now in a week and with the alien technology, in hours. The drilling and blasting was all done out in the open, until they were deep enough to set up a small dome over the shaft. With the one-third gravity of Mars, compared to Earth, it was common for the blasts to throw the rock for a mile or more. One nick in a suit meant almost certain death to the miner that wore it. They had lost a lot of good people in the beginning.

"Ok, I'm right behind you. I make it another half mile to get to the main tunnel. Move three degrees to the left to avoid their shaft. That should put us in the area we're looking for. If this information is correct that should do it."

"I hope you're right," Joe said. "Keep an eye on our heading. We're just kind of winging it here."

"Well, you've done remarkably well so far," Al said. "I don't expect you to fall down on me now."

As they slowed their pace of advance, Al directed them with elevation and direction adjustments. Soon, they broke into the main tunnel of mine number one. Joe and Jim backed off the laser cutting beams as they advanced into the tunnel.

"Come on up, Al," Joe said. "We have company."

"Mr. Adams, I presume," Al said as he climbed out of the cruiser.

"Al, you old son-of-a-bitch, where did you come from?" John Adams, manager of mine number one, said.

"Mike asked us to drop by and see if you were alright. What are your conditions like?"

"Only fair. We'll run out of food and water in just over a week. We were getting worried. I've been going topside to have a look when I can get there. The domes are holding, but I moved my people down here a week ago to be safe. What the hell are those things you have there?"

"Those big things are a Martian Miners, and the small one is my cruiser. We've tunneled almost a thousand miles in about three weeks. This storm is going to change the face of this planet."

"A thousand miles in three weeks? Christ, that's unbelievable."

"Well, it's the only way we could get to the hub and the rest of the mines. We'll arrange transportation for your people and get them back to the hub at least. We're still working on ways to transport everyone to Pavonis Mons. We have food and water there and can outlast this storm. We may have to give up some of the comforts, but we'll be relatively safe there."

"I heard something about what you were doing over there but didn't think we'd get to see it firsthand."

"Al, shall we turn these things around and head back to the hub?" Joe asked as he and Jim walked up.

"Yeah, Joe. You might as well. Let's lay out this map and see where we need to go next."

Al laid out the map on the front of the cruiser and they all gathered around it. Number two and three were well to the northeast of where they were.

"John, you're more familiar with this area," Al said. "We need to get to these other two mines; how would you go if you had to tunnel over there."

"If this is the tunnel you just made, I'd back up to here and branch off. When you get out about seventy miles or so, then I'd split it again. That should get you there."

"Joe, go back to the point where we turned south. Go out at about ninety degrees until I give you a better heading. You probably won't get too far before shift change. In less than a week we'll have this phase completed."

"Jim, let's head these things back out," Joe said. "See you at the turn, Al."

"Ok, Joe. You guys did a great job."

"I still can't believe you went that far, that fast," Adams said.

"We didn't want to be the only ones left on this planet when the storm died out. We've found a lot of alien technology that's pretty much intact, or we couldn't have even thought about trying this."

"This I'd like to see."

"Al, this is Mike. Progress report."

"We connected with number one a little while ago. I'm standing here with John now."

"Can you bring him back here?"

"Sure, it'll take me a couple hours to get there."

"I'd like to see you both as soon as you can get here. Can you make it by 2400?"

"We might be a few minutes late, but we'll be there."

"See you then, Mike out."

"Well, the master has spoken," Al said.

"Give me a minute," Adams said.

* * *

At 0010 Al and John Adams pulled into the tunnel under the hub. They were directed to the bottom of the incline leading up to the hub complex.

"Al, John, good to see you," Mike said. "John, we were worried about you."

"We were getting a little worried ourselves. We were rationing food and water and figured we had enough to last a little over a week if we stretched it. It would have gotten awful hungry after that."

"Thanks to Al and his people, we've all been spared that. Al, are your miners heading back this way?"

"We have them moving out to the spot where we turned south. They'll set up there and go for number two and three. A couple days should have us to both of them. How are Bill and Slim doing?"

"Shit, they're moving so fast I can't keep up with them. They should connect up with three of the mines sometime tomorrow. They've split up and Slim is branching out a little east of Bill. Slim had five more miners brought up and has put them into branches that will connect to the eastern mines."

"I've been afraid to ask this question," Al said, "how many outposts are there that haven't been heard from?"

"Only one," Mike said. "We got the word out at least twelve hours before the storm hit, but Outpost Charlie didn't check in. I'm hoping they were able to get back to number nine before all this hit. If they were still out there, they're gone for sure."

"Yeah, those thirty-man habitats are good, but they won't stand up to this kind of storm. Where were they located?"

"Almost a hundred miles northeast of number nine," Mike said. "They were the most remote outpost we had. There was a full contingent, twenty people, out there. They'd just made a big discovery and were in the process of mapping the perimeter."

"Well, the ore will still be there," John said. "We'll have to wait until we get to number nine to find out if the crew made it or not."

"Slim should be there late tomorrow or the next day," Mike said. "Is there any way to hurry this process along?"

"Double up on the miners is the only way we've found so far," Al said. "We can pull extras from somewhere else, I guess. Is Bill running the night shift?"

"Yeah, Slim went off duty about seven. He's holed up north of here in one of the cruisers. I talked to him about eight this evening and got an update."

"John and I will go have a talk with Bill and see if we can figure out where to get a couple more machines to help get to number nine. We dropped repeaters in the tunnel to number one, so I'll call Joe and check on him before we leave. I can't shut Joe down. We still have two mines to the east to try to reach."

"It's going to take us another couple days to get transports in here," Mike said. "You were right about the blast doors; they weren't big enough. We started on the outside one and we'll get it back up sometime in the morning. Once we do that we can get out of the suits and maybe the work will go a little faster."

"You'd better get some rest, Mike," Al said.

"When was the last time you got a full night's sleep?"

"I don't remember, but we'll have a handle on this soon. Then we can all rest up a little. You know that unless this thing starts to die down, we're going to have to set up everyone in Pavonis."

"Yeah, I'm working on it. We'll need to bring a lot of stuff with them. Don't worry about that now, just get to the mines."

"We'll see you later," Al said. "John, want to take another ride?"

As they pulled away, headed back into the tunnels toward Pavonis, Al called Joe to check on his progress.

"Joe, progress report."

"We'll be back to where we turned south in a half hour or so. What do you want us to do then?"

"Go east," Al said. "If you need a fix, get Dan or Jeff to line you up. John and I are headed north and may not be back until close to shift change."

"Dan, did you copy that?" Joe asked.

"Roger. I'll line you up with a heading of 090 degrees. Just pull in and align yourselves with my cruiser. If you need help, just sing out. We're already there and once I get you lined up, I'm going back to sleep."

"Sorry we had to disturb you," Al said.

"No big deal. See you in the morning."

When Al and John reached the tunnels going north, they sped into the waiting darkness. The tunnels were wide and the going easy. Al and John discussed ways to get to the more remote mines and maybe even to some of the outposts. Through all the years that they had been mining on Mars, they had only established fifteen major mining operations. The complexity of setting up such an operation was what had restricted the scope of the operations.

"Bill, where are you hiding?" Al asked as they reached the first junction.

"Where are you, so I can give you directions?"

"Approaching the first junction."

"Go left. The next junction is about forty miles. Go left again. I'm up close to the machines. We may be able to open up into number six by noon tomorrow."

"We'll be there in an hour or so."

"We?"

"I have John Adams with me."

"Good to hear he's still in one piece. I'll see you in a while."

* * *

When they arrived, Bill was standing by his cruiser looking at the map display. They went and joined him.

"John, glad to see you made it," Bill said as they approached.

"It's good to be here."

"What do you have, Bill?" Al asked.

"I've been laying out the approach to number six. We've been descending for most of the day so we can come in at the right level. We still have to drop another thousand feet though."

"What elevation is number eight?"

"We'll have to come back up almost three thousand feet to get to it. The problem is that they are at such different elevations and fairly close together."

"We'll figure that out," Al said. "We need a couple machines to beef up the tunnel to number nine. Any idea where we can get them?"

"We're spread pretty thin. What's the rush to get to number nine?"

"Outpost Charlie didn't check in after the warning went out. We need to get to nine to see if they were able to get in before it got too bad."

"We'll have to pull someone from here, I guess. We have four machines working and most of the other headings only have two. We're spread out pretty thin now. How about Joe and Jim?"

"They're setting up to go to number two and three. Can you spare one machine? We can make do with that. I'll try to get more brought over from Pavonis."

"I'll send one that way. I think that kid Morrison is running that crew."

"We'll go tell him its coming."

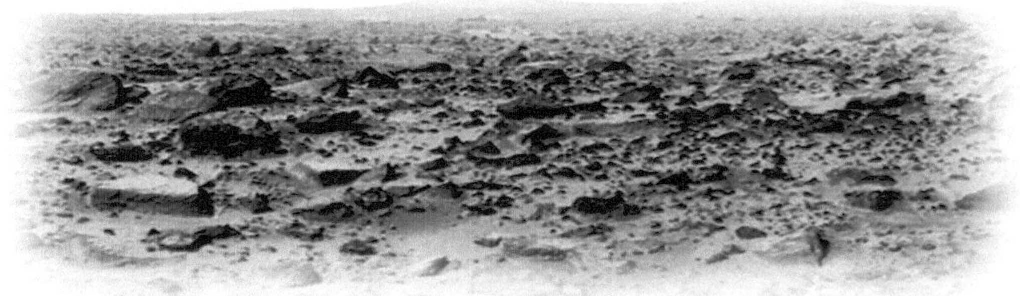

CHAPTER TEN

"Al, this is Lorna. Where the hell are you?"

"You're up early. What's up?"

"Eve and I are headed that way. We don't really know where we're going though. How long will it take us to get there?"

"That depends on where you are."

"No shit. We're in the garden with Martin. We're just leaving now."

"See you about 2100 tonight then. It's a long ways to the hub. Did Martin give you directions on how to reach the tunnel?"

"Yeah, we can find that alright. Where's Brian?"

"He's at the hub working on some blast doors. I'm sure he'll be glad to see you."

"I doubt that I'll be the one he'll be glad to see. Can we have a get together when we get there?"

"Yeah, just let me know when and where. Mike is set up close to the incline going up into the hub. I'm going to crash for a few hours. I've been at it for three days now."

"Dumb ass, you're too old for that."

"No one knows that better than I do. See you tonight."

* * *

"Mike, what are you doing clear out here?" Slim asked when Mike pulled up at 0900.

"I sent Al back toward number one to get some rest," Mike said. "I thought I'd make the rounds myself this morning. How's it going?"

"We're doing quite well actually. I was just going over the map to get things set up to go into number nine. With the extra machine we picked up last night, I think we can be in there in a couple hours. I understand Al sent for several more machines too."

"Yeah, but it'll be a couple days before they can road them over here. I wish we had a way to haul them."

"We're going to have to figure out a way to haul a lot of things. Real soon too."

"Yeah, I know. I have my people working on that now. We'll be able to bring transports into the tunnels in a day or two. That should help."

"I'm sure it will. We can bring some of the alien vehicles out here too. We've established the ventilation system, so we don't have to use suits to get to the hub. Pavonis Mons has enough good air to absorb any bad air that we get."

"That's a good idea. I'll send several people that way to gather some of them up and bring them back. We'll fill every vehicle that goes that way and shuttle them back out here."

"Do you have any rovers at the hub?"

"Six, I think."

"They're a lot faster than anything else we have on the planet. It would be a good idea to get them down here too."

"We've been so focused on getting to the mines that some of these things have slipped past us. Thanks for thinking ahead."

"Al has drummed that into us since we all hooked up together. It's kind of become second nature now."

"You and the rest of Al's crew will be in for a large bonus when we get through this."

"That would be nice, but that's not why we did all we've done. We knew we could make a difference and maybe save a few lives. It's turned out well so far, but we still have work to do."

"And I won't hold you up any longer. I'll get out of the way and let you get back to work."

"See you later, Boss."

"I'll finish my rounds and come back. I'd like to be here when you break into number nine. I've been worried about our people from one of the outposts that should have gone there when we sounded the warning."

"I'll give you a call when we get close."

"Thanks Slim."

* * *

Mike got the call from Slim and returned to the end of the tunnel leading to number nine a few minutes before they broke through.

Slim operated the miner for the last hundred yards and entered the main tunnel of the mine three feet above the ground in the tunnel. He backed up and cleaned the approach and Mike followed him inside. Slim joined him in the cruiser, and they drove the three miles to the bottom of the shaft, the main gathering spot for this mine. The mine was totally dark.

Huddled in makeshift beds were the two hundred people that had staffed this mine. The air was getting bad, and it looked like the crew had abandoned hope of ever seeing the daylight again. When the lights from the cruiser panned across them, they seemed to stare in disbelief.

"My God," Jordon Williams, the mine manager said as Mike and Slim got out of the cruiser.

"Jordon, are you alright?" Mike asked.

"Not really. Are you really here?"

"We're here Jordon. Do you have any casualties?"

"Yes, I think so. We lost power several days ago and then the air started to go bad. We didn't think there was any hope that we'd ever see the daylight again."

"Did the crew from Outpost Charlie make it back to here before the storm hit?" Mike asked.

"Some of them did. I sent the transport out to get the rest of them, but it never returned. I don't know if they diverted to number seven or if they blew away. The winds were too high to risk going out in the rover, but I thought the transport had a chance to make it. Are you really here?"

"Slim, bring up the other cruisers," Mike said. "We need to start getting these people out of here. Call back to the hub and have the rovers brought in too."

"Mike, they can't bring the rovers in until they get the blast doors finished," Slim said a few minutes later. "They won't be able to get them inside until this evening. I have several cruisers coming with air packs. I pulled them from all the other tunnels we're working on."

"Jordon, let's have a look at your people," Mike said as he nodded his head to what Slim had just told him. "Slim, take the cruiser and go gather up your crew. We may need to figure out how many people really need help here. I'll have a look around while you're gone."

* * *

When Al finally woke up it was late afternoon. He had been living in virtual darkness for over three weeks now, but that didn't bother him. It was hard to shake the cobwebs out of his mind. He was alone in the habitat on the back of the cruiser that had been his home for what seemed to be an eternity. As he started his coffee, he got on the radio.

"Dan, how are you doing?"

"Did you finally wake up? We're almost to where we need to split up and go to both mines."

"Ok, I'll come up and get with you. How's the air holding up?"

"Not great, but we can work without the air packs most of the time. By the time we get there, that may not be the case."

"I want you in suits before you break into any of the mines. There's no need in getting stupid at this stage of the game."

"Al, is that you?" Mike called on the radio.

"Yeah, Mike, I just woke up."

"We got to the crew in number nine and they're not in very good shape. We're evacuating them back to the hub. Only some of the crew from Outpost Charlie made it this far."

"Do you need me over there?"

"No, Slim has things handled for now. When you get your crew lined up, go back to the hub, and get them to hurry and finish the blast doors. We need to get the six rovers that are at the hub, down into the tunnels."

"Ok, Mike, I'll be there as soon as I can."

"Al, this is Joe. Go on to the hub. We'll work our way through getting the split made. It sounds like they need you there more than we do here."

"Ok, Joe. I'll be back as soon as I can. You still have almost a day before you get to the two mines. I guess you'll have to go solo after you make the split. Just keep the tunnel big enough to get a rover in there if we have to."

"Got it, Boss."

"If we can get additional miners over here, I'll send you some help."

"By making everything smaller, we should be alright. See you tonight."

Al climbed out of the habitat on the back of the cruiser and folded it up and left for the hub.

Brian was there to meet him when he arrived. They were just finishing the blast doors.

"I heard what was going on," Brian said. "I sent a crew to retrieve the rovers. They'll be back here in a half hour or so."

"Good. When they get here, I'll lead them to number nine. Have they sent any medical help over there?"

"I don't know. I talked to Slim just before noon and he said several of the crew over there were in pretty bad shape."

"Mike, we'll be headed that way as soon as I can get the rovers inside," Al called.

"Good. I sent Slim back to work on the tunnels. Bring Dr. Samson with you. You'll find him about halfway back in the cavern."

"Do we need to bring anything else?"

"Have him call me when you find him."

"Will do, Al out. Brian, your wife will be here tonight."

"That will be nice. When did you hear from them?"

"This morning. They were just leaving the upper garden. They probably won't be here until 2100 or so."

* * *

Al pulled into the main tunnel in number nine at 1800. Behind him were six rovers and five cruisers that he'd commandeered for the evacuation. Dr. Samson rode with Al.

"Mike, we're in the mine," Al called as they turned toward the shaft.

"Good. We're all congregated at the shaft. Is the Doc with you?"

"He's right here. I brought a couple other doctors too."

"Mike, have they responded to the oxygen I had you put them on?" Dr. Samson asked.

"Most of them have. Some of them are coming around a lot slower than the others. We've transported almost a third of them and we're just waiting for a ride for the others."

"Ok, Mike, we're here now." Al said as they pulled up.

As soon as they stopped, Dr. Samson and his two assistants got out and went right to work. Al went to see Mike.

"They gave up," Mike said. "I guess I can't blame them, but that's just not in my nature. I can't see going out like that."

"In their mind they had no chance of anyone getting to them. I'm with you, but I can see their side of things too."

"With the transportation you brought we'll be able to get the worst of them out now, but we'll probably have to make another round to get them all."

* * *

"Al, this is Lorna. We're at the hub. Are you around anywhere?"

"We'll be back there in a couple hours," Al said. "We're loading up the last of the survivors from number nine. I'll find you when I get there."

"We found Brian. We'll be with him. Were there any casualties?"

"Yeah, but we don't have numbers or names yet. Most of them will be fine. I'll see you in a little while."

"He's got to be getting tired," Brian said. "He's been going day and night for almost three weeks now. Mike finally sent him into a dark tunnel with orders to get some rest. I think he might have been able to sleep for six hours or so."

"How are they getting to the mines?" Lorna asked. "On the way in we didn't see any tunnels taking off besides the one to Bill's mine."

"There are two tunnels. The other one is parallel to the one you came in on. The tunnel north takes off from that and then branches off several places."

"Can we help, if we go in there?"

"I doubt it. Mike has been in there most of the day and Al took in the transportation. They came back out once already, and this should be the last load."

"Ok, I guess we'll just have to wait then. How have you been?"

"With the materials that Sean has sent us, we've been able to keep up fairly well. We get enough rest to get by. I do miss the company though."

"I'm here now," Eve said. "We'll take a couple days before we go back to Arsia."

* * *

"Al, this is Joe."

"Go ahead Joe," Al said when the call came the next morning.

"We're getting ready to turn it over to Dan and Jeff. We made the split in the tunnel about 2400 and took one miner each way. It's big enough to get in with a rover, but not anything bigger. With any luck they'll break into both mines in about four hours."

"Which one should be first?"

"Number three, I think," Joe said. "That tunnel is shorter than the other one, but they won't be far apart, time wise. Maybe only an hour or so."

"We'll gather up some medical help and additional transportation and head that way. Lorna wants to see what you've been up to."

"Did she finally decide to grace us with her presence?"

"Yeah, she and Eve got here last night. You guys get some rest. I'm sure we'll need you again over here somewhere."

"Ok, Boss. Joe out."

"Lorna, want to go for the ride with me. Eve can hang out with Brian for a day or two. He's going to be building airlocks in the tunnels going north."

"What the hell. I don't have anything better to do," Lorna said.

"Al, I'll monitor things to the north," Mike said. "If you need any help over there give me a call."

"Good. Slim has his finger on things over there, but a little backup is a good thing. I'll take three of the rovers in with me. There may be a need to transport some of the people back in a hurry."

"I'll position the others to the north where we can call them into wherever we need them. Lorna, do you realize that your efforts on this planet have saved thousands of lives?"

"Well, we do what we can."

"No, I'm serious," Mike said. "If you hadn't developed the ways to get to those wonderful places you found, there'd be a lot of other people entombed here. The discoveries that you and Al made have literally saved us all."

"I know, but we still have a long ways to go to get out of this one. Let's not break our arms patting ourselves on the back just yet."

Thirty minutes later they were headed into the tunnel to the east. Following them were three rovers and two more cruisers. They made the turn toward the two mines and then the fork that led to number three. When they were approaching the miner, they had to stop. The cruiser that Joe was sleeping in was blocking the way.

"Joe, are you awake?" Al asked as he walked up to the cruiser.

"Uhhh, I am now. What's up?"

"We're here to see if anyone needs a ride. Any idea how much longer it'll be?"

"Soon. I mapped it a few minutes ago. They're about a mile away from where we are now. I just figured I'd catch a few winks while he finished it up."

"Sorry to disturb you."

"It's just one of those days. Dan, how are you doing?"

"Good. Can you come up here and give me another fix? I think we're getting close."

"Be right there. Al's here too. We'll be right there."

"We'll follow you," Al said as Joe started to fold up the habitat on his cruiser.

"Dan, you're about a hundred yards or so away," Joe said when he reached the back of the miner. "Your elevation looks good. We'll stand by."

"Ok, Joe. This won't take long."

A few minutes later he broke into the tunnel of mine number three. The others had been walking behind the miner and went into the tunnel as he cleared the way. They were about a quarter mile from the shaft and could see people milling around. They went and retrieved the rovers and cruisers and drove to the shaft.

"Is everyone alright?" Al asked as he got out of his cruiser.

"Who the hell—Al, is that you?"

"Yeah, George, it's me. Are you all ok?"

"Yeah, but how the hell did you get here. We've been cut off since the storm hit. Our supplies are getting low, but we're not whipped yet."

"Good, neither are we. We tunneled from Pavonis Mons," Al said as he started his explanation. By the time he'd finished, everyone had gathered around.

"My God, that's quite an undertaking," George said.

"We thought you were worth the effort. If you're all ok, we'll go to number two and check on them. We'll be back this afternoon to give you a ride to the hub."

"Got room for one more?" George asked.

"Sure, you can ride with me."

"Alistair, take care of things here. I'm going to help them."

"Jeff, are you making any progress?" Al called as they turned to leave.

"Another hour or so, Boss. Have they made it into number three?"

"We're just leaving there now. They're all fine here. We'll be there about the time you get inside."

* * *

They arrived just as Jeff powered his way into the tunnel of mine number two. Al drove past him as soon as he was clear of the new tunnel. He turned immediately toward the shaft and sped on. He found the crew huddled in small groups near the shaft.

"Alicia, are you here?" Al called as he got out.

"She's dead," a voice called from the far side of the shaft.

"What happened?"

"When she decided it was time to evacuate the complex and come down here, she stayed to make sure everyone made it. We couldn't get the shaft seal to work, and she sealed it from above. We haven't seen her since."

"What was the condition of the complex when you came down here," Al asked.

"It was trying to shake itself apart. We'd already lost one dome and the other two weren't looking too good."

"Could she still be alive?"

"I guess it's possible, but there's no way to reach her even if she was. That's the bravest woman I've ever seen, hell, the bravest person."

"It was her mine and her responsibility. Get your people loaded up. We'll see if we can find her. Brian, I need you at number two, now," Al called into his radio.

"Al, what do you need?" Brian asked.

"I need a small blast door as fast as you can get it over here. There may be one person still on the surface. The mine manager, Alicia Sorenson, sealed the shaft from the top. The others are fine and I'm sending them back to the hub. We're going to start a tunnel to the surface and see if we can find her."

"Shit, I'll round up a crew and head that way. I won't be able to get there until late though."

"Do the best you can."

"Roger, Boss."

"Al this is Mike. What's happening?"

"Alicia stayed on the surface to seal the shaft after everyone else evacuated. The rest of them are fine, but she's still up there. We're going to try to reach her."

"Shit, what next?"

"Are you doing any good over there?" Al asked.

"Yeah, we reached three of the other mines today and are in the process of evacuating them now. We still have five more to go, but we should reach them sometime tomorrow. All present at the ones we've reached."

"Ok. I'm going to try to map out a tunnel to reach the surface and come up inside the domes. We can't breach the surface until we have a door in place, so it may be morning before we can get up there. Al out. Who's in charge of the surveying here?"

"I am," a small voice from the back said. A small woman, in her mid twenties emerged from the crowd. She was just over five feet and had light brown hair that hung below her waist.

"And who are you?"

"Rebecca Williams. I've been here for almost a year."

"Good. I'm going to run a tunnel into the center of the dome where the shaft is located. I need all the information you can give me. GPS coordinates, elevation, anything you can think of."

"I was down here mapping when the call to evacuate came. I had my laptop with me. It's tied into our cruiser. Will that help?"

"Damn right. Where is it?"

"Back in the first tunnel. It was in the way here, so I parked it and walked back."

"Does your cruiser have a map that includes the surface?"

"Well, sure. We worked it in the domes before we lowered it into the hole. I didn't see any reason to erase that little bit of information, so I left it."

"Come with us," Al said, leading her to his cruiser. "Everyone else, load up in the rovers and cruisers. We'll get you all back to the hub and decide what to do then. Jeff, you, and Jim come with us too."

The two cruisers went to the first tunnel and turned in. The cruiser for the mine was parked back away from the entrance, sitting in the dark.

Rebecca got out and fired it up. They all gathered around to look at the display of the map of the mine.

"As you can see, the shaft is almost two thousand feet," she said. "I left the mapping system on by mistake when they lowered it down here. Maybe that was a good thing."

"It sure was," Lorna said.

"Can you get up there to check on Alicia?"

"We're sure as hell going to try," Al said. "This information is exactly what we need to pinpoint the location we want. Do you have any idea which dome might be in the best shape?"

"Well, I heard them talking. The big dome, the one farthest from the shaft is the one that failed. Alicia had moved everyone into the one that housed the shaft and the hoist. She thought it would last the longest. From what I heard, there wasn't anyone in the one that failed."

"Ok. We'll aim for that one," Al said. "We're going to need this cruiser for a guide. I'll send you out with the rest."

"I'd like to stay—if that's ok? Alicia was more than just my boss. She was my friend too."

"You're welcome to stay. Jeff, let's back up into the tunnel we just made and start up here," Al said, indicating the spot he wanted them to start the tunnel. "It should be small. Just enough to get the miner through. If the dome is holding, we can always make it bigger. I want to make it small enough that we can put in two sets of blast doors, so we'll have an airlock. Start off level for a hundred yards or so and then angle up at about a seven percent. Rebecca will guide you. Rebecca, I want him to come out as close to center in that dome as you can."

* * *

At 0430 the preparations were complete. The tunnel angled up to within a thousand feet of the surface and Brian and his crew had the two sets of blast doors in place.

"Al, we're going to need to adapt a rover's environmental system to these doors," Brian said. "We have to have a way to equalize the pressure and I don't know if the cruisers have the capacity to handle it."

"One of them should be back here in a few minutes," Al said. "I had a feeling you'd need one. Frankly, I'd like to have one to go topside in too. We should be able to tell the surface conditions before we have to take the cruiser up there though. Jim's ready to make the final push and Rebecca is right behind him. She wouldn't even take a nap last night."

"Maybe you should take her back to our place. She sounds like she'd fit right in."

"I've been thinking the same thing," Al said. "Doctor Samson is going to be in that rover when it gets here. Have him wait here for us. We're going to take it easy the rest of the way. I don't want any surprises."

"Is Lorna going up with you?"

"No, I don't think so. She hates these sandstorms. I think we can persuade her to stay down here."

"What?" Lorna said as she came up behind them.

"I want you to stay here while I go up," Al said.

"Not a dieing chance in hell that's going to happen," Lorna said. "I go where you go."

"Be reasonable," Brian said.

"Reasonable my ass. I'm going."

"I don't have time to argue with you," Al said. "If you're going, get a suit on. Jim, how are you doing?"

"I'll be to the surface in a half hour."

"Ok, we're coming. Don't break through until we get there."

"Roger, Boss."

When Al and Lorna pulled up behind Rebecca, they could see that she had her suit on too.

"How's he looking Rebecca?"

"Right on target."

"Go ahead, Jim."

Jim powered up the laser cutters on the miner again and started to inch forward. Joe had joined him just after they had started this tunnel and he drove the miner while Jim worked the lasers. Soon, there was a hint of daylight ahead of them. First just in the top of the tunnel and then it grew larger as they advanced. There was a rush of air past them when they broke the surface.

"Al, there isn't any pressure in the dome," Jim said.

"That's not good. Get us on up there so we can have a look. Test the winds if you can."

"Ok. We're almost out now. The dome is damaged, but the wind isn't that bad. Only the top is gone. We're sheltered from the full force of it."

"Ok, let's go see if we can find her."

When the miner was out of the way, Al pulled into the dome following Rebecca. They turned around and poised the cruisers to go back into the tunnel. As the five of them started to search for Alicia Sorenson, they looked at the devastation all around them. The top half of the dome was gone and the sand on the floor was almost two feet thick.

"Spread out and see if you can find her," Al said. "Look in and around things; anywhere she might take shelter from the storm."

"Al, do you have any idea where their suits were kept?" Lorna asked.

"I know," Rebecca said.

"Show me," Lorna said. "Al, call if you find anything."

She followed Rebecca into the center dome, or what was left of it. There were areas of this dome that were almost completely gone. There were only a few feet of the walls left. By crouching down to stay out of the full force of the wind, they were able to make it to an area between the outer two domes.

"They're in here," Rebecca said.

"Ok, lead the way."

"My God, Alicia—Lorna, she's in here."

CHAPTER ELEVEN

"Lorna, can you bring her this way?" Al asked. "We'll come to meet you."

"Yeah, hell, she's still alive and mostly mobile. Alicia, can you get up?"

"I think so. Rebecca, what are you doing up here?"

"We came to get you. Shut up and help us get you on your feet."

"Who are you?"

"I'm Lorna. Now do as you're told and help us get your ass out of here. Al, we're on the move. We may need help to get her through the center dome. It's a mess in there."

"We'll help you. Joe, get the miner ready to move, but don't take it into the tunnel yet. We may need to get her out of here first."

"Al, what the hell are you doing clear over here?" Alicia asked.

"We just dropped by for a visit, now get it in gear. This dome may not last much longer. If you get caught by the full force of the wind, you'll go sailing."

"Hell, it's calmed down compared to what it was a few days ago."

"How long have you been stranded up here?"

"I don't know; seven, maybe eight days. I was able to eat and drink for the first three days or so, and then it got to the point that I couldn't open my faceplate. The area around where we stored our suits was the most stable, so that's where I stayed. I didn't expect to see anyone again."

"Ok, girls, we have her," Al said as they took over. "Damn, Alicia, you look like hell."

"Well, you all look like angles to me. I'm still not sure I'm not dreaming."

"We'll get you into the cruiser and pinch you if you want. To tell the truth, I thought we'd be bringing out a body."

When they got to the cruisers, Lorna and Rebecca took Alicia and Al and Jim followed them into the tunnel. Joe brought up the rear with the miner.

"Where did this tunnel come from?" Alicia asked as they started down.

"They made it last night," Rebecca said. "Now, let's get you out of that suit."

"That would be a good thing."

"Brian, we're headed your way," Lorna called. "Are you ready for us?"

"Yeah. Can you all get into the airlock at the same time?"

"I think so. We'll have to wait for Joe."

"I have the rover hooked up to pressure up the airlock as soon as you get inside. With this jury-rigged setup, I don't know how many times I can make it work though."

"Ok, we'll just have to wait. We'll give you the word."

"Brian, I'll get Jim to close the door after Joe gets in," Al said. "Is the doctor there?"

"Yeah, he's right here."

"Doc, you're not going to believe this, but she's in pretty good shape."

"How long was she up there alone?" Dr. Samson asked.

"She said seven or eight days. She survived in a pressure suit."

"My God, that must have been terrible."

It took almost thirty minutes to get the miner moved back down into the airlock. When it was safely inside, Jim got out and closed the door. Brian started the slow process of bringing the pressure up to the same pressure as the tunnel. That took almost an hour.

"Sorry it took so long," Brian said when they finally got the door opened and were able to get into the tunnel. "The rover didn't want to handle the extra load."

"That's alright," Al said. "As it turned out, there wasn't any real rush."

"Alicia, are you alright?" Dr. Samson asked as they helped her out of the cruiser.

"Yeah, great—now. I had made my peace with the Lord and was resigned to my fate, but not ready to give up. I had to keep recharging the oxygen cylinders to keep going. If the reactor had given up, I'd have been done for."

"I'm going to want to do as much of a physical as I can, under the present circumstances. Al, we need to get her back to the hub."

"Now just how the hell are you going to do that?" Alicia asked.

"We've made a few improvements around here," Al said. "From now on, all of the mines are going to be connected by these tunnels. We're completing the last of them now. By this time tomorrow the system will be complete."

"You must know a process that I've never heard of before."

"We do. We've tunneled well over a thousand miles in just under a month. When you get your mine up and running again, I'll show you how it works."

"You're shitting me. A thousand miles in a month; that's impossible."

"Not anymore. Doc, let's get our star of the hour back to the hub. We may need to take her to Pavonis. I'm betting we have better facilities there than you have at the hub now."

"That wouldn't take much. At the hub, it's about as primitive as I've ever seen."

"Mike, this is Al."

"Good morning. When will you be back to the hub?"

"A couple hours. We'll be bringing Alicia and the doctor back."

"I've been monitoring your frequency. Sounds like she faced the beast and fought it back."

"She's a hell of a woman. We're getting ready to leave now. Where are you going to be?"

"I'm in my make-shift office. I'll be here when you get here."

"Do we need to bring these miners back there?"

"No, I don't think so. Leave them there for now. Slim and Bill are closing in on the last locations and we should have them all opened up by the end of the day. We've been very lucky so far."

"Yeah, but there's more to do. Have you figured out a way to get most of them back to Pavonis?"

"We're getting large numbers of the alien vehicles coming over now and we're starting to transport everyone this morning. It may be a slow trip for some of them, but that's better than staying here."

"Ok, we're ready to go here. See you soon."

* * *

Late that afternoon Slim was approaching the last mine location. The rock in the area approaching the location was badly fractured and Slim called a halt to the operations.

"Al, this is Slim."

"Go ahead."

"You'd better come have a look at this. I don't like the looks of this rock around number six."

"What's wrong with it?"

"It's all broken. We're coming in at seven hundred feet and it's trying to cave in on us. We're still six miles from the mine."

"Do you have any blast doors in that area?"

"No, not for a long ways back. The closest one is the other side of the junction to number seven."

"We'd better gather up the makings and get you an airlock before you go on in," Al said. "Fall back and find us a good place to install it. We'll head that way."

"Roger, Boss."

* * *

It was almost 2400 when Al and Mike arrived at the location of the airlock into number six. Brian had been at work all evening and was almost finished installing the airlock when they arrived.

"Brian, you have to be getting tired," Al said when Brian came to meet them.

"Yeah, we're getting there," Brian said. "This will be finished in a few minutes. Are you going to be able to go on in?"

"We don't have a choice. We have to go on."

"Slim's up ahead. He's been walking the tunnel all evening, trying to evaluate the best way to do this. He thinks he may have to back up and go west to try to get around this bad ground. He's afraid it may be broken all the way to the surface."

"That's a bit of a stretch, but we'd better not take a chance. I'll go up and have a look at it with him. Mike, do you want to ride along?"

"Yeah. It looks like Brian has this taken care of."

Thirty minutes later they pulled up to where Slim was examining the rock in the side of the tunnel. As they got out the miners came from the other direction, led by Bill in his cruiser.

"I'm not sure I can afford to pay the overtime," Al said when they all got together.

"You'll figure it out," Slim said. "We've been in here all evening and think this is the best place to branch off. The ground up there is just too unstable."

"How far will you have to go to get there," Mike asked.

"We've had to back up almost ten miles and the route won't be as direct," Bill said. "We're looking at almost twenty miles."

"Will you be there by morning?"

"Around 0800 is my guess," Slim said.

"I want you in suits for this one," Al said. "Don't go any closer than a mile without them."

"Ok. Where will you be?"

"I've been up for a day and a half. I think we'll go back down the tunnel and deploy the habitat and get some rest. We won't be far away if you need us."

"Set your radio to frequency six," Bill said. "I'll call if we need you."

"Ok, good luck."

* * *

"Al this is Bill. We're stopping to put our suits on. By the time you get up here, we should be ready to open into the mine."

"God, what time is it," Al said.

"0700," Bill said.

"Right on schedule."

"Pretty much. See you in a few minutes. You might want to shake Slim out of bed as you come by."

"Ok, we'll do that. Al out."

Thirty minutes later they pulled up behind the miners and stopped next to Bill. Slim was only a few minutes behind them. As they watched the miners work on the last mile of the tunnel, Mike and Al donned their suits. Slim had put his on when he had gotten up.

"We're breaking through," came the call from one of the miners.

There was a momentary rush of air past them as the miners broke into the tunnel.

"Ok, pull into the tunnel and let us get by," Al said. "What does it look like?"

"According to our readings there's still some pressure in here, but the air is real bad."

"Ok, move out of the way."

They sped past the miners and headed for the shaft. The readings on the gages in the cruisers confirmed the readings they had gotten from the ones in the miners. When they reached the shaft area all they found was bodies. The entire crew was dead.

"What happened here?" Mike asked as they got out.

"They must have lost power," Al said. "The oxygen generators couldn't function without it. From that rush of air when we broke in, there may have been a breach to the outside too. It seems to have been resealed somehow. It may take some time to sort out what happened."

"A hundred and fifty-seven people lost."

As they turned to leave, they went around and checked each of the bodies that were laid out in a row. None had any signs of life.

"Ok, let's get out of here," Al said. "We still have thousands of people depending on us."

"Slim, seal this tunnel for now," Mike said. "I'll make the arrangements to get the funerals taken care of."

It was a solemn trip back to the hub. The silence was only broken by the hum of the electric motors in the wheels of the cruiser. The glass smooth surface left by the miners gliding beneath the wheels. As the trip was about to conclude, Al broke the silence.

"We probably wouldn't have been able to save them even if we'd have gone right to them. It looks like they died a couple weeks ago."

"I know," Mike said. "That doesn't make it much easier though. I'll get a medical team to go in and determine the cause of death and when it happened."

"Now that we've reached all of the mines, I need to get back to my other duties," Al said. "Arsia Mons is still a mystery. Lorna has been over there looking around, but we've had to pull all our resources out of there to support our activities here."

"We have enough resources available now. I have the other mine managers to direct things. You've supplied us with enough transportation to get us around. You saved us all from the fate that took number six. All in all, we're in pretty good shape."

"I'm going to give my people a few days off. They've earned it."

"They sure have."

* * *

The area around the upper garden in Pavonis Mons undertook a dramatic change in the next few days. Al and his crews managed to steak out an area close to the main habitat that Martin had been getting ready for the influx of so many people. Sean had come over from Arsia Mons to join them to decide on a course of action for the next phase of operations.

"Mike, how's the evacuation going?" Lorna asked as they sat down for lunch.

"We'll have them all moved in here in a couple more days. We've been running around the clock. Al, I've been thinking about one of your problems. Can you make it possible to get one of the transports into Arsia?"

"I guess we can do almost anything we want," Al said. "We've proved that. What did you have in mind?"

"We need to move some of that equipment over here, right? We have three transports with flatbed trailers that we can bring in this far. All we have to do is get them on over there and your transportation problems are solved."

"That might link the ecosystems together," Lorna said. "Even more than they already are. Is that a good thing?"

"All the information we've gathered so far indicates that they're very close in composition," Sean said. "I don't see any problem with a more direct link."

"We have plenty of qualified crews to run the miners," Al said. "Yeah, we can do that. It'll take a week or two to open it up. That would make things a lot easier to move around. If we can ventilate it well enough, we can even run the alien vehicles back and forth. I'll have Bill work on it."

"Can I play too?" came a small voice from the door.

"Alicia, God, you had us worried," Mike said. "Come join us."

"Three days under the care of the good doctor is enough for me. I need to get back to work. Can you find anything for me to do around here?"

"If you feel like a lot of riding, I think we can find something," Al said. "What do you think of our mine?"

"Mine? What do you mine here?"

"Survival."

"And thank God for that. This is an amazing place. I still can't believe all this is hidden inside of a mountain."

"Oh, you haven't seen anything yet," Lorna said. "When you're up to it we'll take you to our other mountain."

"I've been listening to others talk as the doctor has been subjecting me to all his pagan ritual tests. I think I've been able to piece some of it together, but don't really believe it yet."

"Mike, with all the added manpower, what do you think about assigning teams to go exploring and finish the job in Pavonis?" Al asked. "They don't have a lot to do until the storm blows over."

"I think that's a great idea. If we get this one explored, we can do the same to Arsia Mons."

"Isn't that the volcano to the southwest of here?" Alicia asked.

"That's our other mountain," Lorna said. "It takes us the better part of a day to get there from here. I managed to keep nine cruisers working on mapping the tunnels over there. I need to get back over there and check on their progress. You're welcome to tag along if you'd like."

"I'll have to check with the doctor, but I'd love to."

"That sounds like a good idea," Mike said. "You can recuperate and see the sights at the same time. Al, where is Melissa? I haven't seen her around since I got here."

"She's down at the library with Hollie. They're still trying to sort things out there. Slim and Jim are taking their break down there too."

"Have they come up with anything yet?"

"Not really. It may take a year to process all the information in those rooms. Even then it may not tell us much more than we already know. It'll help when we can get them the equipment to get them up to the upper areas in the libraries. So far all they've been able to do is the lower shelves that they can reach."

"When you all get rested up, I'd like to see that tunnel to Arsia get started."

"We'll move the equipment over there this afternoon and get that started," Al said. "I'll leave that to Bill and take my people over to Arsia Mons in the morning. Can you relieve Melissa, Hollie, and Sharon at the library? I'd like to take them over to Arsia too. They can help lay the groundwork for moving people over there."

"I think that can be arranged. I'll move the computer lab people from the hub down there. That way I won't have to look at them here."

"Lorna, can you gather up our people and have them all back here by morning?" Al asked. "I'll get with Bill and have him ramrod the new tunnel. We'll go down and find a place to get it started."

"We'll all be ready to go in the morning," Lorna said. "Alicia, see what the doctor has to say."

"I'll do that now. Can I bring Rebecca along for the ride?"

"I don't see why not. She sure stuck out her neck to get you out. We might even pair you two up and send you out in a cruiser to help us map Arsia Mons."

* * *

Late that afternoon Al and Bill stopped in the tunnel designated 210, at the intersection of ring sixteen. This would give them the straightest shot at connecting with the Arsia Mons complex.

"Bill, I think we need to start back here," Al said. "By starting back this far, the air will stay good for longer. We need to allow for two-way traffic in this tunnel and we'll close off the other one and use it as a ventilation duct between the two mountains. As we force the air that way, it will flow back through this tunnel."

"How close to the other tunnel will we come up?"

"I'm not sure yet. We're going back over there tomorrow, and I'll scout out a location to shoot for. When I get it mapped, we'll coordinate things with you. I think it will be quite a ways inside the other mountain, but I have to look around. You'll want to angle down on a gentle slope until you get down to at least five hundred feet below the surface."

"We'll shoot for five percent or so," Bill said. "I have six miners headed this way. With all the extra people we have available, it won't be a problem to get crews to man them around the clock. I'll get Johnson over here to help on one shift. Hell, he's not doing anything anyhow."

"I haven't had a chance to thank him for sending me those girls that designed the mapping system. I'll bet he's kicking his own ass for that one."

"Yeah, I talked to him not long after they started distributing them to the mines. He was plenty humble and also pissed off."

"How long before your miners get here?"

"Three hours or so. I still have to give them the final coordinates. They're just coming in this general direction. I sent them to the lower garden area to get them before we left to come down here."

"I'll leave you to it then. I'm going back up and get things ready for tomorrow. When you get to the other end, I'll buy you lunch and show you around."

"That's a deal. Talk to you tomorrow."

As Al left, he heard Bill giving the directions to the crews in the miners. They had four cruisers riding herd on them and leading them to the proper location.

* * *

At 0800 the next morning the excursion to Arsia Mons was about to begin. There were ten cruisers lined up and ready to go. Alicia and Rebecca had one and Lorna and Sean were explaining some of the fine points to them and explaining where they were headed. Rebecca had used the one from their mine and understood it fairly well, but Alicia hadn't had much exposure to it.

"This is your master map," Lorna said. "You can zoom in or out to locate anything you need on it. As you can see by the display, we've covered a lot of ground."

"This is an amazing complex of tunnels," Alicia said. "I never would have believed that these could have existed."

"We're just full of surprises. Al will lead the way and you follow him in about ten minutes or so. The dust in some of these areas is pretty bad and you'll need to maintain your spacing. I'll follow you with Sean. This cursor will indicate your location in the complex at any time."

"Who came up with this system?" Alicia asked. "Who ever it was, I hope they got a hell of a bonus."

"You'll meet them when we get over there. They've been exploring the upper level. And yes, Mike saw to that. Ten figures if I'm not mistaken. Without this system there would have been a bunch of dead people on this planet right now. Without it and the Martian Miners we couldn't have gotten to any of you in time."

"Ok, I guess we're about ready to go," Al said as he walked up.

"They'll be right behind you, and I'll follow them," Lorna said.

"Think you can find your way alright?"

179

"Shouldn't be a problem," Rebecca said. "I've been working with this system for a few weeks. Not on this scale, but I think we can find our way."

"If you have any problems just sing out on the radio. Lorna will be close behind you. I'll get started so the rest can come in their turn."

"See you over there later," Alicia said.

As Al left, Lorna went back into the habitat to talk to Mike. Martin and Jen were there going over food availability with him when she walked in.

"Well, we're in pretty good shape for now," she heard Mike say.

"It's going to tax us if the storm doesn't break soon though," Martin said.

"Are there any other sources we can draw from?"

"Arsia Mons," Lorna said as she walked up behind him. "Martin, did you get a chance to look at those samples I brought you the other day."

"They show a lot of promise. They came from over there, didn't they?"

"Yeah, and there are a lot of others that you'll need to look at. Mike, I'd like to have Martin and Jen tag along to go into the garden we found over there."

"I guess we can take over here. Yeah, that might be a good idea. If this storm lasts very long there may be problems feeding everyone from what's here."

"Pack your bags. You have a new home," Lorna said. "We'll see to it that you get directions to the habitat over there. I'll take you up to the garden tomorrow. Do you think you two can coexist in a cruiser for a while?"

"We'll manage," Jen said, a smile growing across her face.

"By the time we get done with all the projects you keep finding for us, she'll be a first-rate interplanetary botanist," Martin said. "There aren't many of those around either. I guess you've already realized that she works for me now, not you."

"Yeah, I kind of figured that. Mike, you need to adjust her pay grade. What she's accomplished here is worthy of more than a housekeeping pay scale."

"Consider it done. Young lady, you are now a junior botanist, and we'll fill in the dates and pay adjustments when we can. Don't let me forget."

"Don't worry, I won't," Jen said.

"Along with that I hope there's a bonus for her part in the discoveries here too," Lorna said and winked at Jen.

"Done. We'll work out the details when we get the place put back together. Now go away. You're costing me a lot of money here."

"Go pack your things. We'll get you steered in the right direction. I have to make sure Alicia and Rebecca get off on time."

* * *

"How'd you make out last night?" Bill asked as he relieved Albert Johnson.

"Hell, I just sat back and watched them work. We're about ready to level out. I make us at four hundred and eighty feet. Those things work pretty good."

"Yeah, they're miracle machines as far as I'm concerned. We've had one for a while and the production went through the roof as soon as it was delivered."

"Yeah, we were slated to get one when this thing blew in. I'd heard rumors about them but didn't really believe them. It looks like they consume everything in their path."

"That's adjustable. You can alter the focus so that it leaves the good stuff. There are some things it won't penetrate, but for the most part, it can up your production by three hundred percent. Hell, they can't haul it away fast enough."

"After watching them work, I can believe it. What else have they found over here?"

"I don't really know. But they found a way to get to us and pull our asses out of a big jam. Now maybe we can return the favor by driving them a little tunnel. We'll bring in some of the people from each of the mines so we can have them trained for you by the time this is all over."

"That sounds like a good idea. How long will this take?"

"Al said just over a week. That sounds a bit optimistic, but maybe he knows more about it than I do."

"Well, we'll give it hell and see just how long it takes. Where are we going?"

"Arsia Mons. It's several hundred miles to the southwest."

"Oh. Several hundred miles, you said."

"Yeah."

"Shit, that's a long ways."

"Go get some sleep. I'll see you tonight."

* * *

Al and Mona arrived at the habitat in Arsia Mons at 1730 and got ready for the other twenty people that were spread out behind them. He was surprised but glad to hear that Lorna had brought Martin and Jen along. As they were looking into the interior cavern, the crew that had been sending the materials to them came out for the evening.

"You guys did a hell of a job supplying us with materials," Al said.

"Once we figured out what we could use, it wasn't that hard," Bud Williams, Brian's foreman said. "We haven't heard how it all went. Did you get to all of them?"

"No, but we saved most of them. I think the toll stands at about 2200."

"Shit, that's a lot. What happened?"

"Most of them were lost when they lost two of the domes at the hub. We also lost the entire crew of number six. They're looking into what happened there."

"That's still a pretty good score though. 2200 lost and several hundred thousand saved."

"We're bringing in a bunch of cruisers to help with the mapping. Have you seen any of the cruisers that have been working over here?"

"I think Patty and Brittany are due back this evening. The others have been in recently and gone back out."

"Good. We need to get an updated map, so we know where we stand."

"You can pull most of that off the computer in the habitat. They keep it updated fairly regularly."

"We'll do that. Thanks guys."

Al and Mona went into the habitat and downloaded a map of Arsia Mons. There had been dramatic changes since they had been there. As they looked over the map, Alicia and Rebecca pulled up. From another direction came both Patty and Brittany. They went out to meet them.

"Well, look who finally decided to come visit us in the trenches," Patty said.

"I see you didn't get lost," Al said. "This is Rebecca and Alicia. Patty and Alex and the short one over there is Brittany and with her is Johnny. Now that you've all been introduced, what have you been up to?"

"Short one," Brittany said. "You'll pay for that. We found four more ways to get to the upper level. One of them isn't far from here."

"That's great. How long does it take to get up to the garden?"

"About an hour and a half. That's a lot better than a whole day."

"Martin will be glad to hear that," Mona said.

"Is he coming over this time?" Patty asked.

"He's bringing Jen and coming to have a look at this garden. We have a lot of mouths to feed now."

"We've been listening in on the radio some. It sounds like it's getting a little crowded over there."

"Yeah, the population has jumped by several thousand percent," Al said. "They may be moving this way soon. Will ten or twelve extra cruisers help you any?"

"Hell yes. They're doing fairly well on the lower level, but we're just getting a good start on the upper one."

"We looked at the map that's been downloaded since we were here last. You've made good progress. That should be Lorna coming."

In the next two hours the rest of the cruisers filtered in. It looked like a parking lot by the time they all got parked. Lorna had received updates from the other mapping cruisers that were wandering around in the mountain.

"Rebecca, how'd you make out today?" Al asked as they all sat around talking.

"Other than being a long ride, fine. Where do we go from here?"

"We'll assign you an area to map," Lorna said. "You can do it at your own pace. You'll need to stop and stretch your legs fairly often.

When you stop, look around. Look in some of the rooms that line the walls. We'll give you some paint to mark the ones that you look inside. If there's something of interest in there, mark that too. The navigation here is pretty simple. The spokes of our wheel shaped tunnels are labeled with their compass heading and the rings are numbered from the center out. This ring here, where the habitat is, is number one."

"That sounds easy enough," Rebecca said.

"We could use most of you on the upper level," Brittany said. "As you can see by the map, we still have a lot of ground to cover."

"How's the access to the garden?" Martin asked.

"You can get in almost anywhere," Patty said. "The access inside is pretty good too. There are a couple of areas that are hard to get into, but for the most part you can drive almost anywhere."

"Watch out for the birds," Lorna said.

"Birds?" Alicia said. "What birds?"

"We haven't officially named them yet," Al said. "They're flying around in here. They seem to feed on the upper level and nest down here. There's a big hole between the two levels."

"Here's the way to get up," Brittany said. "It's at 025 degrees and ring four. The others are spread around ring four. We can spread out from there."

"You heard the Boss," Al said. "Get some rest and we'll get started in the morning."

"Al, do you mind if we go on up to the garden?" Jen asked.

"No. Haven't you had enough riding for one day?"

"I just want to get an early start. Do you mind?"

"Of course not. That's up to you. Get some rest though."

"We will. Martin, shall we go?"

"Whatever you say."

As they climbed into their cruiser Lorna looked at Al. She knew why Jen wanted to move to the garden, but as usual, Al didn't have a clue.

"Well, I think I've had enough fun for one day," Sean said. "I'm going to lay out the habitat and go to bed."

"What habitat," Alicia asked.

"The one on the back of the cruiser. It has most of the comforts of home," Al said. "Come on. I'll show you how it works."

"You guys are full of surprises," Rebecca said. "I've seen that thing on the back but was never told what it was."

"When we go out mapping, we stay out as much as a week or two. It makes roughing it a little easier. All you do is press these buttons in the right order. When you get a green light after pushing one, you push the next one in the sequence."

As he started the deployment of the habitat, he explained what was happening. Soon it was deployed and inflated. He took them inside.

"The earlier versions slept six, but when we added the mapping system to them, we cut that down to four. There's a double bed up front and two singles in the back. The refrigerator is accessible from both sides. There is a small toilet in this corner, complete with a curtain."

"That could be handy," Alicia said.

"Get some rest and we'll go to work in the morning. We'll keep you fairly close for a day or two. Don't worry, you won't get lost in here."

"I'm not worried," Rebecca said. "I'm pooped."

CHAPTER TWELVE

"God, I feel like hell," Al said as he came out of the cruiser habitat the next morning.

"What's wrong?" Lorna asked.

"Oh, nothing. Just all wrung out. Mona and I are going to go find a place for Bill to aim for this morning. Can you get everyone lined out on a pattern of some kind?"

"That's no problem. We'll lead them all up to the upper level and assign them from there. Jen and Martin won't be up for a while, so I'll just let them sleep until we get set. I may have to keep Eve and Brian down here for a while. I don't know if they're going to need anything from them on the other side."

"Later in the week Brian may need to coordinate that new set of blast doors in the tunnel coming over here. I don't know how we're going to power the fans. I'll leave that up to him."

"I'll mention it to him so he can be thinking about it. I'll just have them work inside here for a couple days until he has to go take care of that. Where are you going to have Bill aim for?"

"I want to bring them up well inside the outer boundaries for the good air. That's one of the things that I need to find. I want the air going into that tunnel to be as good as possible. We'll have to absorb the bad air from the old tunnel. I don't know what that's going to do to us over here, but it can't be helped."

"We could reverse the flow," Lorna said. "Then the air would be good in both directions."

"The problem with that is that the new tunnel is too big to put the fans in. Also, we need that one to get the transports through."

"I didn't think of that. We'll just have to monitor the air a little closer. Any idea how much bad air we'll have to deal with?"

"Not really. Could be a lot. The entrance to the tunnel is in the bad air. We may have to fix that too."

"There are a lot of tunnels that would have to get plugged."

"Yeah, I know. It might be easier to turn the miners around and run a parallel tunnel and abandon the original all together. I'll give that some more thought."

"What the hell. They don't have that much to do right now. That would make everything a lot simpler."

"I'll suggest it to Mike when I talk to him later. Well, Mona is starting to stir. We'll get a bite to eat and get started."

"Ok. I'll go roust the others."

* * *

Lorna and the others didn't get to the upper level until 0930. She led them to where the tunnel intersected the garden and stopped.

"This is where we split up," Lorna said after they had all assembled. "Take a tunnel and map it. We're going through the garden and check on Martin and Jen. Brittany, you can assign the areas to them. You know more about this place than any of us do."

"Ok. Gather around guys," Brittany said. "Patty and I have been working mostly south and east of here. As you can see on the map, we need to work north and west. If we all go that way and split off a team on every other spoke, we can cover a lot of ground. Go out until you intersect the outer ring and then turn west to the next tunnel and come back in to here."

"Alicia, you and Rebecca stay close to the garden for a day or two," Lorna said.

"This doesn't sound all that hard," Rebecca said. "We can join the pattern. It doesn't look like we'll be all that far from anyone if we have a problem."

187

"Ok. Patty, you, and Britt keep them between you for now. Good hunting. Sean and I are going into the garden for a while and will probably come out on the other side. That kind of depends on what Martin and Jen have for us. Remember to deploy the repeaters when you're mapping a new area."

"It's a good thing we laid in a good supply of those before the storm hit," Sean said. "Alicia, do you and Rebecca know how those work?"

"Yeah, they showed us. We're supposed to deploy them in intersections, right?"

"Yeah, if you can. It gives us better coverage."

"Ok, we're all set then," Patty said. "With all this help we may be able to finish this in a couple weeks or so."

As Patty led the way, Lorna and Sean watched until they were all gone, and then drove into the garden. There were fresh tracks in the soggy soil of the garden, and they followed them. They hadn't been to this area of the garden before, but it seemed to be a lot like the areas that Lorna and Eve had looked at when they were in there before. In the outer reaches it was a mess, but the farther they went in, they found less debris.

"Martin, Jen, how far did you go last night?" Lorna called on the radio.

"Uhhh, good morning," Martin said. "We went in a few miles. Where are you?"

"We're inside a few miles, following your tracks."

"Oh, shit. We must have overslept. It was late when we stopped."

"Yeah, I'll bet it was. Ok, I see your cruiser. We'll be there in a minute."

About a mile ahead they could see the cruiser and as they drew closer, through the opaque plastic of the habitat, they could see what appeared to be a scramble to get dressed. Martin emerged first, just as they parked, still pulling his shirt on.

"We didn't interrupt anything, did we?" Lorna asked as they got out.

"No, of course not," Martin said.

"It's almost 1000. We figured you'd be up and around by now."

"Oh, hell. You know what's going on here. We had to unwind when we got here last night."

"Yeah, I know. You two have been dancing around this for weeks now and I thought you could use a little privacy to see if anything would develop or not. It looks like it developed just fine to me."

"Yeah, I guess it did at that," Martin said with a sheepish grin on his face.

"Did you look at the area as you came in last night?"

"What we could see. I still can't get over the way the light in here simulates the sun outside. The plants and trees are different in here and I can't tell you much about them until we've had a chance to look around more."

"I know. I was just looking for your initial impression. Good morning, Jen. Sleep well?"

"The best night's sleep I've had in ages, thank you."

"You're welcome. Just remember that you have a job to do; a very important job."

"We'll hold up our end. How did you know that we were looking for this?"

"I'm old, but I'm not blind or stupid. I'm surprised you two didn't find a way to make this happen sooner. You've been working together for weeks now."

"We came close a few times, but it just didn't seem to work out," Jen said. "Last night, it did."

"Martin, how can we help you?"

"We need a couple days to look around. My first impression is that this garden will compliment what we have on the other side. It's still not going to be a perfectly balanced diet, but I'm sure we can survive on it. It would be nice if we had meat to go along with all of this."

"That's not really an option. The birds in here might be good to eat, but we'd have to kill one to find out. We don't know how many of them there are, and we don't want to eliminate them altogether. My guess is that they're an integral part of the ecosystem."

"What birds?"

"We have pictures of them. Let me bring them up on the computer," Sean said. "Lorna and Eve tried to get up close and personal with them a few weeks ago. There, you can see they're quite large."

"Where did you see them?" Jen asked.

"These pictures were taken on the lower level," Lorna said. "They seem to nest down there and feed up here. We've seen several places where they've been but haven't encountered them up here."

"How big are they?"

"Big. Like a flying elephant."

"I can see how they might be a part of the ecosystem alright," Martin said. "Where were the signs that they'd been up here?"

"Mostly around the big hole between the two levels. They seem to range in for several miles, but don't get all the way to the outer edges much," Lorna said as she pulled up the map on the monitor on the outside of the cruiser. "We saw areas where they had been feeding in this area here, just to the southwest of the big opening."

"Ok, we'll watch for them. Maybe we can document their feeding habits or something."

"Any information you can get on them would be good," Sean said. "I know it's not really your area, but you're the ones that'll be in the right area to do the job."

"We'll see what we can do," Jen said. "Do they bite?"

"They sure tried to bite us," Lorna said. "Keep your distance if at all possible."

"Have you given them a name yet?"

"No, Jen, and I'm not looking for another species named after me."

"Why not?"

"You get some data on them and maybe we'll name them after you."

"Cool."

* * *

Al and Mona found the outer boundary of the good air late in the afternoon. When they determined where it was, they turned and went back halfway to the garden and decided to have Bill aim for that spot.

"Bill, this is Al."

"Go ahead, Boss."

We have the coordinates for you to shoot for. On the map of Arsia Mons they'll be over halfway into the mountain. I'll bring you an updated map and the GPS coordinates so we can get everyone on the same page. For now, just continue on your present course."

"Ok, when do you think you'll have all the information for us?"

"We'll bring it over tomorrow. I think we're going to want to turn the miners around and make a parallel tunnel to the one you're driving. A smaller one for setting up the fans for the ventilation."

"Can we fall back and bring it at the same time? I can get more miners over here."

"Yeah, I don't see why not. We need to keep it small enough to make it easier to install the fans, but large enough to get through with at least a rover."

"Understood. I'll go round up more troops."

"Move it over to the next spoke tunnel to the west. We don't want them too close together. I'll get you the map to that location too before I come back to your side."

"It'll probably be sometime tomorrow before we get it started. It takes a long time to move things around in here."

"Yeah, I know. That will work fine. I just don't want to pull all that bad air over here and screw things up."

"Yeah, we can't afford that. I'll get started on it right away. Bill out."

"Mike, did you copy any of that?" Al asked.

"Yeah, I think so. You're running two tunnels instead of one."

"Yeah, I'll explain things to you tomorrow when we get back. How are things going there?"

"As good as can be expected. I'm leaving a maintenance contingent at the hub to monitor and evaluate things there. We'll need to know as soon as the storm starts to die down."

"What do the conditions look like up there now?"

"Actually, they're improving slowly. We may have another month before we can go topside again, but that doesn't sound all that bad to me."

"No, we can work with that. Have you been able to get a good head count to see how many people we lost?"

"We're still working on that. Best estimate is still around 2200 though. With everybody spread out it may be hard to get that list compiled."

"How many supply ships will you have stacked up in orbit by the time you can contact them?"

"Maybe as many as ten. They usually come in about every two weeks. We have enough minerals to fill eight right now and by the time we get them all loaded and turned around, we should be able to process enough to fill the other two, providing the processing center survives the storm."

"You know the supply chain is going to be disrupted for years to come. I just hope they don't give up on us and call them back."

"I got off a message to them before we lost communications and emphasized that fact. I never received a response, but I think I worded it strong enough to get their attention. I guess we'll have to wait and see."

"Ok, Mona and I will be back over there sometime tomorrow to coordinate things with Bill. We'll come by and you can buy us a salad or something."

"Salad does seem to be the order of the day, doesn't it?"

* * *

As the caverns of both complexes started to dim with the setting sun, Jen and Martin found a spot to bed down for the night. They had covered a lot of ground on their initial inspection of the Arsia Mons garden.

"So, what do you think?" Jen asked.

"There are a lot of species of plants that aren't in the Pavonis gardens, either one of them," Martin said. "We'll have to set up a lab over here to run some tests, but I think we'll find that most of it is good to eat."

"Martin, this is Lorna."

"Go, Boss."

"Did you do any good today?"

"Yeah, I think so. I may have to take some samples back to the other garden and run some tests, but it all looks good to me. I'll have to round up a small lab set-up to bring back over here. I didn't have time to do that before we left."

"Do you think we can grow some of our own food here too?"

"Yeah. The soil is even richer than it is in Pavonis. I haven't found a water source yet, but I know it's here. The soil is wet to the touch."

"I don't remember seeing one either. We're on the western edge of the garden and we're going to bed down soon. Keep me informed."

"Will do. Martin out."

"I guess we have some time to kill now," Jen said. "Any ideas how we can do that?"

"As a matter of fact, I do have a couple ideas on that subject," he said as he took her in his arms and kissed her.

"You dirty old man. It took you long enough. I'll make the bed out."

"That takes too long."

* * *

Late the next afternoon Al and Mona pulled into the new tunnel. They had made good progress. Albert Johnson was sitting at the bottom of the ramp, some ten miles in.

"Bill said you'd be along," Johnson said.

"Where is he?"

"He's getting set up for the other tunnel. The other miners should have arrived over there an hour ago."

"We downloaded the coordinates that you need to shoot for on the other end. You can upload this into your cruiser and go right to it. I'll rig another one for Bill."

"I wanted to tell you how wrong I was about Patty and Brittany. After running around in one of these cruisers for a few days; now I understand what they were trying to get me to let them do."

"Without these wonderful machines, you'd still be stuck in your mine. Hell, let your people have a little space to explore their potential."

"I don't suppose I could have them back. Could I?"

"Not a dieing chance in hell. They're mine."

"I figured that."

"How far have you gotten?"

"Almost a hundred miles. How much farther is it?"

"About three hundred more. Just keep on track and start up fifteen miles before you get to the end. I'm going to go find Bill."

"Ok, Boss of Bosses."

"Smart ass. See you later."

Just over an hour later they pulled up to where Bill had started the other new tunnel. Bill was sitting at the top watching them descend through the rock.

"Are you having fun?" Al asked as he got out.

"Not yet, but soon. We're just getting a good start."

"Mona made you a duplicate of the disc I gave to Albert. This should guide you the rest of the way. The size looks good. When you get down to the bottom and level out, I'll have them start on the blast doors and the fans. Tomorrow sometime?"

"Yeah. This one is a lot smaller than the other one. We'll probably get to the other side before they do."

"That's good. I'm headed back to talk to Mike. We'll get the transports headed this way. They're so damned slow that it'll take them a day to get over here, maybe two."

"They may be slow, but they haul a hell of a load."

"I have Brian getting some of the equipment lined up for them to move. He should have several loads waiting for them when they get there. Is there anything else you need?"

"Just a big steak. I think we're all going to need that before we're back to normal."

"Maybe when you get this tunnel finished, we can go over to your mine and rifle the freezer. You probably have a few in there somewhere."

"As a matter of fact, you're probably right. When we evacuated to the mine, we didn't have much time to gather up the things that we didn't really need. The stuff in the freezer was way down on the list. It wouldn't last long in the mine."

"We have some stuff stashed in a locker in here. We're not racking it out until we have to. There isn't enough to go around."

"I'll watch over this one and Albert can handle the other one. I'm betting we get there first."

"You'll be able to travel a lot faster than they will. I'll leave this to you. Mike's expecting me."

"Thanks for the directions. I'm sure they'll help."

* * *

Over breakfast the next morning Al and Mike went over what needed to be done next. Mona went over the latest maps that the two cruisers that were still working inside Pavonis had brought in the day before.

"I called last night and got the transports headed this way," Mike said. "They won't be here until sometime tomorrow though. They had to work their way into the domes and get them."

"There's no real hurry," Al said. "We have almost a week to go, getting to the other side. I knew it would take them a while. Brian's crew is going to start on the fan set-up today and maybe start installing them by tomorrow. I don't have any idea how we're going to power them, but they said they'd figure out something."

"Have you talked to Lorna today?"

"No, not yet. She was in the garden with Martin and Jen most of the day yesterday. She's still trying to get an idea of what all's in there. They haven't found any water source yet. The ground is soggy, so there has to be some in there someplace."

"I still can't believe the quantity of water you've found in here. You'd think we would have hit some of it somewhere else, with all the digging we've done."

"Yeah, I've been thinking about that for a while. I thought we might have hit some when we were tunneling to the hub. If it was there, maybe the miners sealed it off. I don't know."

"I have Alistair camped out at the hub. I'm sure I'll have to make several trips over there and back. I needed someone I could count on. I have him set up on frequency seven if you need him for anything."

195

"Is he doing any recon inside the domes?" Al asked.

"Yeah. He's going in a couple times a day. He said last night that he didn't trust the weather station equipment anymore. He thinks it's so far out of calibration now that we can do better by looking outside. The winds seem to be diminishing a little, but it's hard to tell the difference between four-fifty and four hundred."

"Alicia said they had died down a little compared to what they were. She should know since she was in the middle of it for a week or more. Maybe we're on the downhill side of this one."

"I hope so. We shouldn't lose any more people, but we're still not in very good shape."

"Are there any small power units at the hub? Portable ones."

"I don't think so. I checked on that for you once before. I don't think we had anything we could use. We've adapted everything we could get our hands on to put in the cruisers. I have a steady supply of them coming, but only a few at a time and we can't get to any of the ones that are on the supply ships in orbit."

"It was just a thought. We're going to need something to power the fans to ventilate the tunnels to Arsia Mons. That's the only way we're going to be able to run back and forth with any machine we have. Right now, all we have are the cruisers and rovers. They may have to tie into one of them for power."

"If the ventilation is that important, do whatever you have to."

"By the time they get to the other side they're going to be on air packs. I think it's that important. We ran into the same problem when we started for the hub. We got around it by connecting the two tunnels together and keeping the fresh air as close to the face as we could. Otherwise, we'd have been in suits or air packs."

"Al, this is Martin," they heard on the radio in the habitat.

"Go ahead," Al answered.

"Are you anywhere around the habitat in Pavonis?"

"Yeah. I'm here talking to Mike. What do you need?"

"Get with my guys there and have them rig me a portable lab set-up. I'm going to need more than I brought with me. I'd rather not have to come all the way back over there to get it."

"I'll have them call you so you can tell them what you need. I'll have it back over there tonight or tomorrow morning."

"That will be a lot faster than if I come to get it."

"Have you found anything yet?"

"It's looking good so far. There's a wide variety of food here. I don't know how fast it will regenerate, but there's enough to do us for quite a while. I brought several varieties of seeds that we've been able to pull out of fruits and veggies. We'll plant some of them and see what happens."

"How's your assistant working out?"

"Hell, she took over. I've just been a passenger and observer. She sees a lot of things that get past me."

"You have a winner there."

"Don't say that so loud. She'll get a big head. Martin out."

"I like that young lady," Mike said. "She has a lot of spunk."

"I'd like to see her rewarded for her efforts."

"We talked about that before she went over there the other day. I elevated her to junior botanist or something like that. Lorna insisted on a bonus for her too. I'll take care of her when we get back into a somewhat normal mode of operation."

"That's good. She's really worked hard and done a lot of the things that we just didn't have time to do and done a good job in the process."

"Yeah, well, you've all done that. So where do you plan to take us now?"

"God, I really don't know. In the next couple weeks, we'll develop a better idea what's going on in Arsia and that may lead us somewhere. If you need us for anything else, just call."

"Things are coming together here," Mike said. "Now if the storm will just calm down, we can get back to work."

* * *

Three days later there was some confusion about what the congregation of cooks and chefs were going to do to feed the mass of humanity. Mike found himself in the middle of it.

"Hey, hold on here," he said as he fought his way into the gathered mass. "What the hell is going on here?"

"Mr. Mike, these rank amateurs are trying to tell me, Franco, how to prepare a meal. This behavior is unacceptable."

"Mr. Franco, can you do all of this by yourself?"

"But of course not. There are simply too many of them."

"Can you explain to all of them what needs to be done? Someone needs to take charge of this mess. People are going to get hungry in here and if that happens, I'm going to kick all of your asses. Franco, you're in charge of this for now. If you screw it up, I'll fire you and get someone else to do it. Now get this mess straightened out. Dinner is in two hours!"

"Yes, Mr. Mike. Franco will take care of it," Franco said as Mike stormed back through the crowd.

"Mike, this is Alistair."

"Yeah, what now?"

"Did we get up on the wrong side of the planet today?"

"Sorry Alistair. I just had a go around with the cooks. What's up?"

"The wind velocity has dropped to half of what it was a few days ago. We may be able to get out and move around in another week or so."

"Damn, that's good news. Can you get into the spaceport and try to reestablish a com link back to earth, or at least to the ships in orbit?"

"We're getting ready to do that now. I had to call in a couple of technicians to take in with me. They should be here in a couple of hours. In the meantime, I'm going to go take a look. When we were there yesterday, we established that the only two domes we lost were five and six. There is some minor damage to several others, but we can have them up and running again in a couple weeks. We'll have to isolate the two bad domes though."

"Keep me posted and if you can get that com link up, get in touch with me immediately."

"We'll have it up by this time tomorrow."

"I'll come over tonight. When you get that up, I need to be there."

"We'll leave the light on."

* * *

"Al, this is Bill."

"Go ahead, Bill."

"This is a nice place you have over here. We just opened up into a big tunnel."

"Damn, you're early. I didn't expect you until this evening."

"We had a good run. I talked to Albert a couple hours ago and he's climbing the grade now. If your directions are right, he'll be breaking through in about four hours. We're going over to wait for them."

"Thanks, Bill. I'll meet you there. Stay back a ways."

"Yeah, we're planning on that."

"I'm about three hours away. I'll be there before he surfaces."

When Al and Mona arrived, they found Bill parked in one of the ring tunnels that connected to the intersection where they figured the other miners would break through. Several of the people with Bill were off exploring the rooms in the area.

"Where's all your help?" Al asked.

"Just being nosey," Bill said. "They asked if they could look around and I told them not to get lost. It'll probably be another hour before they break through. I didn't see any harm in it."

"No harm at all. We do some of that ourselves."

"I talked to Brian a little while ago. He's almost ready to fire up the fans. He had the engineers boost the output of the reactor on one of the cruisers to power the fans. He said they'd have to bring them online one at a time and let them smooth out before they could start another one. It sounds like it might take a couple hours to get them all running."

"The timing sounds good."

Forty minutes later the green glow of the miners burst into the center of the intersection. The five miners pulled into the cavernous tunnel line abreast and stopped after traveling a couple hundred feet into the tunnel. The cruisers that were escorting them soon followed.

"Right on time," Al said when Albert Johnson came over to where they were.

"I see Bill beat us here."

"I told you we would," Bill said.

"I knew I should have taken the smaller tunnel. I thought we had such a head start that I could still beat you."

"Friendly competition, that's what I like to see," Al said. "What do you think, Albert?"

"Cool digs. Where do they go?"

"To an alien industrial complex. We're still exploring there, but it's been a great find so far. That's where we got the materials we needed to get to the hub."

"This I have to see. Mind if we go have a look?"

"Not at all. You're done here. We have a habitat set up that we use for a base camp. Gather your guys together and I'll explain how to get there. Bill, you might want to call yours in too. We could probably use the help over there."

When everyone was assembled, Al went over how to navigate in the catacomb of tunnels and explained where they should end up. Once everyone understood that, Al led the way to the habitat. Several of the cruisers took alternate routes to avoid the inevitable dust clouds that lingered everywhere they went.

The crew that had been working out of the habitat had several machines of different sizes and shapes lined up waiting for the transports to take them to the other side. Among them were cranes and forklift looking machines in several different sizes.

"Damn," Albert said as they all got out and gathered beside the habitat.

"What powers them?" Bill asked.

"We have no idea. The engineers have been trying to figure that out for quite a while," Al said. "It seems to be a self regenerating system of some kind. If we ever figure out how to tap into it, it may be the biggest find of all."

"Uhhh, Al, this is Lorna,"

"Go ahead."

"I'm looking at something that I can't really believe. Where are you?"

"I'm at the habitat. What is it?"

"I don't have a clue. Can you come to the upper level and take a look?"

"Sure. Where are you?"

"Upper level, spoke 270, ring four. Actually, a mile or so west of there."

"It'll take me a couple hours to get there."

"We'll wait. There seems to be a shaft that goes straight up from here and I can see light at the top of it."

CHAPTER THIRTEEN

"What was that all about?" Bill asked.

"I don't have any idea," Al said. "I guess I'd better go up there and find out. Want to come along?"

"Sure."

"Albert, you guys deserve a day off. Mind hanging out here?"

"No. We might even find something useful to do."

"Bill, let's go see what Lorna found."

On the ride to where Lorna was waiting Al gave Bill a rundown of what they had found so far. When they arrived, they found Lorna and Sean standing beside their cruiser, looking up into a large vertical shaft.

"What's that?" Al asked.

"You're the one that knows about this kind of thing," Lorna said. "Any ideas?"

"No, I just got here. Let's have a look."

They all moved to the center of the tunnel and looked up into the shaft. It was about forty feet across and seemed to go up a couple thousand feet. Along one side there were notches carved into the stone.

"We've been looking at it for quite a while," Sean said. "I think we can climb those steps if we can get up there. Any ideas on how to do that?"

"We'll have to get a forklift, or something brought up here. That's going to take some time. What else have you found?"

"Just the usual," Lorna said. "The teams have been out mapping and we worked our way through the garden and started looking over here. So far this is the only thing we've come up with that's any different than the rest."

"We can split up and look around while we wait for the equipment. Maybe this is the area where we'll find some answers to our questions."

"I doubt it," Lorna said. "All we seem to do is find more questions."

"Albert, this is Al."

"Go ahead, Al."

"Can you find us something that can lift us up about sixty feet and bring it up to where we are?"

"Sure, if I had any idea where that was. You blokes have me completely lost in here. Is there any way you could send us a guide?"

"I'll see what we can do. In the meantime, see what you can find. Get with the crew that's working in the area and have them give you a hand."

"Roger, Al. I'll give you a holler when we come up with something."

"Al, this is Brittany. We're about two hours from there. Do you need us to go guide them up?"

"Yeah, you're a lot closer than we are. How's it going?"

"We've been kicking ass up here. At this rate we'll have it mapped in another two weeks, unless you find someplace else that we have to map. Did I hear Lorna right earlier?"

"Yeah, Britt, she's done it again. I'll show you when you get here."

"Al, how long did it take you to get up there," Albert asked.

"About three hours, why."

"It may be morning before we can get there with anything."

"Do the best you can. We'll be in the area somewhere. Just give us a heads-up and we'll meet you."

* * *

"Alistair, how's it coming on that com-link?" Mike asked.

"We should have it up soon. Sorry about the delays. They had to reroute several of the subsystems to get power to the array. As soon as they get the power configured, we can give it a try."

"Have you been able to affect any of the repairs to the domes?"

"We're starting to get them back in shape. The small repairs are going good, but we still have to wait for the wind to die down to get to some of the larger ones. The weather has improved a lot in the last few days though, so it shouldn't be long before we can start bringing everyone back."

"Good. Let's go see if they have that uplink established."

It took almost an hour to get to the top of the space port. The way was still littered with the debris that had fallen from some of the dome structures. The crews had managed to get enough of the dome structures repaired so that they didn't have to wear suits to get to the space port.

"You've done a great job getting us back online," Mike said. "Let's see if we can get a message to the outside now."

"Guys, are we ready to try it?" Alistair asked.

"Yes sir. We just finished."

Mike took the microphone and tried the com-link for the first time. Instead of getting to the home office, his call was answered by one of the ships in orbit.

"Mars colony, this is the Captain of the Orion. We were about to give up hope that there was any life left down there."

"Well, don't give up on us yet," Mike said. "We've suffered a lot of casualties, but we're starting to recover. It may be a while before we can receive your cargo, but we're getting there. I need you to forward a message to the main office and have it routed to the board of directors."

"We can do that. Is there anything we can do to help you now?"

"No, we're doing alright. Just don't give up on us and go home. The storm is losing its punch and we're going to need those supplies."

Mike transmitted his message to the ship and signed off.

"I feel better," Mike said. "Good job guys."

"Did he say how many ships are in orbit?" Alistair asked.

"Eleven, with another one due in three days. We're going to have our work cut out for us when we can get this mess cleaned up."

"We'll rise to the occasion. I'm going to stay here and see to these repairs for a while."

"Ok. I'll head back and see if I can finalize that list of names of the people that are missing. We'll need to get that transmitted as soon as we can. Their relatives will need to be notified. That's going to be a nasty job."

"Yeah, but it has to be done."

* * *

"Al, this is Albert. Are you up and around yet?"

"Yeah, but just barely. Where are you?"

"Well, rise and shine. We'll be at the coordinates you gave us in two hours or so."

"Ok. We figured you'd stopped and would be here early. We're here waiting for you. I'll get the coffee started."

"We've already had two pots but could stand more. See you soon."

"What time is it," Bill asked.

"0600. I guess he's an early riser. We might as well get up and see what there is to see."

When Albert led the forklift up the tunnel a little before 0800 everyone was up and waiting. The forklift was a monstrous machine. It had a boom that stuck out in front of it that telescoped out and they had mounted a platform on the forks.

"Think this thing will do the job?" Albert asked.

"It just might," Al said, still working on his cup of coffee.

"What do you need it for?"

"Up there," Al said, pointing to the roof of the tunnel.

"Damn, that's a long ways up."

"Is that what Lorna found this time," Brittany said as she walked up.

"That's it. It appears there's another level to this place. Want to go for a little climb?"

"Let me think about that for a minute. I'll go into almost any dark tunnel, but climbing that, maybe not."

"Afraid of heights?"

"A little," Brittany said.

"Albert, have him run that platform up there and see if it'll reach."

They all watched as the giant machine started to unfold and extend. It took several minutes to get all the way to the top, but it did reach.

"Who wants to go with me?" Al asked.

They all raised their hands, except Brittany.

"Well, we can't all go. Albert, it looks like we may have another tunneling job for one of your miners. Can you go back down and bring one up here. I'll take Bill and Sean up with me and have a look around. We should have an idea if there's anything up there by the time you get back to where the miners are."

"Ok. Now that we know how to get here, it shouldn't be that big a problem."

"I know that it may be tomorrow morning before you get back with the miner," Al said. "That's fine. We'll have a plan worked out by the time you get back. Have Willie stay here to run the forklift for us."

"See you in the morning," Albert said as he left.

"Willie, bring it back down."

"I think I should go with you," Lorna said.

"Yeah, I know you do, but I'd like to have a look around first. It's going to be a hell of a climb. I'm not sure I'm up to it either. Give me this one, ok?"

"Well, alright, but I'm not happy about it."

"I know, but work with me. You're too important to lose on something like this."

"So are you."

"Maybe so, but one of us has to go. You can do it next time. Bill, there's some climbing gear in the side compartment of the cruiser, can you get it?"

When they were all rigged up, they stepped on the platform.

"Wait, you might want to take some water at least," Lorna said."

"That's probably a good idea," Sean said. "Who knows how long we'll be up there."

"You old farts take it easy climbing up there," Lorna said. "Bill, watch out for them."

"I'll do my best," Bill said.

The platform started its climb as they held on to the rail along the back of the platform. Al watched the ground as they climbed to the point where they would start their climb. There was a small jolt when they reached their objective.

"I'll go first," Al said and stepped onto the toeholds that were carved into the rock.

The climb was almost vertical, but the footing was good. The carved steps had a small lip on the front of them which made it easier for them to hang on. Sean followed as soon as Al was up far enough to give him room to get on the ladder. Bill brought up the rear. They were all lashed together with ten feet of rope between them. That was just enough to give them a little freedom, but hopefully not enough to let them get into too much trouble if one of them slipped.

* * *

Lorna watched them as they made their ascent. Everyone stood back and watched with her. She could see that they were making good progress, but worried that they would get tired before they got to the top.

"God, I need a glass of tea," she said finally. "I can't watch this anymore."

"I should get back to work," Brittany said. "But I can't leave until I know they've made it to the top."

"Come have a glass of tea with me."

"Ok."

* * *

It took over two hours for them to make the climb, but finally Al could see the top getting closer. There was a glow coming from one side of the opening at the top, but none from the other side.

"Almost there guys," Al said. "How you holding up?"

"Only fair," Sean said.

"Me too," Bill said.

"Men of few words. I like that."

"We don't have enough wind left for too many. Just get your butt over the top."

Ten minutes later Al scrambled over the edge and helped the others up.

"Why in the hell would any intelligent race build something like that," Bill asked, still panting from the exertion.

"I have no idea," Al said. "Lorna, we made it."

"Yeah, I can see that. Are you alright?"

"We'll be ok as soon as we catch our wind."

"What's up there?"

"Just a tunnel leading west. It's not very big. Maybe fifteen feet high and ten across. We'll go have a look in a few minutes."

"Kinda makes you wish you had the stairs back at the mine, huh."

"That it does. At least there you could sit down for a minute."

After fifteen minutes they went down the lighted tunnel. At the far end of it, some hundred yards away, there was a winch with a cable leading back to the edge of the hole. The tunnel changed directions to the south and they continued on. After a hundred yards it began to widen.

The first glimpse of the immense cavern that spread out ahead of them was almost breathtaking.

"God, would you look at that," Sean said.

"Lorna, you're going to want to spend some time up here as soon as we can tunnel to this level," Al said.

"What? What did you find?"

"There are enough stone tablets to keep Hollie and her computer busy for a long time, but these appear to be made of gold, or something similar. There doesn't seem to be another outlet that we can see from here. We're going to have a look around."

"Why would they store all their valuables in a place like this?" Lorna asked over the radio.

"Beats me," Al said. "It sure is a sparkling sight though. Damn, talk about a retirement nest egg."

"Describe how it's laid out. Damn it, I could use a little input here."

"You know how hard it is to size these things from the first look. It's big."

"Stay where you are. I'm coming up."

"No, don't do that," Al said. "Ok, it's something over a mile long and maybe half that wide. There's one of those crystal structures that we've seen here and in Pavonis Mons that is supplying the light. It looks muted from down there because there's a sharp bend in the small tunnel that leads in here. In addition to the tablets there are all kinds of urns and plates and such. Money-wise, it's probably the richest find in the history of two worlds. You found it too."

"God damn you. Why did you make me stay down here?"

"For your own good. Let me talk to Willie."

"Al, what do you need?" Willie asked.

"Lower the platform and don't let anyone try to come up here. She's obstinate enough to try and I don't want her to get hurt."

"Got you Boss."

"Lorna, it's for your own good."

"Damn you. I'll get even for this."

"Yeah, I know, but at least you'll be alive to get even. It took all we had to make that climb. I'm not sure you have the strength to do it."

"Lorna, this is Mike. I've been monitoring your conversation and I insist that you listen to him."

"Both of you can go screw yourselves."

"Al, what do you think it is?" Mike asked.

"I don't know yet. We're just standing in the doorway. It's like when we first looked into the pyramid room at the mine. It's that kind of feeling. We know it's wondrous, but we just don't comprehend the extent of it yet. We haven't even gone into the room yet."

"How are you going to get her up there?"

"Albert is bringing one of the miners up here. We should be able to tunnel up here in a few hours, once he gets here, but that probably won't be until morning. We're going to have a look around and see if there's another alternative."

"I'm at the hub. We got a link to the outside established today. There are eleven ships in orbit now and another one due in a few days. All we can do is relay through them to get any word out, but at least we're not completely cut off anymore."

"Damn, that's better news than this find we made."

"I thought you'd like to hear the news."

"Yes sir. Thank you. Lorna, I need you to go back down the tunnel to the east and find a spot about four miles back where we can start the tunnel to get up here. We'll have to have it that far back to get the angle we need to keep it from being too steep. Can you do that?"

"Of course, I can do that. I'm going to get that miner up here tonight though. We can dig all night if we have to. I have to get up there."

"Albert, this is Al. Have you been listening to any of this?"

"Yes, sir. I understand the urgency and we'll get there as soon as we can. That's the best we can do."

"Understood. Thank you, Albert. Ok, satisfied? We're going to have a look around. You go find that spot to start the tunnel. We're not going to have a spot to shoot for, so we'll want to go about this very carefully."

"Are you guys coming back down tonight?" Lorna asked.

"I don't know yet," Al said. "That's a hell of a climb. I'll let you know after we look around in here a little."

They started into the room. It appeared that they had brought all of the riches of the civilization to this one room for safekeeping, but from what. They knew they were all going to die, so why go to all the trouble. It did explain some of the lack of anything worthwhile in the other rooms in the mountain, but the question remained, why?

As they made their way through the center of the cavern, the extent of the find became more evident. There were massive piles of golden artifacts, along with stacks of intricately woven rugs and bolts of cloth. The air was so dry that they showed very little signs of decay. Some of the cloth was deteriorated around the edges, but the bulk of it was intact.

Further on there were arrays of golden tablets, like the ones that they had seen when they had first entered the cavern. These, however, were arranged like they were part of an altar or something.

"Lorna, can you get Hollie headed this way? We're going to need some of her magic with that little computer of hers."

"I'll see what I can do," Lorna replied. "She's in the mountain somewhere."

"See if you can get her here by morning."

"Lorna, this is Hollie. We just got back in the cruiser. Did I hear my name mentioned?"

"Yes, you did. We need you on the upper level, spoke 270, just west of ring four. How long will it take to get here?"

"God, we're clear on the other side and on the lower level. It'll probably be late tomorrow sometime. Will that be soon enough?"

"If that's the best you can do, yeah, that's soon enough. If you come by the habitat, have Brian and Eve come with you."

"We'll try to get in touch with them. See you tomorrow."

"Al, did you hear that?"

"Yeah, I guess it'll have to do. Do you have a scanning set-up with you?"

"Yeah. I always carry one. Do you want me to bring it up to you?"

"Nice try, but it won't work. Tomorrow will have to be soon enough."

"I had to try. Isn't there any way that I can get up there?"

"Not that I can think of," Al said. "It's not going anywhere."

With that the radio went silent and Al and the others continued their exploration of the cavern. It took almost an hour to reach the far end and as they had expected, there was no other outlet.

"What do you think?" Al asked.

"Hell of a find," Sean said.

"It's every bit of that," Bill said.

"Do you think we can get that winch to work, Sean?"

"I doubt it, but it wouldn't hurt to have a look at it. You thinking what I think you're thinking?"

"Yeah, probably. Plus, I'm not looking forward to that climb back down. If we could get that operational, we might be able to bring her up and along with her, maybe some food and water. I'm also a little concerned about Albert being able to target that small tunnel successfully. I don't want him to come into the main part of the cavern and damage any of this stuff before we have a chance to evaluate it."

"You two keep looking around and I'll go have a look at it," Sean said. "I'll have to examine that cable too. It's been setting in here for a long time."

"Yeah, but it should be able to handle a couple hundred pounds."

"Don't let her hear you say that."

"No, I meant her and the gear. Yeah, she'd latch onto that and never let go of it, wouldn't she?"

"Al, I'll skirt the west edge on my way back," Bill said. "There seem to be paths around the sides too."

"Ok, Bill. I'll go up the other side and we'll meet back at the tunnel on the other end. Sean, go back up the middle and see what you can do with that winch."

"See you there," Sean said and left.

The paths around the edges were only a few feet wide, unlike the one in the center that was almost twenty feet. There were other paths that connected the sides to the center also. It looked like everything was stacked in categories. They didn't make any sense to Al, but it appeared that way. Things that looked alike were all neatly stacked together, until they got close to the tunnel where they had come in. There they were strewn, helter-skelter and all jumbled together.

By the time Al met up with Bill at the other end, Sean was putting the winch back together.

"What's the verdict?" Al asked.

"There's nothing wrong with it, that I can find. I've traced these wires back into the cavern, but they go under a pile of whatever that stuff is, and I lost it."

"Have you tried to get it to work?"

"Well, no, but God, it's been sitting here for thousands of years. Do you actually think it might work?"

"All the vehicles did."

"Good point. Here goes," Sean said, moving one of the levers on top of the winch.

"Well, that isn't the one," Al said when nothing happened.

"Give me a minute."

After trying several combinations of levers Sean started feeling around under what appeared to be the drive motor.

"There's something here, like a reset button. There, I got it to stay in. Let's try this again."

The end of the cable that had been discarded near the edge of the shaft to the bottom slithered toward them.

"Cool, can you get it to go the other way?" Al asked.

"Maybe. Let me give it a try. Bill, go put a little strain on that end of the cable."

When Bill was in place, Sean moved a different lever and the cable spooled out. The end of the cable was badly frayed, but the part that had been on the spool of the winch looked to be in good shape.

"What do you think?" Al asked again.

"I think we have transportation. I'll have to do some work with the end so we can tie onto it, but I think we're in business."

"Is there enough cable to reach the bottom?"

"We won't know that until we let it out and see."

"Do something with that end first. I don't want to get anyone's hopes up until we know there's something to cheer about."

It took Sean only ten minutes to tie the end of the cable into a braded molly loop. He attached a short piece of rope to that and then went into the cavern and brought back one of the golden tablets to use to weight the end of the cable. After it was tied in place he stood up and shrugged his shoulders.

"Let's give it a try," he said.

"Lorna, this is Al."

"Yeah, I know who it is. What do you want?"

"A little testy, aren't we. Clear the bottom of the shaft. We're going to try something, and I don't want to drop anything on anyone."

"What are you up to now?"

"Just get everyone out from under the shaft."

"Ok, give us a minute. We're down the tunnel a ways."

After several minutes she called all clear.

"Here it comes," Al said. "If this works, I may let you go for a ride."

"What the hell are you doing?"

"Go to the eastern edge of the shaft and look up. There's a winch up here and Sean got it to work. We have a weight on the cable and are sending it down."

The cable snaked off of the drum and disappeared over the edge. It took almost thirty minutes to reach the end.

"Lorna, that's all the cable we have. Where is it down there?"

"About thirty feet off the ground. We can reach it with forklift."

"Get Willie to get into position. I want to test the cable with a heavier weight before I let you try to come up."

"How heavy is the weight that's on it?"

"Maybe eighty pounds."

"Ok, let me find something to put on with it. Just hang on for a minute."

* * *

Lorna ran to her cruiser and got the climbing gear that was stowed there and climbed into a harness.

"Britt, give me a hand getting into this thing."

214

"He's going to be pissed," Brittany said.

"Yeah, but I'll already be up there."

"Get Johnny to help get that weight off the end of it. I'll just hang there and let them pull it up."

"Al and Sean both are going to kick your ass; you know that, don't you?"

"They're both afraid of me. They'll yell a little and all will be forgiven."

"Al, take it up. I have a heavier weight attached," Lorna said after she was attached to the end of the cable.

"Ok, stand back," Al said.

The cable started up and lifted her off the platform. She shut her eyes as she ascended into the shaft. She started to bump her way up the side and was finally able to get her feet against the wall and walked up the side.

"Lorna, that seems to be alright," Al said. "How much weight do you have on it?"

"You know it's not polite to ask a lady her weight."

"What! Are you the weight?"

"Yeah. Keep it going to the top. I'm just getting the hang of this."

"Damn you, woman."

"Shut up and pull me on up. You can bitch at me when I'm not hanging five hundred feet off the ground."

When she finally reached the top Al and Sean were there to meet her. They stopped the winch just as she approached the lip of the shaft.

"I have a notion to leave you hanging there for a while," Al said.

"Yeah, but you won't. Come on; help me get on up there."

"Up easy, Bill," Al called. "Grab hold of the rim, and we'll pull your dumb ass on up."

"I knew I'd have to endure some verbal abuse for this, just figure out when enough is enough," she grunted out as they hoisted her over the edge. "Now, show me what you found."

"This way, your majesty," Al said.

"That's better."

"I meant it sarcastically."

"I know, but at least it shows you know who the boss around here is."

"Yeah, right. Come on; let's go before I'm tempted to throw your ass back down the shaft."

Al led the way, and they entered the cavern a few minutes later.

"Holy cow!" Lorna said, staring in disbelief.

"Is that all you have to say?"

"Yeah, for now. Wow!"

CHAPTER FOURTEEN

Lorna stood there looking at the massive amount of riches that they had just discovered, still not believing what she saw. The light of the mid-afternoon sun that cascaded through the crystal structure in the center of the cavern accented the sparkle that lay before her.

"Well, say something," Sean said.

"I'm speechless."

"That's a first," Al said.

"Why would they bring it all up here?" she finally said. "What were they trying to protect it from? Damn it, just more questions."

"It's like why they assembled all their vehicles in the rooms just outside the garden in Pavonis Mons?" Al said. "These were a very tidy race of people, I think."

"It has to be more than that. This place is almost as good as a vault. They were protecting it from someone, or something, but what?"

"Didn't you say that they had, like clans, or something?" Sean asked.

"Yeah, but I'd have thought that after they were forced underground that that kind of thing would have diminished, if not disappeared all together. The ancient tribes of the Middle East and other areas of the world were that way too, but they never faced the catastrophic changes that these people faced. They made war on each other and would have done something like this to protect their riches, but they didn't have the technology available to them."

"Well, I know where you'll be for the next hundred years," Al said. "This is going to put a crimp in your cruising."

"Yeah, for a while, but maybe not that long. Hollie's on the way and I'll get hold of Eve and have her come up here too. They can handle this without me, that is after we figure out what we actually have here."

"Have you called Eve yet?" Al asked.

"No, Hollie was going to get in touch with her."

"You might want to try. She'll want to see this too."

"Yeah, and Mike too. Eve, are you close to a radio?"

"Yes, mother, what's up?"

"Where are you?"

"In the habitat on the lower level. Do you need something?"

"Yeah, I need you and Brian to come to the upper level. Tunnel 270, just west of ring four. When can you get up here?"

"Brian's on the other side for a couple days. I guess I could steal a cruiser and be up there this evening. What's the mystery?"

"Just the largest artifact find in the history of two worlds, that's all."

"Oh, is that all. I'll be right there."

"Albert, what's your ETA back at the shaft," Al called.

"It'll be late tonight. Maybe by 2400, if we push it."

"Do the best you can. Joe, where are you?"

"North and east of you. We've been helping with the mapping."

"Well, map your way over to our location. I need a pro to run the miner for a day."

"That's 270 and ring four, right?"

"Right. What's your ETA?"

"Before dark I would imagine. We're only a few hours from there."

"Good, Jim can't get here until late tomorrow, so you're elected."

"On our way. We made the outer ring a couple hours ago and have been headed back toward the center for over an hour. See you for dinner."

"See you then. Mike, this is Al."

"Al, I'm in transit back to Pavonis, from the hub. What do you need?"

"Have you been monitoring any of our conversations this afternoon?"

"No, I've been on another channel. What's up?"

"When you get a chance, you might want to wander over to Arsia Mons and get with us. Lorna has done it again."

"Oh God, what's this one going to cost me?"

"Actually, I think it might pay for rebuilding, and even expanding the hub."

"That couldn't be all bad. I'll get with you when I can get away. Can you tell me what you found this time?"

"A large stash of golden artifacts. Very large."

"Is it accessible?"

"It will be by tomorrow sometime. Once we get a handle on it, maybe we should put a lock on this one."

"Use your own judgment. I'll try to get over there in a couple days."

"Ok, one of us will be here. Al out."

"Al, this is Eve."

"Go ahead"

"I just stole a cruiser from some of Albert's guys. They didn't seem too happy about it, but I didn't give them much choice. I'll be there as fast as I can."

"Do you have any idea when Brian will be back?"

"He said maybe two or three days, but he wasn't sure. I'm sure he's monitoring this frequency if he's near a radio. You could try him."

"Ok, get on up here. If you get here after dark, you'll have to wait until tomorrow to see it. I'll explain everything when you get here."

"See you soon."

"Brian, this is Al."

"Go ahead."

"How soon can you get back over here?"

"Day after tomorrow, why?"

"I need you here as fast as you can get back. If that has to wait for a day or two, then it has to wait."

"My guys can probably finish it up. Carlos is here. He can take over. The only thing left to work out is how to power the fans. We've been talking it over and may have that figured out, but I'll need a rover that can be left here. The cruiser idea didn't work out. Just not enough power."

"I'll arrange that for you. Tie it up and head this way."

"Ok, I'll be there late tonight or sometime in the morning. Did I understand that Eve was going to be there too?"

"She's on the way up now. I want as many of our original group here as I can get. See you when you get here."

"That sounds like you've touched all the bases," Lorna said. "Are you going to show me around, or do I have to find my way on my own?"

"This way," Sean said.

They wandered through the mass of artifacts, slowly but deliberately. Al and Sean steered her in the general direction of the tablets that were arranged like an altar. Several times she was sidetracked by a trip down one of the side paths, but never lingered too long.

"This is the most significant looking thing we've seen in here," Al said when they finally reached the altar.

"It almost looks like it's a place that they worshiped."

"That's what we thought too," Sean said. "Any ideas what it might be?"

"No, but it looks like the place to start. I didn't bring up the computer and all the gear when I came so I'll have to wait to scan this stuff in until tomorrow."

"I'm going to have to go back down," Al said. "Someone will have to stay up here to run the wench though. Any volunteers?"

"We'll stay," Sean said. "Maybe you could send us up something to eat. I'm starting to get a little hungry."

"I think that can be arranged. Do you want to lower us back down?"

"You take care of that, Sean," Lorna said. "I want to look some more."

"Ok. Al, we'll need lights and such too."

"I know, and tea. Lower me back down and I'll gather it up and send it back up. Bill can help get it up and then you can send him down."

"Brittany's still down there," Lorna said. "Give her a call and have her gather it up."

"Ok. Brittany, this is Al,"

"Are you alright?" Brittany asked.

"Yeah, we're fine. Can you gather up food and tea for two? Sean and Lorna are going to be spending the night up here. I'll be down shortly to send it up."

"I'll see what I can find."

* * *

Al tested the line and took up the slack in the cable. Sean let out enough slack to get him poised on the edge, and then paused.

"Any last words?" Sean asked.

"Yeah. Don't drop me. Lower away."

Al eased himself over the edge and walked backwards down the wall of the shaft. It was a slow descent, but it was much easier than the climb they had made to get up there. As he approached the bottom of the shaft, he called Sean on the radio.

"Ok, easy does it. I'm about to run out of places to put my feet."

The pace slowed and there was a jerk in the cable.

"Are you ok?" Bill called.

"Yeah, lower me on down. Bill, watch that last step. It could get you hurt."

221

When Al reached the platform, he regained his feet and unhooked his harness. Brittany was there with a large bundle.

"What all do you have in there?" Al asked.

"Just the essentials. Bedding, lights, food, tea, and toilet paper."

"That should get them through the night. Let's tie it on."

They watched it ascend until it was well up into the shaft and then Al signaled to Willie to lower them to the ground. From off to one side, they watched it go on up until it was hard to see it.

"Willie, Bill will be coming down in a few minutes," Al said. "Can you catch him?"

"No sweat."

"Britt, did you go with Lorna to find a place to start the tunnel?"

"Yeah. It's back in the edge of ring four. Do you want to have a look?"

"I need to know exactly how far it is. Can you get that information on the cruiser nav system?"

"Sure, within a few feet. Is that close enough?"

"That will be fine. Let's go have a look."

A few minutes later they pulled around the corner and stopped in ring four. They got out and walked to the place Lorna had marked.

"This is where she thought we should start," Brittany said.

"Yeah, that should do it. Did you look in these doors?"

"We went through them to see if we needed to move anything, but they're pretty well empty. They go back about a hundred feet and stop. She said we could just go back that far and then start up."

"How far was it to here from the shaft?"

"Four and a quarter miles. That's 22440 feet. Is that close enough?"

"Yeah, I think so. Let's go back and set up camp. You might as well hang around until we get in there. You'd like to have a look, wouldn't you?"

"Of course. I have trouble keeping up with you two."

"No, you've made such monumental contributions to the work

we're doing here that no one can ever repay you," Al said, putting his arm around her shoulder. "Do you realize that without your work on the cruisers, most of our people on this planet would be dead right now?"

"Well, no—I never really thought about it in those terms. We just wanted to try some of our ideas, that's all. If you hadn't backed us, we couldn't have done it."

"You are way too modest. I envy you and Patty. The two of you have written your own ticket with what you've accomplished here. To have conquered two worlds at such a young age, yes, I envy you."

"Bull, we just did our jobs."

"That's all any of us have been doing, but you excelled at yours. That's the difference between you and most of the others. They are just in it for the money. While that's a factor for all of us, it isn't the thing that drives some of us. The work is important to us. We believe in what we're doing and do everything we can to make it happen."

"Ok, Dad. Can we go now?"

"Yeah," Al said and laughed all the way back to the cruiser. "I just wanted you to know how much I appreciate you two."

"Thanks. Coming from you that's high praise."

Bill was just coming down out of the shaft when they drove up. They sat and watched as he flopped around and finally regained his poise as he landed on the platform.

"That's a hell of a ride on this end," he said as he stepped off of the platform.

"I told you to watch your step. Did it bang you up?"

"No, nothing but my pride. That must have looked funny."

"As a matter of fact, it did."

"What now?"

"A little math homework is in order. Let's deploy the habitats and set up camp. It'll be dark in a couple hours. We might want to get a little rest before Albert gets here too. Lorna is going to want us up there as soon as we can cut the tunnel. What do you estimate is the height to the top of the shaft?"

"Maybe two thousand feet, not much more than that," Bill said.

"If we miss it, I want to be high. We can always back up and cut it down some until we find the tunnel into the cavern."

"I see what you mean," Bill said. "I can help Joe with the tunnel if you can navigate for us."

"It shouldn't take more than a few hours to do the actual tunneling. How about getting an early start in the morning?"

"Sounds good to me."

"Ok, let's set up camp."

* * *

As the light faded for the day, the others started to arrive. Joe and Sharon were the first to show up, with Eve arriving just after dark. They arranged the cruisers in a circle just west of the shaft that led up to the cavern. Al and Bill were busy planning the tunnel.

"By falling all the way back to ring four we can maintain a gentle slope," Al said, drawing his plan out on a piece of paper. "I want to intersect the tunnel into the cavern here, between the winch and the opening to the cavern itself. I think we can do that by maintaining an interval of fifty yards off the line of this tunnel that we're in. That should bring us in about halfway between the two."

"Do you have any way of measuring the distance to the top of the shaft?" Joe asked.

"No, not really. We're just estimating it at two thousand feet."

"There's no way to do it with the cruiser?"

"I might be able to give you a closer idea," Brittany said. "I may be able to focus some of the upper sensors and maybe even get a map of it. Would that help?"

"It would make all the difference in the world," Al said. "See what you can do. In the meantime, we'll plan it for the two thousand feet."

"Eve, can you give Johnny and me a hand?"

"Sure. What can I do?"

"Let's use your cruiser. The others are already set up for the night."

"Ok, I'll get it and move it under the shaft."

"Joe, how long do you think it'll take to run just over four and a half miles?" Al asked.

"If we keep the size to a bare minimum, less than three hours. We just need it big enough to drive up, right?"

"For now, yes. We'll probably want to increase the size later on, but for now just get us up there."

"First light is just after six; I can be on the move then. Is that soon enough? We could start earlier."

"No, that should be fine. Lorna has enough tea to last until then. I'm going to go check on Brittany. You guys calculate the angle you'll need to connect."

"Eve, try that," Al heard Brittany say as he walked up behind her.

"Any luck?" he asked.

"Shit, Boss, you scared the hell out of me. Maybe we should put a bell on you, or something."

"Sorry, you were concentrating on what you were doing, and I didn't want to interrupt."

"I've realigned several of the sensors and we're just getting ready to try it. Any luck, Eve?"

"I think so. Move the center one a little, there. I think it's 2100 feet. We have a decent outline of the sides of the shaft, plus it even shows the tunnel that takes off to the west."

"Good going, ladies. We'll use this cruiser to do the navigating. Now, let's all go get a bite to eat."

"Al, this is Lorna."

"Yes, what can we do for you?"

"Just checking in before we sack out."

"Mom, you guys be good up there," Eve said.

"Hi, Eve. When did you get here?"

"A couple hours ago. We'll be up to see you in the morning, about nine, or so."

"Wait until you see this place. You're not going to believe it."

"So I've heard. I can hardly wait."

"Well, we're going to turn out the lights and get some sleep. Just yell if you need us."

"Lorna, where are you bedding down?" Al asked.

"By that altar looking thing. There's a big area for us to set up in."

"Stay in the cavern in the morning. We'll come in close to the opening."

"Don't worry; we have plenty to look at. Good night."

"Good night."

"Al, this is Albert."

"Go ahead."

"Where do you want the miner?"

"Intersection of ring four and tunnel 270. Just park it there and we'll start the tunneling at first light."

"That's just east of where you are now, right?"

"The first intersection east. See you in the morning."

"Not too early. It's going to be late when we get there."

"Sleep in. We'll get things going."

* * *

Al, Bill, and Joe were up early the next morning. Eve had decided to sleep in Lorna's cruiser so she could enjoy sleeping in a little. They took Eve's cruiser and went to where the miner was parked. Albert and his crew were nowhere to be seen. Joe and Bill positioned the miner and started the cut.

It was different, cutting through the rooms of what used to be a home, but that was where they needed to go. Once they had cleared the back wall, they changed the focus and started up. It was a very gradual slope and they had decided to run the tunnel fifteen feet wide and twenty feet high. The arched roof took shape, and they started up.

"That's close to the angle we're looking for," Al said once he was able to get the cruiser all the way into the tunnel. "Go on up with what you have. We can adjust it when we get closer to the other end."

"Albert and his guys must have gone off a ways, so we wouldn't wake them up," Bill said.

"Yeah, I don't blame them. It had to be late when they got up here."

They climbed steadily for an hour and a half before the radio crackled to life again.

"Al, where are you?" Brittany called.

"We're in the new tunnel. Good morning."

"Can I help?"

"We're good for now. We're just over halfway. Give us another hour and come on up."

"Ok, we'll see you then."

* * *

"Joe, if I'm reading this thing right, we should be about the right elevation. Start to level out," Al said at 0830.

"You got it, Boss. How far till we intersect?"

"Maybe two hundred yards, more or less. I don't have an exact target for us to shoot at. Just keep going until I say to stop, or you cut into the tunnel. Lorna, are you up."

"Yeah, of course. Where are you?"

"Knocking at your door. Stay out of the tunnel to the winch. That's what we're shooting for."

"No problem. We're close to the other end of the cavern. Come on in, the door's not locked. Eve, are you up yet?"

"Lorna, this is Brittany, she hasn't surfaced yet."

"Well, get her ass up and tell her to bring that computer and all of the scanning equipment out of my cruiser up to me."

"She's not going to like that much."

"I don't really care. She has work to do."

"We'll be up soon. Brittany out."

"Oh, shit. Al, we just clipped the top of the tunnel," Joe said.

"I'll back up and you can come back and cut it down until you get to where we want to be," Al said. "Come on back. When you get to the tunnel widen the focus so we can have a place to park and turn around. Go on past a couple hundred feet.”

“How high was that tunnel?” Joe asked.

“Twelve to fourteen feet,” Al said.

“Ok, that should be far enough to drop down that much. Here we go again.”

As the miner moved forward it nosed down, just slightly, and then went on. Only moments later Joe crossed the tunnel and opened the focus and enlarged the size of the hole he was cutting. Al stopped just past the tunnel and got out. Joe cut a large room and pulled off to one corner and parked.

“So, where’s all this treasure stuff?” Joe said when he got out.

“This way,” Al said. “Brittany, are you guys on the way up?”

“We’re in the new tunnel, Al. We’ll be right there. There are two cruisers of us. Is there room to park?”

“Joe made a nice big room for us to use. We’ll wait for you here.”

When they arrived, Al led the way down the small tunnel, and then just stepped to one side and let them all file in. The look of astonishment on their faces was priceless.

“Wow!” Brittany said.

“You can say that again,” Eve said.

“Ok, Wow!”

“Joe, honey, this is fantastic,” Sharon said.

“Yeah, it looks like you have plenty more to catalog. I know where I’ll have to go to see you now. It’s simply awesome.”

“Don’t just stand there, come on in,” Lorna called from the center of the cavern.

“Spread out and look around,” Al said.

They all wandered into the cavern, lightly brushing different articles as they went. Al hesitated and just watched them. Eve moved with a little more purpose than the others.

* * *

"Mom, what have you come up with?" she asked when she found Lorna.

"Not much. There's so much of it, it's hard to figure out where to start. I've just been looking around, trying to categorize it in my mind. Did you bring the computer?"

"It's in the cruiser. I wanted to have a look before I started dragging everything out. When is Hollie due to get here?"

"Probably not until late this afternoon or this evening. They were clear on the other side of the mountain when I talked to her yesterday."

"She's made several changes to the scanning program that may be helpful in deciphering all of this. I worked with it a little at the library, but don't really understand that computer stuff that well."

"Did you bring my cruiser up here?"

"Yeah, it's in the room that Joe made for us to park in. I wonder if they could connect us with the cavern. We're going to need to set up a base here. I guess we'll have to use a couple of cruisers for now. There aren't any more habitats that I know of."

"Look, most of this stuff is nothing more than expensive trinkets," Lorna said. "It's like locking up your good silver so the burglars won't get it if they break in. I'm more interested in the reason behind putting all this stuff up here. Who or what were they hiding it from?"

"That's a good question. Maybe the answer is here someplace."

"Well, if it is, then it's probably here. This is the only place in the whole cavern that has any kind of organization to it. It's arranged like an altar or something. Everything else is just stacked in here."

"Then this is the place to start," Eve said. "I'd like to look around for a while before we get down to it."

"Ok, I'll go out and get the computer and scanning equipment."

CHAPTER FIFTEEN

Eve stood looking at the altar, examining the inscriptions that cascaded from the upper tier. They seemed to form a pattern that seemed vaguely familiar. Most of the symbols were somewhat the same as the ones they had worked with at the mine. They still didn't mean anything to her.

"What do you think?" Lorna asked when she returned.

"Most of the symbols look a lot like the ones at the mine, but there some subtle differences that I can't explain," Eve said. "It's like the difference between a New York accent and one from Alabama or something. They probably mean the same thing, but the way they're presented seems all wrong. God, I wish we could learn to read this shit."

"Well, scan them and we'll let the computer chew on them for a while. I'm still trying to figure out why they went to all the trouble to move all this stuff up here."

"Yeah, there doesn't seem to be any real reason for it."

* * *

As the darkness started to descend in the cavern, Lorna and Eve were still huddled over the computer waiting for it to come up with a translation.

"I give up for now," Eve said. "Maybe Hollie can make something out of this when she gets here."

"Yeah, let's go see what everyone is up to. I need to stretch my legs a little."

"Ladies, come up with anything?" Al asked when they got back to the cruisers.

"Not really," Lorna said. "We'll let Hollie have a go at it when she gets here."

"I talked to them a few minutes ago. They're still a couple hours away. I suggest that we go back down to the intersection and set up camp and wait for them. We've done about all we can here. The light's almost gone now."

"Yeah, and I'm pooped," Lorna said. "Sleeping on the rock up here isn't the best night's sleep I've had lately."

"But it's not as bad as when you were locked in the gate room," Bill said. "You had a hell of a time getting any sleep that night."

"God, don't remind me of that. I still swear that place was just a little haunted. Nothing you could see, but I could feel a presence in there. It was the strongest just as I was starting to fall asleep."

"At least they were friendly spirits," Eve said. "What's for dinner?"

"It's your turn to cook," Brian said.

"Ok, cereal it is."

"God, not again."

"Come on guys, let's relocate this party and I'll come up with something," Lorna said.

* * *

At 0700 the next morning the radio startled them.

"Al, this is Mike. Where the hell are all of you?"

"Upper level in Arsia. Why, what's up?"

"I was thinking about heading over there today, but I'm not sure where to go."

"You can use the new tunnel. It's complete and you can also send the transports this way to start moving equipment."

"Yeah, they're on the way now. I talked to Brian yesterday and he said they could get through. I sent him my rover to use to power the fans. Wait a minute; I have a priority call on another channel."

It was several minutes before he came back on the radio.

"Sorry, I'm going to have to go back to the hub," Mike said finally. "Alistair has a problem that requires my attention. I guess the trip over there will have to wait for a few days."

"That's too bad. You'd like what we found this time. Is there anything we can do to help you with your problem?"

"No, not really. He's trying to get the space port operational and there are several things that I need to do. With a little luck we'll be able to resume receiving supplies in a few days; providing the weather cooperates."

"What does it look like out there now?"

"The wind is still up over a hundred miles an hour, but we've received shipments in winds as high as one-forty. There's a problem with the landing bay though, so it's still not a sure thing."

"Let us know if there's anything we can do."

"You just keep doing what you do best. Mike out."

"You heard the man," Al said, turning to the group who was just finishing breakfast.

"I'll get the information that Lorna and Eve scanned yesterday and see if I can get anything out of it," Hollie said. "I'll need a cruiser that has a lot of storage on the computer. Mine is ready to be downloaded. We didn't take the time to do it on the way up yesterday."

"You can use that one over there," Eve said, indicating the one she'd brought up. "It's almost empty."

"Think you can get anything out of it?" Al asked.

"Hell, I don't even have a clue what they scanned. How can I tell if I can get anything out of it?"

"Well, maybe you'd better go have a look before you get started," Lorna said. "Gentlemen, we're going to go up and have a quick look around. We'll be back in a couple hours."

"That sounds reasonable," Al said. "Brittany, have you checked in with any of the others today?"

"No, but I talked to several of them last night. They seem to be doing ok."

"I guess you could go back out now if you want to."

"Yeah, I've done about all I can here. I sure don't want to miss anything important though."

"You won't be far away. If there's anything that you can help with, I'll call."

"Ok, Boss. Hear that, Johnny? It's time to get back out and see what we can find."

"Yes, Ma'am," Johnny said.

"I see you have him trained," Lorna said.

"Not yet, but I'm gaining on it," Brittany said.

"You kids be careful," Al said."

"Always. Call if you need any help with anything. See you later."

As they left, Lorna gathered up the others and started for the cavern above them. Al just watched as they all left.

"What a crew," he said finally.

"Yeah, a hell of a crew," Bill said.

* * *

At 1730 that afternoon, Mike pulled into the cavern below the hub. Alistair was waiting for him at the makeshift office that had been put together earlier. It was still two hours until dark.

"Have any luck today?" Mike asked as he got out of the rover that he'd commandeered.

"Some," Alistair said. "The landing platform is stable and about as good as we're going to get it. The material handling equipment is coming online and the day after tomorrow we should be ready to go. The com equipment is better, but still has problems. We still can't get any farther than the ships in orbit."

"Will they be ready to deliver the supplies as soon as we're ready for them?"

"Oh, yeah. They're ready now. Most of them are ready to turn around and go back without even landing."

"Let's go have a look. What about the ore handling equipment? Will it be ready?"

"It's up now. We may have a few bugs to work out, but that shouldn't be that big of a deal. I'm going to need more people when we start receiving the supplies."

"You'll have them. Can we move them back into the hub?"

"Yeah, that's not a problem. We've been staying inside for a couple days now. The food stores are better inside, and I think in a couple weeks we'll be back on a somewhat more normal routine. What about the people that lived in the two domes, that weren't in there when they blew? What do we do with them?"

"I'll probably leave some of them inside for now. Al could use the help and their accommodations will be better at Pavonis than they will be out here. I think the last head count that I had of those people was eleven hundred. As it turns out our losses weren't quite as bad as we'd thought. The best number I have now is sixteen hundred. We found a bunch of people that we'd though were lost."

"The Captain of the Atlanta is getting pretty antsy about sitting in orbit. I've tried to keep in touch with all the ships to let them know what's going on, but he's being an ass. I was hopping you could talk to him."

"What's his position as far as unloading?"

"He's number seven in line. There are four behind him."

"Ok, I'll have a chat with him when we get to the landing platform."

Thirty minutes later they arrived at the landing platform. The crews were still milling around getting things finished.

"Get the Atlanta on the radio for me." Mike told the operator.

"He's not available," the operator said a few minutes later.

"Let me have that," Mike snapped. "Atlanta, this is Mike Peterson. Get the Captain on the radio, now!"

"Sorry, but the captain left word that he wasn't to be disturbed," the crewman on the Atlanta said.

"You have five minutes to get him on the horn. Do you understand me? He's about to blow all of your futures. This is my planet and he'd better get available, understand?"

"Yes, Sir."

Ten minutes later the radio came back to life.

"What the hell is the meaning of getting me out of bed?" the captain yelled into the radio.

"Captain, this is Mike Peterson. Do you know who I am?"

"No, and I don't give a flying—."

"Captain, you just got moved to the back of the line for unloading. Would you like to try not getting paid for your trip at all?"

"You can't do that!"

"Yes, I can. Now calm down and I might reconsider and let you get half pay. Otherwise, you can walk home."

"Just who the hell do you think you are?"

"I run this planet. I'm God here, understand. You contact your boss back on Earth and he'll confirm what I'm telling you. Look you son-of-a-bitch, I've had it with you. You'll also be the morgue ship to take the bodies of the people that have been killed here. There are a lot of them. Instead of being an ass, maybe you should start the preparations for receiving them and make sure you have the facilities ready. If there's any problem and my people aren't taken care of, you'll never fly again.

"If you decide to break orbit and leave, I'll have you shot. Now, do you have any more problems that we can work out?"

"Go to hell!"

"He cut me off," Mike said. "Get the Atlanta back."

"Atlanta here," a meek voice said a moment later.

"Is the Captain still there?" Mike asked.

"No, Sir. He stormed out of here."

"Get me the XO"

"Executive Officer Saunders here, sir," came the call a few minutes later.

"Saunders, you've just been promoted to Captain," Mike said.

"I don't understand. By what authority?"

"Mine. I want you to give me an hour and then contact your company. By then I'll have made the necessary contacts. As of 1830, this date, you are the Captain of the Atlanta. Can you handle the job?"

"Yes, yes sir; I can handle the job. What about Captain Kowalski?"

"Put him in the brig until we can make the arrangements to have him brought down to the surface. I think he'll be spending a few months with us. Now, son, I don't expect you to do much until you have a chance to verify what I'm telling you, but upon conformation you'd better deal with him as I've prescribed or I'll fire you too, understand?"

"Yes sir."

"You'll be getting a call from your company in just over an hour. It'll take that long for me to get things rolling. Mars out! Now get me Captain Sorensen."

"Mike, good to hear from you," Captain Sorensen said.

"Captain, I need you to route a message to your company office. Priority one."

"Sure, what's the problem?"

When Mike had finished dictating the message Sorensen came back on the radio.

"Damn, kind of stepped on it, didn't he?"

"Yeah, get that off right now and have the response sent to me and to Captain Saunders aboard the Atlanta as soon as possible."

"Consider it gone. Mind if I add a footnote to it?"

"What kind of note?"

"That he was entirely in the wrong and deserves what he's getting."

"No, just get it on the way. I'll be here waiting for the response."

"Yes sir."

"This will get around the fleet in a matter of minutes," Alistair said. "That should take care of any further problems."

"I think that's a fair bet."

* * *

It was almost 2030 when the message was received from the shipping company headquarters. Mike read it and had them contact the Atlanta again.

"Captain Saunders."

"Did you receive the conformation?" Mike asked.

"Yes sir. Captain Kowalski is being escorted to the brig as we speak."

"I haven't made up my mind what I'm going to do to him yet, so just keep him on ice for now. I'll want him transported down to the surface when it's your turn to unload. Is that clear?"

"Perfectly clear, sir. Is there anything else that I can do for you?"

"No, but when it's your turn I'll want to talk to you personally."

"I understand, sir."

"You're back to number seven, but it'll probably be a couple weeks before we can get to you. Is there any problem there?"

"No, sir."

"Good. That's all for now. Mars out."

"Would you like to sleep in your own bed tonight?" Alistair asked.

"God that would be wonderful."

* * *

"Al, this stuff doesn't make any sense," Hollie said late that night.

"What do you mean?"

"Well, it says something about the lowland clan making raids on their complex. It says something like they came here from the northwest to rob them of their valuables."

"Northwest?"

"I think that's what it says. There's also something about the far clan coming to their aid and the near clan helping too."

"Far clan, near clan?"

"Yeah, well, I think that's what it says. At least that's the way I read it. Could the near clan be Pavonis and maybe the far clan, what, Ascraeus Mons? Northwest is maybe Olympus Mons?"

"That's a stretch," Lorna said.

"Hey, I'm the skeptic here," Al said.

"Yeah, but come on."

"This may be enough for you to get approval to try to get to the other two volcanoes." Al said.

"There are other names for the clans here too, but I can't make them out," Hollie said. "Is Olympus lower in elevation than we are here?"

"Yeah, quite a bit," Al said. "If there was a significant amount of surface water here now, the base of Olympus would be almost at sea level."

"Well, could that be considered the lowlands?" Hollie asked.

"I guess it could," Lorna said. "I just have a little trouble with this translation. There has to be more, or you've translated it wrong."

"You're welcome to see if you can come up with something else. This is the best I can do. I washed it through the computer three times and came out with a variation of the same thing each time."

"I just think there has to be more than that," Lorna said.

"I know, but the information that you scanned, that's what I came up with. Is there anything else in there that you haven't scanned yet?"

"Probably. We haven't looked the whole thing over. That's what I want you and Eve to do for the next few days."

"Ok. I guess it doesn't matter where we are; the job doesn't change much."

"No, just the questions change and there get to be more of them."

"Brian, now that you've joined us, I'd like you to figure out a way to lock up this place," Al said. "It's the only place that we've found that really could be spent. I don't think there's any likelihood that that will happen, but let's just remove any temptation."

"That shouldn't be that big a problem," Brian said. "Just a set of blast doors in the tunnel leading up there should do it."

"Yeah, but I want to have it coded so that only a few of us can open it. Also, the tunnel to the shaft; I want that sealed too."

"We won't need it anymore, will we?"

"No, I don't think so. You can just wall it off."

"This'll take a couple days. I'll have to round up the materials for the job."

"No hurry," Al said. "I'll take Bill back to the other side and check on things over there. Mike had to go back out to the hub last night. There may be a few things over in Pavonis that we'll need to look after."

"I'm going to stick with Eve and Hollie for another day," Lorna said. "There may be something I can add to the mix."

"Joe, you and Sharon can go back out tomorrow if you want," Al said. "I don't think they're going to require Sharon's services here for a while."

"No, we can get by for a while," Eve said. "We have to figure out what we have before it'll do us much good to process it."

"I'll get with Brittany in the morning and see where we need to go," Sharon said. "All that riding gets old, but we enjoy the time alone."

* * *

The following morning, they all split up and went their own ways. Al and Bill left for the upper garden in Pavonis Mons and arrived there late in the afternoon.

"Al this is Mike," came the radio call just before dark.

"Go ahead," Al said.

"Where are you now?"

"Back in Pavonis. Do you need anything?"

"We're going to try to land the first of the supply ships the day after tomorrow. Can you get with the administrative people, Sally in particular, and send out the crews for the space port. I've contacted some of them directly and they're trying to gather up their people, but they may not be able to find them. We need to coordinate this better. Can you help me there?"

"Yeah, I think we can get things lined out for you. Bill's here with me. We'll go see Sally tonight and get things started. She's still up here in the upper garden, isn't she?"

"She should be. That's where I left her."

"Where are you going to be tonight?"

"In my apartment," Mike said. "I slept here last night, and it feels great."

"I guess we need to start mass mobilizations again then."

"Just logistics and maintenance types for now. The others will follow soon, but let's not get too carried away just yet. I still have a lot to do here to get things ready for their return. See if you can also round up the other mine managers and have them head this way. We're going to need to get the mines back up and running as soon as we can."

"We know where most of them are," Bill said. "I'll have to get some of them headed back this way. There are two still over in Arsia."

"Just get on the horn and see what you can come up with. I guess that's probably enough to throw at you for now."

"We'll have a good idea of who, what, and when by morning," Al said. "I'll get back with you then."

"Al, I'll see who I can round up," Bill said after Al hung up the phone.

"Ok. I'll go find Sally and get her started on the rest. Then I'll arrange transportation for as many as we need to send."

"Al, when you don't need me anymore, I need to go check on my mine. I need to know want kind of shape it's in before we try to take the people back over there."

"Yeah, I'd like to make that run with you. Get on the horn and get Albert back over here but leave Alicia over there for now. We know they can't get anything going at her mine until she gets the domes repaired. I have a feeling that most of the mines are going to be in similar shape."

"I hope not, but you're probably right."

"You may have to carry the production load for some of the others for a while. We could probably arrange to ship from your mine through the tunnels. It would complicate the handling on your end, but I think it could be done."

"Let's go see who we can round up."

* * *

"Mike, we've sent over two hundred people your way," Al said when he called the next morning. "Most of them are for the space port, but there are

240

several senior maintenance and production people. They'll be able to evaluate their areas and call for the people they need. We've also alerted a lot of the others to check in regularly to see if they're needed. The word is spreading here that it's almost time to relocate back to wherever they were."

"Good, that's a start," Mike said. "We can get by for a day or two with that, but I'll still need to get all of the supply people soon. When we get the ships started downloading, it's going to be a nonstop process for several weeks."

"Sally is rounding them up now and we'll have them over there tonight sometime. As many as we can at least. I left Alicia over in Arsia. Her domes are shot, and it'll be a while before she can get back into production. Is there any way to do a surface survey of the other mines to check their condition? A rover could probably make the rounds now."

"I have a team headed out today to do that. We should know something by late tonight, or tomorrow sometime. We can cover the ones here without much problem. Can you get to Bill's mine from there?"

"Albert should be here in a couple hours. I'll leave him to coordinate things here and Bill and I will go over and have a look. We can get in through the mine. That's a modification that I think we should make to all the mines as soon as they're operational again. It just makes sense to me."

"I see what you mean. We'll evaluate things as we go. I'm counting on you for input on how to keep from having this problem again."

"We have the infrastructure in place now. All we have to do is refine it a little.

"I'd better go. Have Sally contact me in a couple hours so I can get an update on how she's doing."

"Will do. Talk to you later today. Al out."

* * *

Al and Bill pulled into the main tunnel of Bill's mine just after 1400 that afternoon. They drove the cruiser to the portal and looked out into the outside world for the first time in weeks.

"She's still kicking up pretty good," Bill said.

"Yeah, but it could be a lot worse. Let's get our suits on and see if we can find a couple of those steaks you've been hording over here."

"Sounds good to me."

Thirty minutes later they pulled into the maintenance dome of the mine.

"So far so good," Bill said.

"Looks like it held up ok," Al said as they got out. "Let's go see how the rest of it is."

They walked through the airlock between the domes and inspected the entire facility. It showed some definite wear, but structurally it seemed sound. The air quality wasn't as good as it should be, but the power was still on, and the pressure was holding at the reduced setting that Bill had set it at.

"Damn, it looks like we're ready to go back to work," Bill said.

"Just a little cleanup is all I see. Think you can ship ore in a day or two?"

"I don't see why not. We have all the bins full and all we need is to load the transport. Are you still going to need to steal my guys to train anyone on the miners?"

"No, I think we took care of that with all the tunnels we've driven in the last month or so. We have over three hundred people trained on the miners now, but we still need to train them on how to mine with them. They can all drive a tunnel, but to retain the good stuff may be a little more than some of them can grasp yet."

"We can train some of them here. We have plenty of headings that are loaded with ore. I'm thinking that some of the other mines may not be as lucky as we are here."

"I know we lost two of them. Number six is a total loss for now, and also Alicia's mine, number two. She won't be able to do anything until they get her domes repaired."

"How about that steak we've been looking forward to. Do you know how to cook?"

"I can burn a steak," Al said.

"Well, let's go see what we can find."

CHAPTER SIXTEEN

By mid afternoon the next day the space port was operational. Mike had stayed with the crews that were getting things put back together for almost thirty-six hours.

"Captain Sorensen," Mike called on the radio.

"Go ahead."

"This is Mike Peterson. We're ready to receive your cargo."

"Yes sir. We'll work up the navigation and head that way. Do you have anything for us to take back?"

"We do indeed. We have full loads for eight ships and by the time we get that many unloaded we'll have enough to fill the others. No sense going back empty."

"Yeah, and it doesn't pay very well either. I've been in contact with my home office, and they have dispatched four new ships that weren't supposed to join the rotation for several months, but with the gap that we're going to have in the supply chain they thought it best to send them along now. The first one has been on the way now for two weeks and they'll be spaced out to fill in some of the gap."

"That sounds good. Are you coming down to the surface?"

"I thought I would. I'd like to see for myself what you have going on. That way I can send a better report."

"I'm afraid our accommodations are a little lacking right now. We still have most of our population underground. I think we'll have everything back up to speed in a few months."

"I don't mind roughing it a little. I'll see you in about two hours."

"Contact the rest of the fleet and tell them that if everything goes well, we'll get to them soon."

"I'll do that sir. Orion out."

"Alistair, they'll be along soon. Get your people ready."

"We're as ready as we'll ever be. The space port manager has taken most of the load now, so I'd like to go survey my mine."

"Permission granted, and thanks for all of your hard work. Has the rover come back from the surface survey yet?"

"I haven't heard from them yet. I'm hoping they'll have good news."

"I'd better go check on them. They should have reported in by now."

* * *

Two hours later Captain Sorensen called the spaceport control room as he and his crew descended through the outer atmosphere in the supply landing module.

"Mars base, Orion one here. Descending from two-hundred-mile orbit. Permission to land."

"Permission granted, Captain. We'll receive you in landing bay one."

"Understand landing bay one," Sorensen said.

"Affirmative. Standing by."

"ETA twenty-two minutes."

The captain watched as the red glow caused by the outer atmosphere started to appear on the front of his ship. In the distance he could see the great volcanoes of Mars appear on the horizon, marking the way to the landing spot that he and his crew had waited for weeks to see.

"Ease it down, Commander," Sorensen said. "Let's not keep them waiting any longer than we have to."

"Yes sir," the Commander, said. "Holding on glide path."

The giant hulk of a ship slipped silently toward the Red Planet. It was at one hundred-fifty thousand feet when it passed over Pavonis Mons, descending rapidly. The beacon from the landing pad was visible in the distance, a bright green laser against the red background.

"Forward twenty," the captain said as they approached the platform. "Rate of descent is thirty feet per second. Slow it down a little. That's better. Left three degrees. Hold what you have. Ease us down now. Contact, stop engines. Welcome to Mars."

The ship sat atop the structure and soon began to be drawn down into it. When the elevator stopped, the airlock doors closed. It took the customary ten minutes for the pressure to be equalized and the atmosphere to be exchanged for a breathable one.

"Orion one, clear to disembark," came the all clear from control.

When the Captain led the way out of the hatch Mike Peterson was there to greet him.

"Glad you could make it," Mike said as he reached for the captain's hand.

"Glad you're still here to invite us down. I looked over the conditions of your facility as we came in. It looks like you had a tough time."

"That's the worst storm that anyone has ever seen here," Mike said. "It didn't last as long as some, but it was the most intense."

"Are you sure you'll be able to load all of us?"

"No problem. I've just received word that we'll begin receiving shipments from one of our mines tomorrow and they assure me that they have enough on hand to get us by. We're still evaluating the condition of most of our operations, but we'll get everyone turned around and headed home as quickly as we can."

As the crew of the ship emerged from the hatch, the ground crew was already moving the material handling equipment into place. The giant conveyors were run into the ship and in minutes the cargo containers began to emerge and glide toward their resting places in the receiving area.

"Captain, I know that you're accustomed to having a few days on the ground while you're here," Mike said as they went into the control room. "I'm afraid that you'll have to forego that this time. Our facilities are very primitive, and I need you to start your return voyage as soon as possible."

"Can we manage one night on the ground?" Captain Sorensen asked.

"That we can manage. It'll take us until this time tomorrow to get you reloaded and fueled up. Unfortunately, we have no amenities to offer you. We'll manage to find you a room somewhere, but there isn't anything in the entertainment area that we can offer."

"That's too bad. Where are all your people? This place looks like a ghost town."

"It very nearly was just that. A hand full of my people worked for over a month to get to us here in the hub. If they had failed, we'd all be dead. We lost around sixteen hundred people during the storm. Come on; let me buy you and your crew a drink. I'll tell you about it. God, we're glad to see you."

* * *

"Al to hub control."

"Go ahead Al."

"Can you locate Mike for me?"

"I'll patch you right through," the controller said.

"Al, do you have any news," Mike said when he got the call.

"I'm leaving Bill's mine now to go round up his people. I've had a call in to them and they should be headed this way soon, but I want to make sure. I left Bill savoring a big steak that we found in his freezer and he's going to have everything ready to ship the first load by morning. Do you have any more transports that you can send him? He said he can have enough to fill three more by the time you can get them to him."

"None of the other mines are functional yet. I guess I could get their transports to go pick up a load. Are you sure he can handle the load?"

"None of the others can be made operational?" Al said.

"No. We lost portions of the domes on all of them. That will have to be taken care of before we can ship anything they have. How did his facility fair so much better?"

"We discussed that," Al said. "It looks like the winds may have been absorbed by the chasm or something. That's the only thing we could come up with. He assured me that if I could round up a little extra help that he could get you the material you need to complete this round of shipments to Earth."

"That sounds a little optimistic to me."

"I believe he can do it. We're going to get with the other managers and rotate their people through there and train them on how to mine with the Martian Miners. That way, when they go back to their own mines, they'll have the experience to hit the ground running. We'll manage to keep the other people busy until their facilities are up and running again."

"Good. I'll get right on the transports. It'll take a little time to get them there. You may have to dispatch the people from Pavonis Mons."

"I have Albert rounding them up now. I took the liberty; hope you don't mind."

"No, of course I don't mind. I'm sitting in the bar having a drink with Captain Sorensen of the Orion. He's the first off world face we've seen for a while."

"Tell the good Captain to have one for me. I think my crew is going to be due a vacation when you get things back up to speed."

"And your money is no good on my planet. You tell me when you want to start, and I'll arrange everything."

"You have one for me too," Al said and signed off.

The tunnel ahead was smooth, and Al pushed his cruiser up to full speed and headed north. It appeared that things might actually be getting back to normal. This was indeed a good thing.

* * *

As Al made his way back to Pavonis Mons he was lost in thought. The questions of how to get the planet back to a more normal operation danced through his thoughts. Far off in the distance a set of headlights broke his chain of thoughts.

"Al is that you?"

"Yeah, who's that?"

"Dan and Jeff. We heard the Boss wanted us back at our house, so we hijacked a cruiser and headed out. What's up?"

"Bill's getting things ready to ship your first load of ore. I'm going to be sending several crews and miners that way in the next day or so. I'll also send Slim and his crew over for a week or so. You guys can start training the other crews in how to mine with the machines that they've all been running. You may have to support the planet for a while."

"No sweat. How many crews are you going to send over?" Dan asked.

"At least one from each mine; two if possible. We need to get them up to speed as soon as we can. I'm working on a few ideas that may help our current situation, but don't have them worked out yet. When you get to the mine, get with Bill, and give him a hand."

"That's why we got an early start. The others will be heading over as soon as they get them rounded up."

"You may have to take the first transport load to the hub."

"That's ok. We'll turn it in record time. No long layover this time. What are we going to do for Martian Miners? They're scattered all over the damn planet."

"I've been making a list of where we left them. I hope I can remember where they all are. I'll get several loaded up on a transports and sent as close to you as I can get them. They may have to drop them off at the junction in the tunnels. Can you get them moved to the mine?"

"By the time you can get them sent over, I'm sure we can get that part taken care of."

"I'll try to help from the other end too," Al said as Dan and Jeff sped by in the other direction. "Get on over there and give Bill a hand. Tell him I'm working out the details as I cruise back to Pavonis."

"Will do Boss."

* * *

It was late afternoon when Al pulled up to the habitat in the upper garden in Pavonis Mons. There were several extra people milling around, most of whom Al didn't recognize. They seemed to gravitate toward him as he got out.

"Are you Al?" one of them asked.

"Yes, what can I do for you?"

"Albert said you might be looking for miners to go to Bill's mine and get back to work. Is that true?"

"Yes. I'll be putting together crews from each of the mines. I'm calling a meeting of all the mine managers today to get things started. Where are you from?"

"We're the only survivors of number six. We were at the hub when this thing hit and couldn't get back to the mine. We want to be part of whatever you're doing. We owe it to our friends that all died."

"Go inside and write down your names and what you're qualified to do. I'll get back with you this evening or first thing in the morning. Will that do?"

"Well, it's a start. Look, we all want to get back to work, that's all. Our mine won't be operational for a long time, if ever. We want to tie on with another crew and try to put this thing behind us."

"I understand how you feel. I'll see what I can do for you. How many of you are there?"

"Three miners and four support crew members."

"I think I can help you, but you'll have to give me a little time."

"Thank you. We appreciate your help."

As Al stood by his cruiser, they all turned and walked into the habitat. The five men and two women looked totally whipped. Their spirit seemed to have been ripped from them. But in their eyes, he saw a glimmer of hope, one that needed to be fed.

"Al, when did you get here?" Albert Johnson asked as he walked up.

"Just a minute ago. How's it going, getting the other mine managers rounded up?"

"They're all here except Alicia. She's still over in Arsia Mons. I can have her back here by morning if you need her."

"No, that's alright. We need to get the others together and figure out how we're going to get this planet back on a paying basis."

"They're waiting inside."

"Ok, let's go in and see what we can stir up."

As Al and Albert walked in, the seven people from number six were leaving. Al stopped the one who had been their spokesman earlier.

"Come see me in a couple hours," Al said.

"We won't be far away," he said and left the habitat.

"Who was that?" Albert asked?

"The only survivors of number six. They want to get back to work. Do you know any of them?"

"No, I don't think so."

The other mine managers were sitting at a long table in one corner of the habitat. Al and Albert went and joined them.

"I guess you're wondering why I called all of you together," Al said as he took the seat at the head of the table. "Believe it or not, there is some good news for a change. Mike is at the hub right now, receiving the first shipment from the ships in orbit. He's asked me to coordinate getting things back on a paying basis. Unfortunately, all of your mines have sustained damage to your domes. It looks like you'll be here with us for a while. However, Bill's mine is more or less intact. I need you to gather up two crews of three miners and send them to help Bill. We'll get your people trained on the Martian Miners so they can train the rest of your people when the time comes.

"We'll need to move a lot of stuff around in the next couple days. I have to locate several of the miners and get them shipped to Bill. He doesn't have anything to work with right now."

"Didn't he have one of the miners before this all hit?" Albert asked.

"Yeah, he did, but we pulled it out to help us get to the hub and it was left over there somewhere. I've been working up a list of where we left them, and we may need to go get some of them and get them driven or hauled to his mine. We still have several more here in Pavonis and several over in Arsia Mons. I need you to get some of your people back to your mines and see if they can get to any of your transports and take them to his mine also. He has enough ore on hand to ship four or five loads right now. By the time he has that all shipped he thinks he can have that much more, providing we can get him what he needs to work with."

"How's he going to do that?" Albert asked.

"With the miners. He'll start mining around the clock as soon as we get him the equipment to work with."

"Al, we've all seen what these machines can do, but all they do is burn holes. They eat up everything in front of them."

"Not if you know how to operate them. We've found ways to adjust the lasers, or whatever they are, to take out the rock, but leave the ore. I think that we can get all of your mines up again, churning out massive amounts of ore in a matter of a few weeks. The biggest problem I can see is that we'll have to move all operations underground. The only time we'll see the sun is when we go to the hub. That's going to present a whole new set of problems that you'll have to deal with individually, but I think it can be done. Some of these folks don't adapt to life underground very well. They may not be able to take it.

"Look, all we have to do is move the miners to each mine and open up the tunnels so we can get the transports to each mine. We didn't make the tunnels big enough when we tunneled to the mines to reach everyone because it would have taken too long. Now we have time. I haven't cleared any of this with Mike, but I don't expect that he'll have a problem with it.

"You see what this civilization did in here. Why can't we do something similar? It would minimize the possibility of this ever happening again."

"Ok, we're all old miners," Albert said, seemingly speaking for the others. "Hell, we've spent most of our lives underground up until now. I guess we could manage this. What are we going to do for living quarters? We don't have all the comforts that you do here."

"That would take time," Al said. "In time we can develop towns connected to each mine. Everyone would have the comforts of home, in time. We'll need to tap into the water and power from the complexes. Look, I don't have all the answers yet. You're all managers. Manage! The first thing on the agenda is to get the equipment and personnel that Bill needs. Then we can work on this other stuff. Each of you, send a team to your mines. Evaluate the conditions there and get the transports sent to Bill. I'll go talk to Mike tomorrow and see if this is even feasible. He may not allow any of it. Questions?"

"No, I guess not," Albert said. "Look, Al, we all owe you our lives and that's not a debt that can ever really be paid. I can see from the looks that we'll try anything at this point. It's probably the only way to get some of the mines opened up at all. Alicia's mine was almost completely destroyed. From what I've heard mine isn't much better. I can see how this could work, but the planning is going to take some time."

"Yes, it's going to be a lot of work. I'm open to suggestions."

The room was silent. The faces looked at each other in turn, and then turned back to Al. Almost in unison they all nodded.

"Ok, round up your people and we'll arrange transportation for them. Some may have to go to the hub and on the surface from there. Others may be able to get to the surface from the mines themselves. You know your systems better than I do. Do what you have to, to make it happen. I'll get the machines delivered to Bill so he can get to work. I need two crews of miners from each of you. I also want to include the crew that left here as I came in. They're the only survivors of number six. You can all reach me any time."

With that the meeting broke up. Al watched as they left the habitat; Albert was the only one to linger after the others left.

"Was there something else?" Al asked.

"How is it that you stand so much taller than the rest of us?"

"What the hell is that supposed to mean?"

"The rest of us all run tight ships. Our mines are as productive as yours when you had one. Yet we sit around and do little, if anything, while you save the planet. Not that we don't appreciate it, but, well, I want to grow up to be like you."

"Shit, give me a break. I had resources that none of you had. If you'd had them, you'd been the one to save the day. It's all about being in the right place at the right time."

"Yeah, right. You're still doing it and we do all have the same resources."

"I was a Boy Scout when I was a kid. You know, be prepared."

"Ok, be modest if you want. I'll go round up my troops and see about getting my transport moved over to Bill's mine. I'll have two crews here in an hour to go help Bill in the mine. Are you sending anyone?"

"Yeah, Slim and his crew will be going over for a while to help in the training. I still have to get them back from Arsia Mons, so they won't be able to get over there for a couple days. Maybe that'll give us time to get the rest of this set up."

Albert left and Al just watched him go. The radio was going on several channels in the background. The sounds all running together.

"Al, Lorna's trying to reach you," Smitty said from across the room.

"What's she need?"

"I don't know. She just tried to call a few minutes ago. I told her you were tied up in a meeting."

"Lorna, this is Al. What do you need?"

"Al, where have you been hiding?"

"I've been busy. Do you need something?"

"Just checking on you. Things are about the same over here."

"I need Slim's crew to head this way as soon as they can. Mike has the space port operational and has started to receive the supplies from the ships in orbit. I need to get all the miners rounded up and sent this way too. Load them on transports if we have them available; drive them if we don't. Can you take care of that?"

"Yeah, I think so. Is there anything else?"

"No, I'll handle the rest. I'll have to recall Alicia and Rebecca from your explorations. I need Alicia back over here for now."

"Al, this is Alicia. We've been monitoring your conversation. When do you need us there?"

"Just head this way. I'll get things started from this end. Is your transport accessible?"

"It should be. It was inside the outer dome the last time I saw it. What do you need it for?"

"I'll round up some of your people to get things started. I'll explain everything else when you get back over here."

"Ok. We'll head that way, but we're on the northwest side of the mountain. It may be tomorrow before we can get there."

"That's fine. Just do the best you can. I'll be here somewhere."

"Ok, see you tomorrow. Alicia out."

"You need anything else, Lorna?"

"No. I'll get right on things here. Is there any way we can help?"

"God, I don't know. I'm just making it up as I go along. Now that you mention it, I could use you and Sean over here for a day or two. Can you get away?"

"I don't see why not. Sean wants to know what you have that has you all stirred up?"

"Oh, nothing. Just planetary production and mass relocations. No big deal."

"Oh, is that all? What is your thinking on those minor subjects?"

"How to meet our quotas and get all the dead mines back online without rebuilding the domes. Bill's handling the mining part for now, but I don't know how long he can pick up the slack for all the mines that are damaged. I'm still working it out in my head. By the time you can get here I may have a plan. I need to put in a call to Mike and have him meet us all here. When do you think you can get here?"

"1200 tomorrow. Maybe a little earlier. We can make it an all nighter if you need us there sooner."

"No, I still have to survey our resources and get things lined out a little better. 1200 will work fine. See you then."

"Ok. We'll get things rolling and head that way. Lorna out."

"Smitty, can you get Mike for me," Al asked.

"Sure."

Al sat and stared at his list of things he had to do. When Smitty had located Mike, Al took the call.

"Mike, I could use a little help over here for a day or so. Can you get away?"

"I think I could manage that. What's up?"

Al laid out his plan to Mike. The details were still sketchy in his mind, and he left a lot of holes that would have to be filled in later.

"I'll be there late tonight," Mike said. "I think you might have come up with a plan that will get us back up to speed months ahead of where we could be. I'll get on the road and see you tonight. I'll be thinking this idea over on the way."

"I won't have all the pieces in place for a day or two. Hell, I don't even know where all the pieces are."

"We have ten or twelve miners on this end. Do you need them back over there?"

"No. Bill can only handle eight or nine and I think I can supply them from here. There's no need to bring those back here and move them all back again. Do you have any rovers left at the hub?"

"No, I don't think so. They're all in there somewhere. What do you need them for?"

"To get some of the crews to the mines, on the surface. I don't think the cruisers are heavy enough to handle the winds that are still blowing out there. Most of the mines are only accessible from the surface, at least the parts where the transports are located. I'll try to round up what I can. Which mines are the most likely to have transports that we can get to?"

"Two, four, six, eight, and nine. They're the ones that have those parts of the domes still standing. Two's a long haul to get to Bill's mine though."

"Alicia will be here tomorrow. I'll go over it with her then. I guess that's about all I have for now."

"Leave the light on. It'll be late when I get there."

"I'll still be up. I have a lot to do."

* * *

Al put Smitty and Charlie in charge of mobilizing the equipment that Bill would need. The transports that were moving the equipment from Arsia Mons back to Pavonis were about to emerge in Arsia Mons when they got the call to pick up the miners. There were seven of them at the point where they came up into the lower tunnels in Arsia. One cruiser was riding herd on them to be sure they didn't have any navigation problems.

"Al, there are seven of the miners at the point where they go up into Arsia," Smitty said. "They think they can get all of them on two of the trailers. Do you want the third one to go on to the habitat and load up there?"

"No, turn them all around. I'll have something for the other one to haul by the time they get here. This is priority one."

"Al, do I need to plan on going back to the mine?" Charlie asked.

"Yeah, Charlie. You'll need to keep your finger on the pulse of things over there. Bill's going to be busy as hell. We'll get you a ride as soon as some of the others start checking in. Can you go find that crew from number six for me?"

"Sure."

A few minutes later he came back with the seven of them in tow.

"I have a job for you," Al said as they gathered around the table where he was sitting. "I'll find you a rover. I want you to take it to the hub and then go to your mine and get your transport. Take it to Bill's mine and haul ore back to the hub for as long as we have something to haul. Which ones of you are the miners?"

"We are," one of them said.

"When you get the transport delivered to the mine for the first load, you three stay at the mine and get with Bill. He'll get you lined out on the operation of the Martian Miners. The rest of you can split up and work with the crews over there and operate the transport when there's something to haul. Any questions?"

"No, Sir. We'll do our best."

"I know you will. You, what's your name?"

"Jake Stevens."

"You're in charge of your crew. You can reach me anytime, day or night, understand?"

"Yes Sir. Thank you."

"Go gather up your things and report back here in a couple hours. I should have you a rover lined up by them. Oh, I'm Al, not sir."

"A lot of people around here have elevated you to God status," Jake said. "Just thought you might like to know that."

"Get out of here before I change my mind."

"Al, God of Mars," Charlie said as the others left. "Has a nice ring to it."

"Charlie, unless you want to walk back to the mine, you might want to let it drop right there."

"Yes, your Majesty."

"Charlie!"

CHAPTER SEVENTEEN

The next morning the daylight seemed a little brighter than it had been. Al woke up earlier than he'd have liked, but knew he had a long day ahead of him. Mike had come in at 2200 hours and parked next to Al and had just gone to bed the night before. He too was awakened by the first light of the new day.

"Good morning," Al said as he met Mike just outside of the habitat.

"That's easy for you to say," Mike grumbled. "Coffee, I need coffee."

Al led the way inside and they found the pot already brewing.

"Mr. Al, Mr. Mike. It is so good to see you this morning," Franco said.

"What's so damn good about it?" Mike snapped.

"The day is brighter than it has been for a long time, I think. Is that not something to be happy about?"

"Franco, yes, I guess maybe it is," Al said. "Do you have some of that good coffee of yours brewed up yet?"

"But of course. I knew that you would want to get an early start on your day, so I got up early to make sure you had a proper start. Breakfast will be ready in a few minutes. Excuse me please. I must get your coffee."

"God, I hate happy people first thing in the morning," Mike said as Franco left.

"With him, you just have to accept it," Al said.

"I think I must be a little hung over from my drinks with Captain Sorensen. That and the two days that I spent in the space port getting ready for him to land. What's your status here?"

"Not too bad, actually. We have seven miners on their way back from Arsia Mons, on transports. I've had two more moved to the head of the tunnel to the hub. They can pick them up on the way. I have seventeen crews lined up to go to Bill's mine as soon as they get the word that the miners are being delivered. They can pick up the miners and drive them on into the mine from the junction. The transports can't get all the way to the mine.

"Each of the mine managers have dispatched teams to go to their mines to evaluate the conditions and retrieve the transports. I talked to Bill last night and Dan and Jeff have already left for the hub with the first load of ore. He said it's almost completely stuff that they mined with the miner. He's holding off on shipping any of the magnetic rock for now. He doesn't think the conditions are good enough to risk it yet."

"Can you lay out your plan for getting us back on track? I've been so busy with the space port that I haven't really had much time to think about it."

"Move everything underground," Al said. "If we wait for the domes to be rebuilt, it's going to be a long time before we can get back up to speed. We'll need to open up the tunnel system that we made, to handle the transports. We'll also need to establish living quarters around the mines.

"Another thing we'll have to do is figure out how to load the transports underground. Making the extra room isn't a problem, but all of our handling equipment is geared to shipping it to the surface to be loaded. Sean and Lorna are on their way back here now and should be here later this morning. I thought they might have some ideas on how to handle this."

"Sounds like you have it all worked out. What do you need me for?"

"I can't authorize this kind of undertaking. It's going to take a lot of time and manpower to accomplish it."

"Hell, it sounds like you already have. Has anyone come up with any better plans?"

"No, they haven't come up with anything. I think they're all kind of shell shocked or something. They don't have much of a spark left."

"What about power and water? They'll need that at the mines."

"We can tap into the power from the domes. Water too. It may take some doing to get reliable power, but I'm sure that Sean can figure that out."

"What time is Sean due in?"

"Around 1200. They got a late start coming back from Arsia Mons yesterday. There are several of the others that are due in about then too. Most of Slim's crew are on their way back too. I'm sending them over to help Bill."

"Mr. Al, there is a radio call for you," Franco said as he brought the coffee.

"Thanks Franco. Excuse me Mike," Al said as he left the table. "This is Al."

"Al, this is Jake Stevens. We're at the complex at number six. It looks like the domes are a total loss."

"Can you get the transport out?"

"I think so. We're still evaluating the situation. The rover is here too. Shall we try to get it out also?"

"We can always use another rover. How far are you from the location of Outpost Charlie?"

"About forty miles, I think. It's northeast of here. They're closer to number nine."

"But you have two rovers and a transport. Can you go check on the conditions and try to locate the transport from number nine? They went to try and rescue the crew of the outpost and haven't been heard from. After this long, it's doubtful that any of them survived, but we owe it to them to look for them. Get the transport headed for the mine and take the two rovers out and look around for them."

"Yes, sir. We'll report in again this afternoon."

"Thanks, Jake."

"Who was that?" Mike asked when Al returned to the table.

"Jake Stevens, from number six. They're trying to retrieve the transport."

"I thought we lost everyone at number six."

"Apparently not. There are seven of them. They were stranded at the hub when the storm hit. They approached me a couple days ago, wanting to get back to work."

"It looks like my list of fatalities has some flaws in it. I'll have to see about that. It sounded like you sent them somewhere."

"Yeah, I sent them to look for the transport that went to Outpost Charlie. There's a slight chance that some of them are still alive."

"Shit, I forgot about them. God, how could I do that?"

"You've been busy."

* * *

By late afternoon the transports had made their way back into the lower complex of Pavonis Mons. They were accompanied by one cruiser that was responsible for the navigation. Al had instructed them to pick up the other two miners and deliver all nine of them to the junction to Bill's mine. He had then dispatched the teams of miners to meet them.

"Al, I've been thinking about your idea to move everything underground," Sean said as they all sat around the table. "I can't really find a flaw with it. In the short term we can rig ramps to load the transports with the loaders that we have. Later, we can figure out loading stations of some sort if we need to. We'll need to open up some sizeable rooms to handle the stockpiles of ore. We can use the support crews from each of the mines to build the facilities that we'll need to get things livable."

"Is this going to be a workable long-term solution?" Mike asked. "Some of these people have spent very little time underground."

"They seem to be doing alright here," Al said. "I know that this isn't quite the same as in the dark all the time, but they seem to be coping ok. We may have to send them to the hub more often or something, to get them their day-light fix. It's the best shot that we have right now. Once the domes are repaired, we can resume normal operations."

"Lorna, what do you think about all of this?" Mike asked.

"I don't see a problem with it as long as they can have good power to light up their new world. Just lay it out to them and they'll rise to the occasion."

"It's not an ideal fix, by any means, but it will get all of the mines back into production," Al said. "It's the only way that some of them will be able to get back to work for as much as a year."

"Al, there's someone named Jake on the radio for you," Smitty said as he approached.

"Thanks, Smitty. I'll be right there. Mike, you might want to hear this," he said as he got up to leave.

Mike followed him to the communications station and the others did the same.

"Go ahead, Jake," Al said.

"Al, we found the transport. When we got to the location of the outpost it was completely gone. We headed back toward number nine, figuring that was where they would have gone. It's tough going out here, but we found it about an hour ago. There are six people inside, all dead. Looks like they got lost in the storm and ran into a ravine. The hatch seal was cracked, and they've been dead for quite some time. There isn't much we can do for them now. The transport is going to need a lot of help to get pulled out. What do you want us to do?"

"Jake, this is Mike Peterson. Mark the coordinates so we can find it later and head back. I'll send out a recovery team to take care of everything there."

"Yes, sir. We're heading back to the hub. Jake out."

"Albert, sorry," Mike said. "Al, can you get things started here. I need to check with my people."

Al turned to the others, who included all of the mine managers. There was a look of defeat on most of the faces that he saw.

"Ladies and gentlemen, we have our orders. Round up teams of miners and send them to your respective mines. We'll have to relocate several more Martian Miners to assist you with what's ahead. Do you all understand what we're about to do?"

"I think that's pretty clear," Alicia said. "We'll need a lot of transportation support to pull this off. What can we do to handle that?"

"We have a mountain full of alien machines. Find what you need and take them with you. I suggest that you spend a little time planning out what you're going to do at each of your locations. You all know your areas better than any of us. You know where you can establish your new towns, for lack of a better word. Open up large caverns for handling the ore stockpiles. The first thing you probably need to do is open the tunnels to your mines, so we can get the transports to you. Once that has been established, we'll bring in more people to start building your living quarters. This is going to take some time, but we can do it."

"Al, I think it would be a good idea if some of us went to get things started," Sean said as the others left. "They're all good people, but they seem to be lost right now."

"Yeah, I know. When you look at the faces of most of the people in here you see the same thing. I don't understand it. They're in no danger now. Hell, the worst of it is past. They'll be alright once they're back to work. I'll go see about lining them out. Maybe you should go along too. Lorna, can you ladies handle things here and on the other side?"

"Of course, we can."

"I knew that. I don't even know why I asked."

"Just habit. I'll head back over in the morning. Can we come to visit later?"

"We'd be disappointed if you didn't," Sean said.

* * *

Later that evening Bill sat in the control room at the mine. He'd been monitoring the radio traffic for the last two hours and was trying to get an idea of what everyone was doing. There seemed to be a mass mobilization of some kind in progress, but he couldn't figure out what it was all about.

"Bill, this is Slim."

"Go ahead."

"We're downstairs. We'll be up there in a few minutes."

"Who's with you?"

"Just Joe and Jim. The others will be along in a few hours. They're moving the miners in from the junction."

"How many miners did you bring?"

"Nine. Think you can find a place to put them all to work?"

"That's not a problem. Think you can get them lined out on how they work?"

"No sweat. Got anything descent to eat around here?"

"Meet me in the dining hall and we'll see if we can come up with something. I think we can find a few steaks."

"Damn, that sounds good after the rabbit food diet we've been on. See you in a minute."

"It's good to see you back here," Bill said when they met in the dining hall a few minutes later.

"It's like coming home," Slim said. "Looks like it held together pretty good. From what I hear it's the only one that did."

"Yeah, that's what I hear too. Do you have enough crews to get us started?"

"Eighteen or nineteen. I think there are two from each mine and one from number six. They're off trying to get you another transport but should be here tomorrow sometime. They have some support crew with them too."

"What about the rest of my people?"

"They'll be along tomorrow. Al was rounding up transportation for them. Now, where's that steak you mentioned."

"Looks like we'd better dig out quite a few. The others will need to get back on a working-mans diet too. Do you know when they'll get here?"

"My guess would be about three hours. We can check on them later. Charlie's driving one of the cruisers. We'll be able to reach him."

"Good, I need him here to run the lift and all that other stuff that he does. I've been trying to do it all for a day now, but I'll have to be in the hole most of the time."

"That's why Al sent us. Now, do we have to do the cooking, or are you the chef?"

"Come on; let's see what we can find."

* * *

263

Bill found rooms for all of the crews when they arrived and bedded them down. The next morning, he called them all together in the dining hall.

"Ladies and gentlemen, here's how it's going to work," he began. "We have five people trained on how to use these machines. They'll each take a crew and train them. Slim, Dan, and Jeff got in late last night. They'll surface soon and help you and your crew. By late this afternoon we should have everyone trained enough so you can go out and start playing with the machines. It'll take a little practice to get it right.

"The first group will be the night shift. Once you've had a little time to learn the systems, you'll come back up here and sack out. We'll run around the clock and see if we can match the production level of the entire planet, for the foreseeable future. Any questions?"

"We've all had time in the miners," John Anderson, lead miner for mine number two said. "What's the big deal about running tunnels with them?"

"Now you're going to learn how to mine with them," Slim said. "We'll run three men, or in some cases women, to a crew. The tunneling is basically the same, but what happens in the back compartment is what'll make the difference. There are a lot of controls back there that will enable you to get rid of the rock but keep the ore. It's almost pure when it comes out. All we have to do is clean it up behind you. The support crews will be here this afternoon to do that. Let's get some breakfast and get started."

* * *

The loading of Captain Sorensen's landing craft had taken longer than he had anticipated, but the last container of the refined raw minerals was being lifted onto the conveyor that would run it into the cargo hold. The ten large containers were heavier this time than usual.

"It's a good thing that you folks have only one third gravity here," the captain said.

"Yeah, with a load like that you'd have a hell of a time getting off the ground back on Earth," the controller said.

"Well, I guess I'd better go make sure things are all nailed down. Hope things here are back up to speed soon."

"We're already receiving shipments from one of the mines. They'll keep us going until we can bring more of them back online. You have a safe trip back. Contact me when you're ready to launch."

"Will do, son. You take it easy here. See you next time around."

Thirty minutes later he contacted the controller again.

"Orion-one ready to lift off."

"The hanger bay is clear, Captain. It'll be a few minutes to get you moved up into position."

"Roger. Calculating trajectory for return to orbit. Advise when we're clear for takeoff."

"Stand-by."

The giant doors above the ship started to open and the atmosphere quickly rushed out into the windblown cold that was Mars. The controller made the adjustments to the controls and the ship began to rise. Then, minutes later it was locked into position.

"Orion-one, clear for departure. Have a good flight."

"Thank you control," Sorensen said. "Ease us up, son."

The pilot of the landing craft started the engines and increased the throttles. This had become a routine operation but was still nerve-racking. The craft shuddered under the heavy load, but soon gave way and started its ascent into the red dust cloud that engulfed the planet. The captain watched as they rocketed upward and marveled at the progress that had been made here since his first trip to Mars, some six years earlier. The trip back into orbit took only fifteen minutes, but they still had to rendezvous with the Orion.

"Orion, Orion-one. We've achieved low orbit," the captain said on the radio. "We'll rendezvous with you in one hour. Get things ready to leave orbit."

"Roger, Captain. Standing-by to dock. Welcome home."

"Sorensen, you old fart. Are you finally done?"

"Is that you Talbot?"

"Yeah, it's me. We've been waiting for you to reach orbit so we could go on down."

"They have a hell of a mess down there, but they'll get you loaded as fast as they can. You'll only be a couple days behind us on the way back. It's going to get interesting when we get there and have to stack up in orbit again."

"Yeah, but it'll be a short turn-around. Hell, you may be headed back before we even get there."

"That's entirely possible. Talk to you later."

"Kick it in the ass and get out of here. We'll want to make the short turn too."

"See you when you get there. Orion-one out."

* * *

Al and Sean drove toward the hub late that morning. They were on the way to see if they could help with the operations plan that Al had come up with. Mike had left earlier that morning and would meet them at the hub.

"Can you remember where you left all of the miners?" Sean asked as Al drove.

"Most of the mines have at least one," Al said. "We left them there when we reached them. Number one doesn't have one, but I think most of the others do. There are also several in various access tunnels."

"That's probably where we should start. We need to find the resources and get them distributed as well as we can. You said that Bill has nine of them?"

"Yeah, and there are at least ten or twelve sitting around over here. All of the other managers will be back over here by tonight. We'll have to bed down at the hub somewhere. Mike said he'd find us a place."

"I still have my place there. I haven't seen much of it lately, but it's still mine. We can stay there."

"That'll work fine until the ladies show up. How many bedrooms do you have?"

"Two. I have one of the larger apartments. It's one of the perks of being in management."

"Hell, that works for me. We'll get an early start in the morning."

* * *

"Where did you guys spend the night?" Mike asked as Al and Sean walked into his office.

"My place," Sean said. "That was about as far as we could make it last night."

"Have any of the managers checked in yet?" Al asked.

"Just Alicia. She's headed out to her mine to have a look around. She said she'd check in later. The others should be around here somewhere."

"They don't seem to be all that anxious to get started," Al said.

"They're just very disorganized. I hope they get over that soon. Bill can't carry the load indefinitely."

"No, but he can carry it for a while," Al said. "If we can work out the logistics of this thing, we should be able to put as many as four miners in each mine. That would give us the highest production levels that the planet has ever seen."

"Your Martian Miners are going to make my milling operations almost obsolete," Mike said. "I took a look at the ore that Bill sent in on the first load. It was damn near pure right off the transport."

"That's a good thing, isn't it?"

"Cost wise, yes. Production-wise, yes. It's going to leave me with a lot of people and facilities that I don't really need though."

"Now that is a shame. We've always been short of both. We won't be getting the regular influx of new people for a while either. Besides, you have a lot of rebuilding to do here."

"And at all the mines," Sean said. "We'll need all the help we can get."

"This is a problem we can deal with as we go," Mike said. "Besides, it's basically my problem. Do you think this plan of yours will really work?"

"I don't see why it won't," Al said. "It's going to require a lot of work, but it should make it so this kind of disaster never happens again."

* * *

Lorna and Eve started their day at the cavern where the riches had been found. They had been cataloging the contents for several days.

"I think I need a break," Lorna said. "Why don't we go exploring for a day or two and let them finish up here?"

"Sounds good to me," Eve said. "Which direction should we go?"

"West. That's the direction we were headed when we found this."

267

"When do you want to leave?"

"In a couple hours. I want to get things lined out here a little. Sharon can supervise things here. We need to get a status check from all of the teams too. I'd like to have an updated map to send to Al as soon as we can come up with one."

"I'll get on the radio and see if I can arrange for everyone to meet us back here in a few days. How long do you think we'll be gone?"

"I don't know, four days or so. That should be long enough for us to get out to the perimeter and back by a different route."

"Ok, I'll set it up. Shall we have them all meet us here?"

"Yeah, this is as good as anyplace to use for our headquarters."

* * *

"Slim, how'd it go last night?" Bill asked.

"Not too bad. The support crew is having a little trouble keeping up with the miners, but we can fix that. We stockpiled enough to load three transports on the night shift."

"There are three headed this way," Charlie said. "We've been in contact with them through the night. They should all be here by 1000."

"Can we turn them around and get them out again by tonight?" Bill asked.

"We'll have to," Charlie said. "The others will be in by this time tomorrow. With eight of them in the pipeline we'll have to keep them moving."

"Are any of them bringing in supplies yet?"

"We got the first load last night on the transport from number six," Slim said. "We got it unloaded about 0100 and turned the transport, loaded it, and sent it out again. It left about three hours ago."

"Good, we'll need a steady stream of supplies if we're going to support this many people. I'm thinking about trying to get more support people too. Before long we're going to have trouble finding places to put all of them."

"We do need to raise the staffing level on the support side," Slim said. "We may need to bring in support equipment from somewhere else too."

"Well, you had better get some rest," Bill said. "I'm headed down to take my morning tour."

"Ok, see you tonight," Slim said as Bill left.

Bill went to the back of the complex and climbed into his cruiser and started the descent to the mine level, some four thousand feet below. The old crew cars weren't fast enough to cover the ground that had been opened up, but the cruisers were. He had the added benefit of being able to keep the progress in each tunnel mapped as he went. Slim had also been doing the same during the night shift. As he spiraled down, he zoomed the map out and saw that the tunnels were getting awfully long. It appeared that they had started to open up several of the tunnels into rooms. He would hit the main tunnel between number six and number eight, so he decided to check on them first.

As he approached the end of number six, he saw the reason why they had belled it out so much. The mineralization that was showing in the walls and roof was tremendous. Dan was sitting well back from the end of the tunnel when Bill pulled up.

"I see you found us something to send to the hub," Bill said as he got out.

"Yeah, we did. It's one of the richest deposits I've ever seen. I was afraid to let them open it up too much more. What do you think?"

"Let's not get too greedy for now. Is there any information on this area in the surveys?"

"Hell, we outran the surveys several days ago. This is all virgin territory. How are we aligned with number four and eight? Can we cut cross drifts and connect up with them?"

"I have the latest information on my cruiser," Bill said. "Slim made the rounds just before he went up to meet me. Let's have a look."

Bill transferred the display to the view screen on the side of the cruiser and adjusted the view to show a view of the side of the tunnel.

"It looks like you're running a little higher than number four, but not much," Bill said. "It would be easy enough to adjust the elevation and make a connection."

"I was thinking more about turning toward number eight," Dan said. "We're almost a mile farther out than number four and they haven't found this deposit yet. Eight is almost even with us and they belled out about the same place that we did here. If we cut cross tunnels here and here, we could get a better idea of how big this deposit is. That way we could maximize the return without compromising the safety."

"That would give us some giant pillars to deal with later. Have you talked to Jeff this morning?"

"He has a similar situation between seven and nine. They're out about thirty miles on both of those and he said Joe had had them start to open up the size of the tunnels about 0430. They started this about an hour before that. I'm sure Slim was in on that decision too."

"Yeah, he probably was. He didn't mention it this morning, but he had a lot going on last night."

"Are you just getting started on your rounds?"

"Yeah, want to come along."

"Sure. They're going fine here, and I haven't had a chance to look around much this morning."

Bill had Dan and Jeff working as roving supervisors on the day shift and Slim had Joe and Jim doing the same on night shift. They were the best qualified to give any guidance on how to mine with the new machines and they were also the best that he had available.

"God, this mine is getting big," Bill said as they drove to the end of tunnel six before turning back toward the main tunnel.

"By the time they get the rest of the mines up and running it'll dwarf any of them, even the older ones," Dan said. "It almost doubled in size in the last week."

"It's a good thing we have these cruisers to keep track of the progress. If we had to wait for a survey crew to map all this, we'd be lost all the time."

"Dan, this is Jeff, where are you?"

"With Bill in tunnel six. Why, what's up?"

"I'm at the back of number nine and I'd like you both to come over if you have a minute."

"Anything wrong?" Bill asked.

"No, but I'd like you to see this."

"We're on our way."

"Wonder what that's all about?" Dan asked.

"I don't have a clue," Bill said as he kicked the cruiser up to full speed. "Let's go have a look."

Twenty minutes later they pulled up beside Jeff's cruiser and stopped. Jeff had his lights shining on a spot in the wall of number nine.

"What's that," Bill asked.

CHAPTER EIGHTEEN

"Damned if I know," Jeff said, still looking at the wall.

"I've never seen any mineral like that," Bill said. "I wonder what it could be."

"We'd better put in a call to the hub and get someone out here to have a look at it," Dan said. "This could be something significant."

"I'll go get on the horn and have Mike send someone out," Bill said. "Jeff, see if you can get me a good-sized sample and bring it to the top. We have a transport getting ready to leave in about two hours. Let's see if we can send the sample in with them."

"I may have to drill it and shoot it to loosen it up," Jeff said.

"I'll have the support crew load up the small drill and bring it back to you. They can haul it back in the bucket of one of the loaders. Dan, we'd better go get things rolling."

As they left, Jeff was still examining the porous material in the wall of the tunnel.

* * *

"Brittany, where are you?" Lorna called.

"We're just inside the western perimeter, about an hour outside of the light. What's up?"

"Eve and I are about to go into the darkness on a heading of 270. How much more is there to explore on the northern half?"

"Maybe two more spokes. We're at 290, so we're not too far apart. We still have most of the southern half to go yet, but in the last couple weeks we've made good progress. Patty's just north of me and we'll pick up anything between where we are and you. Drop south when you make the turn."

"That's what we were figuring on doing. I'd like to get together tomorrow sometime and compare notes. Let's see if we can arrange to meet somewhere and combine our maps. I really need to get a look at everything we have."

"We can be back to the garden ring by late tomorrow afternoon. We'll be able to have most of the cruiser teams meet us there. Let me know what heading you take when you turn back to the center. We'll meet at the spot where you reach the garden."

"Ok, see you there."

* * *

Alicia rolled southeast toward her mine at midday, the sand still swirling around her rover. She knew that there wasn't going to be much to see when she got there, but it was a trip she had to make. She had to return to the spot that had almost taken her life.

She was almost on top of the tattered domes before she could see them. Rebecca was driving the rover and taking it easy. They pulled to a stop just short of the airlock and just sat there and surveyed the situation.

"It looks like hell, doesn't it?" Alicia said after several minutes.

"Yeah, it's going to take a lot to get it back into shape. Do you think they can fix it?"

"I'm sure they can, but it's going to take a long time. Al's plan to move everything underground is probably the only way we can get back to work here. The other mines haven't faired any better either, from what I've heard."

"What can we do here?"

"Not a damn thing let's go back. Control, this is Alicia at number two."

"Go ahead."

"Can you connect me with Mike?"

"Stand by while I locate him."

It took almost twenty minutes before the controller came back on the line.

"Alicia, this is control."

"Go ahead. Did you locate Mike for me?"

"He's tied up in a meeting. Is it important enough to have me pull him out?"

"No. Just leave a message to have him call me when he gets out. We're heading back from the mine site, and we'll be back late this afternoon. Alicia out."

"I'll leave word for him."

They fell into silence as they drove west to intersect the main road back to the hub. The sand still swirled around them, but the visibility was actually pretty good, and still improving. At this rate it might be back to normal in a couple weeks.

When they made their turn a half hour later, they skirted the edge of the Ophir Chasm for a short distance. They always liked this part of the trip.

"I wish the weather was a little clearer so we could see the bottom of the chasm," Rebecca said as they headed north.

"That would be nice. It's been a long time since we've been able to see all the way to the bottom. I still think there's a spot for a mine down there in the bottom. The way the strata lay and the look of the terrain, I know it's there."

"You geologists are all alike. Prospecting everywhere you go. All I know is the scenery is fantastic, as always."

"Yeah, I guess it does kind of go with the territory. It gets in your blood after a while. When I was your tender age, I made a couple big discoveries in Nevada that way. People had been skirting around a remote area in the center of the state. I flew over the area and saw some potential that no one else had seen. It took a lot of doing to get anyone to listen to me, but eventually they went into an area that I had been pushing. I was on the lead team, and we found what turned into the largest heavy metal find in history.

"It's all about observation and passion. You have some of those skills, although you need to work on them quite a bit."

"If I didn't have a little passion and adventurous spirit, I wouldn't be here. My parents tried to talk me out of making this trip. They thought it was too dangerous. I kept telling them that the technological advances of the last couple generations had made it routine to make the trip to Mars. Now I guess I'm going to have to explain this latest storm to them. I haven't been able to get through to them yet."

"None of us have, but the company has put out the word that everyone is alright. I'm sure they'll handle the casualties separately. That's something we don't have to deal with. All we have to do is get back into production and get back to earning a living."

"How are you planning to do that?"

"We'll go into the bottom side of the mine tomorrow and start laying the groundwork. First, we'll have to get the tunnels opened up. Then make a place to live. Once we have that done, we can bring the rest of our people back in and get to work."

"That's what Al was planning for the rest of the mines too, isn't it?"

"Pretty much. There's only so many ways to get this done. If Bill can hold up the production end of things for a couple weeks, we can get this done and not loose all that much. I still can't believe everything I've seen inside those two mountains."

"Who would have ever thought that that could actually be there?"

"I know. There's so much we have to learn about this planet."

They fell silent and continued north. Alicia was lost in thought. Rebecca drove and observed the terrain that she'd been over so many times before. Surprising to her, she saw things that she'd never seen before. Most of them were small and insignificant, but she marveled at what the increased focus on her surroundings brought to light.

"Alicia, this is Mike."

"Go ahead."

"Did you need to speak to me?"

"We went to number two and the domes are almost a total loss. We'll need to get a maintenance team out there to secure the reactors and make sure we can still use them when we go back in. I'll start back in from the bottom tomorrow. I think Al's plan is the best chance we have to get back up and running."

"Where are you now?"

"About two hours out from the hub. There wasn't anything we could do at the mine, so we headed back. You buying dinner?"

"I think that could be arranged. Call me when you get back."

"Will do. Alicia out."

* * *

Al and Sean finished the last leg of their northern tour late in the afternoon. They had located most of the miners and firmed up their plans for getting into the mines. They entered the dome of the hub just as Alicia and Rebecca came through the airlock.

"Alicia, this is Al. Where have you been?"

"Out sightseeing. I had to go to the mine to see for myself what the conditions were. I haven't been there since you guys dragged me out."

"Is it as bad as I remember?"

"Probably worse. It's salvageable, but it's going to take a lot of work. With all of the other mines in as bad a shape as mine, we're going to have to set up a priority system for the repairs. I'll go in tomorrow and get things started on the lower end. Do you have the miners all located?"

"We think so. How many do you need?"

"I think the stock answer to that question is all we can get. Any idea how many that might be?"

"We can probably scare up three of them for each mine. Bill still has the highest priority on the miners. You can do a lot with three of them though."

They pulled into the parking area and stopped next to each other. Alicia climbed down while Rebecca powered down the rover.

"I didn't really have a chance to look around when we were there," Al said as they met. "Is it really that bad?"

"Yes, and no," Alicia said. "The framework seems to be mostly intact, but the shell is almost a total loss. They'll have to almost start from scratch on that."

"How about your reactor?" Sean asked.

"I'll know more about that tomorrow. I'll have a crew headed that way at first light. I'll take a crew into the bottom and start there. Any chance of stealing on of those cruisers?"

"I think that can be arranged," Al said. "Yours should be at the mine still. But I'm sure we can get you one."

"I'll probably just stay over there for a few days to get things lined out. That habitat on the back sure will make that easier."

"We can relate to that. What are you doing for dinner?"

"I'm supposed to call Mike. I think he's planning something. Join us?"

"We might just do that."

* * *

It was late afternoon when Eve and Lorna pulled up at the junction with the inner ring, just outside the garden. There were already four cruisers there waiting for them.

"Hey there, Boss," Patty said as Eve and Lorna got out.

"How long have you been here?" Lorna asked.

"Not long. Maybe an hour. Brittany should be here in a couple hours. They were running a little late today."

"How's it going?"

"Good. Between us we've managed to get most of the northern half of this level mapped. It's kind of boring. The sights don't change much. You know how it is."

"Yeah, I do. How are your supplies holding out?" Eve asked.

"Everybody's running low, but we're not doing too bad. Any word when we might expect some real food again. This veggie diet sucks."

"I haven't heard yet, but I know they're starting to receive shipments from the ships in orbit. I'll call Al and check on it for you," Lorna said. "Actually, we're kind of interested in that too."

"Can we start the downloads and see where we stand?" Eve asked.

"I've already been working on it," Patty said. "We have the ones that are here loaded into our cruiser. Want to have a look?"

"That would be nice," Lorna said as they moved toward the cruiser. "God, you have covered a lot of ground. How many others are still headed in?"

"Five. The others have all been called back to the other side. What's going on over there?"

"Mass mobilization back to the hub. It's going to take quite a while to get things back to normal. Al and Sean are over there trying to help. I think I'll give them a call now."

"Remember to have them send some real food this way," Eve said.

"Al, this is Lorna, where are you."

"I was just going to call you. Are you trying to read my mind again?"

"No, I'm not into short stories. What's going on over there?"

"Just trying to get a feel for the scope of things. We'll probably need to be here for another week or two. Where are you hiding?"

"Upper level in Arsia. We're getting a map briefing from all the teams. By tomorrow we'll know what we have here. Have the supply ships started unloading yet?"

"Yeah, they're doing good. Do I detect a cry for real food?"

"You damned right. Get us some good stuff headed this way. If it's not here soon, you may have a rebellion on your hands. We need meat."

"Consider it done," Al said. "I may have to pull a few strings, but I think I have a little influence around here. Is there anything else we can do for you?"

"No, I guess not. We've almost finished the north half of the upper level and the lower level is about two thirds done. We're just trying to figure out where to go next."

"If you find anyone headed this way, you might send me an updated map. I'm still interested in what's going on over there."

"Maybe when you send us the food, we can arrange that. We'll compile the update for you and leave it at the habitat on the lower level."

"Ok. We're on our way to have dinner with Mike. Any message for him?"

"Just to make sure you get us some real food. Like Eve says, this veggie diet sucks."

"Understood, Al out."

* * *

By late that evening all five of the other cruisers had arrived and the map showed that the northern half was complete. They would have to run all of the rings to get the final map, but the spokes were laid out and the area was defined. As they sat around and had their veggie dinner Lorna got a call on the radio.

"Lorna, this is Jen, where the hell are you?"

"On the west side of the garden, why?"

"You know those seeds we planted a couple weeks ago; well, they've produced some giant fruits. Some of the trees are already over twenty feet tall and have trunks almost a foot in diameter."

"Are you sure you've got the right spot?"

"Yeah, we double checked with the mapping system. Besides, these are real apples and oranges, not the alien stuff we're used to in here. Want to come have a look?"

"Where are you?"

"We're inside the east entrance at 090 and ring one. About three-or-four-miles in. We'd probably better meet you at the entrance and guide you back in."

"It's kind of late tonight. We can be there by 0900 or so in the morning. Why don't you two hang out and meet us then."

"I think we can manage to find something to do until then. See you in the morning, Jen out."

"I wonder what effect on the ecosystem we're going to cause doing that kind of thing," Eve said.

"It has to be done. If we're going to feed this planet, we're going to have to produce an awful lot of food. I just wish there was a way to raise cows and such."

"I know, but I still have to wonder."

"Lorna, there's a call for you on the other channel," Brittany said.

"Who is it?"

"Team nine over in Pavonis. They've been trying to find you all day."

"They haven't been looking all that hard. We've been close to the radio all day. I don't even remember who team nine is."

"That's Robert and Samantha Jenkins, I think," Eve said. "They stayed over there as one of the last two teams when we all came over here."

"Team nine, this is Lorna. What can I do for you?"

"Lorna, this is Sam—Samantha Jenkins. Are you real busy?"

"No, not particularly. What's up?"

"We're out close to the outer ring in Pavonis. There isn't much to look at over here anymore, but we may have found something you'll want to see. I've been trying to get in touch with you all day."

"We're on frequency seven over here, try that next time. What did you find?"

"Well, we're not sure, but we think there may be a tunnel that leads to the north-east. We went in for about a hundred miles and figured that we had to be well outside the mountain. Isn't that kind of like what you found over there that led to Arsia?"

"That's exactly like what led us over here. What's your exact position?"

"Ring nineteen and spoke 033 on the upper level. We thought about seeing where it led, but we're about out of supplies. What do you think?"

"I think we'll meet you back at the complex in the upper garden in Pavonis tomorrow night. We'll gather up a few things and head that way in the morning."

"So, you think this might be something important?"

"Damn right I do. Good work. Head back now and be sure you mark where you are so we can find it again."

"Oh god, here we go again," Brittany said.

"It does look that way. The only thing out that way is Ascraeus Mons. What are the chances?"

"A lot better than they were yesterday," Eve said.

"I'd better get in touch with Al. Al this is Lorna."

There was no response after several tries.

"Shit," Lorna said. "Hub control this is Lorna."

"Yes, my goddess, what can I do for you?"

"What's this goddess crap?"

"Al's the god of Mars and you're the goddess. You saved our entire presence on this planet. Allow us to worship you."

"Don't give me that shit. Find Al for me. He's probably with Mike. Lorna out."

When she turned around all the cruiser crews were on their knees bowing to her.

"What is your wish oh Goddess of Mars," Brittany said, then broke up laughing.

"Very funny. Just for that you get to go exploring again. Patty, you're in charge here. Eve, pack us up. We're headed out tonight. I want to have time to see what Jen and Martin have found before we go back to Pavonis. Britt, meet us at the upper complex in Pavonis tomorrow night."

"Yes, oh Goddess. We hear and will obey."

"Are you looking for an ass whipping? God, what did I do to deserve this?"

"Lorna, this is hub control. Al's in route to the hotel to have dinner. I haven't been able to nail him down yet."

"Keep trying. I have to talk to him as soon as possible."

"I'm sorry," Britt said. "You have to admit that it's funny though."

"Yeah, I guess you're right, just drop it."

"Yes Goddess," Britt said and took a couple steps backward.

"Patty, I'll need to have a composite map to take with me. Can you arrange that?"

"Sure thing. Anything else?"

"No, I can't think of anything. You can check with the habitat on the lower level in a day or two and go get some real food. You might all want to plan on that. Take a day or two to rest up if you need to. Eve, we'll cut across the garden. When can you be ready?"

"Half hour or so. Britt, can you give me a hand?"

"I'll get that map," Patty said.

"Lorna, this is Al. What's so urgent?"

"One of the two teams we left over in Pavonis has stumbled onto what may be the route to Ascraeus Mons. Eve and I are headed that way to investigate. I'm going to take Brittany and Johnny with me and leave the rest here to carry on until we find out what's there."

"What the hell are you talking about?"

"I just told you. We may have found the way to get to Ascraeus Mons. We're going to meet up with Robert and Samantha Jenkins at the upper garden in Pavonis tomorrow night. I thought you might like to know."

"Hell, yes, I might like to know. When did you find this out?"

"About thirty minutes ago."

"I'll get back to you. Where are you and what are you going to do now?"

"I'm still on the west side of the garden in Arsia and we're packing up to go see Martin and Jen before we head back. Do you think you might want to join us tomorrow night?"

"Want to, yes. Be able to, that's another question. I'll let you know in a couple hours."

"We'll stay close to the radio. It's going to be a long haul to get over there, so you probably have a little time to make your arrangements. Let us know."

"I'll get back to you as soon as I can. Al out."

"Eve, are you about ready?" Lorna asked.

"Ten minutes."

They pulled out at 1930 and headed into the garden. They would have to skirt south of the big hole in the center of the garden, but that would still be closer than going all the way around. It took three hours to reach the south rim of the hole.

"It's 2230," Eve said. "When do you want to stop for the night?"

"I don't think it's a good idea to stop here," Lorna said. "Let's go on for an hour or so."

"Al still hasn't called back. I wonder what's keeping him."

"I don't have a clue. If we haven't heard anything by the time we stop, I'll try giving him a call."

"Lorna, this is Al. Sorry I couldn't get back to you sooner. Where are you?"

"We were just talking about you. We're just on the east side of the center hole in Arsia. We're going to get a ways away from here before we bed down. What did you come up with?"

"I'll be there tomorrow night sometime, but it might be late. I want to go along with you on this one."

"Who are you bringing along?"

"Probably just Sean. Can you think of anyone else we need?"

"No. We've been talking about it and think this first run should just be a small party. If we actually find something, we can leave Robert and Samantha over there with Britt and Johnny. Bring some real food for the group going over there. We may be there for several days."

"I already have that in the works. We'll pick it up before we leave in the morning. Anything else that you can think of?"

"What time are you going to get out of there?"

"Probably not until late morning. Maybe 1100 or so. If you think of anything in the morning, give us a call."

"Al, is there any chance that Brian could come along?" Eve asked.

"I'll check into it for you. He might be handy to have over there with us, but he may be tied up with the mine renovations over here. I'll see what I can do."

"I'd appreciate it. We haven't had much time together since the sandstorm hit over six weeks ago."

"I'll check into it. Talk to you in the morning."

They drove on in silence for a while and Lorna finally pulled up between two trees and parked.

"This looks like as good a spot as any," she said.

"I'll lay out the habitat. I'm pooped. What time do we need to get started?"

"Early. I'd like to be over there by 0800 or so and it looks like we still have over two hours to go. Don't worry; you can sleep while I drive."

"Deal."

Inside the garden it was eerily quiet. The leaves on the trees never seemed to move because of the lack of any wind. In the daytime there was a little movement because of the heating of the air, but at night it was deathly quiet.

Lorna stretched her weary bones as Eve laid out the habitat. It had been a long day and the prospect of the trip clear to the north end of Pavonis was wearing on her.

* * *

"Hey, time to get up," Lorna said at 0530. "We just have time to get over there before we have to go on to Pavonis."

"Just a few more minutes," Eve said, pulling the blanket up over her head.

"Come on. You can go back to sleep while I drive."

Reluctantly Eve rolled out of bed, and they dressed and started folding up the habitat. It was just starting to get light when they finished. From the north they heard a rustling sound in the trees. It sounded close.

"What was that?" Eve asked.

"Just the garden waking up. Come on, let's go."

As they climbed into the cruiser there was a crash just behind them. They looked back and saw one of the big birds coming through the trees.

"Oh shit," Lorna said.

"This would be a real good time to get the hell out of here," Eve said. "Today, Mother."

"Hang on to something," Lorna said as she gunned the cruiser forward, gaining speed and leaving the bird with a puzzled look on his face.

She didn't let up on the throttle for several minutes, careening through the trees, bouncing off of several of them. Eve watched as the bird disappeared from sight.

"Damn, that was close," Eve said.

"It may have just been curious about what we were."

"Yeah, and it may have had us on the menu for breakfast. I for one don't want to hang around and find out which it was."

"Don't be so dramatic, Eve."

"Dramatic, hell. We could have been eaten."

"Well, we weren't. Go back to sleep. I'll wake you up when we get there."

"Sleep hell. I can't go back to sleep now."

"Then help me figure out what we'll need to take with us for the next leg of our trip."

They drove on, discussing the trip north. At 0700 Al called.

"Lorna, are you up and around yet?"

"Yeah. We have been for an hour and a half. What's up?"

"Just checking to see if you need anything else."

"We're just going over that. I think we need to take five cruisers for this one. We have three from over here and you makes four. Can you come up with another one?"

"Brian is coming. He'll meet us in the upper garden in Pavonis tonight. That will make five. What do you think about bringing Jen and Martin along?"

"That's not a bad idea. Is anyone coming with Brian?"

"No, but I see what you're getting at. We're going to be one person short. I'll round up Mona and take her along with me. That should round out the crew."

"We'll be where Martin and Jen are in a few minutes. I'll talk it over with them and see if they can break loose. I don't know what they're working on."

"Let me know. I'll arrange provisions for six cruisers for a week to be delivered to the upper garden in Pavonis by tonight. The relocation of most of the people is continuing and with a little luck they should have several of the mines operational in a couple of weeks. I talked to Bill last night and they're holding their own over there. They're shipping two transports a day. That should be enough to tide us over for a while."

"How are they managing that?"

"Just working hard and having a lot of good luck. The stuff they're shipping is almost pure enough to load onto the ships, as is. Most of it is being sent just that way."

"Ok, we'll be with Jen and Martin in a few minutes. I'll get back to you after I have a chance to talk to them."

"Ok. Talk to you then. Al out."

"Lorna, this is Jen. Where you?"

"I figure we're about thirty minutes from your location. Want to go for a little ride?"

"We do that every day. What's so special about this one?"

"We'll be there shortly. You two talk it over and see if you can get away for a week or so. I think we may need your special talents in Ascraeus Mons."

"Ascraeus Mons? Where the hell is that?"

"North-east of Pavonis."

"Did you find a way to get over there?"

"We think so. We're going to go have a look and I'd like you two to tag along for a few days. We're just getting a glimpse of the edge of the garden. We'll see you in a couple minutes."

Jen and Martin were just finishing folding up the habitat when they drove up. Martin had a puzzled look on his face.

"What are you two up to now," Martin said as they got out. "Jen said you wanted us to go off somewhere else. We still have a lot of work to do here."

"I know," Lorna said, "but we have other irons to put in the fire. We may have found the way to Ascraeus Mons. We're headed back to Pavonis to gather up a party to go have a look. Al thought you two should be along this time. Can this wait for a week or so?"

"Yeah, I guess so. I guess I could get someone else to come over here and watch over the stuff we have going here."

"What needs watching over here?"

"Just the seeds that we planted a week ago. Come on, I'll show you."

They walked into the edge of the garden and proceeded for a few hundred yards. They emerged into a small clearing in the trees and stopped.

"We planted these a week ago and have been coming back every couple days to check on them."

"Damn, the apples are as big as watermelon," Eve said.

"The growth rate is phenomenal," Martin said. "From a seed to this in just over a week. If we only had more seeds, we could produce all the food that any of us could ever eat. We need to make sure that we get them headed this way as soon as possible."

"That's already in the works, but it'll take time," Lorna said. "In the meantime, we need to expand the envelope to see what else we can find. Are you in?"

"Damn right we're in," Jen said. "We'll meet you at the upper garden tonight. We have to make a few rounds to check on."

"That settles it then," Lorna said. "Eve let's get loaded up and head out. We still have a long ways to go."

CHAPTER NINETEEN

At 1800 that evening the crew had begun to gather in the clearing in the upper garden in Pavonis Mons. Lorna and Eve had arrived at 1500 and the others were starting to drift in. First was Brittany and Johnny at 1645. Robert and Samantha Jenkins were next at 1715. Jen and Martin at 1745.

"Lorna, you may not remember us," Samantha said when they finally found Lorna. "We're the Robert and Samantha Jenkins."

"Yeah, I do remember you," Lorna said. "Do you have a map for me?"

"This is the latest and greatest thing we have," Robert said, handing her a disc. "I downloaded it on the way in. Can we find someplace to display it?"

"My cruiser will do," Lorna said. "Eve get things fired up."

They all followed Eve to the cruiser, and she loaded the disc into the computer and switched the display to the external monitor. When it flashed to life, they could see that there were indeed very few holes left in the map of Pavonis Mons.

"Where did you find this other tunnel?" Lorna asked.

"See this line here," Samantha said. "Can you zoom in on this area?"

"I think that can be arranged," Eve said.

"There. That's the place," Sam said. "See how there's an indentation in this view. We drove right past it the first time, but there was something that caught my eye. We went back and found that there was a small tunnel that led to the north-east. As you can see it appears that we were well outside of the boundaries of the mountain."

"Eve, give me a side view of this area," Lorna said. "If it's what you think there should be a sharp decline in that area."

"There it is," Brittany said. "And see this small indentation here. I'll bet that's an entrance from the lower level. It's a lot like the one to Arsia."

"Could be," Lorna said. "How long did it take you to get back here from there?"

"All day," Sam said. "We started out last night but didn't get too far. If we leave here at 0700 in the morning, we can be back to the jumping off point by 1800 or so tomorrow night. It's a long ways up there."

"Yeah, we've been there. Britt, why didn't you find this when you were out that way?"

"We were running the spokes, remember. We didn't get into the rings very much. That was our next chore, but you pulled us off to go to Arsia Mons."

"Ok, good work. Get some rest and we'll get you provisioned with real food tonight and be ready to go first thing in the morning. Everything is big enough that we can all run out there together as long as no one falls behind. Al and Brian should be here in a while. Go get a spot staked out and lay out your habitats. I need another glass of tea. Circle the wagons. Eve, get this uploaded to all the other cruisers, please."

The gathering broke up and they all moved their cruisers a short distance from the main habitat and parked them with the habitats pointed toward the center of the circle. Lorna made her way into the main habitat and found the tea and sat in the corner.

"Miss Lorna, I have not seen you around here for quite a while," Franco said as he approached.

"We've been tied up on the other side. How have you been making out here?"

"It is very primitive, and Franco is not happy at all. Mr. Mike explained the situation to all of us and it did not sit well with me, but one must learn to adapt. We are starting to get some shipments of real food again and that makes it a little easier. Can I fix you something special?"

"A fat juicy steak would be nice."

"We just received a shipment this afternoon. Let me see what I can do for you. Are there any more in your party?"

"Yeah, about ten. Think you can fix us up with something that actually has some meat in it?"

"Franco knows he can come up with something. Just give him a few minutes. It is good to see you again."

"Thank you, Franco," she said as he retreated.

"Miss Lorna. There is a call for you on the radio," he called back as he left.

"This is Lorna," she said when she reached the radio.

"I see you made it," Al said.

"Yeah, where are you?"

"We'll be there in a couple hours. Brian is close behind us. Did everyone else show up?"

"We're all here waiting for you. I talked to Mona right after we got here and warned her that you were headed this way. She's been wondering where you were."

"Yeah, sometimes I have trouble remembering where I left her, but she's used to that by now. I'm looking forward to taking her along on this one."

"That's good because I don't think you're going anywhere without her for a while. She's tired of being left behind. Franco is rustling us up some real food. Do you want us to save you some?"

"Sure. Be there in two hours. Al out."

When she returned to her table the others had gathered there, guarding her glass of tea.

"Al will be here in a couple hours," Lorna said. "Eve, Brian is close behind him.'

"Do they have any real food here yet?" Brittany asked.

"Franco is trying to round us up something. He said he'd try to make it something with real meat in it. That may have to do for starters. I haven't seen any sign of the stuff that Al was supposed to send over for us. After we eat maybe we can go find it."

Thirty minutes later Franco came back out with a big pot of stew.

"My humble apologies. This is the best Franco could come up with. He am ashamed to say that he has let you all down."

The aroma of the stew drifted across the table, and they all smiled.

"Thank you, Franco," Lorna said. "It smells heavenly. After what we've all been eating it will taste like a slice of heaven."

"Where is Mr. Al? Franco thought maybe he would be here too."

"He's on his way. Can you save some for him and Sean and Brian? We're all headed up north in the morning."

"But of course. There was a delivery for you this afternoon. It looked like supplies for the cruisers. I have it safeguarded in the back. Would you like to have a look at it?"

"After we eat. Thank you, Franco. You are a magician."

"Again, I apologize for the humble meal. It is just so hard to make anything palatable out of what they have sent me."

Brittany stuck a spoon in the pot that he had set in the middle of the table and tasted it.

"Wow, that's good," she said and got up and kissed him on the cheek.

"Miss Brittany, you make Franco blush."

"Thank you, Franco," she said as she sat back down and started spooning her plate full.

He bowed as he retreated from the table.

"God, Britt. You're going to give the old fart a heart attack," Eve said after he was gone.

"Hey, I haven't had anything with meat in it for a long time. I'm almost to the point of offering to have someone's baby just to get a pork chop. I need meat."

"We can all relate to that," Lorna said as they all dug in. "Hopefully we'll get back on track with our supplies again."

The table went silent as they all shoveled their plates empty and refilled them again. It was like they hadn't had anything at all to eat for a year. Finally, the pace slowed.

"God, I ate too much," Lorna said.

"Yeah, but it was so good," Eve said. "Think we can manage breakfast in the morning before we leave?"

"If you get out of bed. I'll leave word that we'll want to eat at 0600. That should be enough time to eat and get on the road by 0700. If you don't get up, you don't eat."

* * *

Al and Sean pulled in at 2030. They looked like everyone else felt, tired. They just kind of unfolded from the cruiser and greeted everyone.

"Good to see all of you again," Al said, stretching to get some of the kinks out.

"Al, this is Robert and Samantha Jenkins," Lorna said. "They're the ones responsible for us all being here this time."

"Good to finally get to meet you. I hear you may have found us something else to look at."

"We hope so, sir," Robert said.

"Sir is a little out of place around here. Al will do just fine. Besides, when someone calls me sir, I start looking behind me to see if someone important has just walked up. Think it might be possible to get a bite to eat?"

"Franco is expecting you. We've already eaten, but we can join you and talk," Lorna said. "We've loaded most of the supplies in our cruisers and have some set aside for you and Brian. Mona should be along in a few minutes. She's expecting you about now."

"Sounds like you've got things lined out," he said as they all walked into the main habitat.

"We try."

"Mr. Al, so good to see you. Miss Lorna said you would be here, so I saved you some of my wonderful stew. I apologize that it can not be a more appropriate meal for a man of your stature. It is just that I have so little to work with."

"I'm sure it'll be fine, Franco. Thank you."

"We have a disc to upload the latest map to your cruiser," Brittany said. "Are you going to take point again?"

"Probably. That's one of the perks of being the God of Mars."

"Oh, so you've been getting that too," Lorna said.

"Yeah, a little. Mostly in good fun. I just ignore it most of the time. You're the one that's really responsible for saving every ones lives here. If you hadn't pushed so hard to come here and look around, well, we'd all be dead now. All I did was direct the efforts with what you found."

"It was a team effort. Let's just let it go at that."

"You're being too modest again," Sean said.

"It's a character flaw. By the way, it's good to see you again. Want to go for a ride with me tomorrow."

"That sounds like fun. Do you have our bed made? After we eat, I'm about ready to crash. Al's been dragging me all over hell and gone."

"The bed is made, and you need to watch who you run around with. He can be a bad influence."

"I know, but his credit is pretty good around here now. He can get us almost anything we want. It's a trade off."

"Can I see where we're going?" Al asked.

"I'll get a laptop and load it up," Brittany said. "It's good to see you again, Boss."

"It's good to see you too. Have you been staying out of trouble?"

"No, that wouldn't be any fun. I'll be right back."

"God, I love all these kids," Al said after she left. "They've done monumental work and not asked for anything in return. They just want to contribute. What we're doing here is a tribute to their hard work and resourcefulness. I'm so proud of them all."

"God, are you getting soft on us?" Eve asked.

"No, but I am in awe of some of the things that we've accomplished. Think about it. If you two hadn't deciphered enough of the stuff in the mine to get the go ahead to come over here, we'd all be screwed. If we hadn't been able to get Patty and Brittany and they build the cruiser nav system, we'd all be screwed. If they hadn't found their way into Arsia Mons so we could draw from the resources there, we'd all be screwed.

"It's all tied together. If we had missed any step along the way, we'd all be screwed. With what we've done here we can put this planet back together and make it better than anyone ever thought it could be. It's going to be a hundred or even a thousand times more productive once we get all the mines back up and running. The technology that we've found and figured out has moved us a century ahead of where we might have been."

"Cool," Samantha said. "Can we play?"

"I think you've already answered that question," Al said. "We don't know what lies out there in the dark, but you found the door. Each time we've opened one of these doors we've changed the face of this planet. Hell yes, you can play."

"Here's what they found, Boss," Brittany said, setting the laptop down where he could see it.

"That's the right direction alright. I'm still surprised that we've found both of these tunnels on the top level. Tomorrow will tell the tale."

"Baby, you finally made it," Eve squealed as Brian walked in.

"Well, hello to you too. I thought you'd be happy to see me."

"Join us," Lorna said.

"Eve, go get your husband something to eat," Al said. "He's earned it. Did you get them all lined out before you left?"

"I tried. I'm sure they'll be on the radio wanting me to walk them through every step. God, you'd think they could think for themselves once in a while."

"Not if they can get you to do it for them," Sean said. "If I had half the grit in my people that you all have here, it would be a wonderful place to live and work."

"Well, I want you along on this one," Al said. "They'll just have to deal with it."

"It'll be good for them," Sean said. "Now, Lorna, where did you park our bed? I'm pooped."

"Right this way. See you all in the morning. Franco will have breakfast at 0600. Anyone that oversleeps goes hungry, Eve. Good night."

* * *

At 0600 the next morning Lorna walked into the habitat and to her surprise Eve and Brian were already there. The only ones missing were Brittany and Johnny.

"Well, I'm proud of all of you," she said as she joined them. "Al, I see you found Mona."

"Yeah, she showed up just after you crashed last night. Where are Brittany and Johnny?"

"I heard them rustling around. They should be here any minute. They know the rules. Brittany is so anxious to get at some meat that I don't think she'll miss a chance at some."

"What's your plan for the day?" Al asked.

"I just figured that we'd get up there today. That may be about all we can accomplish. We can all run together. If we stay alongside each other the dust won't be that big of a factor. If we get there early enough, we might decide to go part way into the tunnel. It just depends on how we all feel."

"It would be nice to be able to get all the way across to the other side tonight," Al said.

"Yeah, but I think it's just too far. It'll take us until evening to get to the beginning of the tunnel. Then to take off to somewhere we have no idea about doesn't make much sense."

"I think you're the one that's getting soft," Eve said.

"We'll see when we get there. You mind your manners, I'm still your mother. I understand what you're saying. I just don't feel the urgency this time. Tomorrow is soon enough for me."

"How about if we go up to the point where the light ends and have dinner," Al said. "From there we can decide how far to go. I know it's a long way, but I do feel a certain amount of urgency. I can't explain it though."

"That's fair enough."

"Miss Lorna, Mr. Al, Franco has prepared the best breakfast he could under the circumstances. Eggs, bacon, biscuits, and gravy. I hope you will find it to your liking. Franco is so ashamed of the meals he has put before such fine people."

"It looks fit for a king, Franco," Al said. "Remember what we've been eating. This is wonderful."

"You are too kind. Now Franco must see to the rest of my flock. Please excuse me. If there is anything else that Franco can do for you, just ask."

"Thank you, Franco," Lorna said.

"God, he's so apologetic," Al said. "What's the deal with him?"

"I think Mike jerked a knot in his ass somewhere along the line. He's been that way ever since we got here yesterday. From what I've been able to find out he's been like that for several weeks."

"Well, eat up. We have a long way to go today."

Brittany and Johnny joined them just as they all dug in.

* * *

"Ok, Robert and Samantha, you have the lead," Lorna said as they walked to their cruisers. "You take the center of the tunnel, and we'll all fall in on either side of you. We'll probably need to stop every couple hours to stretch and go to the bathroom. We can play that by ear."

"Yes, Ma'am," Robert said.

The group followed them south toward the opening and then they all turned east. When they reached the spoke where they needed to turn to the north, they all wheeled right and pressed on, as fast as the cruisers would go. They stopped three times through the day and at 1600 approached the edge of the light.

"Let's pull up here for a minute," Al said. "This might be a good place to have dinner and stretch our legs. Lorna, switch your display to the outer monitor so we can all have a look at it together."

When the dust had settled, they all gathered around Lorna's cruiser to look at the map.

"It looks like we're still about an hour from the small tunnel," Al said. "Let's get a bite to eat and walk out the kinks. Then we can figure out whether we want to go on or not."

After they had eaten and walked around for a few minutes Al called them back together.

"Who's up for a run to the other side? I know that it's not very cool to stop out there where it's dark and the air is probably bad, but we've all done it. I'd like to see how far we can get tonight."

"Ok, you win," Lorna said. "I'm good until midnight or so. We all got a fairly good night's sleep last night. Let's go for it. Al, you lead, and I'll bring up the rear."

"Mom, you should be number two," Eve said. "Brian and I will bring up the rear. Robert and Sam, you go third."

"Ok, let's roll," Al said.

As they pulled out Al took the lead. He ran to the center of the tunnel and the others fell into formation. Lorna and Sean to his right, Robert, and Samantha to his left. They accelerated to full speed. Just under an hour later they approached the turn to the new tunnel.

"Al, the turn is coming up on the left," Samantha said.

"What are the conditions in the tunnel itself?" Al asked.

"Dark."

"Sam, I mean is there much dust or any obstructions."

"Oh. The dust didn't seem too bad, and we didn't encounter any obstructions. Sorry."

"Dark. Ok, let's try to stick together. If the dust gets too bad you may have to drop back a ways. I'll be running flat out, so judge your speed accordingly. We have a map to go by for the first leg. You can use that to guide you if it gets too bad. Turning left now. Al out."

"Al, it's about a mile and a half to the entrance."

"Thanks, Sam."

When he reached the small entrance, he slowed and turned right. Lorna fell in right behind him and matched his acceleration. The others filed in one at a time.

"Lorna, can you monitor the air in here?" Al asked after they had started to descend.

"Yeah, so far it doesn't look that bad. How's Mona holding up?"

"She's complaining that her butt is sore. I think it's going to take several days for her to reach the same state of numbness as the rest of us."

"She'll learn like the rest of us have had to."

* * *

By 2300 they had started to ascend again. It took a little over an hour before they leveled out again. They started to encounter scattered tunnels on both sides and the main tunnel started to widen.

"Ok, God of Mars, I'm just a little pooped now," Lorna said finally. "Do you mind if we stop soon?"

"Ok, as soon as I find us an intersection. I seem to be getting a lot of grief over here too."

"Give him hell Mona," Eve said from the back of the pack. "Otherwise, he's going to get in there somewhere and look back and he'll be alone."

"Alright, I get the message. There's an intersection just ahead. We'll stop there."

They gathered around Al's cruiser after the dust had settled.

"It's almost 0100," Al said. "Shall we get an early start?"

"Yeah, about 1000," Eve said. "I don't do well without my sleep."

"Well, we'll discuss that in the morning. We'll split up here and do like we did when we went into Arsia. I'll go straight and the rest of you take a spoke on either side of me. That way we can cover six of them on the way to the center. I guess sleeping in isn't such a bad idea after all. I think we'll still be ahead of where we would have been if we had stopped on the other side."

"I was watching the air on the way over," Lorna said. "It never did get too bad. Not like it was going to Arsia. We could almost drive it without the enclosed cabins. It wouldn't be pleasant, but I think it could be done."

"Get some rest," Al said, as they all started to break up.

* * *

It was 0800 when Lorna emerged from the habitat on the back of her cruiser. There was a hint of light coming from further down the tunnel, but they were still in almost total darkness. The glass of tea she had in her hand was almost half gone when Al came out to join her.

"Been up long?" he asked.

"Just a few minutes. Sleep well?"

"Not too bad. Looks like we have another exploration job for the kids."

"Yeah, I was just thinking the same thing. What on earth are we going to find this time?"

"You mean what on Mars are we going to find this time? That's a good question. I'd say that we'll probably find part of that answer right down that tunnel, later today if we're lucky."

"The air quality here is surprisingly good this far out," Lorna said. "It's way better than either of the others."

"Well, Ascraeus is quite a bit smaller than the other two. Maybe it just hasn't degraded as much as they have. It's a cinch that there's another garden in here. Think there are two levels?"

"I don't see why not. Both of the others have two. How are we going to work this today?"

"Just go with the flow," Al said. "If we find something at the center, we'll probably leave Jen and Martin to look it over. Maybe the best thing is to define the perimeter and meet back at the center in a couple days. What do you think?"

"It would be nice to know the scope of what we have here. Maybe we could send them out to do a quarter of the outer ring instead of the whole thing. Send one north, one south, east and west. When they get to the outer ring, they could all turn right and go until they intersect with the others tracks. Then we could combine them all to get the big picture."

"It might only take two or three days that way. That sounds like a good idea."

"Hey, hold the noise down," Eve called from the back of their cruiser. "We're trying to sleep over here."

"Well, now that you're awake, maybe we should get going," Lorna said. "It's getting late."

"Not late enough to suit me."

Before long the backs of the cruisers started to open, and the bleary-eyed occupants started to emerge.

"That was a little bit of a long day," Martin said. "We're not really used to that."

"You can probably get back to your routine later today," Al said. "We're betting that you'll have another garden to inspect by tonight. All we have to do is find it."

"You guys like to find us challenges, and then drive off into the sunset, don't you?" Martin said.

"It's what we do best," Lorna said.

The radio crackled to life. "Al, this is Mike. Where the hell are you?"

"Morning. We're somewhere in the southern rings of Ascraeus Mons. Do you have any requests on what you'd like Lorna to find over here?"

"Oh God. Here we go again. Tell her that I don't care what she finds. Just make it work for us. What's this one look like?"

"About like Arsia, from what we can tell. We're still well away from the light, but the tunnels look like they're about the same size as the other ones. We got over here late last night and we're just getting around. We'll know more later today."

"How long are you going to be over there?"

"At least a week, unless you need me back sooner."

"No, that should be fine. Johnson and Alicia think they can have their mines up about then. I've moved some stuff around a little to help get them up and running. The others should be getting there a week or so later. They all seem to have some spark back."

"They're all good people. They'll do fine."

"Keep me informed and don't let Lorna lead you astray. Mike out."

"Did you hear that? You're not supposed to lead us astray."

"Yeah, like you guys need anybody to lead you astray. You all find enough ways to do that on your own. Let's get something to eat and hit the road."

* * *

It was late afternoon when Al and Mona reached the inner circle and the garden. The others were behind them by as much as a couple hours. They had all split up and were coming to it from six different spokes. Al and Mona pulled just inside the garden and stopped.

"Martin, I think you're going to like this one," Al said. "It's mostly grasslands. We can't see the other side, but there don't seem to be many trees."

"How high is the grass?" Martin asked.

"Waste high, from the looks of it. Can you figure out something to do with it?"

"In time. We can get cattle sent up and graze them there. That would supply our meat. It'll take some time, but it can be done."

"Come to us when you get to the center ring. Everyone else do the same."

"Ok, Boss. We're probably the farthest out," Brittany said. "We're three spokes to the west. Maybe two hours out."

"We'll wait here for you and have dinner ready when you get here. Keep me informed of where you are."

"We'll give you a call when we get to the center ring. Brittany out."

The light was showing signs of dimming when the last of them arrived. Martin and Jen had been in the edge of the grasslands for an hour or so when Brittany and Johnny showed up.

"What's for dinner?" Brittany said."

"Steak and baked potatoes," Mona said. "Al had them stashed in our cruiser."

"Wow, Boss. I think I love you!"

"You all deserve this. I just wish we could have them every night. The supplies just haven't been distributed fast enough for that. The stuff is available, but there's so much of it that it's taking a lot of time to sort it all out. Mike ordered them to locate these for us. I have one more meal like this that we'll have when we define the edge of this place. Lorna, do you want to lay out the plan while we eat?"

"Might as well. Here's the way I see it. We need to define the edge, so we know how much territory we have to explore. We'll use four of the cruisers this time. Martin and Jen will stay close to the garden, or whatever you want to call this one. Al and Mona will go out four or five rings and make the circle. The rest of us can go to the four compass points and go out to the edge and turn right. That should cut the pie into four pieces. Go until you find the tracks of the other cruisers. Then go to the next spoke and come back to the middle. It should take two, maybe three days."

"That sounds easy enough," Eve said. "Which way do you want us to go?"

"Go south and circle back to the west. I'll take the north and circle to the east. Robert and Samantha go west and circle to the north. Brittany and Johnny can go east and circle to the south. Britt, 090, or as close as you can get to that. Eve, 180. Sam, 270. And we'll take 000."

"Keep in touch every hour or so and let us know how you're doing," Al said. "Take your time but stay after it. We'll have to define it and get back out before we all run out of supplies. There won't be any resupply over here. They just don't know where to find us. We're on our own."

"Now, how do you want your steak cooked," Mona asked.

CHAPTER TWENTY

They all gathered for breakfast the next morning and left at 0700 on their appointed rounds. Al watched as they all left except for Jen and Martin.

"Anything else you want us to do?" Martin asked. "There isn't that much for us to do here."

"Define the inner ring and if you have time, you might branch out a little and map the next ring or two. We're going to go out to the sixth ring and make the loop. Then if we have time, we may drop back in one and check that one out too. Look at the garden from all sides and see if you can figure out what to do with this one. I'm hoping that we stumble onto a way to another level, like in the other two."

"This one has great potential for food production," Martin said. "We still have a few seeds that we can plant around here and see if they grow like they did over in Arsia Mons. If they do, we'll be all set as soon as we can get the raw materials up here to plant. You might want to talk to Mike and see if he can arrange to get some cattle or something up here. It might take a few years to build a herd that we could use for food. The potential is here. All we have to do is figure out how best to use it. Maybe some farmer and rancher types too. Turn this one over to them. Let them have at it."

"I'll give that some thought and talk to Mike. He may have some ideas on the subject. There may even be some farmer types here now that could give us a hand. I don't know. I'm just thinking out loud. Well, I guess we'd better get going. It's not going to get done sitting here."

"Have a good day," Jen said.

Al and Mona climbed into the cruiser and headed south. Al turned east at the sixth ring and accelerated to maximum speed. The large tunnels were much like the ones in Pavonis and Arsia Mons. They arched up to about two hundred feet with rooms climbing most of the way up. Between these three colonies there must have been millions of people.

They would surely have an opportunity to explore some of the rooms before the day was done. They looked at them as they sped past, to see if there were any that caught their eye, but none did.

"Al, this is Brittany."

"Go ahead Britt."

"Just checking in. We're headed east. There just isn't that much to see in here."

"Yeah, we've been noticing the same thing. I guess the thrill of it all is gone for us."

"Yeah, now about all we do is drive around and map it. Let someone else get excited about going in all the rooms. There are just too damn many of them. They all look alike."

"You kids be careful out there in the dark."

"We always are. See you in a day or two. Brittany out."

"Well, dad, they seem to be taking all this in stride," Mona said. "You've raised them well."

"Hell, I didn't have much to do with that. They spend more time taking care of me than the other way around. I just take care of the things that get in their way now and turn them loose."

By lunchtime they were all well on their way to the outer ring. Al and Mona thought that they had made almost a quarter of a loop, because they were now heading north. As they sped forward, they found the tracks where Brittany and Johnny had gone east.

"At this rate it'll take us a long day and a half to make the loop," Mona said. "Do you think we'll have time to do another one?"

"We'll see what we find," Al said. "If it's all as dead as this we may not bother with another loop. We can leave that for the mapping crews when we move them over here."

"Al, this is Lorna."

"Go ahead."

"What ring are you mapping?"

"Six, why?"

"In Arsia the incline that led to the upper level was on ring four. I was just wondering if this one might be the same."

"When we get done with this one, we might drop in and check that one," Al said. "Anything else that I've forgotten?"

"Not that I can think of, but I'm sure we'll come up with something. You've been pretty preoccupied lately, what with saving the planet and all."

"Yeah, I have been a little busy. Where are you?"

"Heading north. I make it almost three hundred miles to the north side of the garden. That's a little bigger than the one in Arsia, but not as big as Pavonis."

"Did you see anything on the way up there?" Al asked.

"No, it just looked like a lot of grass. We stopped a couple times and took a closer look, but it was about the same as the one we saw on the south end. There's water, subsurface, like in the other two, but we didn't see any streams of it running anywhere."

"How far in did you go?"

"Just a couple hundred yards. We didn't want to take the time to go any farther than that. Martin and Jen can have a look at that while we cruise."

"Yeah, they're going to do that. Sam, you've been awful quiet out there. What's going on?"

"Just the same as everyone else," Samantha said. "There just isn't that much to report. Nothing looks any different than it did in Pavonis. Are you finding anything?"

"No, not really," Al said. "We're just mapping too."

"We found one of those light sources at ring nine. That's all we have for now."

"Well, that's something."

"Yeah, but not much."

"Hang in there. Al out."

* * *

By late in the day Al and Mona had passed the northern track and headed southwest. Lorna and Sean were still headed north but were approaching the edge of the light.

"Everyone check in," Lorna called at 1800.

"We're in the beginning of the outer ring," Eve said.

"Lorna, we're getting close to the outer ring, I think," Brittany said.

"We went into the dark about an hour ago," Samantha said.

"Al, where are you?" Lorna asked.

"Still in ring six but heading southwest."

"Lorna, this is Jen. We mapped the inner ring and moved out to ring two and are just getting a good start on mapping it. Is there anything you need us to do?"

"No, just keep after it and find us something to look at. We'll all meet back at the point where we spent the night last night. We had the longest run to get to our spoke, so we'll probably be one of the last to get in. Keep in touch. Lorna out."

* * *

It was mid afternoon, two days later when the first of them arrived at the assigned point. Al and Mona were the first to get there.

"Ok, roll call," Al said as they pulled up and stopped.

"Sean and I are headed west," Lorna said. "It'll be three hours or so before we get back there."

"I figure we'll be there in less than an hour," Eve said.

"Maybe two for us," Brittany said.

"We're just now back in the inner ring," Samantha said. "It may be as much as four hours for us."

"We'll have ring three finished in a couple hours," Jen said.

"Ok, see you all back here," Al said. "We'll camp here tonight and figure out what to do next."

* * *

It was 1700 when Sean and Lorna pulled in. Everyone was there except Samantha and Robert. Al and Mona were busy getting ready for dinner.

"Sam, where are you?" Lorna called on the radio.

"We should be about there. We're well south of the place where we turned west."

"Al's getting dinner started. Can we go ahead with it?"

"We'll be there in less than an hour."

"Ok, we'll plan it that way. See you soon."

While Al and Mona got dinner ready, the others consolidated all of their supplies so they could see what they had. The pile was fairly impressive. Lorna took charge of this part of the project.

"Well, it looks like we could stay out for another three days and still have enough to get back," Lorna said after going over the inventory. "Al, can we find enough to warrant staying that long?"

"It has to be done sometime," Al said as he stood over the small grill attached to the side of the cruiser. "I think we should change tactics though. I think we should run the rings for a couple days and see if we can find another level. After that it's just a matter of mapping it all."

"I guess you're right," Lorna said. "I just get frustrated with all this driving around in circles, never finding anything new."

"Patience is a virtue. Haven't you learned that yet?"

"And haven't you figured out that I'm not all that virtuous?"

"I heard that about you," Al said. "Now, can we get back to business? If we run the rings, we should be able to find another level, if there is one. In the other two mountains we encountered the way to the upper level fairly close to the center. It just makes sense that now that we have the perimeter defined, we should try to find the other level."

"Ok," Lorna said. "I can see the sense to that. I just don't know what we can do in three days."

"Have you lost all your adventurous spirit?"

"No, of course not. It's just that I get discouraged when we just run around in circles. We've covered several of the inner rings here and found nothing to speak of."

"Lorna, we have to get on with it," Brittany said. "Everyone counts on us."

"Oh, Britt—I know. I guess I'm just having a bad day."

"Well, get it together. We have work to do and you're our leader."

"I give up."

"Come and get it or I'll send it to the Lornavulture in Arsia Mons," Al said as he pulled the steaks off of the grill.

"Lornavulture?" Lorna said.

"Well, we have to call it something," Al said.

"Yes, oh God of Mars. I hear and obey. I want mine medium."

"I know how you like it. Just pick through them and find one you like. I just burn them."

* * *

"Ok, now remember," Al said as they gathered for breakfast the next morning. "We go out and complete at least one ring each. We've already covered one, two, three, and six. Lorna, you, and Sean take four. We'll take five, Brittany, seven, Samantha and Robert, eight. Jen, you and Martin take nine and Eve that leaves you and Brian to take ten.

"Logically, one of us should come across the ramp to another level. In the other two mountains we found our way up a lot closer than the tenth ring. Arsia was four and Pavonis was six. We'll meet back at ring ten and this tunnel, 290, when we get done. If you find something sing out and we'll decide what to do. We only have three or four days to do this in, so, let's get to it."

"If you find the way up, go in and start a ring around the inner circle and at least map that," Lorna said. "I know this is going to be a lot, especially for the ones on the outer rings. By coming to ring ten and 290 we'll be where we need to be to head back out. I guess I don't have to tell all of you to be careful but be careful."

"Yes, Mother," Brittany said. "Come on Johnny, let's hit the road."

"Well, here we go again," Lorna said. "Sending the kids off into the unknown."

"Yeah, but they can handle it," Al said. "I'll follow everyone out. Where do you think we'll find it?"

"I don't know, four, five, or seven would be my guess," Lorna said. "I have a strange feeling about this one. I can't explain it and I can't shake it."

"I'm thinking four or five. That's why we have those. They're also the shortest. I may have to bail and go back to the hub before this thing all comes to a head over here. Are you up for it?"

"Of course."

"It's just that you've been sounding like you've lost your edge lately."

"I guess I may have had the edge rounded off a bit," Lorna said. "I have that nagging feeling that something is going to happen, that's all."

"Well, we have to go on. We can't just crawl into a hole and hide. If we did that every time one of us had a bad feeling, where would we be?"

"Arizona?"

"Get out of here. I'll talk to you later."

"Yes, Dad."

* * *

"Al, this is Mike. Where the hell are you?"

"Ring five in Ascraeus Mons. How are things going there?"

"I haven't heard from you for a couple days. I was beginning to worry."

"We'll be here for a couple more days. After that we'll have to come back out and restock."

"Anything I can do for you?"

"No, unless you can come up with a herd of beef. We found a grassland garden over here that we were thinking we might be able to run a good-sized herd in. That would give us fresh meat to supplement our supplies."

"God, how the hell are we going to get cows up here?"

"That's a good question. I knew you didn't have that much to think about, so I thought you could chew on that in your spare time. Any progress over there?"

"Slow, but it's going to come together soon. We'll have two of the mines back up and running in less than a week and two others just after that. I think we'll have the tunnel system connecting all the mines expanded by the time any of them are ready to ship any ore. The hub facilities are coming back online fairly fast, and we should be back to almost normal by the end of next week."

"I'm impressed. What's the weather like?"

"Slowed down to a strong gale. At times we can actually see the sun now. Not all the time, but at times. They're projecting we should be back to our clear weather in two or three weeks."

"What do you think about the cow idea?" Al asked.

"I can't imagine even how they could accomplish it. All the cargo is in a part of the ship that has no gravity and damn little environment. If you put a herd of cows in there they're going to go berserk."

"Well, run it past them and see what they can come up with. We could handle several thousand head in here. Martin planted a few seeds that he carries around with him and they matured to full size in three days. There's no reason to believe that the grass won't do the same thing. All this stuff seems to grow faster when the demand is greater. You pick a tree bare and in a few days it's ready to be picked again. If you leave it alone, the fruit just hangs there until you need it. It's the weirdest thing I've ever seen, and you know that we've seen some strange shit."

"That's a fact. Ok, I'll run it by them when I can get in direct contact. I'm still communicating through the ships in orbit."

"Just do what you can. That's all we can do."

"Every time you guys get out and about you cause me bigger headaches. Do you know that?"

"Yeah, but just think about having a big juicy steak that hasn't been freeze-dried. You know, fresh. If we can do this it would take a lot of the load off of the supply chain and if we ever get in the same situation that we just went through, well, no more veggie diet."

"That does sound pretty good. Is there room to set up a processing plant over there?"

"All the room in the world." Al said. "If you can come up with some farm equipment and seeds to get us started, we could plant some of this one in wheat or whatever. In a couple years we might be able to be self sustaining almost. Think what that would do for the profit margin."

"With the ore that Bill is sending, the profit margin is the least of my worries. Hell, we're shipping it as is. We're not even running it through the mill."

"If you don't watch out this place is going to make you rich."

"Not if I have to keep spending it all on you guys. I have a meeting I have to get ready for. I'll talk to you later."

"You're the Boss. Later."

"It doesn't seem that way a lot of the time anymore. Later."

"That should keep him busy for a while," Mona said.

"Yeah but think of the possibilities. If we can pull this off this place could almost take care of itself."

"Al, this is Lorna. I was eavesdropping on your talk with Mike. You gave him a pretty big undertaking to think about. Think he can make it happen?"

"I don't know. It's going to take time. How's it going?"

"Same stuff different day. Nothing yet. Where are you?"

"Ring five and about 200. We haven't seen anything yet either."

"We're coming up on ring four and 180. If it's in this ring I expect to hit it soon."

"Just keep looking. It has to be here somewhere."

"Later."

* * *

It was late afternoon when the next radio contact was made.

"Uhhh, guys," Brittany said.

"That you, Britt," Lorna said.

"Yeah. We're at ring seven and 165 and we're headed for the basement. We've been descending for twenty minutes."

311

"Going down, that's a switch. How much change in elevation have you had?"

"Almost two thousand feet. I think I can see where it levels back out. It's still a long ways ahead of us."

"Well, when you get to another spoke, hang a right and go circle the inner ring. Al, do we need to backtrack and follow her?"

"She should be able to get to the center in a couple hours. Yeah, I guess we'd better go have a look."

"Wait. I just started to ascend. Shit, do you think there are three levels in here?"

"You follow that one and I'll go check on Britt. Brittany, when you get to the inner ring wait for me. I won't be long."

"Ok, we'll be there waiting. I'll let you know which spoke we take to get to the inside."

"Good. We'll be there as soon as we can. Roll call," Al said.

"We're just getting a good start on our ring," Eve said. About ten and 240."

"Nine and 220," Jen said.

"Eight and 200," Samantha said.

"Ok. For now, just keep after it. We'll check and see what there is in there and get back to you. Brian, I may want you to come in to one of these if there's anything that you might need to look at."

"Got it," Brian said. "We're far enough behind the curve that we should be able to divert fairly easy."

"I'll get back to you. Al out."

* * *

Three hours later Al pulled up beside Brittany who was parked in front of a dense wall of foliage.

"Looks kind of like the first garden in Pavonis," she said. "We tried to get through it, but it's just too thick. We don't have anything we can use to cut our way in."

"Did you look around at all?" Al asked.

312

"Yeah, we went east for about twenty minutes and found two more openings, but they look the same as this. We figured we'd better come back and meet you."

"We only have three hours of daylight left," Al said. "Maybe we should split up and meet on the other side in the morning."

"We'll go east, and you go west," she said.

"Done. See you on the other side."

"Al, this is Lorna."

"What did you find?" Al asked.

"Another industrial site. Kind of like the one in Arsia Mons. It may not be quite as big, but it looks a lot like the other one. What did Brittany find?"

"Another one like the first one we found in Pavonis. It's so overgrown that we can't get in. We're going to make the loop and see if we can get in anywhere else."

"We'll do the same up here. It'll probably be late tomorrow before we can get it all mapped and have a look around a little."

"Yeah, if we can get inside it may take us that long too. We'll still plan on meeting back at ten and 290, maybe day after tomorrow."

"Sounds good. See you then."

"Al, do I need to come have a look?" Martin asked.

"No, I don't think so. Let us see if we can find a way in and then maybe we can have you come back for the next round. For now, it just looks a lot like the one in Pavonis."

"Ok, we'll just keep after it then. Let me know if you need us."

"Will do," Al said. "Britt, you ready?"

"I was born ready."

"See you on the other side tomorrow."

"We'll stop when it gets dark and start again at first light."

"Good luck."

* * *

Two days later they began to assemble at the assigned junction, ring ten and 290. Al and Mona were the first to arrive. Brittany was only a few minutes behind. It was just after lunch time when the others started to filter in.

"Sean, what did you come up with?" Al asked as they all sat down to a late lunch.

"It's a lot like the one in Arsia, but in a lot better condition. After we had the perimeter mapped, we were able to make a couple trips across the area from a couple different directions without much trouble. Thousands of pieces of mobile equipment, manufacturing plants that are almost intact. It's a lot better find than the one in Arsia. There were at least another fifty of the miners in there that we saw, probably more. That's all we had time to look at."

"Brittany, do you have those maps combined into one yet?" Lorna said.

"Just about. I stopped to eat. It won't take long to finish it up," she said.

"Good. We'd all like to have a look at it. Finish eating though. We're not in that big of a hurry."

The radio crackled in Al's cruiser as they were finishing.

"Al this is Mike."

"Good afternoon," Al answered.

"You still hiding out?"

"Yeah, but we're getting ready to head back. We're just about out of supplies. We should be back at the garden in Pavonis late tomorrow. What do you need?"

"Just checking on you. I finally got a direct line to the board and pitched your cow idea, and they have people looking at it, but didn't sound real optimistic. Things here are getting back to normal faster than we'd figured, and I was wondering if you and all of your people might like to take a few days off at the hub. I can clear out as many rooms at the hotel as you think you might need."

"You know—that sounds like a hell of a good idea. Plan on us for the day after tomorrow and I'll see if I can get you a head count. It's going to be big, maybe a hundred or so."

"Christ, that many?"

"You said all of our people. We have more than forty cruiser crews alone. I assume you mean all of them."

"Yeah, I do. Just get me a number for the rooms you need, and I'll take care of it. Shit, this is going to be expensive. What time of day will you get here?"

"We can make it by late afternoon, just in time for you to buy dinner."

"Good. I'll be expecting an update on what you found over there too. Mike out."

"It's party time," Al said. "Any takers?"

"You mean a hot bath and everything?" Brittany asked.

"That's exactly what I mean. Think you can handle it?"

"Oooh yeah! You damned right. These spit baths are better than nothing, but to soak in a big tub for a couple hours sounds like as close to heaven as I can imagine right now."

"Well, get those maps combined and we'll have a look and get on the way."

"Give me five minutes," Brittany said.

"Sam, you and Robert too," Lorna said. "You've earned it."

"That does sound good," Samantha said. "I don't remember when the last time I was actually able to lie in a tub of hot water and soak my bones."

"It has been a while for all of us," Lorna said. "I think we should stay over there for a week."

"Sounds good to me," Al said.

"Guys, the map is ready," Brittany called.

"That was quick," Al said. "Let's go have a look."

"Center on our present location and zoom in a little," Lorna said after they had all assembled. "There, that should do it. The three gardens are almost stacked right on top of each other. The perimeter isn't anywhere near the edge of the mountain either. Not as close as it is in the other two. Ok, let's get a side view."

"The lower one is well below the planet surface," Al said. "Britt, make copies for each of us so we can study them on the way back. Lorna, we need to recall all of our crews and the ones over in Arsia and get them back to Pavonis by tomorrow night. Then we can all go to the hub together. That should be quite a parade."

"I'll get on it as soon as we get started. Are we ready?"

"Let's mount up," Al said.

A few minutes later they wheeled to the south-west and ran line abreast and headed out.

CHAPTER TWENTY-ONE

Al and Lorna watched as their troops began to gather the next evening in the upper garden in Pavonis Mons. There were forty-three cruisers and two rovers that were gathered in small circles around the main habitat by the time they had all been accounted for.

"I called Bill and he's going to bring Slim, Joe, and Jim in tomorrow," Al said as they watched the gathering from the habitat. "He said he could spare Dan and Jeff for a couple days if we wanted them to come."

"Yeah, I think they deserve to go too," Lorna said. "Has Melissa showed up yet?"

"No, but she'll be here soon. I talked to her a few minutes ago."

"God, most of them are so young. They all look like babies."

"I think they are a lot better suited for this than we are. We're getting too old for this shit."

"I can't argue with that. It looks like old home week out there. Just look at them."

"Did you tell them what you called them in for?"

"No, I thought it would be a nice surprise," Lorna said. "I just told them all to be here. Patty and Brittany are getting a head count now, to make sure we have them all. God, I don't even recognize half of them. Where did they all come from?"

"You hired them all."

"Yeah, but since we sent them out, I haven't crossed paths with a lot of them. They come in and download and go right back out and pick up where they left off and just keep going."

"Mr. Al, Miss Lorna, Franco would like to welcome you back from wherever you go to. May I fix you something?"

"Franco, you may indeed, but we'll need a lot of it," Al said. "You have an extra hundred or so mouths to feed tonight. We brought in all of our crews at the same time."

"I had noticed that there were a lot of faces that Franco does not see every day. I called in some help and have enough to go around. You cannot sneak up on Franco so easily anymore. he pays attention to the radio and he watches what is going on around him. Franco's blood pressure is much happier when you do not surprise him."

"Well, we do have a surprise for Franco," Lorna said. "Tomorrow morning after breakfast we're all going to the hub for a week and Franco is going too. After a rocky start you held things together here while we were out doing what had to be done. We think you deserve a vacation too. What do you think about that?"

"Franco is dumbfounded. Franco would love to go and cook in a real kitchen again. We get by here, but it is not to Franco's liking. As you say, we must do what we have to, to get by."

"No, you don't understand. I said a vacation. You don't have to cook. Someone will do all of that for you."

"Franco does not allow just anyone to cook for him. No, the idea of a vacation to Franco is to cook in a shiny kitchen for people who enjoy eating what Franco cooks. That is a vacation for Franco."

"Well, we'll see what we can do for you," Al said. "We'll have to leave ahead of the others, but we'll be sure you have a ride."

"Franco is most grateful. Thank you. Now, can Franco fix you something special?"

"No, we'll have what everyone else is having," Lorna said. "I'm sure it will be wonderful."

"The lady is too kind. Franco must go now and prepare."

"Thank you, Franco."

They just stood and watched as he bowed as he backed away from them. He was almost clear across the habitat before he turned and left.

"God, how did we end up with him?" Lorna asked.

"It takes all kinds," Al said. "Shall we go let the rest of them in on what we're doing?"

"Sounds good. Let me grab another glass of tea."

They went out and gathered everyone together. Patty, Brittany, and Eve joined them as the others gathered.

"What's up Boss?" Patty asked.

"Everyone, gather round," Al called. "We called all of you in at the same time to make a special announcement. We're all going to the hub for a week of relaxation. You've all earned it, and the entire tab is being picked up by Mike Peterson."

A cheer rose from all assembled. They looked at each other and laughed and giggled like a bunch of school kids. Most of them weren't much older than that.

"Now, we're going to drive in there tomorrow and I want everyone to have a good time. That's an order."

"Where are we going to stay?" came from the back.

"I have rooms at the best hotel in town reserved for everyone. I need to know if you need a separate room or if you can bunk in pairs, so we know how many rooms we need. Patty and Brittany will be inside after we get done and they'll take down names and what you need. I'm sorry that I don't know all of you personally, but we've grown so fast and been spread out for so long that I just haven't been able to keep up with everything.

"You'll have the best that there is to offer on the planet. That may not be as much as it would have been in the past, but it's got to be better than what we've all had for the last couple months or more. Hot baths seem to be what most of the women are interested in. I can understand that."

"You've all been such a help that we thought you deserved a vacation," Lorna said. "The work that we have left out here can wait for that long. Go and have a good time but try to stay out of too much trouble. We'll bail you out, but not until it's time to go back to work. It'd be a shame to spend your time in the brig instead of a nice hotel. Mike has arranged a dinner in the ballroom of the hotel for tomorrow night and we'd appreciate it if all of you would attend that and after that you can do whatever you want.

"Now, Franco has us all a hot meal that will be ready soon and then we can all get some rest. We'll leave after breakfast in the morning. Thank you all."

"We heard that you found another mountain to explore," one of the crew said. "Is that true?"

"Yes, it's true," Al said. "We just got back from there. Don't worry about that right now. We'll fill you in on it when the right time comes. For now, just relax, have fun, and get reacquainted with each others. Eat some of Franco's good cooking and get some rest. See you all in the morning. Thank you all."

"That was quite a speech," Melissa said as she walked up behind them.

"Glad you made it," Lorna said. "We were worried about you."

"I got a late start. What's this about another mountain? I hadn't heard about that."

"Ascraeus Mons," Al said. "Come inside and we'll fill you in. Franco has dinner about ready."

* * *

Al sat at the table in the habitat as the light began to filter into the upper garden the next morning, looking over the list of names. They'd need ninety-three rooms at the hotel. That was going to be a large order even for Mike.

"Penny for your thoughts," Melissa said as she approached.

"God, you startled me," Al said.

"Sorry. I guess I should have coughed or something," she said as she sat across from him.

"I was just going over the list of names that we're taking to the hub. Most of them I don't even know. Knowing all of my people personally is one of the things I try to do. It helps me relate to them on a personal level and that makes them feel like they belong."

"Are there any communications with Earth yet?"

"Yeah, Mike said he was able to communicate with them directly a couple days ago. I don't know how reliable they are, but I'm sure that they'll be good enough for you to report in. Is that what you had in mind?"

"Yeah, and I want to get a message to my family that I'm ok. My folks are probably going out of their minds. They didn't want me to accept this job. They thought it would be too dangerous to fly off to Mars and live in this environment. They didn't know that there were people like you and Lorna up here to take care of all of us, I guess."

"Well, we do what we can."

"Your modesty is only surpassed by your superior dedication to your job and the people that work for you. I plan on letting everyone know about it. I don't know what all you've been doing these last couple months, but I have heard enough to know that you saved the lives of everyone on this planet."

"Don't you go off on that God of Mars bit on me too. Look, we just did all we could to get us all through a very bad time. Our training and our people deserve the credit. We were just in the right place at the right time."

"Ok, I'll drop it for now. What time are we leaving?"

"By 0800. That should put us in there by dinnertime. We've found a shorter way to get to the tunnel, so it doesn't take as long as it did a few weeks ago. Mike has a big dinner planned for 2100 and I'd like to get everyone into their rooms well ahead of that if we can. It's going to be a long day, but I don't think anyone will mind."

"Well, it looks like they're starting to surface, Melissa said. "Will Slim be able to make it?"

"Bill will be bringing them over. They should be there when we get there. Are you anxious to see him?"

"Yeah. We've been going in different directions for so long that I really do miss him. Who would have thought that I would go halfway across the solar system to find a man like him. He's one of a kind."

"He is that."

* * *

They all filed out of the garden a little after 0700, an hour earlier than they had planned. Al and Lorna led the way and they all spread out and ran along side of each other. It was quite a sight to see. Forty-four cruisers and two rovers clearing a path as they went. The dust boiling up behind them that would hang in the air for an hour before it settled again.

They all arrived at the hub at 1800 and parked in the maintenance area. After they had gathered, they all went to the hotel together. When they walked in, Al went to the desk.

"We have reservations," he said.

"Yes, Sir. We have everything prepared. We'll just need you to sign in. We have the top two floors reserved for you and your crew. The rest will be spaced out throughout the hotel. Dinner is at 2100 in the ballroom. You should have time to clean up if you'd like."

"We'd like," Al said as he signed in.

"Your room is the presidential suite on the top floor. I have a list of about twenty or so to occupy the other suites. Is this list right? Some of them have already checked in."

"Yeah, that looks right. Good, Bill and the rest have already arrived." Al said as he went over the list of his core group who had seen it all. "Take care of these people and we'll try not to be too much of a disruption."

"It is our pleasure to serve you and your party."

"Thank you," Al said as he took his key card.

* * *

"Mona, are you about ready?" Al asked at 2030.

"Yes. Sorry, but I had a little trouble prying myself out of that big tub. It felt so good."

"We should probably go down a little early so we can be there to greet the others as they come in. I want them to feel at home."

"You're a good dad, you know that. There I guess I'm as ready as I'm going to get."

"You look great. Shall we?"

"We shall."

322

When they stepped out of the elevator there was a mass of people there to greet them. They made their way through the crowd receiving thanks from everyone they came near. Mike was standing in the doorway to the ballroom.

"What the hell is all of this?" Al asked.

"I guess the word got out that you'd all be here tonight," Mike said. "I tried to keep it quiet, but we had to deal with a lot of people to make it happen and somewhere it must have leaked."

"I hope it's not going to be like this the whole time," Al said. "I hate being on display."

"Go on inside and I'll head them off," Mike said. "I'll do the meet and greet for you. You can catch them on the inside."

"Ok. I guess that's the way it's going to have to be."

Just then the others started to show up. Joe and Sharon were the first, Lorna and Sean were next. Lorna stepped up with Al and Mona went with Sean to find their places at the table. There were several tables arranged in a half circle. Mike was at the in the center with Al and Lorna on either side of him. The rest had places marked out for them.

When everyone was assembled and the doors were closed to keep the prying eyes of a grateful public out, Mike took the floor.

"Attention everyone. Most of you know me. I'm Mike Peterson, head administrator of this planet. The reason we've called all of you together is to thank all of you for the great job that you've all done. Thanks to all of your efforts the people of this planet were saved during the storm that has been raging out there for the better part of three months now.

"Some of you may not know the history behind what you're doing. It started almost two years ago when some of Al's crew found a wall buried in their mine. We called in Lorna and her bunch, Al called them the bone chasers, to figure out what we had. Little did we know where she would take us. The facts led them to places that nobody could have imagined just a couple of years ago.

"Now, they have led us all to three different city sized civilizations. Without their hard work, and yours, no one on this planet would be alive today. We, the transplanted people of Earth, would like to thank you all for your efforts. I've arranged for all of your expenses, within reason, to be paid for. The hub operations aren't quite back to normal, but we feel there are enough facilities up and running to give you a good time. Communications have been reestablished with Earth and you'll all have priority clearance to communicate with your families. That seems to be the most requested thing by all the people here. Even though we've put out all the information through the proper channels, everyone seems to need that personal contact.

"Now, I've rambled on long enough. You'd think I was running for office or something. I, personally, thank you all. We're in your debt. Now, let's eat. You'll find the menu much better than we had at Pavonis Mons, not that we're complaining. Enjoy yourselves."

When Mike sat down the back doors of the ballroom opened and a parade of chefs pushing carts full of food emerged. Franco, in a shiny white jacket and a tall white chef's hat led the procession.

"Miss Lorna, Mr. Mike, Mr. Al—Franco regrets that he did not get here in time to oversee this fine feast, but he has been assured that it will be fit for kings, and queens," he said as he stopped at the head of the table. "Franco wishes to offer his services during our stay here. Franco wishes to be allowed to prepare another feast for all these fine people. Franco cannot go out and find fantastic things to save people's lives, but Franco can create wonderful things for you all to enjoy."

"Franco, you're supposed to be on vacation," Mike said.

"Franco relaxes in the kitchen. Franco needs to relax. Franco needs to be in this fine kitchen. Franco begs you to indulge him just this once."

"I'll see what I can do Franco," Mike said. "Thank you."

As he turned to leave, he started barking orders to the others. In just a few minutes there was enough food laid out before them to feed three times that many people.

"I'm having ID cards made up to identify your people. They should be ready in the morning," Mike said. "We took their pictures as they checked into the hotel. I want them to be identifiable to everyone here. It's not much, but it's about all I can do for them right now."

"Just getting out of the cruisers for a few days is going to be enough for most of them," Al said. "It's a hard life out there. The isolation alone is hard for some of them to handle. Now maybe we can bring them in a little more often to let them recuperate. I think the largest part of what we have to do is done. We still need them out there for a month or two, but then it should start to wind down."

"We'll have time to talk later," Mike said. "Now, is that steak big enough?"

"I could eat on this for a week," Lorna said. "I guess the supplies have been replenished."

"Yeah, they have," Mike said. "We have shit coming out our ears. We offloaded twelve freighters in just over three weeks. We're running out of places to put it all. Bill has come through though. He's kept us supplied with enough ore to ship back on all of the ships. I can't imagine what it's going to be like when we get all the mines back up and running. There won't be enough ships to haul it all off."

"Now there's a problem I imagine you can live with," Al said.

"Yeah, but it could get to be a real problem in the long run. Just think about it. It's going to stack up around here so bad we won't have room to breathe."

"Store it in the cave under the hub," Lorna said. "When that's full, just make another one."

"That would solve the problem of storage, but it won't get it back to Earth any sooner. That's the big problem. I've been talking to the board, and they can't believe we have a problem. It's going to take time to solve it and they need to get started."

"Yeah, I know," Al said. "Everything takes time here. Any luck on the cows?"

"You should have heard the howls of laughter when I asked for that. They thought I'd lost my mind, but they said they'd look into it."

"Just think of what it would mean to food production on this planet. We could connect the lower tunnels in Pavonis Mons to Ascraeus Mons, like we did with Asia Mons. That way we could move about at will. We'll have to map Ascraeus Mons first, but we could get over there a lot faster that way. There's a lot of exploring left to do."

"The two of you have changed the face of this planet," Mike said. "No two people in history have changed a world more than you two."

"Aw shucks," Lorna said. "We just went where the clues took us, besides; anyone would have done the same thing. Christ Mike, give us a break. We had a job to do, and we did it well. That's all there is to it. Hell, Franco does his job well, go heap praise on him. We're getting a little tired of this shit. Back off a little."

"Did she get out on the wrong side of the cruiser today?" Mike asked.

"No. She—we—get a little tired of being put up on this pedestal that everyone has placed us on," Al said. "It's getting a little hard to function effectively."

"Well, I have a feeling that you'll have to learn to deal with it. There's nothing I can do about it."

"Would you if you could?" Lorna asked.

"Probably not. These people need a little something extra right now. They've found that in you two. Give it a little time and it'll all blow over. I almost hesitate to mention that the board has decided to give you a proclamation of some kind. I haven't heard just what it all amounts to yet, but you might want to be prepared for that too. They want to have a conference call tomorrow afternoon."

"We can't make it," Lorna said. "We're on vacation."

"Now don't be like that. It's going to have to happen sooner or later, and you might as well get it over with. My office at 1300, shall we say?"

"Oh, alright. Now, can I eat in peace?"

"Of course. During the call tomorrow you can fill me in on Ascraeus Mons. I understand you found three levels over there."

"Yeah, but there's nothing that we haven't found in the other two," Al said. "Martin planted a few seeds over there and checked on them after three days and they already had mature fruit on the small trees. The ground is so fertile that if we can get the seeds to plant and someone to work the fields, well; we can produce most of our own food. The one area is so rich in grass that would support a lot of cattle if we can get them up here."

"They're still working on that. I think we threw them a curve with that one."

The dinner went on for almost two hours. When it was over Mike announced to the gathering that they would receive special ID cards at the front desk in the morning. These cards would give them the run of the place, and everything would be paid for. Everyone filed out and Mike, Al and Lorna were the last to leave.

"Kick back and relax," Mike said. "I'd appreciate it if you'd come by the office for that call. They want to thank you."

* * *

As they finished lunch the next day Al looked at Lorna and shrugged his shoulders.

"Shall we get it over with?" he asked.

"Yeah, I guess so. Anyone want to take our places?"

"It doesn't look like you have any takers," Sean said. "I'll go for moral support, but I don't think you can get out of it."

"Gee thanks, guys," she said. "Ok, I guess I'm ready."

"It's almost 1230," Al said. "Mike's going to be pacing the floor by the time we get there."

"He needs the exercise."

Twenty minutes later they arrived at Mike's office. He was waiting for them, pacing the floor.

"I thought you'd stood me up," he said.

"We wouldn't do that," Lorna said. "After all it's a command performance."

"You cut it a little close. I've already received their first transmission. I'll play it for you and then we can formulate a response."

"There's not much to formulate," she said. "As far as I'm concerned this isn't a beg session like when we were trying to get funding to go to Pavonis Mons."

"They have questions."

"So!"

"You're not going to embarrass me, are you?"

"Probably," she said and smiled.

"Oh God. Ok come in here. This is what they had to say," Mike said and hit the play button.

"Mars Hub, this Randolph Emerson, speaking for the board. While we regret the losses you have suffered; we feared the worst had happened. During the course of the storm, we had a lot of hard decisions to make, as I'm sure all of you did there as well. Fortunately, most of what we had set into action here was recalled when we got the word that you had weathered the storm. We congratulate you.

"We understand that you have made significant discoveries that enabled you to endure what we all thought would be a disaster. We were prepared to start from scratch and rebuild the entire colony on Mars. It obviously would have taken years and cost the company a tremendous amount of money to do that. Thank you for being so resourceful.

"Al and Lorna, we are in your debt. Is there anything the board can do for you to make things easier? We await your response."

"That was short and sweet," Lorna said.

"Now's the time to lay out your shopping list," Mike said. "It'll take time to get it filled, but I think they're very receptive to almost anything you want."

"Crank it up," Lorna said. "I have a few things I'd like to ask for."

"Ok, here we go," Mike said and started the transmission. "Mars Hub to Randolph Emerson. This is Mike Peterson here. I have Al and Lorna with me, and we'd like to say a few words. Here's Lorna."

"Hi, guys. We need more of everything, as fast as you can get it to us. We want livestock and people to tend them. We want upgraded reactors for our cruisers, so we don't spend so much time traveling from place to place. We burn up a lot of time just going from here to there. We want farm equipment so we can begin to grow our own crops up here and become self-sustaining so if this happens again, we can feed the masses on our own without hardship. We want improved dome designs that can be implemented ASAP, so we don't have thousands of people blow away in the wind. I'm sure we can come up with more, but I'm out of breath for now.

"We saved you bazillions of dollars and we want bonuses for all of our people that were instrumental in saving the lives of the colony here. I don't think that's too much to ask for, do you? Here's Al."

"Mr. Emerson," Al started. "The remote nature of this operation dictated that we have the support from Earth. Up until now it has been our life's blood. We now have the opportunity to become almost self-sustaining. We think it is in the best interest of all concerned to make that happen. I know that there will be challenges that must be met, but we also know that they can be overcome. Any group of people that can colonize another world can overcome these challenges.

"In the last year and a half, we have turned science-fiction into science-fact. Not a sole on either planet could have even imagined the advances we've made in that short time. I know I never thought there would be ancient civilizations to be unearthed here. The discoveries that we've made have enabled us to save the lives of most of the people that you sent here to do a job for the company. We all knew the risks when we took on the jobs that you sent us to do, but now we have opportunities that weren't available a couple of years ago. We would like your support in our future endeavors. Thank you."

"In closing," Mike said, "I would like to commend Al and Lorna for giving us this chance to make life here so much more than it could have been until now. We'll await your response."

Mike signed off and turned to Lorna.

"You didn't sound very cordial," he said.

"I don't feel very cordial."

"You can't talk to them like that."

"The hell I can't. What are they going to do—fire me? I've been fired by better men than them."

"I guess you warned me that you were going to embarrass me, didn't you?"

"Yeah, I did."

"She's right though," Al said. "We're in a position that we don't have to beg like we had to when we wanted to go to Pavonis Mons. They allowed us to pursue that, and that decision was the best they have ever made. Otherwise, we'd all be dead right now."

"I can't argue with you," Mike said. "Let's just sit back and see what their response is."

It was almost an hour before the response came.

"Randolph Emerson here. Mars Hub, we understand what you're saying and will attempt to address your demands. When you first found the garden, or whatever you want to call it, in Pavonis Mons we dispatched a large shipment of seeds. Given the amount of time that has passed since then, we believe that you should be receiving them within two to three weeks. This will address one of your concerns.

"We have people working on the idea of getting livestock up there to you but are not sure if it's feasible. We may have some answers in a couple weeks. The problem is getting them off the Earth and into orbit. Once that is accomplished, well, we think it would be possible.

"In all of the shipments that we've sent to you since your first discovery in Pavonis Mons, we've included additional reactor units, more seeds, larger computers, and anything else that we thought you might be able to use to further your explorations. We will continue to do this, as you have proven your worth to the operations there. While I won't write you a blank check, you can rest assured that any and all requests we receive will be given considerable weight.

"The company and the families of all the people there are forever in your debt. We commend you and thank you for your farsightedness. We will be in touch in a few days with further communications and to let you know of our progress from this end. Emerson out."

"Well, there you have it," Mike said. "He didn't even read you the riot act for being disrespectful."

CHAPTER TWENTY-TWO

As the week drew to a close the crew gathered again in the main ballroom for a final dinner. Al and Lorna stood by the door to make sure everyone got into the ballroom unmolested. The accolades had died down some, but it was still hard to move around without being attacked by the adoring public. Mike was one of the last to arrive.

"Sorry I'm late. I just got a message that some of your supplies arrived on the transport ship today," he said. "We have three containers of seed stock for you to take back to Pavonis Mons with you. There may be more, but that's all I know about for now."

"That's great," Lorna said. "Can you fix us up with some way to plant some of them?"

"You may have to do it the old-fashioned way for right now. I can't spare the manpower to build stuff for you right now. We just have too much to do around here."

"That's alright," Al said. "We'll take some of them to each of the gardens and plant them and have them monitored. If Martin is right, they should take off and grow right away."

"Yeah, but it's going to create a whole new set of problems," Lorna said. "How are we going to harvest the crops? How are we going to process them?"

"God, all you do is throw monkey wrenches into everything," Mike said. "Can't you just enjoy the moment?"

"Well, we have to think of these things. I think we're starting a new phase of things here. We still have a lot of exploring to do, but think about it, now we have to expand our thinking to include farming and ranching on a new world. There's a lot to think about."

"Think, think, think," Mike said. "God woman, quit thinking and enjoy yourself a little. It will all shake out as we go forward. It's been a great week having all of you here, but I must admit that I'm ready for you all to go back out into the field. This is costing me a fortune."

"With all the money we've saved and made for you; you can afford it."

"Yeah, I guess you're right. Besides, you've all done more than just make us all rich. We haven't had much of a chance to talk about Ascraeus Mons. Is it like the other two?"

"Yeah. It has another industrial area and two gardens. The one is just grassland, and the other is pretty thick. We haven't really been able to get in there and see much.

"What can we do with it?"

"Develop it," Lorna said. "We can run beef and whatever else you want to. The industrial area can be another source of materials for helping you get this place back on track. You're going to need a lot of materials to get this place fixed up."

"We're going to investigate the possibility of tunneling directly into the industrial area and maybe make some shortcuts from between the levels," Al said. "It won't take too long to open it up. It's a long way over there though. We may need to figure out a shortcut back to here too. We haven't had a chance to think it all the way through yet."

"Well, I'm sure you'll think of something," Mike said. "Just let me know what I can do for you. Obviously, there won't be that much in new toys, but I may be able to come up with some extra manpower if you need it."

"I think what we need to do is go back over there for a few days and see what we can find out," Al said. "Then we can start to formulate a better plan. We spent most of our time over there the other day just mapping some of the area in close to the center. We need more time to explore the possibilities."

"We'll take half of the cruisers over there to start mapping the place," Lorna said. "The other half will go back to Arsia Mons and try to finish up over there. Al can figure out a place to tunnel into and the rest of us can explore the gardens and industrial area. We'll need to set up a supply chain so we can stay over there for a while. All in all, we have a lot to do in the next week."

"Can we steal a habitat from somewhere?" Al asked.

"Hell, I don't even know where they all are anymore," Lorna said. "If we cut back on the staff at the library, we might be able to cut them down to one. They probably wouldn't be very happy about that, but they'd get used to it. They're not getting that much productive information from there anyway."

"We'll head that way in the morning," Al said. "It's been good for the crew to relax for a while, but it's time to get back to work. Shall we go in and enjoy a good meal?"

"I'd like to say a word," Mike said as they took their places at the table. "We've enjoyed having you here for the last week. You've run up a hell of a tab, but we owe you that. I want you each to have at least a weekend a month here at the hub from now on, on me, of course.

"However, now it's time to get back to work. As we rebuild from this disaster, we will all have our hands full. Our task here is one that will take time, but we'll be back up, and fully operational before we know it. Your task is to get back out there and see what else there is to be found. With all of your discoveries you've ensured the survival of the people on this planet.

"Up until now we've been entirely dependent on our supply lines between us and Earth. But with the discoveries you've all made we have the opportunity to become self-sustaining. If we can do that, we can change the destiny of us all. A city, a country, a planet, that can support itself will prosper. We still have a long way to go, but you've put us on the right road. Now go out there and lead us down that road."

With that Franco appeared in the doorway with a cart full of food. He made his way to the head of the table and started serving Al, Mike, and Lorna. Others on the kitchen staff followed him out and started serving the others.

"Mr. Al, Mr. Mike, Miss Lorna, Franco prepared a special meal just for you and your wonderful crew. It has been fantastic to work in such a kitchen as you have here."

"Franco, would you like to stay here and work for me for a while?" Mike asked.

"I would love that Mr. Mike, but Franco's place is where Franco can do the most good. Franco's place is back at Pavonis Mons, or wherever Mr. Al and Miss Lorna need him. Franco has been humbled by these great people and Franco wishes to serve them and do whatever Franco can do to help."

"Well, you'll have to come back and cook for us sometime," Mike said. "I'll see what I can do about getting you a kitchen set up at Pavonis Mons. That seems to be where the center of things is going to be."

"Oh, Mr. Mike, that would be truly wonderful. Franco can hardly contain himself. Now, you enjoy this fine meal and Franco has a surprise for everyone. A special surprise."

* * *

Al and Lorna waited for the others to appear in the dining room the next morning. They had put together an assignment sheet for the next week and arranged for all of the cruisers to be stocked as heavily as they could carry. Patty would lead the team in Arsia Mons and Brittany would lead the exploration of Ascraeus Mons. Brian and Sean would gather up a habitat and move it to Ascraeus Mons as soon as they could. Eve and Lorna would pair up and help Brittany, along with whatever they could find to do in Ascraeus Mons. Martin and Jen would set up a test area in Pavonis Mons to start growing some of the seeds that had just arrived. Slim and his crew would set up and start a tunnel toward Ascraeus as soon as Al gave them a target to shoot for.

As the crew filtered in, they were given their assignments and sent on their way. Al and Lorna were the last to leave. As they were about ready to go Alicia and Rebecca came in.

"Hey, you two," Lorna called to them. "Don't you have anything better to do than hang around here?"

"God, we've been going sixteen hours a day for two weeks," Alicia said. "We heard that there might be a spare room available here after the outland crew went back to work and decided we needed a day off."

"Having any luck?" Al asked.

"Yeah, as a matter of fact we are. The plan you laid out is going to work just fine. We have three caverns opened up and we've widened the tunnels to handle the transports. We should be operational in less than a week. It's going to be a lot like roughing it for a while, but we can handle that. Crew quarters are the biggest challenge for us right now. With losing all our facilities in the domes about all we have are mattresses on the ground. The cooking is a challenge too, but we signed up for challenges when we came here, didn't we?"

"We did indeed. Have you heard how any of the others are doing? Mike has kept us out of the loop for the last week."

"They're all progressing, some faster than others. We should all be up and running in a couple weeks. I think my mine will be one of the first."

"You've come a long ways since we pulled you out of your destroyed domes," Lorna said. "Rebecca, are you behaving yourself?"

"No, that wouldn't be any fun."

"If you ever get tired of working in the mine, give me a call. I think we might be able to find you a job with us. I think you'd fit right in."

"Thanks, I'll keep that in mind, but for now, Alicia needs all the help she can get. She tells me that I'll have a full-time job just mapping the mine tunnels once we get to going again."

"She's probably right," Al said. "But we can always use an adventurous soul who wants to see what's hidden in the dark."

"Stop it, you two," Alicia said. "You can't have her. I know that all you have to do is say the word and anyone on this planet is working for you, but I really do need her."

"We wouldn't do that," Lorna said, "unless we really did need her. We have been known to do that on occasion, I guess. Don't worry. We have a fairly full crew at the moment."

"What's this we hear about a third mountain?" Rebecca asked.

"Ascraeus Mons," Al said. "We just found it before we were ordered in for R&R. We're headed back out there later today."

"It has three levels instead of two," Lorna said. "We don't know what we have over there yet."

"Any chances of it going beyond there?" Alicia asked.

"Who knows?" Lorna said. "We didn't even hope to imagine that it would go this far. I guess Olympus Mons isn't out of the question, but it's not very likely. We'll just have to see where this one takes us for now."

"Well ladies, I have to get going," Al said. "Slim is going to be waiting for some new coordinates to tunnel to and I have to figure out where they are."

"I'll be right behind you," Lorna said. "Eve's getting things ready to go. Sean and Brian left an hour ago. I'm going to stop in Pavonis Mons for the night and see how things are going there. We'll be over to Ascraeus as soon as we can."

"Ok, see you then. Ladies, you be good."

"We're better than that," Rebecca said.

* * *

Two days later Al pulled into the center of Ascraeus Mons late in the evening. Brittany was parked in the inner ring and had a command post set up. Al had been listening to her bark orders to the twenty other cruisers that had followed her over the day before.

"You sound like a drill sergeant," Al said as he and Mona got out of the cruiser.

"They got soft sitting around the pool for a week," she said. "Just trying to get them focused again. Don't get me wrong, I enjoyed the time off too, but it's time to get back to work."

"You'll do," Al said putting his arm around her shoulder. "Where did you send them?"

"Six upstairs, six downstairs, and eight here. It's going to take several weeks to get an idea of what we have to work with here. Four of the ones on the upper and lower levels will define the perimeter first. The other two will go into the center and work their way out. That way we can at least get an idea of where we stand."

"I talked to Brian and Sean earlier and they should be here sometime tomorrow with a habitat and a computer to handle the downloads. Where do you want it?"

"This is as good a place as any," she said. "This is where everyone ends up when they come straight in. I was wondering if maybe we could cut a few direct paths between the levels. It seems like a terrible waste of time to go out several rings to get to the ramps."

"I think that might be a good idea for all three locations. I don't know why we didn't think of that a long time ago."

"You've been busy. So have we all, but now maybe it's time to slow down just enough to have a chance to think ahead a little. We all need to think about where we will go next. We have a lot of exploring to do here and Patty won't be done on the other side for several weeks. It's going to take the better part of six months to map all of this."

"Yeah, I know. Say, when did you get so smart?"

"I had a good teacher. You taught all of us to think for ourselves."

"I didn't think anyone was paying attention."

"We all paid attention. Now, I think it's time to have a snack and turn in."

"It has been a long day."

* * *

"Al, are you out there?" Slim called two days later.

"Yeah. Where are you?" Al answered.

"Sixteen and 030. I have six miners standing by. Do you want to drive two tunnels?"

"Yeah, I think that's best. We'll have to set up ventilation with cross tunnels like we did in the others. Go ahead and start in there and by the time you get set up I'll be there to give you something to shoot for. We're back inside Pavonis now and headed your way."

"Ok, we'll set up here and one spoke to the north. I suppose you want to make it big enough to handle a transport."

"Yeah, but don't go too big. I have another job for you when you get over there. Brittany has requested several short tunnels to connect the levels. When we get done with that, I think we should do the same in the others. It'll make it a lot easier to get around."

"Why didn't we think of that before?" Slim asked.

"According to Brittany we've been too busy. She said it's time to slow down a little and think ahead, like I taught everyone. Hey, that's what she said."

"I guess we'd better listen to her."

"Yeah. See you in about three hours."

"Al, this is Lorna. We're in the industrial area in Ascraeus. It looks like we have several types of farm equipment up here. When is Sean going to get over here?"

"They should be there this afternoon. We met them last night on our way back to Pavonis. They were running a little behind. Do you think we can adapt them to do what we need done?"

"I'm no expert on farm machinery, but yeah, I think we can. It looks a lot like some of the stuff my grandfather used on his farm."

"Brian was raised on a farm," Al said. "I'll have him take a look. Brian, are you listening to any of this."

"I read you," Brian said. "We'll get up there and take a look as soon as we drop off the habitat."

"Do you need any help to get it operational?"

"I have that covered and if I need any more, I can hijack a couple cruiser teams for a while. We'll have it up and running by this time tomorrow if we don't spend too much time in the industrial area."

"Take care of the habitat first and then go up. That can wait that long. Lorna can meet you back up there when you get ready. We can try them out in the grasslands if you think they might work for us. I'll get with Martin and send one of the containers of seeds that way as soon as we get the tunnel finished. I don't think we can get them thru the small tunnel."

"If you get up that way you might want to bring a few bags over with you," Brian said. "If there's a bailer of some sort, we can bail some of the grass and then plow the ground."

"I'll swing by there on my way back. Any preference on what I bring?"

"I don't even know what's there. Corn and wheat or something. If they have any seeds for trees, bring a few of those."

"Al, this is Martin."

"Go ahead."

"I've gone through the inventory, and we have a little of everything. Corn, wheat, rice, several kinds of trees. Just about everything you can think of. Most of it is food related, but not all of it."

"Set aside a variety of things that we can use and don't get too carried away," Al said. "I have to haul it in the cruiser. The bulk of it will have to wait until we can get the tunnel finished."

"I haven't had a chance to plant anything yet, but by the time you get here I may have time to get that done."

"Put Jen on it. I want to see some results as soon as possible."

"Yes sir. She's standing right here, and she'll take care of it."

"I'll be there tomorrow sometime. Al out."

They made good time and arrived at the beginning of the tunnel where Slim was waiting for them.

"I've been waiting for you," Slim said.

"Here's the disc with the coordinates on it," Al said. "Mona rigged it up on the way over. When you get over there go on into the center and get with Brittany. She has some work for you. When you get done with that, I'll arrange to have a couple transports bring the miners back over here. We can do the same thing here and over in Arsia. I think she had a pretty good idea."

"Anything we can do to cut down on the travel time will be great. I have enough people to work it around the clock if you want us to."

"Yeah, go ahead. I have a feeling that we'll soon find a lot of other things to do. It sounds like we're all going to become farmers too. This isn't exactly what I signed up for."

"Well, I guess it comes with the territory."

"On that disc we gave you two sets of target coordinates," Mona said. "Al thought you'd need to run two tunnels. Who's on the other one?"

"Joe and Jim are riding heard on it. We have three miners working together in each tunnel and we'll be there in about four or five days."

"Well, I'd give myself a little leeway," Al said. "It's a long way over there."

"Well, that may have been a little optimistic, but we'll make good time."

"I can see that you have at least four weeks' work ahead of you. I think I'd move one of the miners back over here and use four on this tunnel and make this the primary. The ventilation tunnel can be smaller."

"Ok, I can see that. Why didn't I think of that?"

"Moving too fast, I guess. Slow down a little and we'll think our way through this. Remember, that's Brittany's new motto."

"Yes sir," Slim said and laughed.

"We're headed for the upper garden to gather supplies for Ascraeus," Al said. "Keep me informed. We'll see you on the other side in a week or so."

"We'll be along as soon as we can," Slim said. "I'll go get that other miner moved back over here and have it fall in with the others. We just have enough cruisers to support us, but not to chase supplies. Can you arrange to have us resupplied later in the week?"

"I can do that. Keep in touch."

"Get out of here and let me get back to work."

* * *

The next morning Al and Mona pulled into the upper garden just after 1000. They went directly to the habitat in the main assembly area. Martin and Jen were standing next to their cruiser.

"Hey, you made it," Jen said as they got out.

"Yeah, we did," Al said. "Are you doing any good here?"

"I would say yes," she said. "You told me to get on planting some of those seeds and I did. Want an apple?"

"Where did you get that?" Mona asked.

"I grew it. I planted an apple seed yesterday and picked it this morning. It grew overnight. If you have a day to hang around, I think I might be able to show you some other things too, but I need a little time."

"I think we can spare a day," Al said. "Do you have any coffee?"

"Franco can probably come up with some," Martin said. "Come on inside."

"If all of these seeds grow at this rate, what are we looking at?" Al asked after they had all taken a seat at that the table in the habitat. Franco hurried over with coffee for everyone.

"I think we could feed the planet with very few acres planted, which is a good thing," Martin said. "We don't have unlimited acreage to plant, so we'll have to plan out how we want to do it."

"Mr. Al, can Franco get you anything else?" Franco asked as he sat the tray on the table.

"No, Franco, I think we're good for now. Thank you."

Franco retreated and Martin continued.

"We may have a preliminary idea of what we can do in a couple weeks. We'd like to see what we can do here and then go to Ascraeus and try over there too. We need to figure out a way into the lower garden over there so we can see what we have. God, we have a lot of work to do."

"I can get you some help if you need it," Al said.

"Help with what?" Martin asked. "We don't even know what we have yet. Granted it would be nice to have a little help with the planting, but the evaluation of the results will have to be done by us."

"I'll take a few bags of seeds over to Ascraeus and plant them for you and document the time and date they are planted. Is there any other information you need?"

"Well, that's a good start. Mona, you like working in the garden, don't you?"

"I love it," she said. "Back home I always had a garden while he was off chasing his rocks."

"Maybe you could plant a little garden close to the habitat and monitor its progress for a week or so. Having your input would be invaluable."

"I think I could do that while Al's getting the tunnels connected and everything. As long as he doesn't forget where I am again."

"I promise I won't forget where you are," Al said. "I may even hang around and help you a little while we wait for Slim to break through."

* * *

"Come see what we have!" Jen came running in the next morning as they sat down for breakfast.

"Calm down," Al said. "Sit down and have a bite to eat."

341

"But you need to see this. I just went over to where I planted the seeds a couple days ago and we have fantastic growth. Look. Here's a tomato that I just picked."

She handed them a tomato that was the size of a small watermelon.

"How long did it take to grow that?" Al asked.

"Less than two days," Jen said. "I've got stuff coming up everywhere."

"Can it wait until after breakfast?" Al asked.

"Well, yeah, I suppose it can. This is fantastic growth, don't you think?"

"Yes," Mona said. "Now, please sit down for a minute and get something to eat."

"We've had great results before," Martin said. "Nothing like this though. It usually takes over a week for them to grow to half that size. All the tests that I've run on the past small crops indicated that they were as palatable as any you'd buy at the supermarket back on Earth. The taste is a little richer than some, but I see that as a plus. Franco has been using a lot of them in his cooking for over a month now and he just loves working with them."

"This is promising," Al said.

After breakfast they followed Jen to the area where she'd planted the seeds two days earlier. There was a small apple tree that was heavily laden with large apples. There was a small patch of wheat that was almost thigh high, with large shuts of wheat on top. Carrots, peas, beans, corn, and lettuce grew in their own little areas and showed similar growth.

"That's quite a garden you have growing there young lady," Al said.

"Hell, all I did was shove the seeds in the ground a couple inches and cover them back up," Jen said. "I didn't have a lot of time to mess with them."

"Well, it looks like you did something right," Al said. "Keep an eye on things and let me know how it's going. We'll leave later today or tomorrow morning and take a few things with us to plant over on the other side. I hope it works that well over there."

* * *

"Al, this is Brian," came the call late that afternoon.

"Go ahead."

"We're all up in the industrial area and have found some interesting machines," Brian said.

"Anything that will help us?" Al asked.

"Absolutely. All I have to do is figure out how to run the damn things. There's enough agricultural equipment here to farm half the planet. If it works half as good as the miners, we have it made. Do you want us to move some of it down to the grasslands?"

"Yeah, go ahead. We'll be back over there the day after tomorrow, maybe late afternoon. Jen's having very good success with the few things that she's planted over here. Mona and I will set up a small plot over there and see what we can do."

"Ok, we'll see if we can get some of this stuff moved down to the habitat and meet you there. Brian out."

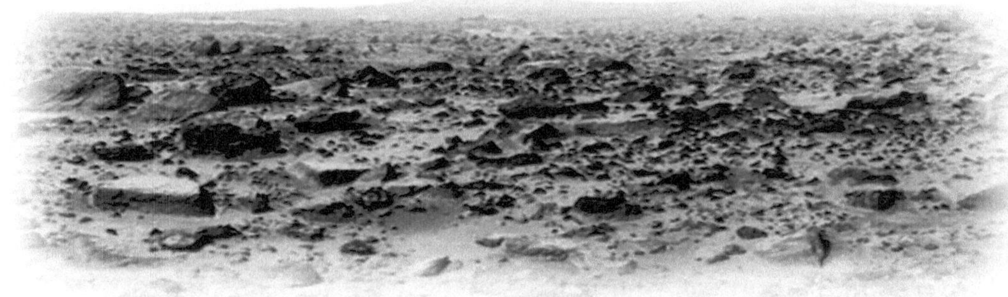

CHAPTER TWENTY-THREE

When Al and Mona arrived back at the habitat in Ascraeus Mons they found that Brian had cleared five acres just inside the opening into the grasslands garden. He had baled the grass and stacked it close to the entrance and cultivated the soil to get it ready to plant.

"You've been busy," Al said as they stood in the entrance.

"Just trying to stay busy," Brian said. "After we cut it the first time, we let it set overnight and had to go back in and cut it again this morning. It grows so fast that it's going to be hard to control."

"It looks like you have a handle on it now though."

"Yeah, after we turned it over and worked it a little it seemed to stunt it pretty good. I don't know if it'll try to come back again though."

"We'll soon find out. We brought all the seeds we could haul. Do you have anything we can use to plant them with?"

"There are three different types of what look like planters to me. Maybe we can adapt one of them to do the job. This soil isn't nearly as sandy as the other gardens we've come across. I hope the subterranean water will still get to it after we turn it over like this."

"Well, that's what we're about to find out. Mona has been laying out what she wants to do with your few acres of soil, so we'll get started tomorrow morning and see what happens. Where's Britt?"

"She left late yesterday to go map a couple spokes. She was bored sitting around here. She should be back here late tomorrow. She said she'd still be hanging in close so she could be around when they come in to download. We have the habitat and computer system up and running. When will we expect to get more supplies?"

"A couple days. I have it arranged, but I'm not real sure when the first shipment will show up. We brought all we could, and I even scrounged up one of your little trailers to bring some extra. We should be fine for a while."

"Don't forget we have twenty cruisers to supply too," Brian said.

"I know, but they all had all they could carry when they came this way, and I told them that they may have to make their supplies last for over a week to begin with. We'll check on them later and see how they're doing.

"I talked to Slim on the way over and they're making good headway. He estimates it will take four or five more days to break through. I think it's a lot farther than he thought it was. As soon as he gets close, we'll call for a transport to bring in the supplies and get this place set up right."

"Do I need to go over and set up the fan system for his tunnels?" Brian asked.

"No, I have Carlos working on that. He's installed enough of them that he can handle it. I talked to Mike, and he's found five portable power units and a bunch of fans in that last shipment. He's sending them to Pavonis, so we'll have them where we need them."

"Sounds like you have everything covered. I guess we'll stay close and give you a hand. I do want to spend more time up in the industrial area so I can try to figure out what we have. It looks like this one is geared more to food production than industrial though. We went through a few buildings and thought we might be able to use them to make flour and such. It'll take a lot of work, but it's better than starting from scratch. There were a few pallets laying around that had a few broken bags of what looked like flour any way."

"Sounds promising. We'll just stick close here until Slim gets here. I want to get him a line laid out so he can come in here and drive tunnels to both the other levels in here. We need to cut down on our transit time a little between levels."

"That's a good idea."

"Yeah, Britt asked if we could do that for her. It'll make things a lot easier and faster getting around in each of the mountains. Slim's going to go do it in the other two after he finishes here. I'll get a couple transports to move him around."

"That'll keep them out of trouble for a while."

* * *

The next morning, they laid out several small plots that were separated by a ten-foot buffer to keep them from mingling. Mona directed things and Brian and Sean did most of the work. Al went up to the upper level and got the coordinates he wanted for the new tunnel and went into the center area and looked around. Brittany showed up just after lunch and joined in with Mona. She bossed Johnny around like he was a rented mule, but he took it all in stride.

By late afternoon they had planted over half of the seeds that they had brought with them from Pavonis the day before. There were plots of corn, carrots, peas, wheat, oats, barley, lettuce, potatoes, and several other food types. They had also planted three different types of trees. Two apple trees, two peach trees and one pine tree.

When they got up the next morning, they already had plants that were a foot high. The tomato plants seemed to flourish in this soil.

"That's the damndest thing I've ever seen," Mona said, standing there looking at the new plants.

"Wow, we may have a fresh salad by lunch tomorrow," Brittany said. "That stuff we had over in Pavonis and Arsia was ok, but I miss a good salad like back home. Lots of tomatoes, a little celery, maybe a sprinkling of cabbage, carrots, you know, just throw it all in there and try to sort it out. Do we have any dressing around here? I don't think I have any."

"We brought some that I stole from Franco," Mona said. "After seeing how Jen's stuff was growing, I thought we'd manage to make us up a good salad to go with some of the steaks we brought."

"Oh yeah," Brittany said. "That sounds good. I want to be sure that I'm here for that."

"You going to help me pick some of it tomorrow?"

"You bet."

"Mary, Mary, quite contrary, how does your garden grow?" Al asked as he walked up behind them.

"Not bad if I do say so myself," Mona said.

"Damn."

"Exactly."

"I thought Jen was pulling my leg," Al said. "How long do you think it'll be before you can pick some of that?"

"I'm not sure, but I'd say maybe late today or tomorrow at the latest. We should have a big salad to go along with those steaks that you brought."

"Martin said the flavor was richer than the stuff we had back on Earth. I wonder just how some of that is going to taste. Getting all of that freeze-dried stuff on the transport ships is one thing, but to have actual fruits and vegetables is going to be a real treat."

"What are you guys looking at?" Lorna asked as she approached. "Damn, didn't you just plant that?"

"What do you think?" Mona asked.

"I'm impressed. The native seeds that we've seen planted didn't grow that fast. Some of the ones we got from our food supply showed good results, but nothing like this. Even Eve could get stuff to grow here."

"She has a brown thumb?" Al asked.

"More like black. If you want to kill a plant, just give it to her for a week. Its days are definitely numbered."

* * *

By mid afternoon the next day they were able to harvest some of what they had grown. That evening they racked out the small grills on the sides of the cruisers and baked several of the potatoes that they had just grown and grilled the steaks that Al had brought. Brittany and Mona worked up a large salad and they all sat down to eat.

"Oh, this is good," Brittany said. "I know that I'm going to eat way too much of this. You may have to roll me to my cruiser later."

"I wonder what cows that grazed on that grass would taste like," Lorna asked.

"I don't know, but I have a feeling that the meat would melt in your mouth," Al said. "Hopefully we can find out one of these days."

"Have they figured how to get them up here yet?" Brittany asked.

"I think they have some ideas. I suggested that they send calves just old enough to be away from their mothers and feed them sparingly on the trip. I have to admit that I wouldn't want to have to clean up after them in an enclosed ship. That would be a very nasty job. I think the plan is to try a hundred in the first round and see how they handle the trip.

"I also suggested that they only send five or six bull calves and the rest female. That way we can breed our herd faster and in a couple of years have a descent sized herd."

"How many do you think we can graze in here?" Lorna asked.

"I'm no expert on ranching, but the grass regenerates so fast that I don't think we will have any problem running a big herd. The problem is going to be processing them."

"There may be something we can adapt up on the upper level," Brian said. "We need to get in there and have a good look around."

"What are you doing sitting around here," Al asked.

"Just making sure you can handle things here before we go off again," Sean said.

"Mona is going to monitor things here and I'll go with you tomorrow. You might as well take Lorna and Eve with you. They'll be hard to live with if I separate you again."

"Yeah, imagine how Sharon, Hollie, and Melissa must feel," Eve said.

"I'll take care of them when I can."

"Al, I've been looking at the map," Brittany said. "If this is going to be the main food area, wouldn't it be a good idea to tunnel toward the hub from here. I mean, we're closer to the hub than Pavonis Mons or Arsia Mons and if you're planning to feed the planet from here it might be a good idea to connect the two more directly."

"You're starting to make me look bad, young lady," Al said. "Pretty soon you won't need me at all."

"You could always tell them it was your idea. I'm just trying to cut down on some of the travel time. God knows we have enough of that already."

"I'll look at it, and if it needs to be done, you'll get the credit for it, for what it's worth. I think we've almost broken the bonus bank."

"I'm not looking for another bonus. It's just that our speed is limited by the cruisers, and we need to find ways to get to certain places faster. The only way we can do that is cut down the distance where we can. You've connected all of the mines with tunnels so that we never really need to go out into the elements again if we don't want to. It just makes sense to do that from here too."

"I can't argue with that. Slim's not going to like it very much though."

"Sorry, but after it's done, we'll all be better off."

"You're absolutely right. I'll see if I can get a handle on it and see if we can make it happen."

"Britt, do you know anything about running a slaughterhouse or a flour mill?" Sean asked.

"No, but driving around out here day after day, we all have a lot of time to think and between us we should be able to make life better for the whole planet."

"You've already done that when you and Patty invented the cruisers mapping system," Al said. "I'm so proud of you two that I can never express it enough. Thank you."

"You're welcome."

* * *

The next morning Al led the way to the upper level, and they went into the industrial area at the closest point they came to. There was an order to it that wasn't present in Arsia Mons. They drove in several miles and stopped in front of a group of buildings.

"This is the area we thought might work for some of our processing needs," Sean said.

"There's a flour mill or something like that over here," Lorna said.

Al pulled out the large map display on the side of his cruiser and studied it for several minutes. He zoomed it out to show the area between the hub and Ascraeus Mons. He took a felt marker and drew lines from the point where they were and the hub area.

"Ok, we need to explore the areas inside these lines," he said. "I want to know everything about all three levels from 130° to 165° and from the edge of the center areas to the outer rings. If we're going to tunnel to the hub from here, we need to have all of this defined, so we don't break into one of the lower tunnels. I'll get with Britt and have her take care of that with her cruisers. As soon as we get that information, I'll map out a way to get there."

"That shouldn't take too long," Lorna said. "She should be able to get that taken care of by the end of the week. She may have to divert some of her cruisers, but that shouldn't be a problem."

"Yeah. We should be ready for it before Slim gets here. I'm wondering whether we might need to go ahead with it before we move them back over to Pavonis and Arsia Mons. I'll have to talk to Mike I guess."

"He's just going to tell you to do whatever you think you need to," Lorna said.

"I know, but it's kind of becoming a habit. You guys look around here. I want to go up north and come in from the other side and see what's there. I haven't had much of a chance to look around in here. Also keep your eye out for something that we can use to get into that lower garden. It's so overgrown that it's going to take some serious cutting to get in there. I don't think whacking it by hand is going to work very well on that one."

"What about one of the miners," Brian said. "Just make it go away."

"That's an idea. We have other things for them to do though."

"We found several more up here the other day," Sean said. "There may be more that we haven't found too."

"You know that someday we're going to have to figure out how those things work, don't you?"

"Yeah, but I think we still have a ways to go before we need to concentrate on that. I also know that sooner or later they're going to want some of them sent back to Earth. I'm surprised that they haven't already been calling for that."

"So am I, but let's not give them any ideas. I want to keep them here for as long as we can. No telling what we're going to need them for next."

"We'll explore here for a few days and see what we can find," Lorna said. "You just go do whatever you need to do. We'll take care of this."

"Yeah, I have another hair brained scheme running around in the back of my mind. I'll be back down below tonight. I need to talk to Brittany about it."

"What's that?"

"It's just an idea that popped into my head. I have to think about it a little before I let it see the light of day. I'll talk to you later."

Early that evening Al pulled in and parked close to the habitat by the grasslands. He had been so lost in his thoughts that he hadn't really paid much attention to what he'd seen all day.

"Al, you're back," Brittany said.

"Yeah, I have a couple things for you to think about. Got a minute?"

"Sure."

"First I need you to map everything in this area on all three levels," he said as he showed her the area on the map. "That way we can have an idea of what we have so we can tunnel to the hub. I really think that's going to have to be done. I haven't talked to Mike about it yet, but I'm sure he won't have a problem with it."

"What else?"

"Well, I was wondering if you could tie video cameras into the nav system so we could have an actual visual record of what the map looks like. Say I select a point on the map and the picture of that point would be displayed instead of just this mass of line-work that we have now. Think you could manage something like that?"

"I don't think it would be a problem. It'll take up a lot of space on the hard drive though. We may have to increase the memory by a bunch to do that. Where can I get the cameras?"

"If you think it might work, I'll get you the cameras. I think we need to map the industrial area upstairs and just the line-work images won't do us much good. I need to be able to see what is actually there. There are hundreds of square miles inside there and it's like trying to map the Los Angeles basin. It would be nice to have them on all the mapping cruisers, but I'll settle for half a dozen for now."

"Do you want a 360° view?"

"That would be ideal, but I'll settle for whatever you can get for me."

"You realize that the rear view will mostly show dust clouds, don't you. I can isolate the cameras so you can select the ones you want to use. Give me a day or two to think about this. I may have to have Hollie come over and give me a hand with the software. Patty is too far away."

"Just let me know what you need, and I'll see to it. How's it going here?"

"Good. Eve's trying to weave some baskets out of the tall grass so we can carry some of the stuff easier. I swear she can weave it tight enough to carry water and never spill a drop. She and Brian came back down a couple hours ago. Lorna and Sean are going to stay up top for a few days I guess."

"Where's Mona hiding?"

"In the garden. She's been out there most of the day. She's been measuring plants and cataloging things every hour all day long. You wouldn't believe that you could measure a plant and go back in an hour and it's tall enough to be able to measure the difference, but she's doing it."

"Well, you give that little project some thought and let me know what you think. I may have to send you and Johnny to the hub for a couple weeks to work with the engineers to get it to work."

"That's rough duty Boss," she said with a big grin on her face.

"Yeah, I know but someone has to do it."

"Al, you're back," Mona said as she came out of the garden.

"Yeah, I just got back a few minutes ago. How's it going in there?"

"Good. It's growing so fast that I can hardly keep up with it."

"Do you think we can feed the planet and graze a herd of cows in there?"

"Yeah, and maybe half of Earth too. I've never seen anything grow so fast and the taste is fantastic. It's better than organic stuff back home. If we plant five hundred acres, we can feed everyone here. I'm telling you that we're going to have more trouble keeping up with it than we are growing enough to do the job. The stuff we picked yesterday has already regenerated and is almost as big as it was when we picked it then."

"I'm sure Mike's going to be glad to hear that. All they have to do is keep the seeds coming."

"We can adapt some of what we grow for seed stock too. That may help. I don't know how the fruit trees are going to fare because there are no bees to pollinate the flowers. There are still a lot of questions that Martin is going to have to answer."

"Why don't you write up your preliminary findings and I'll take them to him. I need to go to the hub for a day. I can drop it off on my way."

"Why do you need to go to the hub?" Mona asked.

"I need to talk to Mike, face to face. I'm getting ready to expend a lot of his resources and need to explain what's going on."

"When do you have to leave?"

"In the morning will be soon enough. This all seems to be in good hands. It'll take me four days to make the trip, plus whatever time I have to spend there. Do you want to ride along?"

"I'd like to, but I think right now I need to be here. Just don't forget where you left me this time."

"Don't worry. I'll check in with you every day," Al said.

* * *

Two days later Al approached the hub in his cruiser. He'd been by the garden in Pavonis the day before and given Martin a copy of Mona's report. He didn't believe what he'd read. The seeds that Jen had planted had only shown about half of the growth rate that Mona was reporting. He and Jen were making plans to go to Ascraeus Mons in a few days.

"Al, this is Brittany."

"Go ahead, Britt."

"I've been thinking about that idea you had, and I probably should plan on a trip to the hub to work on it. I talked to Sean about it, and he had several suggestions that I'm trying to work into the plan. I still have a few days work to get ready for that though."

"Ok, I'll be back over there in a couple days or so. It's a long way to get back and forth. I'll let you know when I'll arrive, and we can make plans from there. I have to talk with Mike before I can do much for you."

"I understand how that works. I'll work on my end and wait for you to get back. Brittany out."

Al checked into the hotel at just after 2100. There was a message from Mike for him to call when he got in.

"Mike, this is Al."

"Good to see you made it. I understand you have another project you need help with."

"Yeah, but that can wait for tomorrow. Is there something you wanted to talk to me about?"

"No, nothing important. It can wait until tomorrow. I just wanted to make sure you got here alright."

"You're going to have to make that trip one of these days. It's a hard two days to get between there and here."

"I hope things will settle down enough here to allow that soon. It's getting better every day."

"One of the things we need to talk about is making another tunnel from the hub to Ascraeus Mons. It's just too far to have to go to Pavonis every time we need to come here. I want to come in and tie into the tunnel close to the hub here and connect directly to the inner circle in Ascraeus Mons. It looks like we're going to do most of our food production over there. The growth rate is double what it is in the other two gardens."

"That sounds encouraging."

"I left Mona up there to watch over things until I get back. Brittany is there with her, working on a special project I assigned her, but that can wait until tomorrow. All I want to do now is get something to eat and go to bed."

"When you get up and around tomorrow give me a call."

"Will do."

* * *

The next morning Al slept in until 0700, unusual for him. As he tried to shake out the cobwebs from his brain he gazed out through the dome. The view to the east was the standard pink of the morning sky. With the CO_2 crystals freezing every night and melting in mid air by late morning, it always had an eerie pink glow to the sunrise. After his morning routine he went down and had breakfast. There was a message for him to come by Mike's office when he had a chance. The waiter delivered it to him as he sipped his first cup of coffee.

An hour later he showed up in Mike's outer office. Sally was busy going through a stack of papers on her desk and was surprised when he walked in.

"Al, I wasn't expecting to see you again so soon," she said. "How's it going out in the trenches?"

"Good, I guess. Is he in?"

"Yeah. Let me tell him you're here."

A moment later Mike stood in the door motioning him to come in with one hand and holding a phone in the other and talking a mile a minute to someone.

Al sat across the desk from him and waited for him to finish his conversation. Mike's desk was cluttered with papers and files.

"Wow," Mike finally said. "That was Alicia. She's shipping her first load of ore today. I've started pulling the crews out of Bill's mine and sending them back to where they belong. She's the first one to bring her mine back online."

"That's great," Al said. "How are the others doing?"

"Better. They seem to be getting some of the old fire back. I think they're going to cover us up with all of the ore they're going to be sending. I've been trying to convince the board that we need to double the transport ships, but they think that's a little optimistic. Even if they could do that, it would take several years. What brings you back so soon?"

"Well, I've been thinking again."

"What's that going to cost me?"

"Not a lot. I think I need to have Brittany and Johnny come in for maybe a couple weeks and work with some of your engineers on developing a new system for the cruisers. She's working on the plans now and won't be here for a week or so."

"I really like her and her sister. What's she up to now?"

"I asked her to come up with a way to interface a video system with the navigation system in the cruisers. I need it to explore the upper area in Ascraeus Mons. I can't take the time to do all I need to do in there, but we think this would give us a video tour of the place. That would be a great help in evaluating what we actually have in there. It's a lot more organized and in a lot better shape than the one in Arsia Mons. I think there's a wealth of recourses that we can draw from in there."

"Sounds reasonable to me. The only problem I have with it is that our engineering staff is stretched pretty thin right now. With all of the repairs we have to do in here and at the mines, it's got them hopping pretty good."

"I know that, and I can send in extra support for that, but there may be some areas that they need the help that only the engineers can provide. I can bring in Hollie and Jim to help them with the fabrication and the programming. I don't want to trust it to your computer people. Sorry, I don't mean to offend you, but I'm not at all impressed with them."

"Neither am I, but I'm stuck with them. Was that all you needed?"

"No. I've been thinking about driving another tunnel," Al said moving to a map on Mike's wall. "It's a lot closer if we come directly from Ascraeus Mons to here. We could connect with one of the tunnels from Pavonis Mons west of here a ways. We have all of the information we need to do that, and I think it's a smart idea, one of Brittany's I might add. It looks like we're going to be able to concentrate our farming and ranching operations mostly in Ascraeus Mons. The soil there is very rich, and the growth rates are fantastic. I think we can use the area to produce almost everything we need."

"So why are you here asking my permission?"

"It's a habit that I may have a little trouble breaking."

"That won't affect what's going on here. It's going to make things a lot better in the long run. Do it. It won't cost us shit."

"I may need to draw on your personnel a little to get it done. We're spread pretty thin. I may need to get some extra bodies to man the miners. My people are all tired and I don't want to push them much harder. We'll oversee it all, but we may have to have bodies to actually do the work."

"I can arrange that. I have most of the mill crews working on repairs. With the amount and the quality of ore that Bill's been sending in, they don't have that much to do. All they do now is separate and melt it down to a form that is easier to handle. There isn't much refining to speak of. Not like we used to have to do."

"We'll have Pavonis and Ascraeus connected in another week or so and then I want to just turn them south-east and head them this way. I may have them take care of a couple little side jobs that I want them to do first, but this is the next priority."

"Do it. I'll get with some of the mill managers and find you, what, twenty people?"

"That should do it."

"Anything else?"

"Not that I can think of. Sean wanted me to go talk to some of the engineers about Brittany's idea, but that's about all I needed to bounce off of you."

"Hell, I thought this was going to be painful, what with you coming all the way in here. I don't need to be consulted every time you want to do something. You know more about what we need out there than I do. Just handle it unless you need me to grease the way for some reason. A couple years ago it was different, but now, you're making us so much money that I really don't care what you do as long as it doesn't interfere with the mining too much.

"Now that we're starting to come back online with some of the other mines, I'm going to bring Bill and his people in for a week or so. They've earned a break. They have us supplied with enough ore to ship for two months. I can't imagine how covered up we're going to be when they all get operational again."

"They have certainly carried the load," Al said. "Well, I'll get out of your hair and let you get back to work."

"You staying the night?"

"Yeah, probably. By the time I get some of the things done that I want to do it'll be late this afternoon."

"Join me for dinner."

"Ok. I'll call you later."

CHAPTER TWENTY-FOUR

Six months later Al and Lorna stood in the edge of the garden in Ascraeus Mons, looking across the vast fields that they had developed. They had been producing almost all of the food for the planet for several months now and they were expecting their first shipment of cattle to arrive any day now.

During the last six months there had been a lot of changes. They had finished the tunnel to the hub and developed several shortcuts in each of the Mons to make getting around easier. Brittany had developed the video mapping system and worked out the bugs with the help of Patty and Hollie. It had given them another tool to use in their exploration of the vastness of the caverns inside the Mons. They had found several people that had extensive farming and ranching experience and put them to work in the center garden in Ascraeus Mons

They had received steady shipments of seeds and equipment to support their efforts. They had managed to set up two camps close to the center garden and were getting ready for the ranching phase of their operation.

The hub was fully operational again and Mike had developed a vast system of storage caves for all of the ore that had stacked up. He'd recently commented that they could all take a year off and still be six months ahead of their production schedule. He'd also managed to convince the board that they would need more transport ships and they should start to arrive in a few months.

"What do you think?" Martin asked as he walked up behind them.

"Unbelievable," Lorna said. "How much area have you planted?"

"About a third of this garden, plus several hundred acres in each of the other two. That should be enough to do what we need to do. We could plant more, but I don't think we need to. We can hardly keep up with what we have. Once we get the flour mill online, we may need to up the production a little, but we've stockpiled a lot already."

"You've done a great job," Al said.

"Well, I didn't really sign on for this, but it has been a lot of fun. Jen's taken over as the field boss and is just having the time of her life. We've been talking about getting married. What do you think about that?"

"I think it's a great idea," Lorna said. "I was wondering how long it would take you two to get around to that."

"The last several months with her have been the best, most fulfilling of my life," Martin said. "We bicker back and forth, but we seem to feed off of each other. She has an energy like I've never seen in a person. A lot of times I'd like to just kick back and relax for a day or two, but no, she gets me up and going every day. She can't wait to see what's going to happen next around here."

"We need to go to the hub in a few days," Al said. "I think you two should go along. I think it's time for another group vacation. I have it arranged with Mike."

"Sounds good to me. When do we leave?"

"I'm not sure yet. I have to figure out where everyone is and get them all rounded up. That will probably take several days. Can you manage to be away from here for a while?"

"Yeah, we have things lined up and we have good help. They can handle things here just fine."

"I hadn't heard about this trip," Lorna said. "When did this come about?"

"A couple days ago," Al said. "I hadn't had a chance to tell you about it. Mike wanted to see our smiling faces again."

"What's it all about?"

"Just a little R&R as far as I know. He wasn't specific. He just wanted us to gather up the main part of our crew and come in for a few days. I'm sure he has an ulterior motive for it, but what the hell, it's a paid vacation."

"Yeah, but I have an uneasy feeling about this. He's up to something."

"Look, it's a few days in the lap of luxury. Just kick back and enjoy it."

"I will, but I still don't trust him."

* * *

Four days later they all pulled into the maintenance area of the hub. They parked and headed for the hotel. It was early evening, 1800, and they were all tired from the trip.

"We'd like to check in," Al said at the front desk.

"Yes sir, we've been expecting you," the clerk said. "Your suites are ready. Again, you will have the top floor to yourselves. There will be a dinner in your honor this evening at 2000. I was instructed to ask you to attend."

"Yeah, we'll be there," Al said. "Right now, all we want to do is go get cleaned up and rest for a while."

"Yes sir. Here are your keys. Your things will be brought up right away."

At 1945 that night they assembled in the dining room and were surprised that Mike wasn't already there. Twenty minutes later he came in, all dressed up and he had someone with him.

"Al, Lorna, and crew, this is Randolph Emerson, Chairman of the Board of the Interplanetary Mining Company," Mike said as he took his place at the head of the table.

"Finally, I get to meet the famous Al and Lorna," Emerson said. "We've talked on many occasions, but this is our first actual meeting where we could actually carry on a conversation. Please, introduce me to your crew."

"Mr. Emerson, this is Lorna and Sean," Al said. "Next are Melissa and Slim. Then we have Eve and Brian, Joe and Sharon, Hollie and Jim, Brittany and Johnny, Martin and Jen."

He continued until everyone had been introduced.

"I've taken the time to come here personally to thank each one of you in person." Emerson said. "I'm not a great one for long speeches, but on this occasion, I may make an exception. During my trip here, which I might add was the first time I've ever been into space myself, I had a lot of time to review all that you've accomplished in the last couple years. I know that a lot of you are due to rotate back to Earth soon. Several of you have already stayed well past your normal rotation times and I understand why, the search must go on.

"I want to thank you all for your dedication and assure you that your efforts will be well rewarded. Accounts have been set up for all the principal parties in this group and several others that have been brought to my attention as well. These accounts will ensure that you will never want for anything ever again.

"We're almost ready to start the development of an engine that will power our transport ships to the brink of light speed, thanks to your discoveries. This will cut the transport times to weeks instead of months. We anticipate that this will all happen in the next couple of years and when it does, we'll be able to catch up with your production backlogs, in a few years.

"I've been here for a week or so now and understand that your first load of cattle will be delivered on the next transport, which is due in a week. I also had several other varieties of livestock included in that shipment, pigs, chickens, and the like. Man doesn't live by beef alone.

"During my brief stay so far Mike has briefed me on most of what's going on, but I want you to give me the grand tour. I'd like to spend a little time with each of you and have you show me what you do every day. I understand that you have developed a new job classification too, interplanetary botanist. Who's the young lady that that was developed for?"

"That's Jen," Lorna said.

"Jen, where are you?" Emerson asked.

"Here, Sir," Jen answered meekly.

"I am honored to meet you. Has Mike taken care of you, financially, that is?"

"Well, we talked about it once, a year or so ago, but we never seemed to get back to it. Even if I only draw my wages as a housekeeper, this job has been wonderful."

"Let me personally assure you that you will be taken care of. I've instructed the board to set up one of those accounts in your name. Given the contributions that you've made I think a good amount is half a Billion. Do you think that's fair?"

"Yes, Sir, that's more than fair. I never imagined that I'd ever get anything like that. Thank you."

"You're more than welcome. Now, besides the obvious contributions of Al and Lorna, I'd like to acknowledge just a few others by name. Patty and Brittany Thompson, are you here?"

"Here, Sir," Brittany said.

"God, you're all so young. You two young ladies will receive five Billion each and the patent rights and royalties for your contributions. I imagine that you can get by on that for a while. The navigation system that enabled this group to save the lives of all the people on this planet has been the most valuable contribution of all. I commend you both. Your farsightedness has been put to work in all of our operations on Earth as well, so the royalties will, over time, be worth more than the meager amount that I've offered you tonight. I want to spend some time with each of you while I'm here.

"Now, I don't want to make this too long, but I want all of you to spend the next week here, on me, of course. Then I want you to take me out and show me this marvelous world you've made for us all. The profitability of the company has been enhanced so dramatically that we want to pass some of it on to you.

"In closing I just want to thank each of you again for the outstanding job. Well, done. Now I think Mike has planned a special dinner for us. Mike."

"Thank you, Randolph. Dinner is served."

Franco burst through the doors leading a group of chefs. He hovered over them as they brought out cart after cart of food. When he reached the head of the table he stood there with his hands on his hips and watched as everyone was served.

"Mr. Mike, Mr. Al, Miss Lorna, Franco is honored to once again be able to serve you. Franco managed to slip away two days ago to begin the preparations for this meal. Mr. Mike has asked Franco to come and make sure this is the best meal that has ever been served on this planet. Franco has surpassed even his high standards. Please enjoy your dinner."

"Thank you, Franco," Mike said. "This is Randolph Emerson. He's the head of the board of directors."

"Mr. Randolph, Franco is honored to serve you as well. These fine people that sit before you are the best that Franco has ever had the honor to serve. Franco has served Presidents and Kings, and Queens, but never has Franco served better people than these."

"I tend to agree with you," Emerson said. "Thank you, Franco."

"It is Franco's pleasure."

"He's a weird duck," Randolph said as Franco made his way around the table making sure that everything was up to his standards.

"You have no idea," Lorna said, "but he's the best chef on the planet. He can work wonders with a can of beans. During the storm he actually made things almost palatable. We were in no danger of starving, but the variety sucked. He made things a little better with some of his concoctions."

"Then he should be rewarded too," Randolph said. "Mike, can you remind me to take care of that?"

"I'll do that. He really has been instrumental in preserving a sense of normality around here, if you can call anything Franco does as normal."

"We had no idea that you would make the long trip to come see this all firsthand," Lorna said. "We're honored to have you here, of course, but it is very unexpected."

"I didn't even tell Mike that I was coming. I decided that after you made the discovery in Ascraeus Mons that I had to see this for myself. I gathered all the data that I could get my hands on and studied it on the trip. We really have to do something to shorten that trip. I'm in constant contact with the board, so there's no real reason that I couldn't make the trip.

"The board has been so astounded with the material that you have been sending back. There are several varieties that we haven't even identified yet. We had Mike send some of the magnetic rock back to us and the ship that brought it had navigation trouble. They were thrown off course."

"We were afraid of that," Al said. "We've been wanting to ship it in bulk but were afraid of that. We decided that the risk was too great. The development may have to be done here. Hell, we had problems just shipping it from the mine to the hub."

"I've directed the necessary staff and equipment be sent here to do just that. They should be here in a month or so. They left not long after I did. With the preliminary studies that they managed to do with the small samples that we received; they have developed a theory about some kind of new propulsion system that will revolutionize space travel. We also think it may be used to power other types of equipment and its entirely Earth friendly. No pollution at all if the studies are correct. It could replace the internal combustion engines back on Earth."

"We could use something like that here," Lorna said. "We're always looking for new power sources. Our engineers haven't figured out the alien power units yet and they probably aren't compatible with our stuff. There are so many questions that we still have to answer."

"Yes, but you've answered many of them too."

"We've been lucky."

"That's not the way I hear it. We've given some of the stuff that you sent to us to select scholars to translate, and they haven't come up with anything that they can make anything out of. Yet here you sit with four major discoveries and technology that has saved the lives of every person on this planet. I'd call that a little more than luck."

"We had a hell of a team to help us through the maze," Lorna said. "All the different areas of expertise can't be figured out by any one person. The captain of a ship doesn't necessarily know how to repair the engines if something goes wrong, but he surrounds himself with people that can take care of that while he does his job. Al and I steer the ship while the others do their jobs. Sean takes care of the engineering stuff; Brian does most of the mechanical, Martin and Jen take care of the gardens. Everyone has their part that they take care of."

"The key to any successful project is having good people working together," Randolph said. "We scour the Earth trying to find those people, hoping that someone can bring out their talents and make them a winning team. You and Al have surpassed all expectations on that. I know this sounds like a pep talk, but it's really only a statement of fact."

As the evening went on Randolph Emerson made his way around the room, talking to each person there. A lot of the conversations were short, but when he talked to Brittany and Patty, he spent a long time. He lingered and kept asking them to explain different aspects of their system and how they came up with the ideas.

"We just look at the situation and try to figure out a way to fix whatever the problem is," Brittany said. "We had this idea a long time ago and worked out most of the bugs on the trip here from Earth. We never had the resources to actually try any of it until we got to Pavonis Mons and Al showed us what we were up against. Frankly, we couldn't have done the job in there without something like this."

"We've adapted your system to map other things that aren't underground too," Emerson said. "It's especially good with the video adaptation added. You can take a virtual tour after you've input the initial information."

"We use it that way here too," Patty said. "That's why we developed it. Al wanted to be able to see all the things that we see, but without the need to actually be there himself. If he sees something he needs to investigate he can just go directly to it and check it out. It saves a lot of time."

"We've developed an extensive video library of the area," Brittany said. "We use it almost everywhere we go now. For the first year or so we didn't have the video capability, but we do have the digital maps that we made during that time. As we go around now, we update the digital maps to video maps. The only problem is that most of the places we go all look about the same."

"Well, it appears that the party is starting to break up," Randolph said, looking around.

"Probably not breaking up as much as just changing locations," Brittany said. "It's kind of become a custom to relocate to the Ophir Chasm Saloon after one of these dinners. Drinks and dancing and such. We don't get to town very often and we all need to unwind a little."

* * *

Five days later Al and Lorna met in Mike's office at 1000 to find out what Mike had called them in for. Randolph Emerson was there with Mike when they arrived.

"Al, Lorna, how is your mini vacation going?" Randolph asked.

"Good," Lorna said. "What's up?"

"Your livestock will be here today," Mike said. "We were just trying to figure out how to get them out to Ascraeus Mons. Any ideas?"

"Just put some rails on one of the flatbed trailers and haul them out with one of the transports," Al said. "We'll need a stock chute of some kind on the other end too, I guess. Martin can call the crew out there and have them set something up. It might take a couple days to get them out there."

"We should probably hold them here for a day or two," Lorna said. "Let them get their feet back under them. I know I needed a few days when I first got here."

"Let's plan on moving them in a week," Mike said. "That will give your people a chance to get ready for them. I'll have them held in the receiving area. It won't be that hard to clean up after them. I called a couple days ago and had some of that grass you have bailed brought in. It should be here this afternoon too."

"Well, it looks like the vacation is about over," Al said. "I guess it's back to work."

"I think we can spare you in the field for a few more days," Randolph said. "Just coordinate things from here. I must admit that I'm getting a little anxious to go see everything."

"I'll take you out day after tomorrow," Lorna said. "Is there anything you'd like to see first?"

"I was thinking probably Pavonis Mons first. That seems to be the logical place to start."

"If we went to Ascraeus Mons first it would cut down on the travel time a little," she said. "That way we could just make a big loop and end back up here in a couple weeks or so."

"Will it really take that long to get back?"

"Yeah, if you want to see everything it will. Would you like us to travel in a group? We can spare the manpower for while if you want to see this all from different prospectives. You said you wanted to spend time with several of the key people."

"Yes, I think that would be a good idea. I know that I have a lot to learn in a short time, and yes, maybe that would be the best way to go about it, at least in the beginning."

"Then it's settled," Al said. "We'll leave at 0800 the day after tomorrow. Lorna and I will get the crew lined up and figure out an itinerary of some kind so you can know what to expect. We'll take eight to ten cruisers. I don't know exactly yet. Some of them may have to join us later. Might I suggest that you ride with Martin and Jen for the first leg? After we get to Ascraeus Mons they may have to break off and get back to their duties. They're the mainstay of our farming and ranching for now."

"That sounds reasonable to me," Randolph said. "I really like those two. That Jen is a ball of fire. I don't know if I could keep up with her for very long."

"We gave up trying to keep up with a lot of our people a long time ago," Lorna said. "Now we mainly try to position ourselves in such a way that we can get out to see whatever they've found in a reasonable time. We're so spread out now that we can't always be in the thick of things like we were in the beginning."

"I can see how that would be a problem. I've gone over the maps of the area and can't believe how much ground you've opened up. By using conventional methods of mining, it wouldn't be possible to do that."

"If all we had were conventional mining methods, we'd all probably be dead now," Al said. "Lorna and her people led us to the Promised Land and literally saved us all."

"Aw shucks," Lorna said. "I've had about enough of this mutual admiration society for one day. Gentlemen, if you'll excuse me, I'll go get things started."

"I'll be along shortly," Al said as she got up to leave.

"Remarkable woman," Randolph said. "I had a sense about her when you were in the first dig. Most capable."

"She is that," Al said. "I don't know how much more there is to find out there, but I do know that she, along with the others will find it. There are still years of work to go through all of the dwellings and such to see if we've missed anything, but I fear that the large-scale finds are behind us."

"I know that you've overstayed your contract by a full year," Randolph said. "Do you have any idea when you might want to rotate back to Earth, and I assume retire?"

"No, not just yet," Al said. "Mike and I have talked about that a few times, but I have a feeling that our work here isn't quite finished. Those people out there are like my children and, God forbid, grandchildren. I can't just walk out on them when there's a possibility that I may be able to do something that will keep them safe from unseen forces that we can't imagine yet.

"The biggest contribution that I can make is to try to see into the future and steer them out of harm's way. We've been very lucky so far. The only fatalities that we've had have been the ones during the storm and that is incredible, given the scope of what we've accomplished here. Our people have been the driving force behind the discoveries. There's no way we could have done all this on our own."

"You are a true leader in every sense of the word," Randolph said. "I've gone over all of the information gathered on this entire operation and can't find one bad decision. I only wish we had more like you."

"You have many more like me that when needed, will step up and do what is needed to get the job done. Some of them haven't realized their potential yet, but when the time requires them to take the lead they will be there and do what's required of them. I'm a pretty good judge of character in most cases and have found that we don't have much dead weight around here.

"We allow our people to go beyond where they thought they could go. Coax them a little when they need it, but mostly just guide their direction and let them go. No leader is any better than the people he leads. If they can't get the job done, he's automatically going to fail. It's just that simple."

"You're right, of course. We spend a lot of time and money selecting the people that we allow to come here. I recently read your initial evaluation. It said that when the chips were down, they had never seen anyone who could adapt faster and move in the right direction more often than not, than you. It seems that you've proved them right."

"Well, that may be, but I've just been doing my job, like everyone else. Now, if there isn't anything else I can do for you maybe I'd better go give Lorna a hand."

"I think we're done here," Mike said. "Thanks for all of your help."

CHAPTER TWENTY-FIVE

At 0700 two days later they all met in the receiving area. Al looked over the mass of cruisers and shook his head.

"God, how many of these damn things do we have now," he asked.

"Almost sixty," Lorna said as she and Sean stood beside him. "We still have most of them mapping in Arsia and Ascraeus Mons. The others are being used for several other projects. The mines all have a couple now too."

"Well, we'd better get this show on the road," Al said. "Do you have the list of who we're taking with us?"

"Yeah, I've talked to them all. They know what to do."

"Good morning," Randolph Emerson said as he came up behind them. "This is an impressive fleet of vehicles you have here. Are these the cruisers that I've been hearing about?"

"Yeah," Lorna said. "Al came up with the concept and Sean and his people made the prototypes. They've gone through several different versions as we redefine the mission for them. They all now come standard with the nav system that Patty and Brittany came up with. We've expanded the area that we have to cover so much that it's real easy to get lost if you don't have that to guide you. We have literally thousands of miles of tunnels that we drive in and we're still mapping more all the time."

"They're not all that stylish though, are they?"

"No, but very functional," Al said. "As you'll see over the next couple days or weeks, they really do the job we designed them for. Is there room for improvement, absolutely, but we'll work on that as we go. The biggest improvement that could be made to them is speed. We have a lot of ground to cover and spend most of our time just getting there and back."

"Is there anything that I can do to help you?"

"No, not really. Just keep the supplies coming the way you have. By the time we formulate an idea and try to figure out how to implement it, well, we just have to do it with what we have on hand. With the fabrication area back up to full strength now we're fairly well self sufficient."

"Who did you say I should ride with first?" Randolph asked.

"Martin and Jen. When we get out to Ascraeus Mons they'll be home. The rest of us will go on from there."

"They're the ones working in the gardens, aren't they? I'm still having trouble putting the names with the various jobs. There are so many."

"Yes. Martin is the botanist and Jen is his assistant," Al said. "They're the ones in charge of growing the food for this planet. The cattle and other livestock are for them. They have a fair-sized crew out there getting ready for the animals."

"Al, the stock is about ready to go," Lorna said. "Eve just gave me the high-sign. We'd better get started. Are you going to lead off?"

"Yeah, I thought Mona and I would take the lead. Martin and Jen can bring Randolph and follow us. We'll all meet at the garden in Ascraeus Mons this evening."

"I'll hang back for a couple hours and fall in toward the back, just to make sure everyone gets out ok."

"We can run in fairly large groups," Al said. "The dust won't be that much of a factor. We have it cleaned up pretty well."

"Yeah. I figured maybe fifteen at a time and space them out about every thirty minutes. The ones going to Pavonis and Arsia can go about any time they're ready."

"Ok. I'll lead out and see you tonight."

After a few last-minute instructions to the group Al and Mona climbed into their cruiser and led the first group down into the cavern below the hub. Al set the pace at full throttle as soon as they were into the large tunnel that led to Pavonis Mons.

"Martin, are you hanging with us?" Al asked as he made the turn toward Ascraeus Mons.

"Right behind you Boss. Mr. Emerson is riding shotgun and Jen is bending his ear unmercifully."

"If that gets to be too big of a problem have him holler uncle and he can ride with us for a while."

"This is Randolph," the next voice on the radio came. "This young lady is remarkably well informed on every aspect of what's going on around here. I'm actually enjoying this immensely."

"Randolph, if she gets to be too much just tell her to shut up for a while" Al said and laughed.

The tunnel stretched out ahead of them and the radio fell silent. They had made this tunnel a little larger than some of the others so they could run two transports at a time through it and be able to pass anywhere. The cruisers fell into a wedge shape screaming down the tunnel with Al on point.

* * *

"So, Mr. Emerson," Jen said over his shoulder. "What do you want to know about next?"

"Please, call me Randolph. I can see that there is very little in the way of formality around here and I do want to fit in. How did you get the job you have now? I don't recall any classification of botanist assistant."

"Well, I was in housekeeping when I first got here," Jen began. "Right out of high school I signed up to come up here and see what it was like. Without a degree or a trade, like a miner or something, the choices were pretty limited. I knew that I could do the housekeeping job and used that to get here. I was doing fairly well with that too, and the job opened up at Pavonis Mons, so I applied for that along with several friends that I'd met on the way up here and right after I got here.

"We thought there might be a way to get in on some of the new ground that the rumors said that was going to open up. Several of us were accepted and made the move to Pavonis when the complex first opened. Two of our group got a bad case of stupidity when they first got the mountain opened up. They almost died when they went into the bad air in the outer rings. Al and Lorna and some of the others had to go in and bring them out. I talked to them as they came out and asked if I could be part of what they were going to do in there and a few days later they called on me to drive one of the crew cars on another rescue.

"God that all seems like a lifetime ago. I had so much fun cruising around in there looking to see what they would find next. When they found the first garden, they asked me to ride herd on the two botanists that they sent out from the hub. They weren't very good in the field and took a lot of watching. They were better in a lab environment, I guess. Martin came out to replace them and I kept pestering him until he kind of took me under his wing and I've been trying to learn as much as I can ever since."

"I understand you were in charge of exploring most of the gardens; almost single handed from what I hear."

"Martin was busy with the tests he had to run, and Al and Lorna were always off someplace doing what they needed to do, so I just kind of took over on that. We went out for a few days at a time and mapped and explored the upper garden in Pavonis and when it was time to move to the others I went with Martin. In Pavonis I had several labor crews that I assigned areas to clean up and as it turned out, that came in handy when we had to move everyone out there during the storm. By then we had the plants fairly well figured out and knew what we could eat and what we couldn't. They all responded to my lead fairly well. They knew that Al had put me there and weren't about to buck him."

"He is a commanding figure, isn't he?" Randolph said.

"He saved a lot of lives when the storm hit," Martin said. "I doubt you'll find a single person on this planet that wouldn't give their right arm to him if he asked them to."

"How did he handle the storm?"

"He evaluated it and decided that he had to act before there was a real problem. He gathered crews and trained them and kept expanding them until he had enough people to do what needed to be done. If he hadn't acted when he did there would be a lot of coffins on the supply ships. By the time we got there they were getting to be in real bad shape. Food was low and the air was starting to turn bad. Water was hard to come by and a lot of them had all but given up hope. He organized the tunneling to the mines and rescued most of them too. We all knew this was going to be like no storm any of us had endured. He had the cool wit to hold it all together."

"This is quite a story."

"Al, God of Mars, is really an understatement. Even the ones of us that were at Pavonis Mons when it hit wouldn't have ever seen the light of day again if we'd lost the hub. There wouldn't have been any way to get there. There wouldn't have been anything if we did get there."

"Now with all of these tunnels, which were made possible by Lorna's discoveries, that won't be a problem ever again," Jen said.

"She's kind of outspoken, isn't she?" Randolph said.

"She's been on her best behavior around you," Jen said. "She can be a little crude at times, but it's served her well. She doesn't pull any punches. If it's in her head, it's out her mouth. That's just the way she is."

"We've had several top people working on translating some of the information that she transmitted back to Earth. They haven't come up with one percent of the information that she and her crew have. I still can't believe how she walked her way through all of it."

"She had a lot of help, but I think she made the really big breakthroughs. She knows her shit. Sorry, stuff."

"No need to apologize, young lady. I must admit that this is an entirely different way of life than I'm used to, but so far, I'm enjoying it. It's kind of back to basics that I'm not used to. I live a good life back on Earth and I'm really glad I decided to make this trip. If it weren't so far and took so long, I can imagine I'd spend a lot more time here. Mike does a fantastic job for us, but I still like the personal touch once in a while. I visit every one of our installations on Earth at least once a year. It just takes so long to make this trip that I have never really considered doing it before."

"I hope you won't be disappointed," Martin said. "We're not doing anything special because you're here. Hell, we didn't know you were coming until you showed up at dinner that first night we got to the hub. Our first job up here is survival, second is production. Actually, they pretty much go hand and hand. Everyone has a job, and we all help out where we can."

"Well, even with the storm the production rate has increased so much that I may have to slow everyone down a little so we can catch up. We don't have enough ships to haul it away as fast as you guys are producing it now. I never thought I'd see that day."

"You can thank Lorna and Al for that too," Jen said. "The stuff they've found in the mountains has made that possible too."

"I've seen their compensation packages, and they are substantial, but I fear they are lacking, even so. Speaking of compensation, how have you faired?"

"I haven't even tried to access that information in the last several months," Jen said. "Mike said he'd take care of me when things got back to normal again and I haven't talked to him about it for a long time."

"Can you access the main hub computer from here?"

"I guess you can," she said. "I've never really tried."

Randolph pulled the computer keyboard to him and started typing. In ten minutes, he'd brought up Jen's personnel records.

"It says here that you are still in housekeeping," he said. "Your base salary is still what it was when you got here. I think I can fix that."

After fifteen minutes of working his way through her records he was satisfied.

"Now, young lady, you are officially a botanist. From what I've seen and heard I think you deserve that title; don't you Martin?"

"She's better than several of the ones that work in the labs at the hub," Martin said. "I don't know what I'd have done without her these last several months."

"With that little bonus that I told you about the other night I will be adding more when I get back to Earth. I only have the authority to do so much on my own. I've gone over a lot of this with the board and they have given me a certain amount of freedom to act on their behalf. Martin, I'll see to it that you will be taken care of also. I'm making quite a list of people that have made major contributions and I don't think it's quite full yet.

* * *

At noon Al called a halt for lunch. They gathered their cruisers in a circle and laid out the noon meal.

"Well, Randolph, how are you holding up?" Al asked.

"This has been one of the most enjoyable mornings I've spent in a long time," he said. "That young lady is fantastic. I don't know how you managed to pull her out of housekeeping, but that was a very smart move. I've elevated her to botanist and seen to it that she's fairly well taken care of. I guess Mike hasn't had time to get around to that recently."

"She's something else alright. She's fearless."

"She and Martin have been telling me all they can about the project they're working on now. I can hardly wait to see it."

"How long are you planning to stay with us," Al asked.

"I was planning on a month and then head back, but I may have to extend that. It's so far out here that I need to see all I can while I'm here. I have no intentions of coming in here and making a lot of changes. I have all the confidence that you all have everything well in hand, but I just wanted to see some of this for myself. So far, all I've seen is the hub complex and this large tunnel, but I'm hopeful that by the end of the day I'll get my first look at what lies ahead of us."

"I guarantee you won't be disappointed."

"Randolph, did you get something to eat," Jen asked as she walked up.

"No, but I'm getting ready to. What looks good?"

"Everything. Franco takes good care of us when he can. He sent all kinds of goodies this time. Once we started getting shipments again after the storm, Al made sure we were taken care of."

She led him to their cruiser and helped him fix a plate. Like most of the other, he decided to stand while he ate. He kind of milled around chatting with several in the crew. Al just stood back and watched.

"How's it going?" Al asked when Martin went by.

"She has him wrapped around her finger. He hangs on every word she says, and we know that she has a lot to say. I truly think he's having a good time. He started to get a little fidgety just before we stopped, but he hasn't complained yet."

"He just told me that he had the best morning he's had in a long time. I have to admit that I wasn't sure how this was going to go."

"I think you can stop worrying about that. If he gets along with the others as well as he has with her, there won't be any problems."

"What about you?"

"I'm doing fine. You know that when Jen is in the conversation there isn't much room to get a word in. I like the old fart. He's loosening up better than I thought he would."

"Don't let her get to him too bad. She has a captive audience, and I don't want him to get scared off the first day."

"No, he'll be fine. I'm actually enjoying watching her work him over and he loves it. He said he wishes his granddaughters had half her spunk. They seem to sit around and feed from the trough, so to speak. By the time we get there tonight I think he'll need a break though."

After their thirty-minute break they all headed out again. Two hours later they emerged into the lower tunnels of the Ascraeus Mons complex.

"Randolph, what do you think?" Al asked on the radio.

"Wow."

"Yeah, that was the first reaction of almost everyone we've brought in here. We're only a couple hours from the garden now. How are you holding up?"

"I've seen pictures of this, but to actually be here is something else entirely. I'm holding up ok, but I have to admit that I'll be glad to get out for a while. This seat gets a little hard after a few hours."

"We all understand that and won't argue with you. We'll be there soon. Al out."

* * *

Early that evening they pulled up and stopped close to the habitat at the lower garden in Ascraeus Mons. They all arranged their cruisers with the backs pointed toward the center of the circle. Jen drug Randolph by the hand into the edge of the garden almost as soon as they were parked.

"The soil here is so much better than any of the other gardens," Jen said as she led him in.

"This is really remarkable," he said.

She reached down and picked a tomato and handed it to him. It was the size of a grapefruit.

"I planted this just before we went to the hub to meet you. The growth rate here is fantastic. We can turn a crop in weeks, or sometimes only days. It's a big job keeping up with it."

Several hundred acres lay before them, heavy with vegetables. Trees lined the edges that bore all manner of fruit. The grasslands were barely visible beyond the groves of trees.

"Makes a hell of a salad," Al said as he walked up behind them.

"Where are you going to put the livestock?" Randolph asked.

"We have a hundred acres fenced off to the west a little ways," Jen said. "We wanted to keep everything close together for a while. That will help us keep things under control until we can see how it's all going to play out. I hope the cows can handle the grass alright."

"Just don't get too attached to them," Al said. "You know that eventually they'll all be on the menu."

"I know. I'll probably have to leave the cows to someone else. I have plenty to do here. Well, I'd better go help get dinner started. It's been a long day, and I was hoping we could eat before it got too dark."

"Thank you for the tour," Randolph said. "And for the insight. Your input has been very valuable to me."

"You're more than welcome," Jen said as she left.

"How does this day and night work in here?" Randolph asked.

"There are several structures in here that transmit the sunlight in from above," Al said. "I'm sure we'll be able to show them to you as we go. We have most of them mapped. They seem to run in groups every few miles and broadcast the light to most of the complex. The outer rings in all three of the Mons are dark, but the rest is pretty well lit."

"Al, you've done a fantastic job here. I want to thank you personally."

"You sent a lot of very good people up here and it has taken all of us to get to where we are today. I can't take the credit for all of their hard work."

"You're very modest. You're a natural born leader and I'm thankful to have you on our team. I was a very young man when it was decided to send people up here. I didn't have the skills to come myself, but I swore that someday I would make this trip. We lost a lot of good people in the beginning and almost closed down this operation several times. I was always on the side of keeping it going.

"With the natural resources back on earth getting harder to find and all of the environmental restrictions it was obvious to me that we needed something like this to sustain us well into the future. The advances that you've spearheaded in the last couple years have insured that we can remain here and supply the Earth for hundreds of years. Perhaps by then we'll find another world to colonize. With what you've found and developed here this world can become self-sufficient in the not-too-distant future. That may present an entirely different set of problems for us, but the financial viability of the corporation is virtually guaranteed.

"You've cost us a lot of money in the last couple years, but you've returned it tenfold. It's impossible to adequately repay you for all you've done."

"It's my job. Now, why don't we go see what else is going on. I don't think I can handle much more of your praise."

Jen came back a few minutes later.

"Randolph, it's time to fix your plate," she said. "I'll give you a hand. We can sit in the habitat and eat."

"Thank you. Al, are you going to join us?"

"In a few minutes. I have a couple things I have to check on."

Slim and Melissa walked over as they left.

"What's up Boss?" Slim asked.

"Oh nothing. I just get tired of getting thanked every hour of every day. It's getting old as hell."

"Al, you may have to live with that for a while," Melissa said. "I know you and Lorna are getting tired of it, but most of the people around here want to thank you in person. They need someone to look up to now. I'm sorry, but you're it."

"Oh, hell, let's get something to eat. I give up."

* * *

The next morning Al and Lorna took Randolph Emerson to the industrial area one level above where they had spent the night. The tour took only about four hours, and they went back to the habitat for lunch.

"That's an impressive find," Randolph said as they sat down to lunch. "How big did you say it was?"

"Over a hundred miles across," Al said. "There's a wealth of equipment and facilities in there that we plan to use to support and enhance the way of life here. We still don't know what all we have up there, but we learn more each day."

"Adapting the alien technology to our needs is quite a challenge," Sean added. "It works well on its own, but when we try to mix it with our technology, well, it doesn't always come out the way we want it to. They're just not compatible."

"Is there anything I can do to help with that?" Randolph asked.

"Short of sending us several nuclear physicists that are up on all forms of alien technology; I don't see what you can do," Sean said.

"I don't know where I can lay my hands on any of those, but I can have a search started and see what we can find. It intrigues me that you have not been able to work your way through this problem when you've done so well in all the other areas."

"We can take them apart and put them together and they work fine, but understanding what makes them work is where we come up short. They don't seem to follow the same laws of physics as we understand them. Hell, we can't even measure the power output from them."

"Would it be possible to send some examples of what you have back to Earth and let them have a look at them? We've never really talked about that before, but we all know that it has to happen sooner or later."

"If that's what you want, we can do that," Al said. "To this point we've been trying to avoid getting this stuff out into the public eye. There are questions that may have to be answered first. Is it to our advantage to go public with this technology? What would be the long-term effects of introducing this into the economy of Earth? Will it irreparably damage the current status quos as we know it today?

"If we send one of the miners back to Earth what's it going to do to our industry there? We know from experience that it will revolutionize it, but is that necessarily a good thing?"

"Keeping it all to yourselves isn't going to last forever," Randolph said.

"We know that, but so far, we've needed almost everything we have just to stay alive and we don't know what else is out there in the dark. I have all of these kids risking their lives every day doing our work, work that they never really signed up for in the beginning. Granted the environment in here seems to be relatively benign, at least so far, but we're not sure what else we're going to run into out there."

"I can't argue with that," Randolph said. "What about a couple of the smaller jeep looking vehicles. That couldn't hurt you that much, could it? Are the power sources in them similar to the ones in the miners?"

"Yes," Sean said. "So far all of the power sources we've found are similar in design. The only big difference is the larger units are in the larger vehicles. The design is basically the same."

"I would like to see that happen," Randolph said. "It's not an order, but I think it might be to everyone's best interest. I can have a lid kept on it for a time, but sooner or later it's going to get out. Now, what are we going to do tomorrow?"

"I thought we'd go to Pavonis Mons in the morning," Al said. "It'll be a long day for all of us but it's the next stop on the tour. You might want to ride part way with Patty and the rest of the way with Brittany. I know you want to spend a little time with them."

"That sounds like a great idea. What about the rest of today?"

"I think rest up a little and maybe look around in Jen's garden a little," Lorna said. "For now, I think we need to think about lunch."

CHAPTER TWENTY-SIX

The next morning Al and Lorna were sitting in the habitat when Brittany and Johnny came in. They gathered their breakfast and joined them.

"You're up early," Al said.

"Yeah, it was one of those nights," Brittany said. "We slept good, but the thought of spending the day with Randolph is a little disconcerting."

"Don't worry about that," Lorna said. "Just be yourselves and things will be fine. Hell, he can kill you, but he can't eat you."

"That's comforting. I just don't like getting the third degree all the time."

"We know what you mean," Al said. "It's kind of like what we have to put up with. It comes with the job. Speaking of the devil, here he comes."

"Good morning, Randolph," Lorna said. "How'd you sleep?"

"Quite good actually. I'm looking forward to continuing our tour today."

"We'll get started in an hour or so," Al said. "Brittany and Johnny will be your chauffeurs for this leg of the trip. We'll head for Pavonis Mons and spend a couple days over there before we go on to Arsia Mons."

"That sounds fantastic to me."

"Al, there's a call for you," Martin said as he approached the table. "It sounds like our cows were making a mess at the hub and Mike sent them out early. They should be here in an hour or so."

"Well, are you ready for them?"

"Yeah. We have a stock chute about three miles west of here and a hundred acres or so fenced off so we can keep them in close."

"Do they know how to get here?"

"Yeah. They've been running supplies out here for several months. Shorty's driving the lead transport and June is following right behind him."

"We'll go over and help them get unloaded before we leave. I'd kind of like to see how this goes."

"I'll direct them on over there. We can meet them after we all have breakfast."

"Thanks, Martin. Where's Jen this morning?"

"She's already over there. She left early this morning to make sure things would be ready for when the stock arrived."

"You might want to let her know it's coming early."

"Yeah, she doesn't like surprises."

* * *

"Shorty, this is Al."

"Go ahead Boss."

"See where all these cruisers are parked up ahead of you?"

"Yeah, I see them. I have to unload these critters from the left side. Is there room to turn around there?"

"Plenty of room. Just take your time. Did you bring them all?"

"Yeah, I have most of them and June has the rest plus the chickens and such. I wish I'd a known you was going to have stock up here. Hell, I grew up on a ranch back home."

"Don't say that too loud. You might end up with a new job."

"Shoot, I'd like that just fine. This truck driving is ok, but I love working with the animals."

"We'll talk about it. Can you get in close to the chute?"

"No sweat. Be there in a minute."

They all watched as Shorty swung the transport around in the intersection and backed up to get lined up. It took two tries to get the trailer to within a few inches of the chute.

"Am I lined up with the gate?" Shorty asked.

"Looks good. Let's let them out," Martin said.

Shorty joined the rest of them and opened the gate. The yearling calves shied away from him, but he soon had them moving down the chute. When they reached the edge of the grassland they stopped. The grass was almost as high as their backs. They waded into it slowly, testing the morsels as they went.

"They may have a little trouble with that grass," Shorty said. "It's a lot different than what they've been eating. It might give them the shits for a time."

"You sound like you know something about this," Randolph said.

"Yeah, I ought to. My daddy had a big spread up in Wyoming when I was growin up. He was kinda pissed at me when I said I was coming up here for a spell. We never had this kind of grass to feed with there either. We had to raise our own hay and such."

"What do you think we need here to keep the cows happy?"

"Hell, they look pretty happy to me. All they do is eat, drink, and shit. It'd be nice to have a few good cutting horses and several herd dogs, but other than that it looks like we could get along just fine."

"Shorty, this is Randolph Emerson," Al said. "He's the chairman of the board of our little operation on this planet."

"Pleasure to meet you," Shorty said. "Sorry about my language."

"That's perfectly alright," Randolph said. "Do you think you could help us develop a herd up here that could feed the people on this planet?"

"Shoot, I don't see why not. Where was you planning on doing the butchering?"

"We haven't got that nailed down yet," Al said. "We have some ideas, but nothing definite. Do you know anything about that side of it?"

"Some. My Uncle had a slaughterhouse in Sheridan Wyoming. I used to help out there some when things was slow. You're going to need to get in several breeding seasons before you get there though, unless you plan on bringing up a lot more cows."

"This is our starter herd," Al said. "They're not quite a year old. It's going to take some time to develop our herd. Would you be interested in helping out? We've been looking for someone to take care of this."

"Hell yes! Where do I sign up?"

"I think you just did. After you complete your rounds on this trip, I'll have you transferred out here."

"How many acres of grass do we have?"

"Over a thousand square miles." Al said.

"Damn, that's a lot. How big a herd do you need?"

"Eventually we want to feed a million people with it. We know we can't do that with a hundred head, but someday we'll get there. Still want in?"

"Hell yes!"

"Done," Randolph said. "You might just be our new ranch foreman. I have to check on a few things before I can offer you the job for sure, but as I see it, you're our best bet for now."

"I agree," Al said. "I'll get a hold of Mike and have you transferred out here. In the meantime, Jen can watch over them with a little help from her labor crews."

"They seem to be content enough," Lorna said. "Al, we'd better get started to Pavonis."

"Shorty, help June get her load off and make a list of anything you might need to get things started," Al said. "You can bunk in those rooms across the tunnel. You'll need mattresses and such and you can eat at the main habitat for now. It's going to take us a week or so to get things set up. Will the herd be alright for that long?"

"Yeah, as long as they're contained. We wouldn't want to have to cover all that ground looking for them."

"We have a hundred or so acres fenced for now. We can expand that as we need to."

"Looks good to me."

"See you soon. Randolph, you can go with Brittany for now. We may put you with Patty after we stop for lunch. Even with the new tunnels we've made it's still going to be a long day to get over to Pavonis."

"Mr. Emerson, our cruiser is right over here," Brittany said, leading the way.

"Randolph, please."

"Yes sir."

As Al led the way away from the transports the others fell in with him. It was 0915 and they were already an hour late. This was going to be a long day indeed.

* * *

"You seem a little uncomfortable, young lady," Randolph said after a half hour of silence.

"Well, I guess I am," Britt said as she drove south. "I just function better in the trenches, I guess. You make me nervous. I guess I'm a little in awe of you."

"Nonsense. I'm just an old fart that has been doing his job for a very long time and have managed to get to the top of my company. You, on the other hand, have surpassed many in your field at such a young age. I am the one who is in awe."

"We're just doing our jobs here and managed to contribute a little extra; that's all. We're not looking to get rich, but like the idea of the bonuses that you've given us. This was an adventure for Patty and me. We wanted to come here and see the wonders and have a good time before we settled down to start a family. We had no idea that we'd change the planet and save thousands of lives."

"But you have done just that. You have no reason to be uneasy around me. Now, tell me a little more about this wonderful new invention of yours."

Brittany started in on the explanation of the mapping system. It took her two hours to run through all of the features. Randolph asked questions as they went. Johnny sat in the back and was for the most part silent. After the break for lunch Randolph set his sights on Johnny.

"Son, what's your part in all of this?" he asked.

"She's the brains, I'm the muscle," Johnny said. "I'm a mechanic by trade. That's how I got involved with all of this. I was working at Pavonis Mons when Brian assigned me to help them develop the system. We fought and argued all the way through the process, but I have to admit it works pretty well."

"So, you helped develop their idea?"

"Well, the idea was theirs and the design was theirs. I just helped get it off the ground. When we had the first two systems installed, I went along for the ride to test them out, just in case we needed to make any changes. We kind of hit it off after a while and we've been together ever since. We've seen a lot in here."

"I'll bet you have. I hope to see more of it myself."

"I think we've gone far enough for today," Al said on the radio, as the light started to fade that evening. "We still have a couple hours to go to get there and it's been a long day. Let's pull into one of these side tunnels and call it a day."

* * *

"Randolph, would you like to ride with me this morning?" Al asked as they got ready to leave the next morning.

"Yes, I think that's a great idea. Let me get my things."

About an hour into the trip the radio crackled.

"Al, this is Sharon. I may have something that needs to be checked on. I've been running a systematic search of the outer rings in Pavonis and have found what may be another small tunnel leading off to the west."

"What are the coordinates?" Al asked.

"It's between 280 and 290 on ring nineteen. You might want to pull it on the map and have a look."

"We'll get back to you in a minute," Al said.

After a long pause he came back. "That looks a lot like what we saw going to Arsia and Ascraeus Mons. We're almost to the upper garden in Pavonis; we'll take a closer look there. Are you looking at this, Lorna?"

"Of course. I think we need to get out there and have a look."

"Let's restock in Pavonis first. If it's like the others we may be there for a while."

"What's this all about?" Randolph asked.

"Sharon found what may be another tunnel leading to the west. There's only one thing west of here; Olympus Mons."

"You mean there may be another complex like these?"

"That's exactly what I mean."

"We'll need to contact Mike and let him know what's happening. Of course I'll want to go along."

"We'll take care of all of that when we get to the habitat in a few minutes. I need to get a closer look at it on the map and see if it's even worth going out and having a look at. At first glance, I'd say it was."

* * *

Two hours later, with the area of the map displayed on the large screen in the habitat, they all studied the area.

"I think we have to go have a look," Lorna said. "That's exactly what we saw when we ended up in the other two mountains."

"I can't argue with that," Al said. "We'll need to round up supplies for two weeks and maybe several of those trailers to haul part of it on. I want to take all ten cruisers this time. It may just be a pipe dream, but we won't know that until we get out there. Brian, do you know where any of those small trailers are?"

"There are five over in Arsia and three in Ascraeus Mons," Brian said. "We may have to have them brought over. I don't know of any around here."

"We need to get out there and have a look at this," Lorna said.

"It's been there for thousands of years," Al said. "It'll still be there in a day or two. Randolph what do you think of all of this?"

"Of course, I think we need to go have a look. I'm very excited that I may actually be able to participate in one of your discoveries."

"Smitty, can you get Mike on the line for me?" Al asked. "By the way, where the hell have you been?"

"Cruising with Alice. That's where you left me, and I didn't have a control room to go back to. After we got everything moved inside the mountain, I just stayed with her. I'll see if I can find Mike for you."

"Shit, I forgot all about him," Al said.

"You've been busy," Lorna said.

"Mike, this is Al," he said after Smitty had found Mike.

"How's it going out there?"

"Good. Sharon may have found us another dark tunnel to go explore. Randolph wants to go along on this one. Do you have any objections?"

"What do you mean another tunnel?"

"Going west from Pavonis. The only thing out there is Olympus Mons."

"Oh, God. Here we go again. Is Randolph there with you?"

"I'm here Mike."

"You see what I have to put up with all the time. It costs me a lot of money to support them in their little quests into the darkness."

"I'm just thankful that you decided to continue their funding. It's paid off. Is there anything I need to know about?"

"No, not really. I have a conference call later today that may bring up something, but everything is ok for now."

"Good. As soon as Al can get the supplies we need, we'll go have a look at this new tunnel."

"Are you sure you want to go out in the dark with that crew? They'll lead you astray if you don't watch them."

"I really would like to be part of this. You may have to delay my departure date a little. I may not be back as soon as I'd planned on."

"I'll put it on hold for now. I understand the need to go on one of those. I wish I could join you."

"Mike, I'm going to call in a supply list," Al said. "Can you have it delivered to Pavonis tonight?"

"I'll see to it. Is there anything else you need?"

"Ten of those small trailers would be nice. We can round up six or so here, but it'll be late tomorrow before we can get them here. They're spread all over the place."

"I'll see what I can do. If I can't get them there, I'll get back to you."

"Thanks for the help, again. Al out."

"What do you think about taking Franco this time?" Lorna asked.

"Now why in the world would you want to do that?" Al asked.

"So we don't have to eat Eve's cooking."

"That's almost tempting. Could we send him with someone who knows their way around a little?"

"He's been seen around with Jessica Arnold," Eve said. "I think they're kind of sweet on each other. She was in here when we got here. She's been running supplies for him."

"Go see if you can find her," Lorna said.

"Are you match making again?" Al asked.

"Could be. He's a pain in the ass, but you have to admit that he can cook anything, and he makes all of us laugh."

"Smitty, would you and Alice like to come along on this one?" Al asked.

"Sure, why not. I'll have to arrange to have someone take over our route for us."

"See what you can do. I think we're going to need all of the help we can get on this one."

"Eve said you wanted to see me," Jessica Arnold said when she came back in a few minutes later.

"Jessica, what would you say if we asked you to pair up with Franco for a week or two and go exploring with us?" Lorna asked.

"Oh, wow, that would be fantastic. He's so funny and I just love him to death."

"Literally. You love him. You wouldn't have a problem being cooped up with him day and night for a while. He's going to bitch at everything we do, you know that."

"He's a little temperamental, but he's a genius in the kitchen. And the answer is yes, I do love him. We've been spending as much time together as we can lately."

"So, if I go ask him these same questions, you're ok with it?" Al asked.

"Absolutely."

"Eve, can you call him for us?" Lorna asked.

"This should be interesting," Eve said as she left the table.

"Mr. Al, Miss Lorna, what can Franco do for you?" he said a few minutes later.

"Franco, what would you say to going exploring with us?" Al asked. "You and Jessica."

"Franco would like that very much. Franco could cook for you on this trip, yes?"

"Yes, but you'd have to do it in a cruiser. We don't have a big fancy kitchen for you."

"Franco has used the facilities on the cruisers many times to help when we had so many people to feed. Franco can do very well if we have several of them together."

"When we're all together there may be as many as twelve cruisers," Lorna said. "Twenty-four people. Can you do that?"

"Franco would love to go along. Miss Jessica is a special lady that I am very fond of also."

"So, you wouldn't mind being cooped up with her in a cruiser for a couple weeks?"

"Franco would like that very much."

"Can you help her with the driving if she needs you to?"

"But of course."

"Make out a supply list for twenty-four people for two weeks. Get it back to us and we'll see to it that it's delivered later tonight. We'll have several trailers so we can take extra for that long of a stay, but don't get too carried away. Keep the menu simple."

"Yes, but of course," he said as he backed away bowing.

"Jessica, you might want to go ride herd on him for us," Lorna said. "You do have a cruiser, don't you?

"Yeah, it's parked out back. That's where I've been delivering the supplies. I just unloaded a little while ago."

As she headed for the kitchen Randolph looked at Al and Lorna with a puzzled look on his face.

"What?" Lorna asked.

"Do you promote promiscuity here?" he asked.

"Look, we're a long way from home and these things will develop," Lorna said. "We don't promote it, but we don't always stand in its way either. If it gets to be a problem, there are enough ways to separate them and let things play out. We've been lucky so far. A lot of our cruiser teams are married couples, but a lot of them aren't. We've had a few weddings come out of it and we think that's great, but not essential. As long as it doesn't get in the way of the job, who cares? Everyone on this planet is an adult."

"Well, I guess I can't argue with your results," Randolph said. "I just assumed that they were all married."

"Not even close," Melissa chimed in. "There are only three married couples in this group in front of you and Slim and I aren't one of them. The system works well, don't screw with it. These people have made the company bazillions of dollars, and I won't sit here and have you question their methods or their morality. Just drop it."

"I stand corrected. The subject will never come up again."

* * *

Late that afternoon Al and Lorna sat in the habitat working on a list of the people that they wanted along. They had cut it down to ten cruisers and twenty-one people, including Randolph.

"That should be enough," Al said. "We have a couple rookie crews that we'll have to keep an eye on. I know that Smitty and Alice will do fine, but I'm not so sure about Franco and Jessica. We'd better get Britt to check them out on the nav system. I know they know how to use it to get around, but to actually map anything with it may be another story."

"I called in the supply list and Mike said he had ten of those small trailers ready to load on a flatbed behind a rover. They should be here late tonight sometime. We may not get out of here as early as we'd like in the morning."

"I know. We can take this one a little easier. Everyone is going to be pulling a trailer and that's going to slow us down. We'll probably just go out to the edge of the light and bed down. That will give us a good start for the next day. You and I may run on out ahead of the others and see if there's anything to look at."

"If we can get out as close as we can and still be in reasonably good air, that would help," Lorna said. "What do you think we'll find this time?"

"God, who knows. We've talked about the possibility of going to Olympus, but neither of us actually thought it would happen. I'll tell you one thing though; I'm about ready to retire. This last year has been hard on me."

"I know that feeling. I do want to see this one through to the end though. I can't see where it could possibly go from here. There's just nothing left out there."

"Yeah, but even if they find something else, the youngsters may have to do the exploring. I'm tired."

"We'll take this one a little slower and get more rest than we're used to. Besides we'll have Randolph along this time. I don't think he can take the kind of hours that we usually run."

"Deal."

* * *

It was 1000 the next morning when they finally got loaded and Al led the procession out of the upper garden in Pavonis Mons. He led them around to the west side of the garden and turned into the spoke that was designated 280. It took until late that afternoon to get out to where the air started turning bad. They were just an hour or so from the mystery tunnel. The light had dimmed but wasn't completely gone.

"I think we'd better stop here," he said.

"It's still early," Brittany said.

"It'll still be there in the morning. Find a place to park and make camp. I'm going to go see if there's even a reason to go on. Joe, can you come up and help me drop this trailer. It'll just slow me down."

"Sure Boss. Need me to go along?"

"No, I think Lorna and I will go have a look. The rest of you help get Franco lined out so we can have something to eat when we get back. We'll only be gone for a couple hours."

A few minutes later Al and Lorna pulled out in their two cruisers. An hour later they turned into the notch in the side of ring nineteen. It began to slope down almost as soon as they entered it.

"Looks like we have a winner," Al said. "I don't think there's much sense in going too far. We can do that in the morning."

"Yeah, but at least we know that we have somewhere to go. When you find a place to turn around, go for it."

"You sound hungry."

"Yeah, a little."

Just over an hour later they pulled back into the group of cruisers and parked. Franco had three cruisers parked close together. He was scurrying back and forth between them getting things ready.

"What did you find?" Brittany asked when they got out.

"Have a look," Lorna said. "It was right where we thought it would be. See how it angles down. If we continue this line, it takes us to the center of Olympus Mons. It's a hell of a long ways out there. We may not get there in one day."

"If we can't make it in one day we may have camp in the confines of a small tunnel in the bad air," Al said. "Most of us have done that, but some haven't. There won't be any fancy dinner out there in the dark. Franco, can you join us for a minute?"

"Mr. Al, Franco's meal is almost ready. Franco needs to tend it."

"Alright, I'll go over it with you after dinner. The rest of you have all done this except Smitty and Alice. I'll go over it with them when I talk to Franco after we eat. I want everyone to get a good night's sleep. We have a long day ahead of us tomorrow."

* * *

"Franco, you're up early," Lorna said when she emerged from her cruiser well before the tunnel began to show any signs of light.

"Franco wanted to make sure everyone had a good breakfast before our long day," he said.

"That's a good idea," Al said coming out of his cruiser.

"Where's Randolph?" Lorna said.

"He's trying to pry himself out of bed. I don't think he's use to getting up so early. Mona's trying to gently prod him."

"You going to take him with you today?"

"Yeah, I thought I would, unless you want the pleasure of his company."

"That's ok. I'll take my turn when we get there. Just throw him into the back seat and let him sleep for a while."

"Let's roust the others," Al said. "Franco, how long until you're ready for them?"

"Maybe fifteen minutes or so. Franco will be ready."

"Fifteen minutes to chow call," Lorna hollered. "If you don't get your asses out of bed you don't eat."

The habitats on the cruisers all started to show life and in just a few minutes everyone was assembled.

"That's better," Lorna said. "Guys, Franco has your last good meal for a day or two just about ready. Eat it and enjoy. Once we go into that tunnel we'll pretty much be confined to the cruisers. If you have to get out remember to monitor the air first. We've done a little calculating and figure that it's probably a three and a half days of hard running to get all the way to Olympus Mons. It's a long way over there. When we get there, we'll split up like we did in Ascraeus Mons and map as many spokes as we can on the way in. Any questions?"

"This isn't any different than any of the others we've gone into," Al said. "If it follows the pattern of the others, you may find that the central area, or areas, will be a lot larger than what we've seen before. Christ, Olympus Mons makes the others we've been to look like an ant hill. It's almost seventy thousand feet tall and covers almost as much area as Texas. There's a mapping nightmare for you."

"One more thing," Lorna said. "A lifetime ago we found three of those rock structures that we found at Pavonis. Two were down low and the other one was miles up the side of the mountain. I believe that there are going to be a lot of levels in this one. Maybe three, four, five, ten, hell your guess is as good as mine. If it's what we think it is, it will dwarf the other three finds. Be careful in there. Let's eat."

At 0700 they eased out and followed Al toward the new tunnel. Franco and Jessica were second, Lorna and Sean third. The others fell in line. At 0815 Al made the turn and started to descend into the darkness of the new tunnel.

To Be Continued in
MINES OF MARS:
OLYMPUS MONS
Part One